The Mahdi II

The Mahdi II

KARL MAY
TRANSLATED BY HERBERT WINDOLF

ISBN-10: 1515172007
ISBN-13: 9781515172000

Publications by Herbert Windolf
Translator of Karl May

Published by Washington State University Press:
The Oil Prince

Published through BookSurge:
Black Mustang

Published by Nemsi Books:
The Treasure of Silver Lake
The Ghost of Llano Estacado
The Son of the Bear Hunter
Imaginary Journeys I
Imaginary Journeys II
Imaginary Journeys III
Thoughts of Heaven
Winnetou IV
Pacific Shores
The Inca's Legacy
The Scout
Deadly Dust
The Mahdi I

Published through CreateSpace:
One more Day . . .
as Translator of Isabell Steiner

As Author:
Observations and Reflections
Pondering What Is

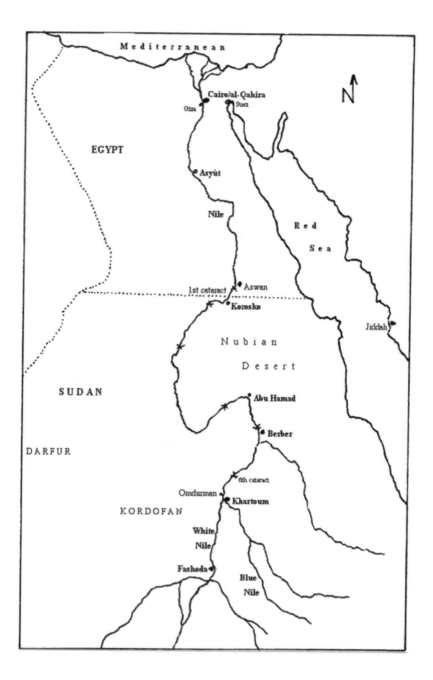

N

Mediterranean

Cairo/al-Qahira
Giza   Suez

EGYPT

Asyût

Nile

Red
Sea

1st cataract   Aswan
Korosko

Nubian

Desert

Jiddah

SUDAN

Abu Hamad

DARFUR

Berber

6th cataract

Omdurman
Khartoum

KORDOFAN

White
Nile

Fashoda

Blue
Nile

Table of Contents

Acknowledgments

I GRATEFULLY ACKNOWLEDGE MY download of "Der Mahdi" from the Karl-May-Gesellschaft Website.

General editing was thoroughly executed by Zene Krogh with my great appreciation.

Manfred Wenner edited Karl May's Arabic language terms. However, not every Arabic term could be properly identified and was left as May used them, except where transliteration from his German to English was called for.

Dr. Johannes Zeilinger, Chairman of the Karl-May-Gesellschaft, kindly permitted the extraction of materials and insights from several of his writings on the Mahdi and Karl May.

Thank you all.

Introduction

IN VOLUME I of "The Mahdi" the narrator, Karl May, made his way from Cairo up the Nile into the Sudan. In the course of his travels, he became involved in many adventures. At the end of this story, he liberated a group of enslaved Fassara women and returned them to their tribal homeland.

In Volume II of "The Mahdi," he has left the Fassara settlement and is traveling with his detachment of twenty *asakir* south to Khartoum. Waylaid by one of his adversaries in an oasis, he vanquishes the group, taking everyone captive, including his adversary, Abd Asl. He also shoots a lion.

He meets Muhammad Ahmad Ibn Assayyid abd Allah, "The Mahdi," at about the time when "The Guided One" begins calling himself by this name. This tells us that Karl May placed the events of his stories in the years 1880-81.

Having spied on both Abd Asl and the Mahdi, he learns that there is a big slave hunt in the making. Ahead of his slow-moving prisoner group, he travels to the Nile, where he insinuates himself into Ibn Asl's camp, the chief villain and slaver. He is subsequently captured by him, but is soon able to escape from the bandit's ship. Together with his Egyptian friend, the raïs effendina, he entraps Ibn Asl's group at the Fever Swamp, where Abd Asl is killed and the Mahdi, severely injured, is left behind.

The friends now separate with the raïs effendina traveling by ship to Khartoum, and the narrator by camelback to Fashoda. Both intend to pursue the escaped Ibn Asl on his slave hunt into southern Sudan.

On his way to Fashoda, he encounters another slaver group. Arriving in Fashoda, he is asked by the local administrator to seek out the leader of the local rabble of soldiers to convict him of being in cahoots with the chief villain, Ibn Asl. He is found out, captured, and taken to Ibn Asl's ship from which he and his companion, Bin Nil, escape again.

Continuing his pursuit of Ibn Asl, he travels with the raïs effendina up the Nile and succeeds in capturing the arch villain's Saribah Aliab. However, Ibn Asl has already left on another slave hunt, requiring his continued pursuit. The story proceeds in The Mahdi III.

The reader of Karl May's stories is well aware of his two famous rifles, the 'Henry Carbine' and the 'Bear Killer'. In the trilogy of "The Mahdi" it is peculiar that the narrator, aka Karl May, refers several times to "his rifles", but rarely mentions them by name.

In "The Mahdi I", chapter 5, "In the Desert", he tells of putting several shells ready for reloading of his two-barelleled rifle, implying it to be the 'Bear Killer'. Then, in "The Mahdi II", chapter 1, "The Mahdi", he again employs his two-shooter when he kills a lion, and that he quickly reloaded, subsequently referring twice to his use of the 'Henry Carbine'.

This is all, no more. A mystery!

Karl May wrote and published his trilogy, "The Mahdi," under different titles in the years 1890 to 1896, two years before the Mahdi's uprising and subsequent rule of the Sudan came to the end in 1898. In 1899-1900, traveling as far as Sumatra, in Indonesia, Karl May also visited Egypt, gaining a brief impression of its condition and its people.

The Mahdi's original name was Muhammad Ahmad Ibn Assayyid abd Allah. He was born in 1844 in Omdurman, Sudan, in the Dongola district of Nubia, the son of a ship builder. He died, probably of typhus, in 1885.

Growing up in a strict religious setting, he gravitated more and more to the mystic Sufi tradition. At the time, the Sudan was ruled by Egypt, itself part of the Ottoman Empire. Strong British interests in the area demanded, together with others, the abolition of slavery. The European influence over the corrupt Ottoman administration became ever stronger, while the discontent of the lower classes increased. They objected to the un-Islamic behavior of the foreigners.

Mahdi means "The Guided One," who was thought to be the redeemer in Islamic belief. It was thought he would rule for a few years, ridding the world of all wrongdoing before the Day of Judgment. On June 28, 1881 Muhammad Ahmad proclaimed himself "Mahdi," revealing to his followers his divine mission to purify Islam and to establish Allah's rule, first in the Sudan and then in other parts of the world.

He gathered a ragtag army of followers, armed only with spears and clubs, and in the course of four years defeated several Egyptian armies, commanded by British generals. Eventually, he captured Khartoum in 1885, where the British General Gordon was decapitated after his defeat. Abandoning Khartoum, he established his administrative center in Omdurman with a state encompassing most of the Sudan. It is thought that the Mahdi died in 1885 from typhoid fever with his organization living on for a short while afterwards. It was the British General, Herbert Kitchener, who defeated the Mahdi's armies in 1898 in the battle of Omdurman, which put an end to the theocratic empire.

1

The Mahdi

KORDOFAN, THIS PECULIAR country, has always been a transit area for many itinerant tribes, which is why its people were already of a mixed heritage prior to Muhammad Ali's conquest. Then the *falla-hin* and *bashibozuks* of the Viceroy introduced the bloodlines of Asia Minor's races. Greeks, Levantines, Armenians, and Arnautlar mixed with the black tribes of the south, and between their descendants lived the pureblooded grandchildren of entire nomadic tribes who drifted in from the *Hijas*.

Kordofan is part of the Sudanese lands. The term 'Sudan,' in use already in the Middle Ages, is now often heard, but a short note about it may be in order. Balad al-Sudan is its full name, with *"balad"* meaning "land," and "al-" being the article. Sudan is the broken plural of *"aswad,"* meaning "black," with *"sud"* its plural. "Balad al-Sudan" means therefore "Land of the Blacks." Emphasis is not placed on the first, but on the second syllable.

Kordofan is pronounced with emphasis on the last syllable. Its northern and western parts are covered by an enormous savanna, resembling a desert during the dry season, but richly vegetated in the rainy season. Broad, grassy areas are interspersed by mimosa woods. There are about nine hundred wells with adjacent villages. During the rainy season itinerant tribes graze their livestock there, only to move on with the beginning of the dry season. There are also giraffes, ostriches, birds of various kinds, and enormous antelope herds.

The southern part of the country has soil which is rich in clay, and holds water. From this results a truly wonderful richness and magnificence of plant growth, with wide areas covered by palms, cassias, adansonias, and tamarinds. In these areas, animals of many kinds are hunted by leopards and panthers, and often enough one can hear the roar of the lion, the King of Beasts.

Wadi Malk is thought to be part of Kordofan, and since we were now between it and al-Safih, we had left Nubia behind. You will recall that I had freed the abducted Bedouin women from the slaver Ibn Asl and, accompanied by twenty *asakir*, returned them to their homeland at Bir al-Sarir. We had been jubilantly welcomed by the relatives of the women and girls and had been richly hosted and presented with gifts, at least by their standards. Upon our departure, the men had accompanied us for two days. Now, we wanted to take the shortest route to Khartoum, where I was to return the twenty soldiers to their commander, the *raïs effendina*, Ahmad Abd al-Insaf.

It was not too long past the rainy season, which is why the savanna still sported a juicy green. Had I not been riding a *hajin*, but a horse, I could easily have imagined riding across an American prairie. Once the grass has withered in the dry season, one must plan one's trips via wells as much as possible, but at present there was no need for this. Traveling from well to well takes up much time. However, with the rich grasses still available we did not need water for our animals, and for us we had filled our water bags. Thus, we were able to travel in a straight line until our water was depleted and we were forced to head for a well. By doing so, we arrived at Bir al-Atshan a full day earlier than if we had taken the mentioned detours. Bir al-Atshan means "Thirsty Well," since it does not hold water during the dry, hot season. Presently, it held more than enough water to refill our bags. It was located in the midst of the savanna, not marked by a rock, tree or bush. I would not have found it had our hosts not assigned us a knowledgeable guide. He was to take us to Khartoum and was as familiar with the area as with the poor characteristics of his long-barrelled, Arab shooting device.

This musket was his heartache, yet he seemed to love it beyond measure. He always kept it in hand and loved to talk about it. And now, sitting next to me by the well, looking at his musket and embracing it lovingly, he said:

"Have you ever seen such work, *effendi*? Is it not marvelous?"

The butt of the musket was inlaid with ivory, but its imagery was incomprehensible to me. I therefore asked:

"It is very tasteful, even magnificent! But what does the figure represent?"

"What it represents? What a question! Don't you see it?"

He held the butt before my nose and asked: "Here, look closely! Well, what is it?"

I made an effort to puzzle the thing out, but did not succeed. It had no lettering, no picture, nothing!"

"You are blind," he said. "May Allah illuminate your eyes! But since you are a Christian, it is no wonder that you do not recognize the figure. A faithful Muslim knows its meaning at first sight. Don't you see that it represents a head?"

"A head? Not a trace!"

At best one could have thought it to be the misshapen head of a hippopotamus. Thus, I shook mine.

"No?" *Allah, wallah, tallah*! It is the Prophet's head, who sits in the heavens with Allah."

"Impossible! There's nothing like a head! Where is the nose?"

"That is missing, *effendi*. The Prophet needs no nose. He is now the purest of spirits and consists of tens of thousands of fragrances."

"Where's the mouth?"

"It is missing, too, for the Prophet does not need a mouth any more, since he speaks to us through the Qur'an."

"I also see no eyes."

"What are eyes for? The Prophet does not need to see anything, since all is evident to Allah."

"I also do not find any ears."

"You cannot find them since there are none. The Prophet need not hear our prayers, having prescribed them so precisely."

"And where is the beard?"

"It is not visible. How could it have been desecrated by ivory, with the oath 'by the Beard of the Prophet' being the most sacred!"

"Not even the forehead can be seen?"

"That neither. With the forehead being the seat of the mind, one cannot depict it."

"Then there's nothing there of the head?"

"Nothing at all," he nodded. "But I recognize every feature of the face."

"Without being able to see the head? Whoever can comprehend this."

"Yes, of course, a Christian will not comprehend it. You are all smitten by incurable blindness!"

"You are, too, but your blindness is more psychic than the healthiest eye. You see a head where just about everything is missing? By the way, isn't it forbidden to depict a human? How much more punishable must it then be to portray the Prophet!"

"The artist who fashioned this picture did not know of the prohibition."

"But he must have seen the Prophet."

"In his mind. The musket is ancient, as you can see. The man who made it surely lived long before the Prophet."

"Impossible. There was no powder at this time."

"*Effendi*, do not rob me of my delight in owning such a precious musket! What is powder needed for? If Allah wills it, one shoots even without powder."

"I admit that Allah works wonders. Here, we have two: first, a bang-bang-gun from a time when there was no powder yet, and second, a picture of the Prophet when he wasn't yet alive."

"I told you already that the artist saw him in his mind. It was a vision, which makes this musket a vision musket."

"Ah, a vision musket. Wonderful, unique!"

"Yes, it is unique! You are right, completely right, and I am glad that you finally arrived at this insight. It is the only vision musket there is, which is why I hold it sacred and am very proud of it."

"How did you get it?"

"Through inheritance. The artist passed it on from child to child. You must know that I am his descendent and one day will bequeath it to my oldest son. Yes, look at me wonderingly. I am truly the great-grandson of the grandson of a man, whom Allah granted the grace to see the Prophet before he was born."

"Then you are the most famous man of your tribe. I'm not simply glad, but find it an inestimable honor to have made your acquaintance."

"Yes," he confirmed entirely serious, "it is an honor for everyone to meet such a grandchild of a great-grandchild. I am known far into the Sudan, as far as there are true believers and my musket has a reputation which echoes even in the lands of the heathen."

"Then it must shoot well?"

"Regrettably, no. It was Allah's will to heighten the Heaven's excellence and that nothing on Earth was to be perfect. This is also the case with my vision musket, something I must admit truthfully. It has some characteristics that fill my heart with sorrow."

"I know all kinds of rifles and muskets and am quite knowledgeable in their treatment. If you name its failures, I may be able to give you some advice."

"There are several. First, the musket has the temperament of a wild ram. It kicks terribly, and has often given me a deft kick in the head."

"That is, of course, not very nice. When shooting, you must put it so that it cannot box your ear."

"Then it kicks me someplace else, it being just the same. Then it wobbles mightily."

"Wobbles? What do you mean by this?"

"I mean that the bullet does not travel in a straight line but snakelike."

"Impossible!"

"*Effendi*, do not doubt it! Anything is possible for a vision musket. I have observed it plenty of times. I must never aim for the target, but, depending on the distance, must aim more toward the right or left, or higher or lower."

"So the musket "twists." To my knowledge there's no other means to alleviate it then to have a new and better barrel made for it."

"How can you expect me to do this? It would totally mess up the precious musket. Allah save me from such a misdeed! The musket must remain as it is."

"Then it's superfluous to tell me its other characteristics. In my opinion, the best gun is one which satisfies its purpose best."

"That it does! My vision musket proves that my ancestor saw the Prophet, which is entirely enough."

"So it is irrelevant how it shoots?"

"Yes."

"But the purpose of shooting is to hit a target!"

"You are no Muslim and therefore cannot provide this musket with the necessary respect."

"No, that I cannot. But should you shoot in my presence, I beg you to protect my life. Do me the favor to aim at me, so that you won't hit me for sure."

"Are you kidding me by chance, *effendi*? I tell you that . . ."

He stopped in mid-sentence, jumped up and peered to the east, shading his eyes with his hand.

"What is it?" I asked. "Do you see something?"

"Yes, I noticed a dot above the grass that was not there before. It must be a rider."

Now I also rose, extended my telescope, and saw a man on a camel coming straight for the well. Once he had approached close enough, he stopped to observe us. Then he rode up, stopped his camel before me, and greeted:

"*Salaam alaykum!* Permit me, sir, to water my camel at this Bir Atshan and to still my own thirst."

"*Wa Alaykum al-Salaam!* The well belongs to everybody, so I cannot prevent you from doing whatever pleases you."

I responded coolly to him, without welcoming him, since he did not make a sympathetic impression on me. He was dressed like a common Bedouin and armed with musket, knife and pistol. While his face did not show repugnant features, I did not care for the sharp, questioning, even piercing look with which he observed us. Accustomed as I was to paying attention to the least detail, it was conspicuous that he had addressed me with his question. My *asakir* wore the Viceroy's uniforms, while I, like our guide, was dressed in civilian clothing. Considering the situation, it would have been proper to turn to the soldiers. This, together with his searching looks, filled me with a slight distrust which did not subsequently lessen but even grew.

He dismounted and led his camel aside to graze after he had removed its saddle. Then he drew some water, drank, took a seat opposite me and pulled a *tshibuk* and tobacco bag from under his *haïk*. Once he had stuffed his pipe and had lit the tobacco, he offered me the latter, saying:

"Help yourself, sir, and stuff your pipe! It is the pipe of greeting I offer."

"Thank you for your kindness but I do not wish to accept it," I responded.

"Then you do not smoke? Are you a member of one of these strict sects whose members are forbidden even tobacco?"

His tone was that of a man who, although he asks, knows already the answer he will receive. It was obvious to me, which is why I felt like remaining even more reserved than before.

"I do smoke. But it wasn't up to you to offer this greeting, but to me. The one present welcomes the later arrival. This it the rule everywhere, and here in the *chala* (land, green savanna) even more so."

"I know it and beg your forgiveness. I have the weakness of carrying my heart on my tongue. I liked you on first sight, and I felt driven to demonstrate this by my offering tobacco. May I ask where you and your *asakir* come from?"

"May I ask you first how come you know that I am with them?"

"Your sharp-sightedness is admirable. I, in your place, would not have guessed it."

"Then you are a stranger in the *chala*, while I cross it frequently."

"Not only am I a stranger here, but *asakir* have never come through here before. It is that much more commendable that your assumption was right on. Although you asked me before, but since I was here before you, you should find it is only right and proper if I, before answering you, would like to know where you come from," I asked.

"I have no reason to keep this a secret. In the *chala*, and even more in the desert, everyone must know who the other is and what he is doing. I come from al-Faky Ibrahim at Bahr al-Abyad."

"And where's your destination?"

"I am headed for al-Fashir."

"Between the places you named lies a much-used caravan route through al-Awid and Fodsha. Why did you not take it? Why did you deviate so far north?"

"Because I am a trader and must get to know the needs of the area. I intend to purchase goods in al-Fashir and sell them on my return. This is why I ride from well to well to learn from the people camped there what they require."

"You seem to be a novice in trading."

"How so, sir?"

"An experienced trader would not venture empty to al-Fashir, but equip himself with imported goods in Khartoum to sell on the inbound trip, making good business. But you want to trade only on the return trip and thus abstain from half of the profits from such a journey. No real *tajir* (trader) does this."

"I wanted to reach my destination quickly, which is why I did not burden my camel with freight."

"A merchant has only one goal: to make a profit. By the way, you ride a *hajin*; a *tajir* commonly uses a donkey."

"Each according to his means, sir. Not that I am poor. Now that you have heard my answers, will you respond also to my questions. Where do you come from?"

My questions had been such that he had to discern my mistrust. They had been even insulting to every honest man. Several times, his eyes had flashed angrily, but the tone by which he answered, had always been polite and seemingly unconcerned. This difference between looks and tone told me that he kept himself under control. Self-control can be a disguise. If the man had a reason to pretend, he gave me every reason to be cautious with him.

I never believed him to be a *tajir*. I was also convinced that he was not coming from al-Faky Ibrahim, but from Khartoum. Meeting us had not surprised him, and his entire behavior let me guess that he had expected to meet us here. But how to explain this? For now, I did not bother with guesses but rather thought to observe him closely. He had lied to me, which is why I thought it best not to tell him the whole truth and replied to his question:

"I come from Badyaruya."

"That is also where the *asakir* come from?"

"No. I met them here, and they allowed me to use the well."

A cunning smile twitched at the corners of his mouth, but he acted as if he believed me, and continued asking:

"Where do they come from? Where were they?"

"I don't know."

"You must know since you talked with them!"

"I asked their permission to camp here. I did not ask about anything else. I think it also impolite to ask strangers right upon meeting them about all kinds of things."

"In the desert and on the savanna curiosity is a duty one must maintain. This is why I ask your permission to ask for the destination of your travel."

"I am headed for Kamlin by the Blue Nile."

"Then you will cross the White Nile at al-Salayiah?"

"Yes."

"And the *asakir*; where are they headed?"

"I do not know. I told you already that I did not ask them."

Now he did a quick turn to the guide, sitting next to me, and asked him:

"And who are you? You must be a Bin Arab?"

I hoped that the guide had observed my mistrust and would beware from providing the correct information, but against my expectation he answered:

"I am indeed a Bin Arab, since I belong to the Bani Fassara."

"You are coming from your home country?"

"Yes."

"Where are your herds presently grazing?"

"Between Bir al-Sarir and Jabal Mudyaf."

"I have heard of the Bani Fassara. They are brave men and fortune dwells in their tents."

He wanted to pump the guide. Since he had been so incautious to name his tribe, it was all the same to me what other information he was still going to provide. I stretched out, put my elbow in the grass to support my head, and gave the impression of indifference, while I kept close watch of every word and expression of the supposed *tajir*. The guide responded to the last remark:

"Yes, fortune dwelled with us but then forsook us."

"Allah may return it. What happened?"

"Ibn Asl abducted our women and daughters."

"I do not know any of this."

"But you must have heard the name of this slaver?"

"Certainly. His deeds are such that one hears of them. So he attacked you? This is unimaginable. You are Muslims, which is why he cannot make slaves of your people. You must be mistaken. It must have been a heathen tribe who committed the deed."

"I am not mistaken. There is proof that Ibn Asl did it. If you do not believe me, I can easily prove it to you, for this . . ."

I noticed that he was going to point at me and say "this *effendi*." Luckily, he looked in my direction, enabling me to give him a warning signal. He stopped, and correcting himself, continued:

"This event can be confirmed by the *asakir*, who visited with us, and whose guide I am."

He began to tell of our adventures. Of course, my person occurred in his narrative, but he was cautious enough to always call me the "foreign *effendi*," without giving away by looks or by pointing that I was the one. Finished, the stranger exclaimed in surprise:

"One cannot imagine a foul deed like this! Ibn Asl abducted your women and daughters and murdered the others he was unable to sell! This is a damnable crime for which Allah will punish him."

"Yes, Allah's arm will surely find him, and the *effendi* and the *raïs effendina* swore him revenge."

"But Ibn Asl is not just bold, but also cunning, and will likely escape them."

"I don't believe so. The foreign *effendi* is a man who finds everyone he is looking for."

"Then he would be all-knowing!"

"That is not necessary. His eyes see everything, and from what he sees, his acumen explains the connection. He did not know the path the abductors would take, but figured it so accurately, as if he had been told."

"Where is he now?"

"He is . . . is . . . still in our village," he replied hesitantly.

"Still in your village?" the stranger repeated with a faint smile while he critically glanced at me. "I would like to see this man for once. If I had the time, I would ride just for this purpose to Bir al-Sarir, but my hours are few enough that I cannot remain even here much longer but must take off again."

He rose and walked to his camel. While I had observed him continuously, I had also looked closely at his animal. By doing so, I had noticed that it had a defect, called 'plucking.' Such an animal alternately opens and closes its toes when walking, causing them to pluck grass blades that remain stuck between its toes. This defect does not cause any harm, but my noticing it on this animal provided me with an advantage and later ruined the plans of some others.

The man saddled his *hajin*, mounted up, drove it over to us, and said to me:

"*Salaam*, sir! Although you told me where you come from and where you are going. I do not believe you. You did not tell me who you are, but I think I can guess it, also that you will soon get to know me."

Not moving, I remained in my previously mentioned position and did not reply.

He nodded derisively and waving a hand contemptuously behind his back, rode away.

"What was that?" the guide asked. "What did he mean? This was an insult!"

I shrugged my shoulder.

"He did not believe you and guesses who you are. Do you comprehend what he wants?"

"Most likely my life."

"Allah 'l Allah!"

"And that of the *asakir*."

"*Effendi*, you scare me!"

"Then mount your camel and ride for home! There will probably be a fight soon, and since your vision musket will not obey you, I advise you that it's best to head for safety."

"Do not shame me! I am to take you to Khartoum and will not leave until we have arrived there. How can you arrive at the thought that we must expect hostilities? Presently, the tribes of this area live in the best of peace with each other."

"The *tajir* told me so."

"I did not hear a word of it."

"He told me so less by his words but by his behavior. Did you really think him to be a *tajir*?"

"Naturally! Why should he claim to be one if he isn't?"

"To deceive us. A scout has every reason to hide what he is."

"A sc . . out? You think him to be a scout? Who would have sent him?"

"Maybe Abd Asl, who wants to avenge himself."

"How can he know that you are here?"

"It must not have been too difficult to find out that I took the freed slaves back home. Just as easy is that I am heading for Khartoum. Thus, I should be found along the way between these two places."

"Talking like this, I am beginning to understand. He wants to satisfy his desire for revenge; yes, yes, one can imagine it. Most likely he went to Khartoum where he knows many people. He has many friends mong the tribes living here, who gain from his business and support him. If he wants to attack you, he will find enough men ready to help him. But he will not succeed. I will show you a way where no meeting will occur."

"I am grateful for it, but cannot agree."

"Why not? It is for your safety."

"How could I get the idea to depart from my way just to avoid a man! Now that I know that he lies in wait for me, I will not be caught. Were they even a hundred, I would be vastly superior to them with my experience and cunning. I will not try to evade them, but literally seek them out. Of course, I'll leave to you whether you want to expose yourself to this unavoidable danger."

"I will stay with you, *effendi*. Do not mention it again. We owe you much. How could I abandon you! But you spoke of looking for them. How can you know where the enemy is?"

"Did you not earlier say that I found the slavers, although I did not know the direction they had taken? Here, it is even easier than before since I have a guide."

"Do you mean me? I have no idea about where to find them."

"I did not refer to you, but the *tajir*."

"Him? You call him your guide? I do not understand. He left west for al-Fashir, while you must search to the east."

"He lied. He isn't going to al-Fashir. As soon as he is out of sight, he will turn to those who dispatched him to scout. We only need to follow his tracks to find what we are looking for."

"If only you are not mistaken, *effendi*! It is still possible that he told the truth."

"It is possible, but most likely I am not mistaken. How long does it take for the ride from al-Faky Ibrahim to al-Fashir?"

"About twenty days."

"Can one do this without a water bag?"

"No."

"So, he cannot be going there since he did not carry one! Furthermore, if Abu Asl truly plans to attack us and commands the necessary men himself, he will expect me to engage a guide, even several, for my trip."

"That in any case, since you are a stranger in this area."

"And these guides must be men who are not only familiar with the area but are also known by the people there. If he'd send us scouts who are just as well known, they would be recognized by my guides."

"That is correct."

"What's the conclusion? What kinds of men must his spies be?"

"Men who are unknown here, strangers."

"A stranger can become lost, or something could happen to him. Does one dispatch such a man without water for such a long distance?"

"No."

"The supposed *tajir* was a spy. He did not have any water with him and, accordingly, wasn't far from his comrades. They are nearby, and will post sentries along a line cutting across our way. When such a sentry sees us coming, he will quickly gather the others to set up an ambush on our way. The *tajir* is one of these sentries. Now, they are waiting for us. The line across our path will not be far from here. The *tajir* will turn and alert his comrades. Our adversaries will expect us at a place we will arrive straight on. If we ride straight ahead, we are certain to meet them. Since we know the direction but not the exact distance from here to their ambush, we must expect them to attack us at any moment. In the open, this does not pose any danger, as we would see them coming. This is why they will select a place with brushwood, a woods, or rocky area, where we would run into their hands without becoming aware of it beforehand. There's the question then whether there's such a place along our today's route. You, as our guide, must know this."

"I know the area very well. It is noon now. If we leave right away we will reach a cassia woods in one-and-a-half hours prior to sunset."

"Then, I give you my word that these people will be waiting there for us."

He looked at me in surprise, shook his head, and said:

"You say this with such certainty!"

"Indeed, and you will see that I am not mistaken. We will first follow the tracks of the false *tajir* until we reach the line of scouts, then . . ."

"How will you recognize that we are there?" he interrupted.

"I will show you. Once there, we take a turn, and countering their expectation arrive from a different direction. While they will be on the lookout to the west, we will attack them from the rear, coming from the east. But before this, I must get a general orientation from you. How large is the cassia woods?"

"As wide as it is deep. It takes an hour to ride through it."

"Are the trees tall?"

"In places, very tall."

"Is there brushwood?"

"Quite a bit. There is a well which provides plenty of water to nourish bushes and lianas."

"Can one cross it on camelback?"

"Yes, if one looks for the open places through the woods."

"Then I know enough for the time being. Let's leave!"

"Shall we not first ride west, following the *tajir*, to see whether he will truly turn?"

"That's superfluous. I am convinced that he will do so. We shall quickly come upon his tracks."

Since he had ridden fast, he had soon disappeared from sight. We saddled, mounted up, and rode eastward with our guide next to me, the *asakir* following in the customary beeline of caravans. They had been sitting close enough to hear what had been said. They were curious to find out whether my prediction would turn out correctly and were eager to put their muskets to work, should everything turn out in that way.

We left the well, following the tracks the *tajir* had made coming toward us. Half an hour later, we saw other tracks coming from the right, joining the incoming ones. I dismounted to check them. Curious, our guide joined me. Looking at the tracks bent down, I straightened up and explained:

"It was the *tajir*, just as I thought."

"How can you say this, *effendi*? It could have been someone else."

"No, it's him. Note the grass on the first tracks! Single grass blades have been plucked. Observe the same on the second tracks."

"This is true, but . . ."

"There's no but. The *tajir's* camel has sensitive hooves and 'plucks.' The second track shows clearer, backward-tossed impressions. From it, we can conclude that he's riding much faster now than before. He turned here and is now in a hurry."

The guide shook his head, but did not say anything. We mounted up once more and rode on, now following the twin tracks. An hour might have passed, when we came to a spot where the rider had halted. The grass had been trampled in a wide circle. Straight ahead the old tracks of three camels and a new, single one led eastward. To the right and left a single track each led south and north. When my companion did not understand the situation, I explained:

"What you see here is proof that my assumption was correct. Far ahead of us, our opponents lie in wait in the cassia woods, from where their leader dispatched a line of sentries. Three men came here. Two of them camped here, while one, the *tajir*, the most enterprising, rode on. When he returned, he reported that he had found us and rode back on the threefold tracks to the woods to report to his leader. The two others rushed off, one northward, the other southward, to order the remaining sentries to return to the woods. Look at this place with its trampled grass! These fellows must think that we are either blind or stupid. With three men posted here, it can be expected that the other posts were manned alike. Since the actual number of warriors is always larger than all sentry posts together, we can calculate the number of men we will have to deal with. We are facing an incautious but numerous enemy. Considering this, I shall hold back with my own wishes and ask for your opinion, men. Do you want to enter into the fight or evade it which, now that the enemy has gathered at a point, is quite easy."

"Fight, fight!" came the general reply.

"All right. Then let's turn left to enter the woods from the north, since they expect us to come from the west. This being a detour, we must ride faster than before."

We hurried on, as fast as our camels would go; the less fast were driven on with rods. After a while, we came across another track, then a second, third, fourth and fifth. All of them led in a southeasterly direction to the woods. Without dismounting, I saw that each set consisted of the hoof prints of three camels.

"Were these all sentries?" the guide asked, riding by my side.

"Of course!" I replied. "You can see that I was correct. Assuming that we found the *tajir's* tracks in the middle of the sentry line, it makes for a total of eleven tracks, each made by three riders. That makes it thirty-three men. How many may then be hiding in the woods? We can assume that we will have to deal with twice that number, that is sixty opponents."

"Then we can expect a tough fight."

"None at all! We will be smart enough not to give them any time for defense."

"You mean that we encircle them and gun them down before they are able to use their weapons?"

"We will probably encircle them, yes, but not kill them. I don't want to spill blood. In any case, we cannot attack them before we have proved that they intend to attack us."

"How can we prove this?"

"Leave that to me! Even if we can tell their hostile intent from their faces, they have not yet committed to it, and we don't have the right to take the life of even one of them. Had we even this right, I would prefer to spare them, to deliver them to the *raïs effendina*."

"This is too bad! Of course, we must obey you, but when I think of what happened in our villages, I am gripped by such anger, which does not want to hear of sparing them."

"The actual culprits have been punished, their crime paid with their death. Consider that the men we are facing are not the ones who abducted your women and daughters."

"Fine, but let me tell you that your decision endangers us all. If we quickly clean up with our bullets, we will not be injured. But how do you plan to catch them alive, without them defending themselves and killing or at least injuring some of us?"

"I do not know yet what I will decide. I must act according to the situation we find. You know that I caught the slavers in Wadi al-Bard without a single *askari* getting a scratch."

He shook his head doubtfully, but preferred to desist from any further objections that would, in any case, have been unsuccessful.

At first, we kept to the northeast, then straight east, and after about two hours turned south, following our guide's opinion that the arc would now take us straight to the woods. We soon spotted a dark stripe on the horizon, a bit to the right from us. We had ridden so fast that we were almost halfway around the woods. This got me to thinking. With sufficient time until sunset, we could approach the enemy not from the side but the rear. For this reason, we now kept more to the left until we saw the strip of wood more to the west of us. That's when we came across a broadly trampled passage, something I had expected, which led from the east toward the woods. The grass had been trampled, and although it had risen again, its buckled tips clearly stood out from the rest of the *chala*. They were the tracks of our enemy group. I could see that they must have passed here by early morning. They then camped in the woods and dispatched their scouts to the west.

Of course, we now turned in this direction and arrived at an opening in the woods, where even a larger group than ours could easily pass through. Now, it called for great caution. I dismounted to walk ahead. Our guide, leading my camel by its holder, followed with the *asakir* some short distance behind. He had told me that the well was located roughly in the middle of the woods, and I thought it obvious that the bandits would be close to it.

We passed by tall cassia and mimosa trees. The shrubs were mostly rhododendron and prickly-trunk bauhinias, which climbed up the tree trunks and branches, dropping their dense growth of beautifully blooming twigs and branches. Behind the densely entwined bushes we were invisible. At one of these thickets my companions dismounted and lead their camels inside to wait there for my return while I went to reconnoiter.

Faithful Bin Nil offered to accompany me, but I declined. Our guide wanted to join me, too, and when I also turned him down, he said:

"But you are unfamiliar with the woods and the path to the well, *effendi*. I must point it out to you."

"Don't worry about me! I know what I'm doing. And you are also mistaken if you think the enemy is camped by the well."

"Where else?"

"Anywhere but not there. Yes, earlier, they will have been there, but with the return of the sentries they will have vacated the place."

"Why so?"

"They must assume that we will head for the well, where it is best to attack us. If they'd attack us when we are still in the saddle, traveling in a rather long line, they would hardly accomplish their purpose. Most likely, they will wait for us to settle down, which is why I'm certain that they won't be at the well but somewhere close by. How's the path to the well from here? Does it make turns?"

"No, it runs in an almost straight line."

"That is to my advantage. I will go now. You have nothing to do but remain quiet."

"But what shall we do if you do not return?"

"I shall return!"

"You speak so very confidently, *effendi*. May Allah lead you!"

By leaving my bright *haïk*, my dark gray suit did not stand out from the rich vegetation. Of course, I took care not to walk on the broad pathway, where I could easily be spotted with the trees spaced apart there. Rather I kept to the side, parallel to the trail, walking in the cover of bushes.

A quarter of an hour on I thought I heard someone speak to my left. The well had to be to my right. I stopped to listen. Yes, indeed, there were subdued voices, indicating that they were not far from me. I lay down and crept on on hands and knees. The farther I crept, the clearer the voices became. Oddly enough, one of them sounded familiar. I was still unable to understand the spoken words, but from their sound the speakers had to be hidden behind some impenetrable brushwood. I crept closer and recognized the other voice, that of the make-belief *tajir*. And if I wasn't mistaken, the other was no one else but – Abd Asl, the father of the slaver, the holy *faqir*, who had tried to see me perish in the subterranean well near Asyût.

The senna brush could not be very deep, since I heard and under-stood their words now so clearly that I figured the distance between me and the two speakers to be at most three to four yards. From various noises coming from there, I could guess that the two were not alone.

"All, all of them must go to Hell. We keep only the German alive!" I heard the *faqir* say, while I was now comfortably listening.

"Why so?" the *tajir* asked. "He should be the first to be hit by our bullets and knives."

"No, I want to save him to bring him to my son. He is to suffer long, long pains. I do not want him to die a quick death."

"Then expect him to slip away again."

"Slip away? Impossible! I know that he is a devil, but there are plenty of means to tame even such a Satan. I shall cage him like a carnivore. No, he will not escape me now or ever! Were it up to me, I would spare also the *asakir* to torture them slowly to death, but since we are pressed for time, we must dispose of them quickly. How I would torment these rogues who killed our fellowmen and took away the great profit we were going to make!"

"Yes, much would have been paid for these Fassara slaves. We ought to cut off the hands and tongues of these men so that they can neither speak nor write and cannot betray anything. Then, we ought to sell them to the most cruel Negro ruler!"

"Not a bad idea. Maybe, we will do it. And, maybe, a better one will still come to us. There is no pain too large, too terrible for them. They must die daily, hourly, without really being able to die. They deserve it, especially this foreign dog, who knows how to guess every one of our plans only to escape with the aid of the Devil when we think we have him cornered."

"This is precisely what should urge us to be very cautious. Just think he could escape us again."

"Do not worry! The orders I have issued are carefully thought out so that no failure is possible. I will fire the first shot, aiming for the German's leg. When he is injured, he will not be able to escape us now or later. Once I have fired my rifle, the rest of you fire, too. Close to seventy bullets ought to be enough to bring them all down."

"I should think so. It is actually a shame that we had to gather such a number of warriors against those few *asakir*."

"This was not because of the *asakir* but the foreigner. Under his command twenty men are as good as a hundred. Let me tell you that we will only be victorious because of the unexpectedness, the suddenness of the attack. If we let them mount a resistance our success will be in doubt."

I laughed softly. Neither the *tajir* nor the *faqir* possessed the smarts required for the execution of their plan. They had not even posted a guard to warn of our approach, which I learned from their next exchange. I also heard that their location was so close to the well that they hoped to hear the noise of our arrival.

The *faqir's* words told me that his son, the slaver, had set a trap for the *raïs effendina*. This concerned me, and I was determined to act quickly here, then speed up our ride to arrive as soon as possible in Khartoum to warn the *raïs*. Most of all, it required a good overview of the situation. Where I lay the brush was so dense that I was unable to peer through it. I crept on to the left where I found an opening providing the desired view. I faced a glade where the seventy men rested, many only partly dressed, but all well armed. I noticed faces from a light brown to the deepest black. Their camels lay next to each other at the edge of the glade, across from my position. The *faqir* and the *tajir* sat separately from the group at the proximal edge of the glade. It had been a stroke of luck that I happened to hit this spot, or I would have found it difficult getting to it.

The men did not sit or lie close to each other, but had gathered in groups of twos and threes. This ought to facilitate our attack. At my present location, there was enough space to post my twenty men. Also, they could see the enemy, and it would be possible for me to give instructions to each of them. Every one of my men had to know which opponent to attack since, otherwise, chaos might erupt, allowing the majority of the enemy to flee.

Since I needn't see or hear anymore, I returned to my companions to inform them of the good results of my reconnoiter. No one was more pleased to hear of the *faqir's* presence than Bin Nil who, barely had I finished, called:

"*Al-Hamdulillah*, the *faqir*, the *faqir* is here! *Effendi*, you must leave him to me; I will shoot him!"

"There will be no shooting," I replied. "We will not kill these men but deliver them to the *raïs effendina*."

"Even the *faqir*, who is mine?"

"He's mine, too, but I abstain from revenge."

"But I don't!"

"We will talk about it later; for now I strongly forbid you to kill him!"

"*Effendi*, consider that you are denying a right of mine which no one can take from me!"

"I won't do that, I only want some delay. The *raïs effendina* is in some danger which I'm ignorant of. The *faqir* knows it and must tell me. If he's killed, I will not learn anything and the *raïs* will be lost. Whatever happens, I must talk with the *faqir*."

"If that is so, I will comply. But later, you will not be so unjust as to prevent me from executing the law of the desert. Well, then, *effendi*, how are we going to overcome these seventy warriors if we are not allowed to kill them?"

"We club them with our musket butts. If one dies from such a blow, it cannot be helped and we will not be sorry for it. But you must hit them hard enough that the victim collapses and can no longer resist. I will lead you and show each of you which group he is to turn on, so that one doesn't hinder the other. I will take on the *faqir* and the *tajir* myself. The moment I break through the brush you follow me. No commands will be given; no one is to shout. Everything must happen in total silence, which will make the surprise even more effective than when the enemy is warned by untimely screams. Consider that each of you must club three to four opponents! You must therefore work quickly, which is only possible if you remain totally quiet. The fellows must literally stiffen from fright. Battle shouts would only make them alive and agile."

Since our camels' legs had been tied, a single man sufficed to guard them. All others followed me.

"I like your plan, *effendi*," our guide remarked, when we took off. "I am not so sure about not shooting, but now these dogs will get to taste the butt of my vision musket."

We arrived unnoticed at the place I had picked earlier. Nothing had changed there in the meantime. Some time passed until I had shown every one of my men where to turn. Then I went myself to the opening I had earlier peeked through. My companions stood, eyes on their specific victims, to my left where the bushes could readily be penetrated. Once I saw that everyone was ready, I rushed through the bushes into the glade, turned to the right – two rifle butt blows, and the *faqir* and *tajir* were taken out of action.

Behind me it sounded like a storm in the bushes; the *asakir* had followed me. A few paces from my two victims sat four men, so terrified by my appearance that they gaped at me motionless. I clubbed the first and the second; the third raised his arms in defense, I still got him. The fourth was going to jump up, but did not make it. I downed him with the others. In consideration for the victims, I had hit them with the broadside, not the edge of the rifle butt. This stunned, but did not kill.

Six men – my quota. Now, I made it my task to keep possible escapees at bay. This is why I turned toward the place of action I had, until now, my back turned to, and readied my multi-shot Henry carbine.

A never-seen sight presented itself. The *asakir* had kept to my orders; they worked quietly, the expected effect showing. Precisely their silence increased the terror of the attacked; they, too, remained silent. Only here and there one of them screamed or jumped up to flee, at which none succeeded. But then, had any threatened to get away, I would have given him a bullet in the leg to drop him.

The knocking down of people is nothing to be pleased about, but for a battle-happy eye, it was a joy to see the *asakir* at work. Bin Nil was the most agile; I believe he struck down six or seven opponents. From the moment I had penetrated the bushes to when the last of the enemy fell, hardly one-and-a-half minutes must have passed, and not a single stab had been made or shot fired by our opponents. This was the consequence of our surprise, a complete, paralyzing surprise like I had never experienced before.

Even now, with our success complete, the *asakir* remained silent. They all looked at me to learn what was to happen now.

"Quickly, tie them all up," I shouted. "Use ropes, ties, or scraps of cloth, whatever you can tear from their clothing! There's no longer any need to be silent; you can talk!"

Talk? How, in such a situation, can one speak about "talking" to an African *askari*? Had I said, "you can scream," the result would not have come close to what I got to hear now. The twenty voices broke into a literally superhuman screaming, as if a thousand devils were rejoicing. Still, they did not miss quickly following my order.

Of course, I first turned my attention to the *faqir* and his scout. Their mouths were open and they breathed noisily. I tied their hands behind their backs, also their legs. There was plenty of material for ties, since every Bedouin carries cords, he often has need of on a ride. Furthermore, every *kuffiyah* (headscarf) and hood comes with a string with which to attach the head cover, all well suited for binding a man.

There were some who were only partially stunned. They were recognized by their movements and, naturally, tied up first. Five or at most six minutes later, we were done and could now check whether one or another had been struck dead. Unfortunately, the *asakir* had not been as kind as I had been. They had hit with the edge of their butts, which is why we found several shattered skulls. To my sorrow we found eight men dead. Three of them fell on our guide's conscience, who said, while he wiped the blood from the butt of his musket.

"*Effendi*, my vision musket has done its duty. Of the four I clubbed, only one will rise again."

"Was that your intention?"

"Yes, I wanted to kill also the fourth."

"Hadn't I forbidden this?"

"Am I forbidden to avenge myself? Did I promise to obey your prohibition? I saw our murdered people lie in the sands of Bir al-Sarir and took revenge, which is nothing to what happened there. You have no right to take away mine!"

I preferred not to answer him and returned to the *faqir* who, as I saw, had his eyes open and, terrified, was now looking over his surroundings. The *tajir*, too, had recovered, and just as frightened looked around. While the *asakir* searched the captives and their camels for booty, something I could not forbid, I sat down by the *faqir*. He kept his eyes closed, whether from weakness, anger or shame was not my concern.

"*Salaam, ya wali al-kabir al-Mashur* (be greeted, you great, famous saint)!" I told him. "I'm glad to see you here and hope that you, too, are happy to see my face."

"Be cursed!" he hissed half-loud without opening his eyes.

"You misspoke. You were going to say 'be blessed', for I know how much you longed to see me. You even sent out scouts to search for me. Unfortunately, your longing was to your detriment. You wanted to shoot the *asakir* and cut off my tongue and my hands, then to sell me to the most cruel Negro ruler."

"He is all-knowing!" the *faqir* uttered to his companion, while he opened his eyes. The *tajir* looked at me with an expression of deadly hate. I nodded kindly to him and said:

"You were totally right when you told me that I would soon see you again and then get to know you better. It took so little time for us to see each other again, although you wanted to get to al-Fashir. I am really delighted, since it is proof that I judged you correctly. You are the one who came up with the idea to take my tongue and hands, and you aren't mistaken when I won't withhold my gratitude for this pleasant idea of yours."

"I do not understand you," he replied. "Why have I been tied up? Why did you attack us? What can you prove? I demand to be untied."

"Your wish will be gladly fulfilled the moment you are turned over to the hangman."

He made a hasty movement, as if wanting to contradict me, and opened his mouth for a reply, but I did not let him get to it by quickly continuing:

"Don't get worked up! You are much too stupid to deceive me. A man like you ought to stay home and not do anything else but bemoan his silly behavior. When you came to us today, before you even dismounted from your camel, I knew already what kind of fellow you were. Do you know the fable of the *Buqqa* (bedbug), who wanted to outwit the *Abu Husayn* (fox)?"

"That is no concern of mine. It is known to every child!" he barked at me.

"But it concerns you very much, for you resemble this *Buqqa*, by arriving at the crazy idea that you can fool me. At this, an even thousand times smarter man would not have succeeded. How you, whose head does not hold a trace of brain, could hope to trick me, can only be explained by your infinite silliness. Ha, you outsmarting a German *effendi*! This is exactly as it is told in the fable – the *Buqqa* who dares to tackle the *Abu Husayn*."

It wasn't arrogance of mine to talk so big; a less haughty way of expression would not have served its purpose. I did not have to wait long, for he replied angrily:

"How can a *giaur* elevate himself above a true believer! Were you as smart as you think you are, you would long since have left your misconception. Remove our fetters, which have been dirtied by your hands, immediately or . . ."

"Shut up!" I interrupted him. "Don't try to threaten me or I will answer you with the whip! Dog-like rabble like you gets beaten when it barks. And since you comprehend your present condition so little that you dare to demand instead of begging, I shall get you to realize it in some way such that your haughtiness will quickly dissipate!"

"You will desist, for I am a *shaykh*!" he objected.

"Bah! A miserable Bedouin *shaykh* is nothing to me. By the way, you claimed to be a *tajir*, while you are in fact a member of a murderous gang. You will be treated accordingly."

"Woe to you then! You will be lost. My tribe will destroy you all!"

"What, this fellow is so impudent to threaten you, *effendi*?" Bin Nil exclaimed, who had walked up and had heard the exchange. "Shall I stuff his mouth?"

"Go ahead!"

With his foot, he turned the *tajir* on his back and pulled the whip from his belt. I turned away. I could not bear watching this punishment, but my ears told me that Bin Nil vented his anger leaving nothing to chance. In the meantime, I told my men to take the captives and their animals to the well. Once done, our camels were also brought there.

Where the well was located, trees and bushes had been removed to make room for even more people than we were. Water was plentiful.

My *asakir* had made some good booty and were therefore in an excellent mood. Each of them received the camels, weapons, and other bits and pieces of at least three of the captives. I, of course, claimed nothing, with Bin Nil, although he was a poor Devil, following my example. When I asked him the reason for his abstention, he answered:

"Why do you not take anything yourself, *effendi*? Is it from generosity toward the *asakir*, that they also get your share? Or is it pride? I learned from you that warriors of the Occident do not take any spoils. I, too, disdain owning items that were in the dirty hands of these sons-of-bitches."

This showed a most decent mindset and devotion and deserved my friendly consideration.

We had to make sure that the captives were secure. They were placed in our midst and kept under close supervision. Guards were posted for the night. While there was still daylight, dusk would fall within half an hour. I thought it wise to check the well's surroundings before nightfall. This was a precaution which I omitted on my travels only when I was absolutely certain of being safe. To check for possible tracks and to orient myself in general, I walked slowly around. Before doing this, I had sent several men into the woods to collect firewood. With the number of captives three times that of the *asakir*, we needed to maintain not just one but several fires. Enough material was quickly gathered. I returned from my walk without seeing anything suspicious. Instead, one of the wood gatherers brought me two items he had found below a tree that had caught his attention.

"Look at these two bones, *effendi*. They seem to be the remains of a calf, and since no one takes a living calf onto the savanna only to butcher it there, the people who camped here and did this must have been cattle rustlers."

I took the bone fragments from him to look at them more closely and was shocked. One was half a shoulder blade, and the other the upper part of a thigh bone.

"These are not calf but human bones!" I told him.

"Allah! Then a man was murdered here!"

"Actually not murdered, but torn apart and eaten."

I was quickly surrounded, with everyone shouting that I must be mistaken.

"I am not mistaken. I know how to differentiate between the bones of a human and those of an animal. This shoulder blade and the thigh bone were crushed by the teeth of a very strong, wild animal. Are there lions here on the savanna, or even here in the woods?"

"May Allah protect us and bless us with his mercy!" our guide now screamed. "This is no other devil than Khazaq al-Jum'a (Weekly Tearer to Pieces), the Lion al-Taytal!"

"Why is he named after this place?"

"Because he takes turns visiting all wells between al-Taytal and the Nile."

"And what's the reason for his other name?"

"Not a week passes that he does not tear a human apart and eat him. He's lived in this area for more than a year."

"Has he not been hunted; did people not try to shoot him?"

"Hunted? What do you think? May Allah protect every human being from this mighty devourer, who is larger than an ox and stronger than an elephant!"

"Is his den known? Has he possibly been seen with a lioness or cubs?"

"No. This is why he does not stay in one place, but sleeps once here, then there, and in between, travels from well to well."

"Ah, a *wahid* (solitary)! I know these solitary creatures, hostile even toward their own kind. They are the worst. If one of those has once tasted human flesh, he will stick to this kind of food and kill animals only when he is extremely hungry."

"This is correct, *effendi*, and this vagabond of al-Taytal is such a man-eater. It has happened that he killed two in one week. When might he have been here?"

"Four or five days ago, as I determine from the condition of the bone fragments."

"Oh, Allah! This is bad! He could be here again tonight. Had he been here yesterday or the day before yesterday, he would surely be somewhere else, but after such a long time, he may have completed his round already."

"That depends on how many wells he visits and whether he has found another victim by now. He cannot devour a human being in one setting, and will leave it only when he has cracked the last marrow bone. He may have stayed here for three days."

"Then Allah was merciful to us. This man-eater could have attacked us at one of our last night camps. The bones are four days old; he was here for three days, which means that he is gone for only a day and we need not fear anything."

"Your conclusion may be correct but could be deceptive. The lion prefers, like any other carnivore, the places where he finds food, versus those he visited in vain. He could easily return sooner than you imagine."

"All saints and *Khulafa'* may prevent this! He may still be here and lie in ambush!"

"In that case I would have spotted his tracks. Still, we must be cautious, since such solitary lions are cunning and deceitful and do not announce their approach like other lions by roaring. Rather, they creep up like panthers and leap silently onto their victims. I once shot one of these obdurate sinners, who roared just once from joy when he came across our tracks, and then approached us in total silence."

"What, *effendi*, you shot at lions?"

"Several."

"And did you hit them?"

"Only when I was still a novice did my bullet sometimes not hit home."

"And did you kill lions?"

"Yes."

"With how many shots?"

"With one. Only once did it take two."

"Oh, *effendi*, what a wonderful liar you are, how magnificent!"

I did not hold this exclamation against the man, since I was familiar with the ways and means that the desert and savanna dwellers hunt lions. Once a den has been discovered, the warriors of a tribe gather, joined by those of other tribes, and then ride there together. The den is surrounded and pelted with rocks. Everyone screams as loudly and as much as he can, until the lion makes his appearance. Now every musket cracks without anyone taking care to aim properly. Most bullets miss; maybe a single one will hit by chance, after which the wounded animal leaps roaring into the crowd to tear one or two riders from their mounts and kills them. The others leap back to reload, stop, and shoot again – with the same result. The lion will advance once more to tear another apart. Salvo upon salvo is fired until the animal riddled with bullets collapses. It is not yet dead, but exhausted from loss of blood. And yet, many men pay with their lives for this inglorious victory. The others fall upon the corpse of the 'Desert King,' beat and kick it, spit on it and demean it with all kinds of terrible curses. This is never done at night, always by day. That a single European waits or even looks for a lion at night, to kill it with a shot through an eye or the heart, is a fable to these people – a total impossibility. They simply do not believe it, which is why I did not hold it against the guide, when he believed that I was entertaining him with a beautiful lie."

"He killed lions!" he continued laughing. "With one shot! At night! And all alone! Oh, Allah, oh Muhammad, what a mighty hero our *effendi* is! I would love just once to see him as such an Asad al-Sabbad (Lion Hunter)!"

"Don't wish it," I warned him without feeling insulted. "Your wish could be fulfilled if the lion comes, and I don't think you'd like it."

"But I would!" he replied, still laughing. "I am as little afraid as you. The man-eater is an enormously large animal, and if I let him come close enough, I will not miss him. What a German can do, who was not even born here, I can do, too, being a son of these lands. I will make you a bet that, should the lion come, I will do the same as you do."

"Fine. What are we betting for?"

"Will you put your watch and your telescope against my vision musket?"

"Yes."

"You are not kidding?"

"No. So you will bet me?"

"Yes. I swear it by Allah and the beard of the Prophet. Do you want to withdraw?"

"No. You swore by Allah and the Prophet's beard, so you also cannot withdraw. At first you contradicted me from disbelief, but then came your desire for my watch and the spy glass. You are certain of getting these two items, since you think that, when the lion comes, I will sit quietly and cautiously by the fire. You are mistaken, though!"

He looked down for awhile, then said:

"I do not want to insult you, but I just don't believe it."

"And while I don't think the animal will come, should it, I shall prove to you that you are mistaken. Is the bet on?"

"Yes, since I swore to it."

"Then ask your Prophet to keep the lion away. If he doesn't grant you your wish, your famous vision musket will be gone. Let's have a look at our captives . . ."

I was interrupted by the appearance of a camel rider at the western opening of the glade, who, seeing us, seemed to be rather perplexed. He appeared to be in doubt as to whether it was more prudent to ride past us or to head for the well. He decided for the latter, drove his animal toward us, dismounted, and said:

"Before 'salaam' crosses my lips, tell me who your leader is!"

"I am," I told him.

"These are *asakir*, but you do not look like an *askari*. How does this explain you calling yourself their leader?"

"Does a uniform make the *askari*?"

"No. You are right. Why are the people tied up, lying here on the ground?"

"They are captives of ours, slavers."

"But this is no crime?"

"Well, then abduction!"

"Slaves, especially Blacks, are not true human beings. You will set these men free!"

The lean man seemed to be a little over thirty years old, and wore a dark, not very dense beard. His cloak had once been white, but now did not look too clean anymore. His facial expression was stern, grimly ascetic. He stood straight and proudly before me, his eyes almost threatening, as if he and not me was the one to command. I could not imagine that this man was later to play such a prominent role as the Mahdi.

"Will I?" I asked him. "So! By what rights and for what reason do you expect me to do this?"

"Because I say so, I, the *Faqir al-Fuqara*."

"Fine! And I am the *Askari al-Asakir* and do as I please."

Faqir al-Fuqara means *faqir* of *faqirs*, the best, the most superb *faqir*. This is why I had called myself the 'Soldier of Soldiers,' the most excellent soldier. He must not have expected this response, for he asked:

"Don't you know me then? Did you not hear yet of the *Faqir al-Fuqara*?"

While he said this, I noticed his look of tacit understanding with the old, 'not so honorable' *faqir*, lying there tied up. They had to know each other, which is why I replied:

"No, but my captives know you."

"How do you know?"

"You told me so yourself."

"I am not aware of it. When?"

"Just now. Your eyes told me. You made a promise to this old Abd Asl which you cannot keep."

"I shall keep it. Ask your captives, and they will tell you that I am powerful, and they know very well that I keep a promise once I make it."

"Ask them first about me, and they will tell you that, at this time, it is I who hold the power here. Who and what you are is meaningless to me. I stand here in place of the *raïs effendina*, who is in the place of the *Khedive*. That should suffice for you."

"It does not suffice at all, but has a different effect than you intended. The Viceroy, as well as the *raïs effendina*, are nothing in my eyes. I would not think of following their directions."

At the time, I did not know his background. Later, of course, I learned why he had used this disrespectful, even condescending expression. He had been a tax collector for some time and was forced to relinquish his position, only to become a slave trader. At the time I was ignorant of this and thus, answered him with a superior smile:

"Nevertheless, you shall follow their directions by following me, who is executing their orders."

"You shall see right away how much I respect these orders."

He drew his knife and bent down to Abd Asl.

"Hold it! What are you up to?"

"Free this friend from his fetters."

"I won't permit this."

"I did not ask for your permission."

He put his knife on the cord. I, too, put something on, that is from behind. With my hands on his hips, I lifted him from his bent-over position and tossed him several paces across the group of captives. He had held onto his knife and quickly got up again. Raising his hand to stab me, he rushed at me with the words:

"You dare lay hands on the *Faqir al-Fuqara*? Here, take this!"

I didn't even think to use a weapon, neither did any of the *asakir* think of coming to my assistance. Only Bin Nil's hand reached for his belt, while he remained standing. They knew that I would take care of the attacker. My fist went from below into the armpit of his raised arm. My blow was so hard that it lifted him up once more and dropped him to the ground. When he jumped up to attack me anew, I drew my revolver, pointed it at him, and shouted:

"One more step and I will gun you down!"

"Stop, or the *giaur* will truly shoot!" Abd Asl warned him.

The *Faqir al-Fuqara* withdrew the already raised foot, whether from fear of my weapon or surprise to hear me called a *giaur*, I do not know; probably for both reasons, and asked:

"A *giaur*? He is no Muslim?"

"No, he is a Christian," the old fellow replied.

"And this dog dared to . . ."

Instantly, Bin Nil stood behind him, the whip raised, asking:

"*Effendi*, shall I whip his skin to shreds, since he gave you the name of a despised animal?"

"Once he will be forgiven, since he spoke from excitement," I replied. "But should he insult me one more time, he will receive the *bastonnade*, and he will remain lying here to perish miserably!"

"Allah! Me, the *bastonnade*!" the man grated. "By a Christian! What an outrage, what daring!"

"Don't mention daring," I laughed at him. "I wouldn't be afraid facing ten of your kind, but here you are alone and, in addition, have twenty *asakir* against you."

"But they are Muslims?"

"Indeed, they are."

"Then they must take my side, not yours! How can a Muslim tolerate a Christian threatening another true believer with the *bastonnade*, yes, when he even lays hands on him and tosses him to the earth?"

Now, Bin Nil stepped in front of him, speaking in my place:

"Listen, we love this *effendi* from the bottom of our hearts and are prepared to fight anyone threatening him. Ten, even a hundred *Fuqara al-Fuqara*, are not the equal of him in our respect. Let me tell you that you are not the first who insulted him and received a whipping. Watch out, therefore! The *bastonnade* hovers over your head, and by Allah, if you do not keep your mouth in check, it will instantly descend on you!"

"Boy!" the *Faqir* barked. "Beware your tongue! What are you and twenty *asakir* against the followers who will rush to my aid, should I raise my voice?"

"Raise it! We will see whether the woods come alive!"

"You can say this because I have no one with me today, but later I can squash you like worms under my feet!"

The soldiers raised an angry murmur, but the fellow did not pay attention to it and continued:

"By serving a Christian against these Muslims you disavow the Prophet. Do you have any right to keep these true believers captive? If they captured slaves, where in the Qur'an does it say that slave trade is forbidden?"

Obviously, it was his intention to incite the *asakir* against me. He may have thought this possible. I had no need to prevent him from his intentions with any words, for Bin Nil, who spoke once again for everyone else, told him:

"You do not understand your situation. Ibn Asl, the son of the old *faqir*, has attacked the Bani Fassara, killed many, and abducted their young women and daughters, to sell them into slavery. But we have liberated them and returned them to their home. From anger and to avenge himself, he sent his father with these men against us. They lay in wait here to murder us, and the *effendi's* tongue and hands were to be cut off. Is it permitted to abduct true believers to make them slaves?"

"No," the newcomer admitted.

"Are the Bani Fassara true believers or *giaurlar*?"

"True believers."

"Then Ibn Asl committed a deathly sin and the men here are his accomplices. They must be punished for it, not to say that they are murderers, since they intended to do what I told you."

The youngster's statement did not miss making an impression. The *Faqir al-Fuqara* turned to the old *faqir* Abd Asl and asked:

"Is it true what I was just told?"

"Let them prove that we intended to kill these *asakir*," Abd Asl replied. "It is a dastardly lie!"

"Do not deny it!" I barked at him. "I heard it with my own ears while spying on you. I lay behind the bushes where you sat with your supposed *tajir*."

"You were mistaken," said the *Faqir al-Fuqara* to me.

"I heard correctly and there is other proof."

"What is it? I must hear it."

"You must? Who made you judge over me? I must only what I want, and I tell you my will right now, which is, that you do not concern yourself with this situation. You burned your fingers already, touching it, so that I advise you to stay away from the fire. Without knowing me, you conducted yourself like a master. Continue on your way or camp here with us at the well, both are fine by me. But as soon as you involve yourself in my duties, I shall prove to you that, due to my authorities, I am the present master at this well."

"How are you going to prove this?"

"By no longer tolerating you, but by chasing you away. No more words now! Step back! You can camp with the *asakir*, but keep away from the captives."

He must have seen that I would tolerate no contradiction anymore, but anger lay like a thundercloud on his features. He took the saddle off of his camel and let it run to graze. Then, he unpacked some of his provisions, took a cup from the saddlebag and settled down by the well to eat his evening meal. Before doing so, he made up for the evening prayer he had missed. The sun had set since his arrival, and the time of *maghrib*, the prescribed first evening prayer, had passed. The *asakir* prayed, too, since they had also committed the same omission.

Four fires had been lighted. Between this illumination lay the captives, so that we could readily see each individual's movements. Around them, the *asakir* formed a chain, surrounded by our camels whose forelegs had been tied.

I, too, sat at the well to eat. Bin Nil and our Fassara guide joined me. The *Faqir al-Fuqara* sat so close that he could understand our conversation. I had no reason to keep secrets; he might otherwise have thought that I was afraid of him. I guessed that Bin Nil would use the opportunity to once more present his demand concerning the old Abd Asl, and rightly so. Barely had I put the last bite into my mouth when he said:

"*Effendi*, I had to honor the meal, but now, that you are finished, I hope to speak. You promised me the old *faqir*."

"It wasn't as final as you seem to think."

"Yes! You wanted to find something out from him, after which I would be permitted to punish him."

"But I haven't learned what I want to find out, and there's still time."

"No. Consider that you could get his information too late. I know that you do not want to see him die, which is why you hesitate."

— 38 —

"Allah will punish him!"

"Yes, but through me!"

"Look at him! He is an oldster, a weak, defenseless man. Do you have the heart to stab your knife into his chest?"

"He had the heart to capture you and me in the well and leave us to perish there. Today, he was once more ready to commit a more than twenty-fold murder. If you pardon him, you sin against Allah, who is also your God."

"That is correct," the guide agreed. "I, too, was in mortal danger, including every one of the *asakir*. We all have therefore the right to demand the blood of this mass murderer!"

"Right on! This is it; very much so!" the *asakir* now shouted.

"Did you hear it, *effendi*?" the guide asked. "Do you want to neglect our well-earned right? Then you must expect that we will take it ourselves."

I had thought of that. The soldiers were angry at the captives. Only the respect they had for me, made it possible for them to obey my command and only club the surrounded men instead of killing them. I could not guarantee them that the guilty would truly be punished in Khartoum. Should they avenge themselves against my will; what could I do about it? Use force against their threats? Then my authority would be gone. It would be better to sacrifice a single one, than many would fall from the stabs of the avengers, and, of course, this had to be the old *faqir*. I had already halfway decided to say "yes," when the oldest of the *asakir* walked up to me to say:

"*Effendi*, I have been charged by my comrades to present you with a request."

"Speak!"

"Tell me first whether we have obeyed you and whether you are satisfied with us."

"I can give the *raïs effendina* a good reference for each of you."

"I thank you! Yes, it is true that we always did what you demanded, although your decisions were often incomprehensible to us. Afterward, we always realized that you had done the right thing, which is why you earned our respect. But, with your permission, there is one shortcoming we must reproach you for. Being a Christian, you have always been very lenient with our enemies. Enemies must be destroyed to stay alive oneself. Should I catch my deadly enemy today and let him get away by mercy, he will attack me again tomorrow. We were doomed to die, but your cunning and prudence saved us. The enemy is ours now, but you do not want us to lay hands on them. All right, we will also obey you this time; we shall take them to Khartoum and turn them over to the raïs effendina, but one must die, Abd Asl. We insist! We do not want to rise up against you, but if you do not allow us this small request, you will be unable to prevent that here and there some knife will find a heart and many of those you intend to save will no longer be alive in the morning. Decide!"

This had been straight talk! What was I to say? Was I truly obligated as a Christian to save Abd Asl, the monster, and by so doing endanger many others? But, maybe, I would be able to achieve my purpose by cunning, relying on Bin Nil's good heart!

No blood was to flow while I was still in command. What happened later could not be on my conscience. This is why I replied, seemingly agreeing to his demand:

"You spoke quite reasonably stating your point of view, but how can I decide the life of the faqir since it isn't mine any more? Bin Nil is the first to avenge himself."

"But you do not allow it, as we heard."

"No. He is to have his right, if you agree and waive yours."

"Then we are immediately agreed, effendi."

"Then you put the faqir's life in Bin Nil's hands?"

"Yes."

"Then we are agreed. Tell the others!"

Satisfied, the askari left. Bin Nil offered his hand, and said:

"I thank you, effendi! Now, the law of the desert will be satisfied and no new foul deeds will be committed by this monster."

"Go then and stab your knife into the tied up old man's breast, so worthy of a brave man!"

He dropped his head, and I saw that he struggled with himself. Then he raised his head and asked:

"The old man is truly mine and I can do with him as I please?"

"Yes."

"Well, then I will take revenge."

He rose and drew his knife. That's when the *Faqir al-Fuqara* jumped up, too, held him by his arm, and shouted:

"Stop! This would be murder I cannot permit it to happen!"

Bin Nil shook the man off with a force I had not thought him capable of, telling him:

"Shut up! You do not give orders here! I pay attention to your words like I do to the buzzing of a fly!"

"Shut up yourself, you wretched boy! If I like, I will squash you in my hands!"

"Try it!"

Bin Nil had drawn his knife, now the *Faqir al-Fuqara* also drew his. I leapt between them and tore the weapon from the hand of the latter, demanding:

"Get back or you will have to deal with me!"

"But you also with me," he shouted angrily.

"Bah! You've seen already what you can do against me."

"That was coincidence. Do you think you have more courage and are more agile than I am? A *Faqir al-Fuqara* isn't afraid of any enemy, not even the strongest, whatever he wants to do!"

Just when I was going to answer, a distant sound caused me to stop. It sounded like remote thunder, yet also like the yawning of a close-by, awakening hyena. I knew this sound, had heard it in similar situations when I was facing the king of beasts for life or death.

"Are you neither afraid of this enemy?" I asked the *faqir*, while I pointed in the direction from where the growl had come.

"No, not at all."

"And you are prepared to fight him?"

"Yes," he laughed, "under the condition that you take me to him."

"Come then! I'll take you."

I took my rifle and checked that it was properly loaded.

"What a hero you are!" he shouted derisively. "To fight a hyena!"

"A hyena? Are you deaf or have you never heard the voice of the 'Lord of the big Head'?"

"The Lord of the big Head? You mean the lion?"

"What else?"

"It was a hyena. You are deaf and so fearful that you think a hyena to be a lion. And if it were truly the 'Strangler of Herds' we heard, I would walk with you toward him, to prove to you that . . ."

He stopped. The roar sounded once more, now much more clearly than before. This was proof that the animal was approaching only slowly. But it had sounded just a touch louder, for the camels began to snort, and the Fassara guide shouted fearfully:

"Allah *karim* – Allah be merciful! This is truly a lion, the great lion of al-Taytal. He will devour us."

"Yes, he found our tracks and also that of the bold *Faqir al-Fuqara*, which is why he roared twice," I replied. "But from now on he will remain silent and approach stealthily to catch himself one of us."

"May Allah protect us from the cunning of this tailed Devil!"

"Ah, you are afraid! How about our bet?"

"Oh, *effendi*, this terrible bet!"

"Weren't you going to do what I was doing?"

"Yes, I will," he replied; but I saw the 'vision musket' tremble in his hands.

"Come, then! Let's go to the lion."

"Are you mad"

"No. If I walk toward him, I'll find and kill him. If I stay, one of our people will fall victim to him."

"But not you or me!"

"One will be eaten for sure, who, is all the same to me."

"It is not all the same! Whether I am eaten or whether he favors another is a big difference to me. I beg you to stay here! If everyone hides behind a camel, we should be safe."

"The lion will catch his victims also from behind a camel. I will go and this great *Faqir al-Fuqara* will accompany me."

"Are you serious, *effendi*?" the *Faqir* asked.

"Didn't you want to accompany me to the lion? Or should I, who you doubted so proudly, possess more courage and skill than you? Every coward can brag, but a *Faqir al-Fuqara* ought to . . ."

"Keep your mouth shut," he interrupted me. "I will come along."

"Then let's go! And how about you, Bin Fassara?"

"I will remain here," the guide replied.

"I knew that. You are brave with your big mouth. Because of it I will win your vision musket."

"Oh, Allah! Oh, Muhammad! Oh, Abu Bakr and Uthman! My beautiful, famous vision musket," he whined.

"If you stay, it will be gone!"

"Then . . . then . . . I will come along, *effendi*, always behind you. You just go ahead, I will follow!"

He trembled uncontrollably, but followed way behind me after all, so that the lion would get me instead of him. I felt sorry for him and would have loved to send him back, but he deserved the punishment. Furthermore, I was certain that he would disappear a few paces on.

"Put more wood on the fires for the flames to rise higher!" I ordered, before I had left the circle of men and camels behind.

Not a sound was heard from the *asakir* and the captives. Fear had silenced them. For protection everyone pressed close to the bodies of the camels. Of all of them, I was probably the calmest. When the moment of danger arrived, any earlier fear must be abandoned or one is lost. The *Faqir al-Fuqara* must not have thought that his bragging would result in this consequence. He had been convinced he was dealing only with a hyena. Now, fear to be thought a coward drove him to follow me. The Fassara guide had traded places with him and now was the last. When we had crossed the glade about halfway he noticed at its border a movement in the bushes. Terrified, he ducked behind a freestanding bush we were just passing, and screamed:

"There it is, there! Oh Allah, oh merciful one, oh you compassionate one! I will stay here courageously. You run off to save yourself!"

Yes, we were to go on, to be spotted by the lion and for him to leap on us, while he remained "courageously" hidden behind his bush.

I had also seen the movement that had terrorized him so, but it could not have been caused by the lion, which is why I called to the coward:

"Keep on going with us or your gun will be lost! You must do as I do!"

"No, no. I stay here and gun him down. You go ahead! And scream aloud so that he becomes scared of you!"

He only asked us to scream so that we would attract the lion's attention. But the animal could not have arrived yet. When it roared for the first time, it must still have been at least two miles distant. This is why I had taken my time for my ironic summons to my two escorts. By now the animal might have covered three quarters of this distance.

With the roar having come from the west, I had, of course, turned to that side of the glade, where I stopped looking for a favorable position. I assumed that the stalking lion would avoid the undergrowth to avoid making noise. On this side, there was only one spot free of bushes, from where I could expect him to break out. I had to post myself nearby.

Two sturdy thalha trees (Acacia gummifera) stood there close to each other, and luxuriant sunut bushes shielded the light from the fires, throwing deep shadows over the place.

"We will lie down here," I told them. "This is the best spot."

"Why here?" the *Faqir* asked, while he crouched down next to me.

"Because the lion will come rushing out about ten paces from here."

"Allah *karim*! Why so close! We must get farther back! Maybe fifty to sixty paces."

"No. The closer the better, and the more secure the shot."

"*Effendi*, you have lost your mind!"

"No, only that I am more courageous than you. I hear your teeth clatter."

"I cannot help it. Suddenly, my jaw became unhinged."

"Is your hand also trembling?"

"Yes, a great cold is penetrating my arms."

"Make sure then that you do not shoot when he comes, but leave it to me! You would hit poorly or not at all and thus increase the danger to us tenfold."

"Would Allah have only prevented me from following you! I am undaunted, but to draw the attention of the 'Human Strangler' purposely onto oneself is simply too daring. Let us not talk any more! He might hear us."

"We were only whispering, and he hasn't even arrived yet."

The *Faqir al-Fuqara* was terribly afraid. I clearly heard the clatter of his teeth, and when I now put my hand on his arm to feel whether it trembled as much, he emitted a fearful shout. He had thought the soft touch of my hand to be the heavy, deadly paw of the lion.

But it appeared that the Fassara was planning something.

I saw him crouching behind his bush. The distance from me to him was forty paces, eighty to the well, to where I could send a clean shot, should the lion make it there. At first he had lain on the ground, but now he was crouching, busying himself with his vision musket. Now he peered around the bush, raised his musket, aiming it at the spot where we had earlier seen the movement. What was he up to? Was he really going to shoot? Should I prevent him by a shout from doing so? Even had I wanted to, it was too late. He fired. The vision musket banged like an old blunderbuss and hit his head so hard that he collapsed. But he quickly recovered, jumped up and screamed, while he windmilled with both arms, rejoicing:

"*Al-Hamdulillah* – Allah be praised! I got him, I got him! I shot at him and hit him! He collapsed over there, lies in his blood, this devourer, this murderer, this 'Human Strangler' and 'Killer of Herds'! Rejoice, you men, shout, scream and sing to his end, an end without glory and honor, an end to cowardice and shame! *Effendi*, come quickly so I can show him to you!"

The behavior of the incautious man could almost be called insane. He gesticulated like a madman. In camp, the *asakir* rose, believing his words. But what might he have shot at? At all kinds of things, but not the lion, for just then a breeze carried the unmistakable, pungent odor to me, characteristic of the great wild species of cat carnivores, ten, even twenty times stronger than found with the half-tame animals living in menageries and zoos.

"He shot him. We must get over there, *effendi!*" said the *Faqir al-Fuqara*.

"Nonsense! The lion is coming from the opposite direction. He's directly ahead of us. I can smell him already."

"Oh Allah, oh mercy, refuge and comfort of the faithful! You are mistaken. The Fassara has won, and I will walk over to him."

He jumped up and left. I could not have held him back, had I even wanted to. I did not have the time nor the hand for it. The lion had arrived! I saw him appear below the first trees of the opening, illuminated brightly by the flaming fires. He was a one meter tall, surely two-and-one-half meters long, uncommonly mighty animal with a very long and dense, dark mane.

I had my rifle at the ready, but the lion was poorly positioned for a shot. I could not risk missing him. There was no time for long considerations, for the animal, seeing the running *Faqir al-Fuqara*, turned to leap after him. I screamed at the top of my lungs to attract the beast's attention to me, but it did not seem to have heard my screams, or at least not pay attention to them, and leaped, in one, two, three bounds, after the *Faqir*. Now, the lion was seen in camp and the *asakir* howled from terror. The Fassara, too, jabbered as if exposed to hellfire, causing the *Faqir al-Fuqara* to take notice, stop and turn. When he saw the pursuing carnivore, he collapsed to his knees in mortal fear and lifted his folded hands, unable to even utter a sound. Three more leaps and the lion would be on him.

They were only several blinks of an eye, but I had used them. With the rifle in my right hand I ran after the 'Strangler of Herds'. With my left hand, I drew my revolver and fired the six shots, screaming at the top of my lungs. That helped. The lion heard me and reversed himself. Instantly, I dropped to me knees and aimed my rifle. The two others were safe for now, I was certain of this, for the lion throws itself onto the man aiming at him. What was I facing now? It was either him or me!

He took measure of the distance, knowing that he could not reach me in one leap. He had to take two, and as soon as he touched the ground from his first leap, my bullet had to get him, or I would have no time for a second shot. These were hellish moments, especially with the mighty cat not making the least sound. Now, he leaped, the front paws spread far apart. Twelve paces from me, he touched down and received the first bullet. A jolt went through the lion's body, as if he had been pushed from the front. He had been well hit, but the once gathered force of will and muscles pushed him on. The mighty body rose once more toward me, had to reach me. But before this happened, my second bullet got him in midair. I threw myself aside, dropping the rifle, and drew my knife from my belt. Raising it to stab, I turned lightning-fast, but saw that further defense was, fortunately, no longer necessary. The lion lay on his back, his legs convulsively pulled to his belly. He moved once to the right, then to the left side, stopped, then, with a final move, the paws spread far apart and bloody foam dripped from his half-open jaws. He was dead!

There was no need for a detailed check. I knew that the two bullets had reached their target precisely, that is, the first through an eye into the brain and the second from below, the heart. Nevertheless, I still did not dare touch the animal. It has happened before that a seemingly dead lion, with several bullets in his head, leaped up again. I picked up my rifle, reloaded, then stabbed the lion with its barrel. Had he still shown life, I could have given him another two bullets before he would have been able to leap up again. But he didn't twitch; he was truly dead.

All that had happened so quickly that it found the *Faqir al-Fuqara* still kneeling and the Fassara still standing hollering by his bush. The *asakir* had stopped screaming, seeing themselves no longer threatened. I walked to the *Faqir*, took him by his arm to help him up, and said:

"Why are you still kneeling and praying? The 'Devourer of Humans' is dead."

"Dead?" he repeated my last word absentmindedly.

"Yes, dead. You need no longer be afraid."

"Al-Hamdulillah!"

Uttering only this single word, he rose and walked off into the woods without bothering to look at the lion, a certainly peculiar behavior to deal with the savior of his life. The Fassara had heard me and asked:

"Is it certain that he is dead?"

"It is!"

"Can I look at him and touch him?"

"Naturally!"

"Then I will get the *asakir* so that they can celebrate our triumph."

He had said "our" triumph. Now I was curious to see the lion he had slain! First, the men came to inspect mine, but not in a rush or tumultuous joy, but hesitantly and silently. Even in death, the size of the lion's corpse called for respect still, and it took several assurances of mine until an *askari* dared grab the head of the beast to turn it from side to side. When this handling had convinced everyone that there was no longer any danger, the, at first, so diffident silence changed into one of high-spirited enthusiasm. The Fassara guide began by appointing himself speaker, stepped onto the lion's body, and said:

"Allah be praised and hail to the Prophet! This is a day of triumph. Confirm it, you faithful!"

"Yes, hail, praise, triumph!" the *asakir* shouted, who had all gathered around. Only Bin Nil, the dutiful, had remained with the captives to guard them.

"You heard," the speaker continued, "of the 'Lion of al-Taytal', which opened its maw and devoured each week a follower of the Prophet. Confirm it, you friends and followers of the two heroes of the day!"

"We confirm it!" came the answer.

Obviously, by the 'two heroes' he meant himself and me. He continued:

"Many hundreds of Muslims are buried in the belly of the 'Lord with the big Head'. At times, he may even have swallowed an infidel, which might have caused him indigestion. Today, he came to this well to continue his crimes. But anger erupted in the minds of the most famous fighters of Africa, and the *effendi* and I rose against the 'Devourer'. Shout hail and glory to them, you witnesses of the deed!"

"Hail and glory!" it sounded.

"The 'Strangler of Life', did not come alone, but brought a godless companion for his foul deeds. This companion, whose soul Allah may turn into the body of a lame dog, was reckless enough to put itself up against me. I was overcome by the brave desire to kill this monster, which is why I drove it from the land of the living, by aiming my vision musket at it and bumped it off. It lies there at the edge of the bushes, illuminated by the beams of my heroism. I shall show it to you in a minute so you can shout shame and disgrace upon it! But I, the victor, praise with a threefold triumphal shout!"

They followed his request. Then he found it appropriate to deal also with me:

"Since I killed the 'Living Grave' of so many faithful, the watch and spy glass must be awarded me. I won them, since I did the very same the *effendi* did. Just like him, I downed a four-footed 'Lord of Thunder'. Yes, I killed mine even before he did his, which now lies here under my feet, prone in his hide, which should have been pulled of while he was still alive. The *effendi* needed two shots to kill it, while I required only one. Nevertheless, this victor shall also be given his reward. Shout to him a threefold hail!"

"Hail, hail, hail!" was given.

"Thus the heroes and victors have been honored, and it is the fate of the vanquished to be derided and to be spit upon. Beat this murderer of the human species; push, pinch and kick him; pull his tail and his ears; give him the names he deserves, so that his cowardly soul quivers and suffocates in infinite shame! Fall upon him, tear out his hair and tear up his hide as a warning example to his kind that they will no longer dare attack the followers of the Prophet, but satisfy themselves with the meat of goats and sheep! I have spoken. Praise to the victors! Hail, hail, hail!"

While the *asakir* joined him in the shouts, he climbed off the lion on which all now threw themselves. The dead animal was punched and kicked so much that I had to put a stop to this mistreatment to protect the beautiful hide. The fastest way to achieve this was to drown out the general screaming with my voice:

"Up, up, you faithful! The 'Strangler of al-Taytal' has been shamed enough! Let us now look at the famous lion whose life was taken by our Bin Fassara. I'm eager to delight in his sight."

"Oh, you will enjoy yourself mightily, *effendi*," the Fassara said. My lion is almost twice the size of yours, for its head reached even above the bushes he was hiding in. I won our bet and you shall not take it from me, just as I would have handed you yours. I will walk ahead, you men! Follow me and form a triumphal march to the place of battle, where my fame won first prize!"

I was not all concerned about the result of our bet. I knew that I had won and the 'first-prize Fassara', as he had called himself, was headed for a great, unavoidable embarrassment.

I guessed what his lion was, whose head had shown high above the bushes. Our camels lay by the well, but the *Faqir al-Fuqara's*, which had been grazing freely, was no longer visible. Eating the young leaves of the bushes, it had entered the brushwood, and our hero of the day had thought it to be the lion, and had injured or, maybe, even killed it.

The group walked silently to the spot. They had to be cautious, since it was not known whether this second lion was dead or only injured. The closer we came to the place, the slower the Fassara proceeded. Finally, he halted and turned to address me:

"*Effendi*, you are convinced of my bravery, are you not?"

"Completely, for you killed the greatest and most famous beast of the desert. Unfortunately, I don't think that the *Faqir al-Fuqara* will be grateful to you for your accomplishment."

"I do not expect this, since he was not threatened by my lion but by yours. He ought to thank you for it. But my lion threatened the well with all the *asakir* and the captives. This means that there is greater grateful-ness due me than your single one of the the *Fuqara*. But come now and walk ahead! I know you have sharper eyes than me."

"You are mistaken. At times, I see poorly, and it can easily happen then that I take a lion for a camel. What insult it would be to you if pre-cisely today and here I would commit such an error. You are the victor; you go ahead!"

He had to comply, but his courage seemed to have reached 'Cape Finisterre', for he now moved forward as if walking on eggs of which he wasn't allowed to crush a single one. Only six or seven paces farther he stopped again, pointed ahead, and said in a low voice:

"Allah *karim*! There he lies. I see two of his feet moving. *Effendi*, what can be done?"

"You just go ahead!"

"But he will bite! He is not dead yet, only injured."

"Then step up to him and give him another bullet! Of course, this reduces your fame, since you can then no longer claim that I needed one bullet more than you."

"I do not care for that fame and will prove it to you. I have only one bullet in my gun, while you have two. You are in a much better position than me to finish off this 'Devourer'. Go ahead, *effendi*, I let you go first!"

"My modesty doesn't allow me to accede to your wish."

"This is very nice of you, *effendi*, but . . . Oh, Allah, he moved his legs again, and do you hear his snorting? He is angry. I will stand behind you."

He slipped past me and the *asakir* in order to seek protection from the imagined lion.

Indeed, the creature had given a audible sign of life, which was, however, not the angry snort of a wounded wild animal, but the painful rattle of a wounded camel. The *asakir*, too, backed off fearfully, while I stayed put and said to the Fassara:

"Fine, I'm willing to avert the danger from you, but under one condition. I will walk around him and drive him toward you. Then, when he leaps at you, you will have a magnificent shot."

I took a few steps as if following my suggestion, when he shouted:

"By Allah's will, don't do it. I do not wish to have anything to do with it!"

"Aha, you are afraid. Well, then I'll show you how great the danger is. These are not the hind paws of a lion, but the feet of a camel."

"You are mistaken, you are! Your eyesight is poor. You said so yourself that at times, you think a lion to be a camel."

"And you, a camel for a lion. I'll prove it to you in a minute. Yes, this animal was substantially taller than the lion I killed, but it was no lion but the *Faqir al-Fuqara's* camel. Here, look at it! I walked over and pushed the branches apart with my rifle. Now, they saw the camel lying there, shot in its right hind leg. The *asakir's* fear had suddenly evaporated. They pushed closer and erupted in booming laughter.

"What a lion, what a dreadful beast!," one of them shouted. Had the Fassara's bullet not downed it, this 'Devourer of Humans' would have gotten us all. Yes, the Fassara freed us from a terrible danger and saved all our lives. He is the most famous lion hunter in the country. Raise your voices, men, to praise him! Shout a threefold 'hail' to him!"

"Hail, hail, hail!" all of them laughed and shouted.

The so praised did not reply, but protected himself from further praise by running away to hide in the bushes. The camel was unable to get up; its right thigh bone had been shattered; it needed to be killed. Just then, its owner, the *Faqir al-Fuqara* returned from the woods. He walked to me, offered his hand and said for all to hear:

"*Effendi*, forgive me for leaving you standing there without express-ing my gratitude. It was too terrible. I had risked too much. My limbs trembled and my soul shook in my body. The 'Devourer' was after me and without you, he would have torn me to shreds. Terror had robbed me of speech, so that I was unable to say a single word to you. I escaped into the darkness of the woods to praise Allah in silence. I can now speak once more to say "thank you" to you. You are my friend and brother; the enmity I showed you has vanished, and I wish to give you proof that my attitude toward you has changed completely. Will you forgive me?"

"Gladly," I answered, while I shook his hand.

"Tell me then how I can serve you or do you a great favor."

"There's no need for it. You did not know what it meant to be attacked by the 'Lord with the big Head'. I demonstrated it to you and am satisfied. Would you dare to face a lion again?"

"Never, no! Seeing him, my blood curdles, and it feels as if all flesh falls off one's body."

"That's the fear. But why did I remain calm? Had I also been afraid, things would have turned out badly."

"Yes, *effendi*, I cannot comprehend how you dared draw the lion's attention in your direction and allowing him to throw himself on you, especially since I had been so hostile toward you. Is this possibly pre-scribed by your faith?"

"No, a good Christian will indeed forgive even his worst enemy, for Christ, the Son of God, asked us to love even our enemies. But to have myself torn to pieces to save a Muslim's life is not required by my faith. In this case, I acted less as a Christian than a man, a hunter, who even the 'Strangler of Herds' cannot cause to lose composure. Being unafraid, I killed the lion; as a Christian I am prepared to reconcile with you. I shall take the lion's hide and will be entirely satisfied with this reward."

"I can understand this only if I assume that, from pride, you reject the gratitude of a man who insulted you. But I, too, am an honorable man, prohibiting me from accepting such rejection. I will give it some thought and hope to find an opportunity to be of service to you, which you then must accept. You do not understand yet who you rescued. Later, when you learn more about me, you will realize that all of Islam and the entire Orient is obligated to you. There lies my camel. What happened to it?"

"The Fassara shot it, thinking it to be a lion."

"Such a fool! Fear turned him blind. Is it severely injured?"

"Yes, it cannot get up. With your permission I shall relieve it from its pain with a bullet."

"Why do you want to waste precious powder and bullet? Leave it be; it will die by itself."

"That would be cruel. An animal is just as much God's creature as is a human."

"Do as you wish; I do not mind. But what will I do without a camel? Must I walk?"

"No. I will make one of the captured camels a gift to you. Let's first get the lion to the well that I can skin him."

I gave the camel the mercy bullet. Then, eight *asakir* dragged the mighty corpse of the lion to the fires where I pulled off his yellow-brown 'coat', as Bin Nil called it. Of course, everyone talked about the lion, while all else was left waiting. The Fassara returned very depressed and was inundated with ironic praise. He let it wash over him without making any comment. This was the best he could do. He put his famous musket aside, and said:

"Here it lies. I cannot present it to you, for this would make it a sin to the ancestor of my forefathers. If you are truly so cruel as to rob me of it, go ahead, take it."

"Yes, I'll take it. It is now my rightful and well-deserved property."

He had figured on my forbearance. When he now saw it in my hand, he threw his hands up above his head and lamented:

"Oh Allah, oh heavens, you deep heartache of my soul! I have been robbed of the glory of my ancestors, legacy of my forefathers and never again can I let myself be seen in the villages of my tribe. Wherever I go, they will point their fingers at me and shout: 'This is the man who gambled away the jewel of his tribe and honor of his ancestors; shame on him! Nothing is left to me then but to fade away and dissolve in tears. My heart swims in a flood of grief, and my life is submerged into the waters. Oh, the pain of my soul, oh Allah, Allah, Allah!"

I had no intention of keeping the musket, but took it only for the time being to make him suffer a bit for his bragging. No harm in that. He stretched out on the ground, covered his face with his head scarf, and now kept totally quiet. The asakir were loud and animated, and did not tire of discussing the lion adventure again and again. They did this in their effusive Oriental manner and, judged by their expressions, I was not only the greatest hero on Earth, but of Man in general, such there had never been and would never be again. When, toward midnight, the subject seemed to be exhausted, Bin Nil found the time had arrived to address his. He demanded the punishment of the old faqir Abd Asl. It had been interrupted by the lion attack; now he pressed to finish the subject. When the Faqir al-Fuqara heard this, he rose and said to me:

"Effendi, earlier I posed to defend the life of the one you were going to judge, because he is my friend. We know each other much more than you can know. But I now realize that I am too weak against you. My opposition would be of no use to him. As you said, you alone are capable of taking on ten Fuqara al-Fuqara. Furthermore, you saved me from the lion, for which I owe you my gratitude. This is why I will not resist you. Therefore, I will not get involved in this matter, but my eyes do not wish to see the death of my friend, which is why I will withdraw until it is done."

He left to sit beyond the circle of camels, turning his back to us. Bin Nil still stood, knife in hand, and asked:

"Then you permit me to take revenge now, effendi?"

"Yes. As I told you before: If you think it worthy of you to kill a weak, tied-up old man, unable to defend himself, go ahead!"

"I know what I owe my honor, and will demonstrate it to you by acting accordingly."

"Do as you wish! The old one is in your hands. He's yours; no one else will lay a hand on him. To this the *asakir* agreed. What you do, will be final. I am telling you this once more with all certainty. But before you take revenge, I must have a talk with him."

I went with him to Abd Asl, who had heard everything and knew what he faced. His face was unmoving so that it was impossible to guess what was going on inside him – whether he felt fear or not.

"You know what's going to happen to you," I said. "Settle your account with life and Allah!"

"Whoever kills me is a murderer," he replied in a voice sounding like the hiss of a threatened snake.

"Think and say whatever you wish; it will not save you. In a few moments, you will cross *al-Sirat*, the road to death. Relieve your conscience, maybe Allah will then be merciful with you."

"I need no mercy. It is no sin to exterminate infidels and their followers but a merit Allah rewards."

"Keep to your view! If you think death by knifing to be a reward, I don't mind. You not only were after my life, a Christian, but also after that of my companions who are Muslims. Furthermore, you know that the *raïs effendina* is to be killed. For this, you cannot take responsibility before Allah, and I call on you to keep this guilt away by telling me the danger he is in."

A derisive grin now swept over his face. He spit and answered:

"I spit at you and death, for I fear neither it nor you. My days are recorded by Allah, and without his will you cannot take a single minute of my life. If he has decided that I am to die here and now, you cannot prevent it. I will therefore not utter even a single word of that which you endeavor to learn."

"I can force you to speak."

"Try it! As I laugh at you, I shall prove to you by admitting: yes, the *raïs effendina* is in great danger. He is lost and with him all that are with him. You now know enough!"

"He will escape the danger just as we did yours."

"No. There is no escape for him. He and his men will be killed for having our companions shot at the well at Wadi al-Bard. Yes, if only you knew what he is threatened with, you might be able to help him. But because you are a brazen Satan who seems to live only by danger, you will not learn it."

"How then, if I have you whipped long enough to talk?

"I will stay mute, nevertheless."

"Oh, pain opens even a closed mouth!"

"This time, your famous acumen escapes you. If you have me whipped, I will give you some kind of answer. But will you know whether it is true or not?"

"I think that I can judge this quite well, but I will desist from having you beaten. I would be ashamed to torment a frail, old man, standing already by his grave."

"Do not shame me! I am not frail, and were I not your prisoner, I would prove it to you. Kill me, you dogs; but I will keep silent!"

"All right, he will get his will," Bin Nil said. "To learn what threatens the *raïs effendina*, we are smart enough without this old man's murderers' information. May he go to Hell."

The youngster knelt next to him, opened his garment and put the tip of his knife on his chest. Abd Asl had not expected that we would be serious and screamed, terrified:

"Stop! Consider that I am a holy *faqir*, that no one can put his hands on. Allah would avenge this murder with the eternal pains of Hell."

"You, a saint?" Bin Nil replied. "You are a monster, a thousand times worse than the lion we killed. And how could Allah avenge your death on me, when you said that you would die only with his permission? If I stab you now, it will happen according to his will and command. Head down to Hell then, where millions of devils expect you joyfully."

He stabbed the knife point slowly, very slowly – only through the skin, as I could see. The old fellow rolled to the side and howled, demonstrating his, until now, restrained mortal fear:

"No, no! I do not want to die; I do not want to! Spare me; spare me!"

"Look, how you pretended, you old coward! Now, terror befalls you," Bin Nil told him.

"Mercy, mercy! Let me live!"

"Maybe, I will spare your life, but tell me of the danger threatening the raïs effendina!"

"I will tell you. I will tell you everything!"

"Out with it, then, or I will stab!"

"He is to be poisoned in Khartoum."

"By whom?"

"By . . . by . . . the muza'bir."

"By the pickpocket who was repeatedly after our effendi's life. How is he going to do it?"

"He bribed an askari, a faran (baker) with the troops of the raïs effendina. He will give him the poison, the faran will mix into the dough, when he bakes kisrât (millet buns) for the raïs effendina."

"Do you swear that you are telling the truth?"

"By Allah, by the Prophet and by the lives and teachings of all Khulafa'."

"See, how quickly I learned what you did not want to spill. We will now dispatch a messenger to warn the commander. Mortal fear opened your mouth. Let me tell you, though, to your annoyance, that you actually had no need for this admission, since I could not imagine soiling my honor by stabbing an old, cowardly, tied-up man. Yes, I want to avenge myself, but not by butchering my opponent. Allah is to decide between you and me. I want to fight, but not against you, since I am young and strong. Select one of your men. I will untie him and give him a knife. I, too, will arm myself with a knife, after which we will fight for life or death. Should he overcome me, you will be saved, but if I kill him, you both die, for he will fight for you and you will suffer the same fate as he. Effendi, I hope you will not deny me your permission?"

This was very decent of the good fellow! But how about the result of this duel? Bin Nil was courageous and for his age unusually strong and agile, but whether he could win, I was unsure of. It was obvious that the old man would pick his best warrior. But could I refuse my assent? No. Bin Nil could do as he pleased. In an undertone, I tried to discourage him, but he replied:

"Do not worry for me, *effendi*. I know what I am doing. You have not seen me in such a fight and are thus concerned for me. But let me tell you that I do not sense a trace of fear."

"You will be facing the strongest man. Remember that!"

"I prefer this to fighting a weakling. Well, will you agree?"

"Yes, keep yourself well. Don't be rash, and do not look at the knife but the eyes of your opponent. Try to position yourself for the light to hit him from the front, but you from behind."

Something I had not expected: the *faqir* chose the supposed *tajir*. There were stronger men among the captives, but, maybe he possessed greater agility and experience in man-to-man combat. They may have also agreed on some kind of deceit. They had lain next to each other, and I had missed their secret conversation. I readied myself for whatever was to come.

Once the *tajir's* fetters had been removed, he received a knife. He stretched and bent and rubbed his legs to limber them up from being tied.

"We will strip down to our pants and fight with bare upper bodies," Bin Nil told him.

"Why? Let's stay as we are."

"No. We will do as I say."

The *tajir* objected once more, but had to submit. Why did he not want to take off his upper garment? Without it, it was easier to fight. Did he want to flee? Bin Nil continued:

"So, if you kill me, Ibn Asl will live. But if I kill you, he, too, will die by my knife. You are, therefore, holding not only your own, but also his life in your hand. Say when you are ready."

"I am ready; we can begin."

They stood amidst our circle, facing each other. No particular rules had been agreed upon, still, I gave the *tajir* the brief warning:

"Watch your legs!"

"It is superfluous to tell me this," he laughed. "Life dwells in the heart; he will not stab me in the leg."

He did not pay attention when I took my Henry carbine in my hands, so that I could shoot instantly.

"Let's go," Bin Nil said. "Come!"

The other had no intention of starting. Neither one wanted to try for the first stab. They moved several times in a circle, keeping close eye contact. Then, the *tajir* jumped at Bin Nil, who slipped aside to avoid the knife thrust. But the attack had only been a feint, for barely had Bin Nil stepped aside when the *tajir* leapt over him and over the heads of two *asakir* blocking his way. He then ran off between the tied-down camels, trying to reach the woods. My assumption had been correct. But my rifle was ready, and I fired before he had covered three quarters of the distance. He stumbled, scrambled up, and collapsed again. I had aimed for his leg and had hit him. I had not wanted to kill him for another reason.

The *asakir*, with Bin Nil in the lead, ran after him, while I stayed put. They dragged the injured man back, but without giving him much consideration. When he dropped down before me, I told him:

"You laughed when I warned you. Still, I was right when I told you to watch your legs. You should realize again that it isn't easy to outwit a Christian *effendi*."

I checked his leg. The bullet had exited, but had smashed his shinbone. I dressed him provisionally.

"We must tie up this dog twice as well and keep him in our midst," Bin Nil commented.

"No," I told him. "He will soon suffer from wound fever, and when he then begins blabbing, he will disturb our sleep. Carry him over there to the two kafalah trees (Boswellia payfera). Put him against one of them and tie him with his back against it, so that he cannot move his head! In the meantime, Abd Asl may assign another man to fight against you."

This order struck my men as odd, but they took care of it without making contradictory remarks. They knew that with everything I did, even if it seemed inexplicable, I pursued a particular purpose. And because I also had such a purpose here, my bullet had only been meant for the escapee's leg.

The escape attempt of this man was clear to me. He was to have gone to Ibn Asl, the slaver, the son of the old *faqir*, to inform him about what had happened, that the attack had misfired, and that he was to come and liberate the captives. The old man was angry about the failure of his plan. I noticed it from his eyes. He chose another man for the fight who seemed to be more dangerous than the *tajir*, who had been previously selected because he was probably a good runner.

Bin Nil's new opponent had almost the deep, dark color of a Negro. He had a broad chest and sturdy build. Nevertheless, Bin Nil did not seem to be the least concerned. They stood motionless about five paces apart from each other. Neither one left the other from sight. Suddenly, the Black took a tiger-like leap at Bin Nil, ready to stab him. He had intended to surprise him, to catch him unawares. Lightning-fast, the youngster threw himself aside, made a quick sideways leap and got behind the Black. Before the man could turn, Bin Nil thrust his knife to its handle into his opponent's back. The man dropped to the ground right where he had stood. As it turned out, the blade had entered his heart.

"*Afirin, mashallah alayk* (Bravo, bravo)!" the *asakir* shouted, pleased. "This was good, this was magnificent! The first thrust felled him. Who would have expected it of you, Bin Nil, you son of bravery!"

Bin Nil turned quietly to me: "*Effendi*, do you realize now that you need not fear for me? I would have downed this man even had he been twice his size and strength. My eyes are sharp, my hand steady, and my heart knows no disquiet, darkening my sight. Is Abd Asl also mine now?"

"Yes," I said, eager to learn what he would do now.

If he was really set to kill him, I had to ask for a delay. He bent down over the Black and pulled the knife from his back. Looking at the bloody blade, he softly shook his head, then said:

"You are correct, *effendi*. It is a great responsibility to kill a human being. This blood is repulsive to me. Do you think the *raïs effendina* will punish the old man severely, his life being mine now?"

"Most severely, I'm certain!"

"Then I give him his life. The Black fought for the old man and died for him, which is why I am satisfied with what happened. Do you agree?"

"Entirely! I am very glad to hear this. Your decision honors you more than what you would gain from Abd Asl's death."

"But I demand that he will later be punished most severely!"

"I shall make sure of this. And so that he cannot make another escape attempt, take him over to the *tajir* and tie him to the other kafalah tree."

The old *faqir* was taken over there by some asakir. Surprised, Bin Nil asked me:

"Why do you have these fellows taken over there. Wouldn't they be more secure here?"

"That is true. We will bring them back, but before, I wish to learn what is planned for the *raïs effendina*."

"But you know this already!"

"No. The story of the poison and the baker is a lie. Go over there now and sit by them as their guard. I shall creep up behind them, and then, when I lie at their back, you leave. Once they think they are alone, they will talk."

He left to sit by the two culprits. The kafalah trees stood close together to the side of our camp. The two captives had been tied to the trunks, so that they looked toward us. They could clearly see anyone getting up, but could not determine whether one of us was missing from where we were sitting. I based my plan on this.

Several *asakir* had to form a dense group around the Black's corpse and act as if they were talking about him. The group offered me cover to get away. When the men had gathered, I left. The two captives sat to the right under the trees. I turned to the left, with the *asakir* standing right in the middle, so that the two culprits could not possibly see me.

Only when I reached the woods did the soldiers sit down but remained ready for my return.

I walked along the edge of the woods under cover of trees and bushes, until I had made a semicircle and arrived behind the two captives. I crept toward them and lay down. Of course, Bin Nil had seen me coming, sitting facing me. When he knew that I had arrived at my listening post, he rose, paced back and forth a few times, then left like someone bored, taking a short walk. This was inconspicuous and had the intended result, for I heard the *tajir* say to Abd Asl:

"Quick, quick, before he returns! What is it we must discuss?"

"Nothing, nothing at all," the old man grumbled angrily.

"But we must arrive at a plan!"

"I do not know any. Allah may curse this seven-times wicked *effendi* to the deepest abyss of Hell! If only you had gotten away! How quickly you could have been at the Jazirah (island) Hassaniah and informed my son. He and his men would have quickly sailed downstream on the Nile and approached us from Makawi or Katana, where he would have left his ship in order to liberate us. But now that is over."

"Is there no other rescue possible? Think of the *Faqir al-Fuqara*! How often did he conduct business with us and gained handsomely. His chance arrival at the well is fortunate. He will do everything to save us."

"That is over. The Christian dog saved his life, which is why he will leave him be."

"He will not do anything personally for him, but can help us indirectly. If he knew that your son is on the *jazirah*, he could inform your son. You should talk to him!"

"They will not permit it, and if so the *effendi* will stand next to us to hear everything."

"What about it? Two or three words in the Shilluk language are quickly said. The *effendi* does not know this language, but the *Faqir al-Fuqara* does and will know what to do."

"This is true. I will give it a try. Should it work, rescue will become possible, but the *raïs effendina* will slip through my son's fingers."

"How so?"

"He lured him to the *jazirah*. There are deep, dark woods which the *raïs effendina* is not meant to leave. Should this ambush succeed, and we accomplish our attack, we will be rid of these two men and can freely hunt and act as we did before. It is the leaders, not the *asakir* we must fear."

"If there is no way out for us, what do you think we can expect in Khartoum?"

"Well, I do not think it will turn out too badly. Supposedly, we will be delivered to the *raïs effendina*, who will not be there, but has fallen under my son's blows. We need not expect severe judges, especially with our main accuser being a Frank, a Christian. If we deny everything, they will hopefully believe us more than him."

The two continued talking, but I figured that any further words would be of no consequence and quickly withdrew. When Bin Nil, who had kept watch, saw this, he returned to the kafalah trees and the *asakir* gathered once more to provide cover for me. I returned to my place without the two culprits knowing that I had penetrated their secret. Shortly thereafter, Bin Nil came, telling me that Abd Asl wanted to talk to me. It appeared that they would make their attempt to deceive me immediately. I went to the two and asked the *faqir* about what he had to say.

"You gave my life into the hands of your Bin Nil," he said, "who gave it back to me. Will I be able to keep it?"

"You needn't fear anything from us anymore. Later, the decision lies in the hands of the *raïs effendina*."

"And you will take us to Khartoum?"

"Yes. Why do you ask?"

"For a reason, dear to my heart. If you deliver me to the *raïs effendina*, I will be lost. You made an effort to, at least, save my life; he, however, is severe and unrelenting and I know that he will have me shot or hanged without mercy and compassion."

"That is indeed likely," I confirmed.

"If you say so yourself, it is assured. I must therefore prepare for my death, and I expect you to help me with it, since I know you to be a Christian whose faith teaches that eternal bliss depends on one's preparation."

"That is correct. Whoever leaves this Earth without remorse and penance for his sins, will be lost eternally."

"I repent and want to remove in particular one deed from my soul that presses heavily on my conscience. You are not the servant of revenge. Will you help me?"

"Gladly," I answered, curious of what he would come up with in his attempt to fool me. He began the matter very piously and seemingly resigned to his fate, which only increased my loathing for him. He presented a very sad face and continued with the softest voice he was capable of:

"Yes, a great, heavy sin rests on my conscience. I want to remove it, but am convinced that the *raïs effendina* will not give me the opportunity to do so. This is why I am asking you. It is fortunate that the *Faqir al-Fuqara* happens to be here. He is the only one who knows the situation well enough, which is why I must turn to him. Would you permit me to speak with him?"

"Hmm!" I said, my face critical. "You are asking for something that I actually cannot allow."

"Only a few words!"

"Whether many or few is all the same. You know how low my trust of you is."

"You can stand next to us and hear everything."

"That's no assurance. What if you intend to deceive me and convey certain signs to the *Faqir al-Fuqara* meant to free you?"

"That is totally impossible with you being present!"

"Oh, it is easily accomplished. You only need to use words I do not understand, but he does."

"I am not such a wordsmith, *effendi*. Relent! You are a Christian!"

"Yes, now you call on my faith, while you earlier derided it. A Muslim would not relent."

"But you! I will speak so slowly and clearly that you can weigh every word. Consider that it will be like a testament, me a dying man facing certain death. What I request from you is something simple and easy. You are strict and fearless, but not cruel. Do you want to be so for the first time? There is no one equaling you in cunning, acumen and circumspection. Do you think you are unable to rely on these characteristics now? Had I ulterior motives, you would catch them much earlier than the *Faqir al-Fuqara*, against whom you are far superior in shrewdness."

He flattered me in order to overcome my apparent concerns. I did not do him the favor, acting as if his praise had not impressed me, but replied:

"What you say there is superfluous. I know myself and my strengths best. But neither you nor the *Faqir al-Fuqara* can manage to deceive me, for this you are both far too stupid. I will therefore go along with your request which presents no danger to me."

"I thank you," he said quietly and modestly, although I had called him stupid. "You are correct. There is no danger to you, since you can listen to everything."

"I will not listen at all, and will not desecrate your desired conversation by my presence."

"Then, I will be able to speak with him without witnesses and supervision?" he asked, while barely hiding his delight.

"Yes, none of us will bother you. Whether this so-called *tajir* listens in is your business. I shall now send the *Faqir al-Fuqara* to you and give you ten minutes to talk. You see how considerate I am. Do not misuse it; it would not become you. I would notice if you wanted to deceive me."

"Do not be concerned, *effendi*! I am honest and your benevolence touches me so that, had I truly planned deceit, I would now abstain from it."

"Fine, if that truly be so. Did you hear of the pious and famous *marabut* to whom a spirit brought the tongues of twelve talking ravens and the ears of twelve young eagles?"

"Yes. He had to eat them, after which he spoke the languages of all men and animals, and heard everything his enemies planned for him even from the farthest distance."

"Well, then, let me tell you that I, too, have eaten such tongues and ears. Beware, I hear everything!"

I left and received proof that I had no need to eat magical eagle ears. Mine were good enough to understand when the old man whispered gloatingly to his companion:

"What good luck; it will work."

The *Faqir al-Fuqara* was quite surprised when I told him that the old man wanted to talk to him and that he could do so without supervision. He walked over and sat down by the two. The *asakir*, too, were unable to understand my behavior, and even Bin Nil opposed my decision. I rejected his concerns telling him that I knew very well what I was doing.

Ten minutes later I saw the *Faqir al-Fuqara* rise and walk back to his place. He had spoken of his gratitude, so now was the time to see whether he was sincere. If he wanted to repay me for saving his life, he had to inform me of the old man's intentions. However, I did not give him this opportunity right away. The old man was to see that I did not talk with his confidante, which would frighten him all the more when he found out that I knew everything. This is why I let the *Faqir al-Fuqara* return to his place on the right, while I went to the left side to the kafahla trees.

"Well, did the *Faqir* agree to your request?" I asked the old man.

"Yes, *effendi*. He promised to make good my mistake. I thank you so very much for making it possible!"

"Now your heart beats quieter?"

"As lightly as it has not done for a long, long time."

"I believe you and know its reason."

"How could you? You do not have any idea of the deed."

"Don't be so sure! I told you that I, too, ate eagle ears and warned you of this. Of course, we are not dealing with a deed you committed in the past, but one the *Faqir al-Fuqara* is yet to perpetrate."

"*Effendi*, you are mistaken. I do not understand what you mean."

"Don't pretend! Earlier, I told you openly that you are too stupid to deceive me. And yet you talked about such an attempt."

"This is not true. What kind of an attempt could this be?"

"The *Faqir al-Fuqara* is to help free you by going to your son Ibn Asl."

"No one, not a single person has thought of this, *effendi*! The *Faqir al-Fuqara* does not even know where my son is."

"You told him."

"No. We did not even mention him."

"Neither the *raïs effendina*?"

"Him, neither."

"No."

"Remember the eagle ears! You told him of the danger the *raïs effendina* is in."

"Not to him, but to you. I told you that he was to be poisoned in Khartoum."

"Yes, you even swore to it, a false truth, Allah will not forgive."

"It was the truth!"

"So? Why then did you tell the *Faqir al-Fuqara* that the *raïs effendina* is to be lured into the sunut woods by the Jazirah Hassaniah?"

"Allah, Allah!" he exclaimed frightened, staring at me like someone before whose feet a lightning bolt had suddenly struck.

"You are shocked? Yes, your son is at the Jazirah Hassaniah, and the *Faqir al-Fuqara* is supposed to inform him as fast as possible that your attack did not succeed and that you have fallen into our hands."

"I . . . do . . . not . . . know . . . a single . . . word of it!" he stammered.

"That is not required," I laughed. The main thing is that I know. I heard even more. Your son Ibn Asl is supposed to head downstream on his ship with his men to Makawi or Katena, then head west into the savanna to attack us and liberate you. You can see that my eagle ears served me well."

"You are a Devil, yes, you are the true Satan!" he exclaimed most angrily. "You did not hear anything; I know this for sure, yet you are informed about everything. This can only be because you are in league with Hell!"

"Or with Allah. You are a most appalling villain, which is why the power assisting me against you cannot be an evil one, but must be a benevolent one. Your attempts are revealed, and I shall take care to shatter them. I will pay your son a visit without asking whether I'm welcome, and woe to him should I find that even a single hair has been touched on the *raïs effendina's* head! You two will be taken back to the fires. You have too few brains to guess why I isolated you from the others. Had you given it some thought that everything I do serves a particular purpose, as you have experienced now so often, you would not have entered the trap I set for you."

When the two were back by the fires, I looked more closely at the *tajir's* injury. At best, he would remain lame for the rest of his life. However, since the least injury hereabouts could easily take on a more dangerous character, a turn for the worse could not be excluded.

I was curious now how the *Faqir al-Fuqara* would behave. If he informed me of the old man's plan, that would be fine. Should he not, I had to prevent him from following through on his assignment. Once more, he had found a place away from the others and when the *asakir*, not needed for guard duty, settled down to sleep, he signaled me to come to him. When I followed his request, he said:

"Sit with me for a moment, *effendi*. I would like to talk with you about an important matter."

With the expectation that he was going to tell me about his conversation with the old man, I sat down next to him, but the beginning of his report showed me that I had been mistaken, when he said:

"You are a Christian. Do you know the Kitab al-Muqaddas (Holy Book = Bible) well?"

"Yes. I've studied it extensively."

"And do you know the explanations your scribes have added?"

"Yes."

"Tell me then, whether you think Muhammad to be a prophet?"

"According to our thinking, he is not a prophet, but a simple human being."

"Then there are no prophets at all with you?"

"Oh, yes! We consider prophets to be men illuminated by the Holy Ghost, whom God sent to his people, to teach them about eternal truth and lead them on the way to salvation."

"But Muhammad did this, too!"

"No. The path he showed his followers is wrong."

"So your people think his teachings to be entirely false?"

"Of course I do not wish to answer this question with just a brief "yes." He mixed up right and wrong. Where he lived, Jews and Christians dwelled, as well. He got to know the Bible's content from them and con-structed from it and various heathen notions the teachings you now call Islam. What he took from our holy book is correct, the other is wrong. Since even the purest truth, when mixed with a lie, is no longer truth, the Qur'an must be rejected, despite its many passages we can agree on."

"*Effendi*, you commit a grave error by condemning the Qur'an with-out knowing it."

"This is untrue. Rightly so, I can turn your claim back on you. Is there a single Islamic *madrassa* (university), where your students can get to know our Bible?"

"No, since it is forbidden to our teachers and student to occupy themselves with the teachings of other believers. They would commit a grave sin, should they do so."

"At our *madrassas* work many educated and famous men, who, with their students study the Qur'an and know it at least, I say at least, as well as your professors. You cannot know the Bible, yet call us *giaurlar*, while we know the Qur'an and are in a very good position to judge Islam."

"Were you also the student of such a teacher?"

"Yes, and that of the most famous. He translated Abu 'l Fada Aidhawi, Ali's hundred Sayings, and others of your scholars. I learned your language from him, studied the Qur'an, the Sunna, and the explanations given by your religious teachers. I am prepared to provide you with any desired elucidation on Islam."

"Wonder of wonders! A Christian wants to explain to me, the learned *Faqir al-Fuqara*, the Qur'an, the Sunna, and the holy scriptures! Should it be possible! You are not only daring in actions but also in words, *effendi!*"

"There's no talk of daring. What I say is well-founded and completely justified. Try me!"

"No. I shall beware of debating Islam with a Christian. You would not let yourself be converted anyway. There are only a very few questions I would like you to answer. Even the wisest of the wise is incapable of making a final judgment about our faith, for Muhammad only began this work. Another will bring it to its conclusion."

"Who?"

"You ask that? This, while you claim to know the Qur'an with all its explanations! By asking this question you prove that you do not know it after all."

"You are again mistaken. I know that you mean the Mahdi, who many of you await."

Let me explain here that this word is derived from the Arab verb *hada*, 'leading', and means: the one led on the righteous path, the helper, the intermediary.

"So you know it after all?" he asked. "Have you heard that a Mahdi will come?"

"Heard and read. The Qur'an does not mention anything of him. Such a harbinger is also unknown to its commentators. He lives only in verbal transmission which I do not give a damn about."

"I do the more though. Allah will send a prophet who will complete the work Muhammad began. This prophet will either convert the infidels, or, if they cannot be converted, destroy them. He will then distribute the goods of this Earth for each to receive according to his piousness."

"These are more worldly than religious hopes and wishes. Were I a Muslim, I would keep only to the Qur'an, where, according to its teachings such a Mahdi cannot be expected."

"How so? If the Qur'an does not mention a Mahdi, this is no compelling reason to assume that there will not be such a personality."

"Oh, yes, because the Qur'an's prophesy is completed. According to Muhammad's own words, he, himself, is the last Prophet Allah sent. His teaching, Islam, is complete in itself, and cannot be amended by additions or even improved. He states that only one will follow him, Isa Bin Maryam (Jesus, Mary's son). He will appear on the Day of Judgment, when he will descend onto the Umayyad Mosque in Damascus to judge the living and the dead. Apart from Muhammad putting the savior of Christendom as the global judge high above himself, he totally wrecks your hopes for a Mahdi."

"You, the infidel, say this!"

"No, I do so as a scholar of Islam, putting myself into the belief of a Muslim. If a Mahdi would arise now, intending to destroy the so-called infidels provided they would not convert, it would be simply ridiculous. There are far more than a thousand million people on Earth, who aren't Muslims. But I want to speak only of us Christians. How would your Mahdi even begin to destroy us?"

"With fire and sword!"

"May he come! But this is precisely why he cannot come, that is, to us. Can a desert spring arrogate to devour the Nile? Can it overcome the desert, then the mountains, by which it is separated from the Nile? As soon as it dares to leave the oasis, it will shamefully disappear in the sand."

"Allah will magnify its waves and strengthen it so that it will become a thousand times wider than the Nile!"

"Indeed, God is almighty, but He will not, for the sake of a Muslim make an ocean spring from barren ground and flood the mountains."

"You do not know us. We will be irresistible when at war we pour across your countries!"

"Bah! Your torrent would miserably seep away long before it would reach our borders. Are you familiar with our countries? Where are they located? Do you know of our peoples, our organizations, our armies? A desert flea has the idea of tackling the elephants and hippopotamuses of the Sudan, the bison and bears in America, and the lions and tigers of India! Madness! If you came, even thousands of you, you have no idea how quickly we would wreak havoc on you."

"Allah, Allah! Have you ever seen a Muslim in battle? We would crush you in a minute!"

"But an instant before you could do this, you would taste death to the last man from the muzzles of our rifles and cannons. Before you talk of 'crushing', visit the Christian countries to look around! You talk like a fish about a desert storm, but as soon as it gets out of the water, it will all be over. Count the millions and millions of warriors we have. And what kind of men they are! What are ten of you against one of them! You ask me whether I have seen a Muslim in battle. Not just one, but many. I have fought Muslims myself and are surprised that you say this. Take only the closest example, myself! I was to be, and still are meant to be killed. Did they succeed? Did these great heroes not all fall into their own traps? I am the only Christian among you. Did Abd Asl not say himself that I was more to be feared than all *asakir* together? I was to be captured. What happened? Instead, I took these sixty brave Muslims captive, here, in their homeland, which they are familiar with. Your Mahdi may come and try to destroy us. Do you think we need to defend ourselves against him? Oh, no! We would laugh, only laugh, and from the sound of this laughter he, together with all his heroes, would run head over heels away."

"You are talking big, *effendi*, but should you see him coming, your teeth would clatter from terror."

"So? Does he look so terrible?"

"Yes, you have no idea how terrible he can be."

"But you have this presentiment? You know him?"

"Precisely because you do not believe in the coming of a Mahdi, precisely because you mock me, I shall answer this question: yes, I know him."

"Then he's already here?"

"He is here already and has received Allah's directive to ready himself for the conquest of Earth and the annihilation of the infidels."

"Would you care to give him some good advice of mine?"

"Which?"

"May he tend to his herds and till his fields in peace but abstain from his imagined prophesy. He is beholden by a mighty self-deception. His followers, should he find any, would pay with their property and their life."

"You err, not he! His mission came from Allah, and he will obey the command from Heaven."

"Let me tell you then what he can expect. First, he will rise against the Viceroy. Maybe the insurrection will be successful. Khartoum is far from al-Qahira, and before the *Khedive* can dispatch troops, he may have conquered the areas along the arms of the Nile. But this will be only for a short time; he will soon have to retreat again."

"Surely not! He disdains the *Khedive* and shall subjugate him. Then he will take Mecca. And after that Istanbul, where he will depose the Sultan and declare himself the true ruler of the faithful."

"He will leave it alone! You don't have the least idea of the conditions and obstacles he is going to meet. Here, on the upper Nile, yes, here he could fight a bit of war. But as soon as he sticks his nose beyond the Nubian border, it would be slapped."

"By whom?"

"By the powers who would not like to see the Viceroy or the Sultan deposed. There are still other men than the Mahdi, who don't like the Sultan in Istanbul. For instance, there's the Emperor of Russia, who would love to possess Istanbul. It's not even very far from him, for his empire borders Turkey. He has several million soldiers, yet does not take Istanbul, not for fear of the Turks or other Muslims, but because other Christian rulers would not allow it. And what the great Czar cannot do, the Mahdi is to accomplish? This is like a child reaching with its hand for the moon. It may desire it, it may clamor and scream, but it cannot obtain it. Tell this man, therefore, that his plan will not come to pass, that behind the *Khedive* stand powers that will not want to see him fall. A Mahdi would at best make it to Aswan, but there would meet European, that is Christian troops, by whose cannons and bayonets his might would falter."

"But what if he had a friend in the army of the *Khedive*, he could rely on?"

"Are you referring to a high officer who would revolt in al-Qahira once the Mahdi rose up in Khartoum?"

"Yes."

"Even if this officer were fortunate in the beginning, luck would soon leave him, for European troops would land and his followers could not resist."

"But if they would not let him land?"

"What could they do against them? They would land under the protection of their ships."

"He would destroy them."

"With what? How? These would not be wooden Nile barges, but immense giants made of steel. Your bullets would ricochet, while their cannon balls would travel all the way to al-Qahira to clean the entire area in a quarter of an hour. If your Mahdi wanted to conquer the Sudan to convert the heathen Blacks to Islam, he would be dealing with people and conditions he is familiar with and success might eventually be possible. But he better not try for other conquests, if he does not want his fingers slapped. A Mahdi wanting to conquer the globe would not only have to have taken in all of contemporary European knowledge, but would have to surpass it. Where is there such a man?"

"There is one!" he replied, self-assured, "who is ten times smarter than all you Europeans together."

"Hmm! Are you referring to yourself? It almost sounds like it."

"Who I mean, I will, of course, not say, but Allah has given him the mind, the knowledge, and the characteristics required for such a sacred mission. Soon the time will come when the news about him will sound across all lands, and the emperors, kings, and counts will dispatch messengers to him, bringing gifts and ask for peace. Believe what I say on my most sacred oaths!"

"Concerning this, I've often, and again today, experienced what the oaths of Muslims are worth. Was that all you were going to tell me?"

"Yes. I wanted to hear the opinion of a knowledgeable Christian of the Mahdi's mission."

"You heard it. Now, I still have something to ask. What did you talk about with Abd Asl?"

"Of a great mistake he once made. He asked me to atone for it."

"Will you do this?"

"Yes."

"But it is a question whether you will be able to."

"I can, for he gave me the necessary information."

"May I hear of it?"

"Why do you ask this, *effendi*? It was the request of a man, who is to die, and you yourself were kind enough not to listen in. Are you suddenly regretting your magnanimity?"

"No, I'm just afraid that I can't be indifferent about this matter."

"It is none of your concern."

"Nothing's planned against me?"

"How do you arrive at this question? You saved my life for which I owe you gratitude. I would therefore warn you, should Abd Asl plan anything against you."

"But he is your friend!"

"My gratitude to you is greater than this friendship. I ask you to trust me!"

"I trust only whom I know, but you, I have only met today for the first time."

"Then I am sorry if you cannot find the time now to get to know me better. I have rested and shall continue my travel to Khartoum. I ask you to select a camel for me."

"I shall do so, but only at daybreak."

"Not now? But you promised me!"

"Indeed, and I shall keep my promise."

"Then, it is all the same, whether you give me a camel now or later."

"Also to you."

"No, because I must leave now."

"And I am saying that you will leave only by morning."

"But I tell you that . . ."

"And I tell you," I cut in sharply, "that what you say, means nothing at all to me. I am certain that you will remain here until we depart."

"*Effendi*, what do you think you are doing! I know what I want. Or am I no longer master of my myself?"

I had risen. He, too, jumped up and faced me threateningly.

"I won't let you leave."

"By what right?"

"The right of the stronger. I am the master at this well and for everything that happens here, my permission is needed."

He had his rifle. I was ready for anything, but most of all that he might suddenly run off. Since I had left my rifle at my place, he might think that running off would succeed with no bullet following.

"You promised me a camel to continue my ride," he again said very determinedly. "I am relying on your word."

"You will get it and can continue your ride, but nothing was said about when. You will leave with us in the morning!"

"But I am in a hurry and cannot wait for you."

"Why did you not say so before? Earlier, you did not seem to be in a rush. Rest assured, we will ride very fast, and you will not miss anything if you wait for our departure."

"*Effendi*, I have no need for traveling companions and protectors. Alone, I travel much more safely than in the company of a Christian, whose presence can only bring danger to me."

"With the *asakir present*, it is different. I really must insist that you wait until we leave."

"By what right to you treat me a prisoner?" he flared up.

"By the right that everyone has who is concerned for the safety of his life."

"Do I, by chance, threaten your safety, even your life, by leaving?"

"Yes."

"Allah 'l Allah! This is done to me, me, the Mahdi, before whom millions will grovel in the dust!"

"Ah, now you come clean! So, you are the chosen Allah spoke to! You want to depose the *Khedive* and the Sultan? You want to conquer the Earth and destroy the Christians? You want to finish the Prophet's incomplete mission and carry the Sword of Islam from one end of the globe to the other?"

With each of these questions I looked him up and down, while emphasizing the word 'you', and then added:

"Honestly, you do not strike me as the man who can command even ten *asakir*, and yet you intend to rule the faithful, even the entire globe!"

"Do not mock me. It will ill become you. I have been illuminated by the Spirit and know all things. I know what has happened and what is going to happen, and see the flocks of mortals gathering about me."

"So, you know all that has happened, and you can also peer into the future? Then you possess the same sharp eyes I do! We both know then that you do not intend to head for Khartoum but to the Jazirah Hassaniah to see Ibn Asl. But do you also know that I will be there before you? Your gratitude to me is truly great, so great that, overcome by my great love, I do not want you to leave me. You will stay with us and . . ."

I did not get any further. He suddenly turned and ran away toward the edge of the glade. I quickly followed him, caught up, and took him by his left arm. He carried his gun in his right hand and reached out to stab its butt into my chest. I pulled him down and knelt on him to keep him put. The man literally fell into a foaming rage and uttered a stream of curses, undignified for a future Mahdi. Anyway, I had not taken his discourse of the 'Mission' seriously.

The *asakir* were no little surprised when I suddenly treated the *Faqir al-Fuqara* as an enemy, but when I informed them of his intention to betray us to Ibn Asl, they would have liked to kill him, this ungrateful man.

From what I had learned, our destination needed to be changed. It was necessary to come to the aid of the *raïs effendina*. Given enough time, he had to be warned, and if too late, to free him from Ibn Asl's clutches. Speed was called for, and since the transport of the prisoners could not proceed that quickly, I decided to leave right away to ride ahead without sleep.

It was not advisable to ride alone, but who should I take along? An *askari*? No. I likely was going to face some unusual situations. They would call for cunning, decisiveness and courage, which called for a traveling companion I could rely on. I would have liked to transfer command of the *asakir* to Bin Nil. I trusted him to bring the group safely to its destination, but he was even more important to me. Better, the prisoners escaped than a misfortune would happen to the *raïs effendina*. This is why I asked Bin Nil to accompany me and surrendered command of the group to the oldest *askari*. He had an experienced assistant in the Fassara guide, who was to take the caravan to the village of Hagasi near the island of Hassaniah, where I hoped to meet it again. I returned the famous vision rifle to the Fassara guide, which delighted him immensely.

"*Effendi*," he rejoiced, "your soul overflows from kindness and your compassion refreshes my heart. Trust me and be unconcerned, I shall safely guide the *asakir* with the captives to Hagasi. Ride confidently and may Allah bless your journey and protect you."

2

Captured

THE DISTANCE FROM the well, where the last events took place, to the Jazirah Hassaniah, is almost thirty miles. Our excellent camels covered it in two days, but when we closed in on our destination, they were so tired that we had to let them walk slowly. I thought I had headed exactly toward our goal but had actually drifted a bit to the left. I found this out when right ahead of us rose Jabal Arash Qul which was located rather to the north of Hagasi.

It was evening when we arrived. Hagasi is a miserable *quaryah* (village), consisting of only a few huts. It is situated on the high bank of the Nile, thus rather well protected from flooding. A path leads from the *quaryah* to a place down by the river where boats land and animals are watered. Such a path, including the watering and landing place is called a *mishrah* at the Upper Nile.

I was delighted to see the river, which I had not seen since my trip to the Fassara. The village residents gathered around us and asked where we were from and where we were going, as well as what our needs were.

Of course, I took care not to provide them with information and avoided their inquiries with countering questions.

First, we led our camels to the river to drink. Afterward, we took them up to a grassy area whose owner allowed us to let them graze there for a small payment.

Above the *mishrah* sat a man who did not appear to be a village resident. He was heavily armed and dressed better than the residents of the *quaryah*. When I inquired about him with one of the villagers, the man replied:

"We do not know him. He came here yesterday and sits at the same spot, looking downstream."

"Is he expecting a ship?"

"Probably, but he did not answer us when we asked him. He keeps a saddled horse outside the village which he rented from our *shaykh al-Balad*."

"Has he ridden it?"

"Not at all, but it stands ready since he arrived."

"Where does he want to go?"

"We do not know. He may have told the *shaykh al-Balad*, since he would not have given him the horse otherwise."

I found the stranger conspicuous. It was obvious that he was on the lookout for something and, once that something appeared, was ready to ride off to report on it. I would have loved to know whom he was to report to, but asking the *shaykh* would have been a bit too conspicuous. This is why I kept asking the man:

"When did the last ship come upstream?"

"Yesterday morning."

"And when did the man come to your village?"

"At the same time. He arrived with the ship. A boat dropped him off at the *mishrah*."

"The boat did not stay here?"

"No, it was rowed back to the ship."

"Whose ship was it?"

"I do not know."

"What was its freight?"

"That, too, I do not know."

"Can you give me its name?"

"It was *Hirthawn* (Lizard). It was not a *dahabiyah* but a *noquar*."

"And when did an earlier ship pass through here?"

"The day before yesterday. It, too, was a *noquar*. It was empty and went south to pick up goods."

"Did a ship sail past that looked neither like a *dahabiyah* nor a *noquar*, but looked very peculiar?"

"No."

His answer reassured me, since it told me that the *raïs effendina* had not passed the dangerous place. His "Falcon" was of such an unusual build and rigging that everyone here would have noticed it.

Bin Nil lay in the grass, watching the villagers' activities. I walked slowly up to the stranger, who kept a close eye on me. Then I sat down by his side and greeted him:

"May Allah bless you with a pleasant evening!"

"Pleasant evening!" he responded briefly.

I had spoken the greeting in full, something done only if one wants to be especially polite. His brevity meant that he did not care for my company. I acted as if I had not perceived it and continued:

"I have no netting with me to protect myself against mosquitos, which is why I cannot sleep in the open. Is there a hut in the village where I can stay?"

"I do not know; I am not from here."

"Then you, too, are a stranger here? May Allah be with you on your journey!"

"May his blessing also be yours! Where do you come from?"

"From Khartoum," I replied, forced to tell an untruth.

"Where is your tent?"

"I do not live in a tent, but in a house. It stands in Suez."

"What are you?"

I made, as much as possible, a crafty face and replied:

"I trade in all kinds of things, but preferably in . . ."

I stopped and with a move of my hand indicated that it was not advisable to complete the sentence.

"In forbidden goods?" he said in my place.

"If that were the case, would I admit to it?"

"You can tell me. I would not betray you."

"In any case, silence is better than talking."

"Not always. If a trader wants to do some business, he must talk about it."

"Obviously, I will talk about it when the time is right. But there's no business now."

"Maybe there is, if I understood you correctly. You arrived on camels. Where are you going?"

"Buying."

"What?"

"That." I nodded, remaining vague.

He had not just become more friendly but, as one says, had become "warm." He thought me to be a slave trader, and I was certain that he was a subordinate of the slaver Ibn Asl who I was looking for. It was important now to reinforce his opinion, but without admitting right away that it was the correct one, for no slave trader will tell the first man he meets what he is and does. In any case, the man's task here was to await the arrival of the *raïs effendina*, then to report it. That meant that the *noquar* "Lizard" was Ibn Asl's and would not anchor too far from here, most likely by the Jazirah Hassaniah.

"You are discreet, something I like very much," the man opined. "One can only do business with discreet people."

"Ah, so you, too, deal in things not everyone need know about?"

"And if that were so?"

"Then we would be a match."

"Really? Are you aware that it is very dangerous business to get *arqa'* (slaves)?"

"Bah! Why would it be dangerous? One heads for a village of Blacks, surrounds it, sets fire to it, then collects the Negroes when they come running from their burning huts. The old and weak are knifed or shot, and the others one takes away. Where's the danger there?"

"Indeed, not with that; it begins with the transport."

"One mustn't be caught, which is why it's best to sell the slaves then and there."

"That is impossible if there is no buyer."

"Then one brings someone along who will buy the Blacks right after the hunt and assumes the danger of transport"

"Where does one find such a man?"

"Where? Hmm!" I mumbled meaningfully.

"Who could he be?" he asked.

"It is likely of no interest to you."

"More than you think. Is the man rich?"

"He has as much as he needs."

"He must also be courageous!"

"That he is. He has been in Ethiopia several times to buy slaves. That takes something."

"Indeed. Where is he now?"

"At the White Nile, maybe not very far from here."

"You are being exceptionally cautious. Are you referring to yourself?"

"Of course I won't say that."

"You can tell me, because . . ."

"Because . . .? Why don't you say it?"

"Because, I, too, must be cautious. But If I am not mistaken, I could possibly tell you from whom you can buy *arqa'*."

"Well then, from whom?"

"From Ibn Asl."

"Allah! From this famous slaver? Where is he?"

"Where your trader is, at the White Nile."

"In what area?"

"Maybe not far from here," he replied, repeating my earlier words.

I acted as if I was happily surprised and exclaimed:

"This is fine; this is very good! I heard talk about him. A Turk trader I know, told me that he had bought plenty from him."

"Do you mean Murad Nassyr? So you know him?"

"Very well. I often bought *arqa'* from him."

"Ah, at last you admit that you were talking about yourself!"

"Ya Allah! It just slipped from my mouth."

"Not to worry! No harm was done, and I can now also speak openly, and can tell you that I am in the service of Ibn Asl."

"Is that so? Or are you only testing me?"

"It is the truth. What reason should I have to falsely my claim to be a servant of the slave hunter?"

"To catch me. You could easily be in the service of the *Khedive*."

"Even if that were the case, I could do you no harm now. I would need to catch you in the act. So, honestly! Tell me whether you want to buy *arqa'*?"

"Well, then, I'll risk it and trust you, although I've never seen you. Yes, I buy slaves when I can get them."

"Where did you plan to go from here?"

"Upstream, far beyond Fashoda, until I find a *saribah* and what I'm looking for."

A saribah is a slave hunter settlement. Such settlements are built like forts, at least what is understood as such in these areas. Their huts house the slavers or hold provisions and are often surrounded by mul-tilayered, dense thorn hedges.

"You need not travel into the blue," the man suggested confiden-tially. "Do you carry money with you?"

"Enough."

"Then I will take you to Ibn Asl."

"I am very grateful to you for doing this and will give you a nice *bakshish* later. But does Ibn Asl have slaves at the moment?"

"Not yet. We were just going for *arqa'*. Murad Nassyr wants slaves, and if luck is with us, more than enough will be left for you."

"Then Murad Nassyr is with Ibn Asl?"

"No, he went ahead to Fashoda."

I was pleased to hear this. I entertained the daring idea of visiting Ibn Asl, a venture that would be like entering the lion's den. He would not know me, since, at Wadi al-Bard he had seen me only from afar. Had Murad Nassyr been with him, I could not have let myself be seen, or would have been done for. Of course, the *mukkadam* and the *muza'bir* could also be with the slaver. These two crooks knew me as well as the Turk. I therefore had to inquire unobtrusively about the presence of these two.

"Do you know what the Turk came for, actually?" the man continued, having become quite confiding.

"No."

"Do you know his family?"

"I only know that he has two sisters."

"That is correct. From this, I know that you are telling the truth and are truly the one you claim to be. He brought one of these sisters to Ibn Asl as his wife. The wedding will take place at a *saribah* on the upper White Nile. Should you come along, you can take part in the festivities. On such occasions, Ibn Asl is always extremely generous. His father will also be there."

"His father?" I asked, pretending not to know.

"Yes, his father is still alive. He travels up and down the Nile pretending to be a pious *faqir* to promote his son's business under this disguise."

"Is he here already?"

"He actually should be, but he is presently absent, since he went with a group of our slave hunters out onto the savanna to hold judgment."

"Judgment?"

"Yes, to punish a foreign *giaur*, who has done us great damage."

"This makes me curious."

"Ibn Asl can tell you about this himself, if he cares to. I do not know whether I am permitted to talk about this man. This Christian is a rogue, a devil who we must destroy."

Had he only known that I was this very devil! He continued:

"He was pursued all the way from al-Qahira to here, but in vain. He even escaped the *mukkadam*, when he . . ."

"The *mukkadam*?" I asked. "Which *mukkadam* are you referring to?"

"The one of the holy Qadiriyya."

"Whose name is Abd al-Barak? Ah, I know him very well. I met him in al-Qahira."

"Really? The more glad I am to have met you here. You will find friends, although the *mukkadam* joined Murad Nassyr to go to Fashoda. He was accompanied by a *muza'bir*; both will come along on our slave hunt."

Now I knew what I needed to know. No one knowing me was with Ibn Asl, which is why I could risk going to him. Just then the sun was touching the horizon, calling to perform the *maghrib*, the sunset prayer. Impersonating a Muslim, I was forced to perform at least the external movements. I thus went to Bin Nil, who was already engaged in prayer and knelt next to him.

I could have stayed with the stranger, but had good reason to perform the apparent prayer next to my companion, who had to learn what I had discussed with the man. Otherwise, should he misspeak, it could easily wreck my plan. Of course, I could not talk with him at length. The stranger could come over to us at which time I had to be finished informing Bin Nil. This is why I told him once the prayer was finished:

"Listen! I am a slaver trader from Suez by name of Amm Silad. You are my servant, called Umar. We know Murad Nassyr, from whom I've bought slaves, also the *mukkadam*. We are on our way upstream, coming from Khartoum."

"All right, *effendi!*" the youngster nodded.

"For Allah's sake, don't say the word *effendi* again except when you are totally sure that we are alone. You have courage. I'm planning something that takes guts. It carries great risk. If you do not want to partake,

I won't hold it against you, and you can stay here in the village awaiting the arrival of the *asakir*."

"Sir, wherever you go, I shall go! Even if that meant death. If there is danger, I shall not leave you."

"Very well! You are a good, faithful fellow. Ibn Asl is nearby, and I will go to him to find out what his plans against the *raïs effendina* are and attempt to wreck them. I will act as if I want to join him on a slave hunt which he is planning, and that I wish to buy Blacks from him."

I was unable to keep talking. The stranger had walked up to us, and said:

"You asked me whether you could sleep in one of the huts. You will not sleep here; after the evening prayer I shall take you to Ibn Asl."

"Why only then?"

"I am still waiting for a ship. You are aware that ships do not usually travel by night but anchor at the bank. At most, they travel for an hour past sunset. Until then, I must wait here. If it does not arrive by then, I will know that it is not coming today and can leave my post."

"What kind of ship is it?"

"Is this young man permitted to hear everything?" he asked in return, pointing at Bin Nil.

"Yes. He is the most faithful and discreet of my servants. I hold no secrets from him."

"You heard of the *raïs effendina*?"

"I even saw him in al-Qahira."

"Then you know also what he wants to accomplish?"

"Everybody does. He is to pursue and catch the slave hunters and traders. I heard that he has been given exceptional powers."

"So it is, indeed. May Allah curse this dog! He has brought much harm to the hunters and recently murdered an entire group of our comrades in Wadi al-Bard."

Had he only known that I had not only been along, but had tracked down and captured this bunch!

"He will not call this murder but simply punishment," I responded.

"Do you agree with him?"

"No way! I, a slave trader, can't possibly be his friend. If he continues as he has, there will soon be no more slaves to buy."

"The *giaur* I mentioned earlier is his friend and helper. Soon, one or the other will be put a stop to. Most likely, the *giaur* has already fallen into our hands. We are now waiting hour by hour for the *raïs effendina*."

"So it is his ship you want to spot here?"

"Yes. He is coming, with Ibn Asl lying in wait for him."

"Is he going to attack the ship of the *raïs*?"

"He would not think of it. The ship is so strongly built and armed, that we could easily come away worse off. Why fight, when the victors might be wounded, and dead. There are other ways to put an enemy out of action."

"How then?"

"One takes, for example . . ."

I was excited to hear what he was going to say. Should the man complete this sentence, I would learn everything I needed to know and did not need to endanger myself by going to Ibn Asl. Unfortunately, he stopped at the fourth word and, shocked, put his hand over his mouth. He added:

"I almost said more than I should. You have such a trustworthy face that I could tell you everything without wondering whether I've got the right to do so. But I must keep silent. Ibn Asl may tell you himself, and I ask you, please, not to let on that I had been so forthcoming with you."

"I am not very talkative, rest assured of that. Are you certain that the *raïs effendina* is coming? The man is supposed to be not only smart but also very cautious."

"As to that, this *giaur*, the Christian *effendi*, must be feared even more, as we were told. Ibn Asl has set a trap for the *raïs effendina* which he will surely enter."

"Do you know what kind of trap it is?"

"Yes. I should actually not talk about it, but you are a slave trader and will travel with us, and since you know already so much, you may as well learn this, too. We conveyed to him in a way that he had to believe it, that a large slave transport will be shipped across the Nile at the Jazirah Hassaniah. It is certain that he will come to intercept this transport at which time he will find his ruination."

This concluded our conversation, at least as far as it was important to me. Although I would have loved to learn the way the *raïs effendina* was to be overcome. Once I had this information, I would have learned everything. I would only need to find and warn him. But I could not press this man much more. He could easily have become suspicious.

We sat together for another hour with our attention focused downstream. Possibly, I was even more expectant than the scout for, if the *raïs* would pass by now without me being able to warn him in some way, he would be lost. Fortunately, he failed to arrive.

'Isha, the evening prayer, would arrive an hour past sunset, after which we could leave. I had not asked how this was to take place, but learned it now when the man said:

"We shall ride. We will go to the *shaykh al-Balad* who will give us horses."

"Will he give us some not knowing who we are?"

"He will not mind, since your camels remain here. They are not, as I noticed, worthless animals. But he will do it also for Ibn Asl's sake."

"Does he know him?"

"He is a secret ally of ours. You know that we slave hunters need helpers everywhere to advise and warn us. He is one of them. When I return here before daybreak, I shall return the horses to him."

The *shaykh* was indeed willing to rent the animals to us, even refused the payment I offered. We mounted up and rode off into the dark of night, since starlight had not yet assumed its full strength.

For an hour, we headed south onto the savanna, then turned east to the river. Individual trees appeared. They gradually increased in number until we found ourselves in the woods. We stopped below a big tree, while our guide left, as he said, to inform Ibn Asl of our arrival and to ask whether he could bring us to him. We dismounted.

"Are you afraid, *effendi!*" Bin Nil whispered to me.

"No, but I'm very tense."

"Me, too. If we are recognized, we are done for."

"There's no one there who has seen us. Nevertheless, we must be extremely cautious. By no means must we become separated, because then one can help the other should it become necessary."

"Do you think it is far from here?"

"Most likely not. We will not have to wait long."

This was true, for only about ten minutes later our guide returned and said:

"My master is willing to receive you. Take the horses by their halters and follow me slowly and carefully. You will quickly need to go downhill."

It was pitch dark, with the trees standing apart. Already, after a few paces, the terrain dropped and soon we saw fires burning, whose light was very helpful. The flames were close to the river bank, where the waters were colored golden by their light.

Not a tree stood there. It had been an *Umm Sufah* place, but the grass had been cut and collected in several piles above. *Umm Sufah* is a swamp grass, a type of sacharum, which grows in enormous swathes in shallow, swampy water along the banks of the Upper Nile. Waves tear it off and carry it from place to place. It collects in bays, from where it is carried away again, forming islands that drift downstream. Often, the river's entire breadth is covered with *Umm Sufah*, which forced hard work on the boatmen in order to get their vessels through.

When we stepped from beneath the trees, I saw about a hundred men lying and squatting by the fires, half and fully dressed, many wearing only a loin cloth. Every kind of skin color was present, even to the deepest Negro black. Internally, however, each of them had to be as "black" as the other. Next to the *Umm Sufah* piles stood six large barrels, and past them rose the outline of the *noquar* from the water, which was so deep there that the vessel lay very close to the river bank.

Nearby a small fire burned, separate from the others where three men sat. When they saw us coming, they rose.

One of them was of mid-size, but broad stature, with a full black beard, and wore a white *haïk*. I recognized him immediately. It was the man on the white *Jabal Garfah* camel I had pursued at Wadi al-Bard without being able to catch up with him, Ibn Asl, the most infamous of slavers. He sternly took our measure, with the other two doing likewise, almost sinister.

"*Salaam*," I greeted, and was going to continue. He, however, waved his hand for silence, and asked:

"Your name?"

"Amm Salad from Suez."

"And this young man?"

"Umar, my assistant."

I did not want to call him my servant, since Bin Nil would then not be allowed to remain with me.

"How many slaves do you want to buy?"

"As many as I can get."

"And where do we deliver them?"

Was I to let myself be questioned in this way? The more modest I remained, the less my security would be. He was not to think he was facing a subordinate person, which is why I replied briefly:

"To where I get money. Do you expect me to instantly tell anyone my business secrets?"

"Amm Salad, you talk very confidently!"

"Do you expect anything different from a man in my business? How about your manners? Does one ask a guest in such a way without offering him a place to sit?"

"Who said that you would be my guest?"

"No one, but I think it is obvious and natural."

"This is not understood. Someone like me must be cautious."

"Me, too. If I don't please you, likewise I don't need to make an effort and can leave at any time. Let's go, Umar!"

I turned with Bin Nil following. That's when Ibn Asl stepped quickly up to me, put his hand on my arm, and said:

"Hold it! You do not understand your situation. Whoever comes here to me is not going to leave."

I looked at him smiling and replied:

"And if I leave anyway?"

"Then I know how to hold you."

"Try it!"

Saying this, I took Bin Nil's hand and ran away into the trees, pulling him after me. Fortunately, he had the presence of mind to immediately match my speed. Ibn Asl had not expected this; we were gone before he was able to hold on to me. Now, he shouted:

"Get them, men! Go after them!"

Whoever had legs ran into the woods, including Ibn Asl and his two companions. I had run only about twenty paces when I turned in a short arc to where the *Umm Sufah* glade ended. Fire light did not penetrate there. I pulled Bin Nil with me into the rushes where we ducked down. Behind us sounded the shouts of the searchers, looking for us in vain.

"Why did you not keep running?" Bin Nil asked. "They would not have caught us."

"Because I don't want to get away."

"Do you want to remain in here?"

"No. I only wanted to demonstrate to Ibn Asl that he cannot order me about. They all disappeared under the trees. Let's go!"

We crept from the rushes, ran to the fire where Ibn Asl had been sitting, and sat down. There lay three muskets and three tobacco pipes next to an earthen vessel holding tobacco. We quickly stuffed a couple of pipes and lit them. That's when a surprised exclamation arose from behind us: "They are sitting over there by the fire!"

This exclamation traveled from mouth to mouth, with everyone returning as quickly as they had run off. We sat there smoking quietly. The men did not know how to respond to this. They raucously shouted and laughed. Ibn Asl had to blaze a trail for himself to get to us.

"Allah *akbar* (God is great)! he exclaimed. "What happened to you? We were looking for you while you sit here!"

"I only wanted to demonstrate to you that I can leave whenever I want. You would certainly not have been able to catch us. I've come, however, to do business with you, and will not leave until it has been consummated."

I said this so confidently that his earlier sinister face turned to a smile and, shaking his head, he said:

"Amm Salad, I have not seen a man like you before. You are exceptionally cocky. Since this happens to please me, I will not hold the prank you played against you. Return to your places!"

This order was for his men, who instantly obeyed. He lowered himself to my right with the others following his example. Yes, I had been cocky, and had to wait now to see whether it's consequence would turn out to be beneficial. We had neither been greeted nor welcomed and as long as this was not done, we were not safe. Ibn Asl took the third pipe, stuffed and lit it, then said, while he blew his smoke almost into my face:

"What just happened, I have never experienced before. You are either a reckless jester or a much-experienced trader."

"Not the former, but the latter," I answered. "I have experienced many dangers and am unafraid when someone receives me without welcoming me right away."

"Can I say "*Marhaba*" (welcome) to you, without knowing you?"

"Yes, but also no. Everyone does it his own way. I welcome everyone visiting me."

"And if he is an evil person?"

"Then, there's always time to chase him away."

"After suffering harm! No, first scrutiny, then the decision!"

"Go ahead then; check me out! It will be my pleasure. But let me tell you that I am very tired. We rode for quite some distance today and are in need of sleep. Be so kind not to extend your examination through the night."

He looked at the two others, who returned his gaze. They were unsure whether to look happy or grim, until Bin Nil added seriously:

"And we are also hungry!"

Now, Ibn Asl laughed out aloud and responded:

"By Allah, you are peculiar people! But I shall diverge from my customary habit and trust you."

"This should not be difficult for you," I said. "It is actually more problematic for me to trust you. We took the risk of calling on you. Is this not the best proof of our honesty?"

"I should think so!"

"Do it, and you won't be mistaken! I was delighted to learn that you are here at the *jazirah*. I was headed for Bahr al-Ghazzal, even up to Bahr al-Jabal, to look for a *saribah*. This would have been a long journey into the unknown. Now I can, with your permission stay with you, and am certain that we will enter into a continuous business relationship."

"The question is what you are prepared to pay."

"As the goods are, so the price! I buy the *arqa'* freshest from the catch and transport them myself."

"But you have no men for it!"

"I will hire them later. I think I can get enough warriors from the Shilluk or Nuer."

"That takes a lot of money, meaning plenty of trade goods, because, up there, payment is only in goods."

"Those I will buy in Fashoda. I've got the money."

"You risk much, then. What if I kill you in order to take your money?"

"You are too smart to do this."

"Do you call me smart to let you keep your money?"

"Yes. If you rob me now, you make a single profit; but if you remain honest, you will earn often and plenty from me."

"You have figured it right. Nothing will happen to you."

"I'm pleased not to be mistaken about you. Concerning myself, Murad Nassyr will vouch for me."

"This is what moved me to let you come. You know him and have bought from him. This leads me to believe that I will be satisfied with you. I do not mind if you accompany me."

"Where are you going?"

"Later about that. Let us first get to know each other. I welcome you, you and your assistant. You shall sleep with us and also eat with us."

A very appetizing scent wafted from the other fires. I learned that they had butchered a cow that afternoon. The meat had been cut into strips they were presently roasting. We received our share and ate heartily. In its course, we conversed, that is, I had to talk because Ibn Asl quizzed me. He wanted to learn as much as possible about me, my past, my situation, as detailed as possible. I provided him with the most extensive information. Of course, everything I told him, was invented. I imagined a slave trader in Suez, dreamed up his conditions, figured his possible business connections, and thought about the travels he might have taken. Since I was sufficiently familiar with these situations, I was able to project, with some luck, an acceptable image which Ibn Asl became more and more interested in. The man thawed and subsequently told me about various things in his life.

What I heard Ibn Asl say made me shudder. This man had never shown a heart or a conscience. His soul did not seem to hold anything human. He carried a true lust for evil and the more and longer his stories became, the more my revulsion grew. He, on the other hand, seemed to find ever more pleasure in me, his sincerity growing. Eventually, he talked about me, and the damage I had caused him by liberating the women and girls of the Fassara. He described me, of course, from his point of view. Each of his words dripped with such hate and anger that they would have caused another to tremble. He told me that he had sent men to intercept me on the savanna, and concluded:

"I gave these men my father as a leader, making certain that nothing would be missed to catch him."

"But he could easily detour around them," I commented. "Did they know what direction he was coming from?"

"Rather well. Surely, he would have taken a guide from the Fassara, and we know the direction the Fassara take when they travel to Khartoum. This time, he will be unable to escape us, after which you will see how many pains a man can bear before he dies."

"Then you intend to torture him to death?"

"Yes. He must lose every member individually. I shall remove his nose, the ears, the lip, the tongue, and the eyes one after the other."

"And what is to happen to the *asakir* accompanying him?"

"I issued orders to kill them. He will be the only one delivered to me. My father is expected to return at any moment."

So, every one of my body parts, every sensory organ, was to be cut off, one by one, stabbed or torn out! It was an exceptionally comforting thought in case he discovered who I was! My hair could have risen, contemplating this! Nevertheless, I risked an inquiry that could easily do me harm. I mentioned the *Faqir al-Fuqara* and asked whether he knew him.

"Of course, I know him," he answered. "He, too, was a slave hunter."

"Was? Not any more?"

"No. He became pious in order to prepare himself for the future."

"Does he have particular plans for it?"

"Possibly, but he does not talk about it. He reads many books, worldly and spiritual ones, and many unknown people come to visit him, with whom he conducts long, secret conversations. Maybe, be wants to become a great *marabut* or itinerant preacher of Islam. On the other hand, it may also be just a disguise below which he conceals entirely different plans. He hates the Viceroy, who chased him from his position and likely will want to avenge himself in some way."

Could this man with his Mahdi idea be serious? Were this actually the case, I would need to inform the government. He had talked about that the Mahdi was going to ally himself with high-ranking Egyptian officers. Possibly, the visitors he received served the purpose of establishing such connections or even to have cultivated them already. I resolved to first inform the *raïs effendina*, who could assess this situation better than I. Much later, when the revolt in the Sudan was under way, I learned that the officer mentioned may have been Arabi Pasha, but it is doubtful that he was in contact with him already.

Unfortunately, I was still unable to find out that which was more important to me. Ibn Asl did not return the conversation to the *raïs effendina*. I took pains not to direct our conversation to him overtly, but made every effort to return to the subject indirectly, without him noticing, but it was in vain. Time passed until close to midnight, when he said he was ready for sleep and asked me to accompany him.

"Where to?" I asked.

"Onto the ship. We find better protection there from the insects and I shall give you some netting. You will sleep with me. You can see from it that I like you."

I believed him, although he could easily invite me for the reason to keep an eye on me.

"I don't want to burden you," I objected. "On my travels, I'm used to sleeping with my assistant. Allow him to stay with me."

"There is only room for you and me," he objected. "He, too, will get a good spot, sleeping with my officers, who have their own cabin."

I did not press the issue further. Insisting on my request could easily cause suspicion. I had to submit. I also had no reason to push for Bin Nil's presence. Everything, so far, had gone well, and I did not have the least reason to believe that danger would threaten us before morning.

In the course of our conversation, I had observed that many of the slavers had gone aboard the ship, likely to escape the mosquitos. Thus, its hold had to be empty in order to accommodate that many sleepers.

A kind of ladder led from the bank on board. Arrived there, the two other men, he had called his officers, went forward, taking Bin Nil along. There was no time nor opportunity to give him any cautionary instructions. Ibn Asl went with me to the stern.

The difference between a *dahabiyah* and a *noquar* is that the latter has an open deck, at least the middle section of the vessel remains open. The kitchen is usually up front, operated by some slave women, while a small cabin is found at the stern, where the ship's master, the *raïs*, lives.

Whether the "Lizard" was furnished like this, I was unable to make out despite the now relatively bright starlight. There was a cabin in the stern, which I discovered right away, since Abd Asl took me there. It consisted of two rooms, the one in front being the smaller, with the larger one behind. He stopped in the first to light a lamp. Although I had little time to look around, I saw a floor cushion to my right, and a wooden chest on the left, holding various kinds of tools, as needed on board a ship. This latter fact would become very important to me.

"Enter quickly, so that the mosquitos will not come in!" he requested, while he pushed the mat aside that separated the two rooms from each other. I followed his request, and when he had the lamp suspended from some string dangling from the ceiling, I was able to see the room's furnishings. It consisted of pillows lying along the wooden walls, and a most inartistically painted box that might hold his clothing. He took two fly nets from it, handing one to me. I wrapped myself elaborately into mine with him following suit.

If I had been of the opinion that we would sleep now, I had been mistaken. He rather told me that he would like to continue our conversation until the oil in the lamp was depleted. This was fine with me; this way I might yet learn what I had tried to find out before.

"You said that you are tired," he commented, "but you can sleep into the coming day, for as long as you like."

Saying this, he provided me with an excellent reason for my comment:

"If you aren't sleepy yet, I will be glad to keep chatting with you, but I won't sleep into the day."

"Why not?"

"Because you are expecting the *raïs effendina* to arrive; you intend to engage in battle."

"Are you afraid of it?"

"Not at all! I've smelled enough powder already, am not a poor shot, and even wish to partake when it starts."

"There will not be much powder used. All is to take place as much as possible in silence. But if you would like to bash the skulls of a few *asakir*, I will not mind."

"So there will not be shooting but clubbing and stabbing? It's all the same to me; I will join in in any case. But how will we get from your *noquar* onto the ship of the *raïs effendina's*?"

"We will beware of entering it. Fire is better than powder."

"Ah! You intend to incinerate the *raïs effendina's* ship? That will be difficult. Might you have a man on board who is going to light it?"

"No. I could not achieve my purpose in this way. The fire would quickly be noticed and extinguished, and I would be left empty-handed. I will start it quite differently, so that not a single man is going to escape and not a splinter of the ship remains."

"That I don't understand."

"Yes, while you have seen and experienced much that others did not get to know, you are still lacking the right style and trickiness. A slave hunter must not show any mercy. We are dealing here with to be or not to be. Either the *raïs effendina* or I must perish, and since I do not care to do so, it will have to be him, and in a way that makes rescue totally impossible."

"You are right there. From everything I've heard of you, I would act just as firmly in your place. I only lack the insight as to how you intend to achieve your goal so quickly."

"You could actually guess it, but I will tell you. Did you notice the *Umm Sufah* piles?"

"Of course, they are large enough."

"I had the *Umm Sufah* cut down, first to make room for our camp and second for fire material. Did you see the barrels nearby?"

"Yes."

"They are filled with a material that will destroy the *raïs*. They hold *gaz* (petroleum)."

"*Gaz*? Ah, I'm getting it. But how will you bring this dangerous oil onto his ship?"

"Onto? I need not bring it onto his ship, but only close to it. It's much easier than you think. I am convinced that he will land at Hagasi. This gives me time for my preparations. You know that I keep a scout in Hagasi. As soon as the *raïs* arrives there, he will ride up here to report it. The *jazirah* divides the Nile into two arms, of which the one here is the quieter and safer, which will cause the *raïs* to steer his ship to our side. I will divide my men into three divisions. The first stays with the barrels; the second will occupy the bank downstream, as far as possible, and the third will take over the bank of the island over there. In this way the river arm, the *raïs* needs to use, is occupied by my warriors on both sides, and they, of course, will not let themselves be seen right away. Once the ship has come so close that it can no longer escape, the men will toss the petroleum barrels into the river, followed by the dry, quickly burning *Umm Sufah*. The oil will spread across the water, and lit by flaming torches, will form a wall of fire around the ship from which he will be unable to flee. What do you think of my plan?"

I shuddered from this man, but forced myself to reply in an admiring voice:

"It is magnificent, singular! Was it your idea or someone else's?"

"I thought it up myself," he commented, obviously proud.

"Then I admire you. I would never have come up with this idea. At most, I would have ambushed the *raïs* and secretly given him a bullet."

"And his followers would have remained alive. No! All, all of them must go to Hell!"

"But what if they find the time to steer the ship to the bank?"

"Let them try! Remember that within a few minutes they will be engulfed by flames, in which they must suffocate. The ship will immediately be ablaze. Nevertheless, I thought about the possibility that some will jump into the water, trying to reach the bank. Should they escape the fire and the crocodiles, which I think impossible, my men will stand at the ready, here and over there, to kill them dead with the butts of their muskets. So you see, not a single one is going to escape."

"Can the fire not endanger your *noquar*?"

"No."

"But what about the consequences? You will be chased by the Viceroy's soldiers until they get hold of you; then three times woe to you!"

"Will they learn how the fire arose?"

"Maybe. Some may drift all the way to Hagasi. It will be noticed that it was caused by oil and the question will be raised who dumped the oil into the river."

"Let them ask; no one will answer!"

"Are you sure of your men?"

"Yes. None will talk."

"Since I feel so well disposed toward you, let me draw your attention to something else. What if another ship shows up in addition to that of the *raïs*?"

"Then it will perish, too."

"Or if another ship comes downstream? It could stop and become a witness to the sight. You would be given away."

"Hopefully, this will not be the case, but should it happen, I cannot prevent it. I would try to get this ship to land, and then continue with my plan. It is not my fault should my petroleum catch fire and the *raïs effendina* is stupid enough to risk entering the fire with his ship. Who can punish me for this?"

"Hmm! Let's just hope that there won't be any interference."

"And should it happen, it will not matter to me. Have I not been pursued enough? Can I let myself be seen in Khartoum? Am I not already hunted these days? I am an outlaw. No one except myself knows where I live. I am against the law and the law is against me. I must still take care of a number of things hereabouts after which I shall disappear. I am therefore indifferent as to whether it becomes known that the *raïs* died by my action. It is only too bad that his ship will have to burn, without me being able to capture the least bit of booty. But what I will miss there, my slave hunt will bring. I shall go on a *ghazwa* (a slave hunt) like there has never been before. You will see. Let's not talk about that now. The lamp is going out, and we shall sleep now."

Not much oil had been in the lamp. The flame became smaller and smaller and then went out. It became dark in the small room.

What had I learned there! Was it possible for a human being to arrive at such a devilish idea? The execution of this terrible plan had to be prevented. But how? The simplest and best would be for me and Bin Nil to secretly disappear from the ship and return to Hagasi to warn the *raïs* there. But where was Bin Nil, and would it be possible to get him away from his two fellow sleepers without being noticed? I had to try, but naturally, I could not attempt it until Ibn Asl had fallen asleep.

I waited eagerly for this to happen. Minutes passed, long, long minutes. Finally, I noticed from his soft, regular breathing that he was asleep. I unwrapped myself from the netting and crept over to him. With my ear close to his face, I listened. Yes, this was the breathing of a truly sleeping person. He did not pretend. Still, I took one of his legs to shake it softly. He did not wake up and was therefore asleep. I crept to the front room. I had deposited my belongings there, but left them now, since they would have been a hindrance in the search for my companion.

When I reached the open deck, I stopped first in the deep shadow of the cabin to orient myself. Most of the slavers had entered the hold. In there, the air was more stifling, but the men were bothered less by the annoying mosquitos. Only a single fire still burned, the one most distant from the ship. Next to it lay several sleepers, protected from the insects by its smoke.

Had guards been posted? I neither saw nor heard any. Likewise, there was no movement on the semi-dark, starlit deck. I lay down in order to creep forward and passed by the hatch and the mast. There wasn't a man in sight.

I arrived up front where there was also a cabin. On this ship the kitchen was located amidships and not, as is customary, at the very prow. I heard subdued voices coming from the cabin, and crept to the thin board wall to listen. The two officers and Bin Nil were not asleep yet. They were talking with each other, still awake. I was able to understand quite well what they were talking about, and realized that Bin Nil was trying to pump the two officers. The eagerness of the young man to be of help to me was so great that he sacrificed sleep, while he tried to keep the two men awake. This wrecked my plan. They might talk for a long time yet. Would it then be possible to leave without being seen? The bird-life along the Nile awoke well before daybreak. Once the birds became noisy, the sleepers would awake and it would be too late for our escape.

Then, too, I heard from the voices that the three speakers were not positioned advantageously for my purpose. Bin Nil was lying in the back, and the room was so small that he, even if the others were asleep, could not have left without needing to climb over them. That had to wake them up. At least, it was likely.

What to do? I could not get Bin Nil out, but I could not leave without him; it would mean certain death for the good fellow. I had to stay. But what about the terrible danger the raïs effendina was headed for? It had to be prevented, and quickly. He might come sailing up the river by early morning, at which time it would be too late. Yes, if it were an assault by men, but not this hellish petroleum attack! I had to render this scheme harmless. If the raïs then came, he would at least not be incinerated and could defend himself against an attack.

Should I get off the ship and roll the barrels into the water? No, that would have caused a noise, and I could not be certain how far they would drift downstream. If they were soon caught by the rushes along the bank, Ibn Asl would have them returned and execute his plan after all. They had to stay put, yet the petroleum had to disappear. To drill holes into them? Ah! I remembered the tool box. Maybe it held a drill. This was the only way by which I could prevent the ruin of the *raïs* and his *asakir*.

But what would Ibn Asl say when he found the barrels empty in the morning? I could care less!

I could not think of myself and had to risk being thought of as the perpetrator.

I returned as quickly as possible to the stern cabin. Ibn Asl was breathing as before, being fast asleep. I went for the tool box and removed one tool after another. It was very difficult, since I had to avoid making the least noise. I succeeded, finding some drills. Some were too big. The hole, or rather the holes, could not be too large so that they would not be spotted right away. At the bottom of the box lay one with not quite the diameter of a pencil. This was the right one. I pocketed it and returned the other tools very carefully. I now listened once more for the breath of the sleeper, then slipped outside onto the deck and headed for the boarding ladder.

Arriving there, I first peered cautiously down to see whether a guard had been posted, and when I did not see one, climbed down. I quickly covered the short distance to the barrels and began my work. Each barrel needed to get two holes, one at the top to provide entry of air, and one at the bottom for drainage. I put the holes at places where, in my opinion, they were not easily spotted. I had to take great care not to come in contact with the draining oil. The smell of oil, or oil spots, would have instantly betrayed me.

In order that the barrels could quickly be opened and tossed into the river, they had been placed close to the water's edge. The liquid had to run only three to four feet before entering the water. I was done in less than a quarter of an hour. I cleaned the drill in the water, wiped it carefully on some rushes and then went back on board. Once in the cabin, I returned it to the tool box and crept under my mosquito netting.

My heart beat easier. I had saved the lives of many men and prevented a serious assault, more contemptible than any other I had ever come across. But what would the consequences be for me! Well, I was unable to avert them under the circumstances, and so waited quietly to see what would happen next. After the excitement I had experienced, I eventually settled down and slept. I awoke not by myself, but by Ibn Asl.

"Get up, Amm Salad!" he said. "You must have slept well for it is late morning, and there will be lots to do very soon. The *raïs effendina* is coming."

In an instant, I was fully awake and jumped up. My first look went to his face. Nothing showed that let me assume that my deed had been discovered. His eyes shone brightly; he even nodded pleasantly at me. Then he continued:

"Yes, you seem surprised. It is time to get up. Go outside where there is some coffee waiting for you."

Outside the cabin was a cushion on which I sat. An old, ugly Negress brought me the morning beverage. The slavers were gathered on the bank, just as I had found them yesterday. I, therefore, said: "The *raïs* is coming, you said. But your men aren't at their posts."

"That is not required yet. I just received the message that he arrived at Hagasi and landed at the *mishrah*. It is not known how long he will stay there. Hours could pass before he leaves. This is why I dispatched another scout who is watching, halfway between here and Hagasi. Only when he returns will the time come for everyone to assume his post."

"No other ship will arrive about that same time?"

"Not upstream, or my scout would have seen it. And downstream . . . Hell, that would be fatal if one came now!"

"Would you let it pass?"

"Certainly not. In passing, it's crew would see us and the *noquar* and report it to the *raïs*."

"This is not certain. Maybe they would sail past without talking to him."

"There you do not know this dog. He hails every passing ship, forces it to stop, to check it for slaves. He would surely learn that a *noquar* is banked here. He would become suspicious and be on guard, after which my beautiful plan would come to naught. No, if a ship came downstream, it would be stopped and made to wait until the event is over. To make sure, I will dispatch another scout upstream. The time for action has arrived, and I will not be put off by anything turning up."

He went on land to dispatch one of his man. That's when Bin Nil came to me. With no one nearby, we were able to talk undisturbed.

"You slept long, sir," he said. "I almost became concerned for you. Did you not think of what is at stake here?"

"I not only thought, but acted, and more than you know."

"And I didn't sleep at all. I was unable to close my eyes from concern for the raïs effendina."

"I also had trouble sleeping for awhile."

"The two officers became very talkative last night and told me that the raïs is going to be burned. Imagine!"

"By the petroleum in the barrels down there."

"You know?"

"Yes, Ibn Asl told me."

"Sir, what are we going to do? The raïs effendina is coming and there waits the petroleum. It is terrible, infinitely terrible, to think about it. And with all that, you slept and did not bother about anything!"

"Don't quarrel! It isn't as bad as you think. I drilled holes into the barrels last night. The oil ran out."

"Ya Allah! Is it true?"

"Yes. It wasn't easy to do. I wanted to escape and take you along, but heard you talking. You lay in the back of the cabin and would not have been able to get out. I therefore had to act without you."

"This is why it smelled of petroleum when I got up. The men ascribed it to the fumes coming from the barrels. But there are dead fish drifting in the rushes."

"There will be more downstream. Was the water colored?"

"No."

Then the oil was either very pure or the strong morning breeze flushed the residue away from here, all to our good."

"I don't see anything good in it, sir. When they discover it, suspicion will obviously fall on us."

"Very likely. But who can prove it?"

"None of these people will ask for proof. We must get away as quickly as possible."

"It would indeed be best for us, if we could leave, but I have some reservations."

"What are they?"

"First, we cannot do so unobserved and, once they see us trying, they will stop us after which our game is over."

"We can do it like last night: we simply run away."

"Then they will demand that we stop, and if we don't, they will send some bullets after us."

"They did not do so yesterday."

"It was night and dark, but now it is day and bright. There's a difference, consider it! We could have escaped last night because of the dark. No one could have properly aimed at us, but now, we would soon be hit by a few bullets. And to where should we flee? To Hagasi, across the open savanna, where any pursuer could shoot us easily?"

"We can shoot, too!"

"Yes, but if we want to shoot, we must stop and will allow our pursuers to catch up. No, no, that won't work. And our escape is to serve a dual purpose, which is to extract ourselves from the noose into which we voluntarily stuck our heads, while simultaneously be of service to the *raïs*. If we run away now, he will come here unsuspecting. Although he can no longer be destroyed by fire, an ambush can still be laid that will be to his detriment. On the other hand, if we stay, we may be able to prevent this by some ploy or at least warn him."

"Warn him? As soon as we hail him, we will be lost."

"Bah! The warning can be made by a rifle shot that happens to be accidentally released."

"But the moment they discover that the barrels are empty, won't it then be best for us to have disappeared?"

"That I agree with. Let me think! Maybe a thought will occur to me."

"It needs to come quickly or we will lose precious time."

He sat down next to me awaiting the arrival of my thought. Unfortunately, it often happens to people that precisely when an idea is urgently required, none is found. Such was the case. I thought and thought, but in vain. Five, ten, fifteen minutes passed. Ibn Asl stood with his men by the bank, talking urgently to one of them. It seemed to me that they frequently looked up to us during their conversation. Then he came aboard. His face was as friendly as before when he said to me:

"Amm Salad, you were correct when you said that the petroleum fire would endanger my ship. I shall have it pulled some distance upstream. I hope the raïs effendina will not come while we are doing that."

So, that is why the men had looked at the ship. Their looks had not been for us. A number of them now came on board to erect the mast.

This puzzled me, since the draw rope could also be attached someplace else. In so doing they came closer to us and . . . suddenly threw themselves on us. This happened so unexpectedly and quickly that I did not have time to offer any resistance before my legs had been tied up and my arms tied to my back. Now I lay next to Bin Nil on the deck. What had happened? How come this sudden hostile surprise? Some suspicion must have arisen against us.

The expression on Ibn Asl's face had turned quite different. His men had retreated a couple of paces, while he stepped close to me and said threateningly:

"You did not expect this, did you? You seem to have a clever mind, but this is why I, too, must be clever. I had to both deceive and overcome you quickly."

"I'm surprised," I replied. "What was the reason for the attack?"

"Yes, that you do not know, which is, that you two were overheard earlier."

"Whatever we said could easily be heard," I answered calmly. "We did not talk about anything that would have given you reason for this sudden hostile behavior."

"So! Do you really think you can deceive Ibn Asl? If so, you are extremely stupid. This man – he pointed to a man, who had grabbed me first – lay, without you knowing, on the roof of the cabin. He overheard everything. So as not to be seen by you, he climbed down the rope to which the boat was attached and told everything. Are you denying it?"

"Not at all! But what was it we were talking about?"

I relied on the fact that the man could not have understood everything. Although we had not spoken softly, but also not any louder than two men do who are sitting next to each other, talking about matters not everyone is supposed to hear.

"Of many things," Ibn Asl replied, "but mostly of falseness and betrayal."

"Prove it!"

"You demand proof? Is it up to you to ask for proof? Did you not talk of petroleum?"

"Indeed. Why should I deny that? You, yourself, told me about it."

"But you claimed there was none in the barrels. How come you spoke such silliness?"

"It was, of course, a jest," I replied, pleased how I had been misunderstood halfway and not at all the other way.

"You shall soon learn that it was no jest but serious! You also talked about fleeing. Why would you want to flee if your conscience is clean?"

"We spoke of fleeing from the fire, should it ignite your own ship. Did we flee last night? Did I not prove to you that I want to remain with you, and that I have no wish to get away from here?"

"You seem to be the master of excuses! But what are you going to say, when I ask you why your rifle should misfire once the *raïs effendina* shows up?"

"Should? It should not! And my rifle, mine? I spoke of guns in general. I feared some incautiousness, some hastiness, by which the *raïs* could be warned. You will position your men far from the bank, about which I said, 'hopefully, no musket will discharge by accident'. Although

— 110 —

this man listened, he only understood some of our words, and wrongly at that. Next time, I advise that he listens somewhat better."

Ibn Asl's looks went searchingly between me and the listener. My audacity impressed him. It was obvious that he was becoming confused and began to believe me. But he kept asking:

"But you were afraid for the *raïs effendina*?"

"Here, again, your famous reporter misunderstood me. I wasn't afraid for the raïs but of him."

"How does that jibe with you telling me yesterday that you were not afraid?"

"At that time, I did not know what was to happen. Now, that I know your intentions, and when I talked about them with my companion, I was concerned that they could be thwarted. That's what I meant."

"Thwarted? Who could do that?"

"The *raïs*. He went on land at Hagasi. You lured him here by erroneously informing him that a slave transport would cross the Nile here. He must therefore be aware that traders, even slavers would be here. Do you expect him to travel here as if on a pleasure cruise?"

"What else?"

"I think it quite possible that he will leave his ship in Hagasi and take his *asakir* here by land in order to attack you from the rear. While our eyes are focused on the river, he will creep up on us from the savanna and attack. That's why I was afraid of him, but in no way for him."

"Allah! That is true, that is very true. I did not think of this. We must also direct our attention inland and . . ."

He was interrupted. The scout posted upstream came running to report an approaching ship. A boat under the command of the two officers was manned at once and sent toward the vessel to make it land.

I was hoping to be untied again, when he asked me:

"How do you know what we told the *raïs effendina*?"

Unfortunately, the guard at Hagasi had asked me not to give him away. I was obligated to the man and did not want to harm him, which is why I replied:

"It was mentioned last night by the second fire. While we sat by the first I heard it, nevertheless."

This untruth came from good intention, but immediately found punishment when he answered:

"This is a lie. It could not have been mentioned at the fire. Only four people knew what I passed on to the *raïs effendina*, the two officers and the guard at Hagasi. None would have talked about it. Who told you? Maybe the *raïs* himself? I was ready to trust you again, but I realize that your excuses are hairsplitting and ambiguous. Before I let you go free, I shall check this situation carefully, and woe to you, if I find the least bit of suspicion in your tale! But I do not have the time for it now. You will remain here under guard."

He turned away, since his attention was drawn upstream from our anchorage, where the other vessel appeared. It was hailed by the boat sent toward it, and the crews of the two vessels entered into a discussion. Then we saw a man climb into the waiting boat, which was now returning to us, while the other ship was steered toward the bank to land there.

Our guard kept a sharp eye on us. I was unconcerned. I figured that the excuses I had presented would yet produce their intended effect. They could not prove anything. While the listener had presented some serious charges against us, the true connection had escaped him. He had understood only individual points from which no conviction could be forthcoming. My only concern was the moment when they discovered the empty barrels. Having become distrustful once, suspicion would most likely fall on us. But, here, too, we could not be proven guilty. Unfortunately, it would turn out differently, quite differently.

The boat landed and the officers brought a man on board. Imagine my shock when I recognized Abu al-Nil, the helmsman of the *dahabiyah* 'Al-Samak', with whom I had experienced the nightly adventure at Giza. This *dahabiyah* had been intended for the slave trade and had been confiscated by the *raïs effendina* that night. Out of pity, I had enabled the helmsman to escape, had even given him some travel money, and had received his assurance that he would head north to his home. And now I saw him here upstream from Khartoum in the deep south!

Surely, the man still remembered me. He had to, since I had often found that my face was not one to be easily and quickly forgotten. People who had seen me only once and in passing, had years later recognized me instantly. Worse was the fact that this helmsman, Abu al-Nil, was the grandfather of my companion, Bin Nil. It could be expected that, once he saw us, he would come instantly running to us and give us away.

Bin Nil did not lie on his back like I did, but was rather turned on his side, away from the side the men had come up, which is why he had not seen his grandfather. I needed to prepare him and turning to him, whispered:

"Don't be startled and stay as you are! Your grandfather came on board."

I saw that he was going to make a move of surprise, but controlled himself. It took him awhile to ask:

"Both my grandfathers are alive. You mean the helmsman?"

"Yes. Abu al-Nil, the former helmsman of the *dahabiyah* 'Al-Samak'."

"Oh Allah, what joy!"

"No, what misfortune for us! He will give us away."

"Heavens! This is indeed likely. How did he get here? What is he doing here?"

"He was on the ship Ibn Asl forced to stop. One of the officers brought him here, most likely to give orders on how he is to conduct himself."

"Where is he standing?"

"Over there, to the right. He hasn't seen us yet. Ibn Asl is talking to him."

"Can we not signal him to remain silent?"

"Were we not tied up, it would be possible, yes, but as it is, we must let this misfortune develop as it may. How did he get to the White Nile? He wanted to go to Gubator."

"Originally, yes, but things turned out differently. Did I not tell you that I met him in Asyût?"

"No, I do not recall this."

"I lost him there. I was lured by the old Abd Asl into the subterranean well, where I was to perish, until you saved me. If only he will be cautious – may Allah so provide – and not let on that he knows us!"

"Do you think we can expect him to have such presence of mind?"

"Likely not. The joy of seeing me, and the shock of finding me tied up, will affect him such that he will be incautious enough to call us by our names. Turn aside that he cannot see your face!"

I followed his request, although I did not expect it to help. On the *dahabiyah*, the old helmsman had not acted such that I could trust him to have the self-control required.

Our guard had not paid attention to our exchange, rather he looked toward Abu al-Nil than at us. Ibn Asl had been speaking with Abu al-Nil, but since I was talking with Bin Nil, I had been unable to catch their conversation. Now, that they fell quiet, I heard the old helmsman say:

"But I still do not see any reason why we should interrupt our travel. We are not in your way."

"You are! Remain here for a short time, at most a few hours, and then you can continue."

"Why not now?"

"I need not tell you that."

"You will have to, or we will immediately set sail again."

"You must listen to me, for if you do not obey, I will simply hold you here for the time being."

"You have no right to do so."

"You think so? I am the *raïs effendina*, whom you must have heard about."

"No, you are not. I not only have heard of him, but have even seen and talked with him."

"So! Well, then I tell you that I am his lieutenant. Whether that or he himself, is all the same. You must obey!"

"Prove to me that you are telling the truth! The *raïs effendina's* men wear uniforms, but not yours. I noticed that your ship's name is 'Lizard', while the *raïs effendina's* ship is called 'Falcon'. You are lying."

"Me, lying? Beware of insulting me! Indeed, the *raïs effendina* commands the Falcon, but since this ship was insufficient for his purposes, he hired the 'Lizard' and assigned command of it to me. It should be obvious to you that hired men do not wear uniforms."

"If what you say is true, you must have written authorization from the *raïs effendina*. I do not owe you obedience until I have seen this authorization."

"And I don't care to show you this document. You must believe my word and obey."

"Then I shall return to continue my travel."

"Hold it, oldster. Not so fast! You will not leave this ship without my permission. You are the helmsman of the stopped vessel. What is your name?"

"Himyad al-Bahri."

Having turned around, I could no longer see the old man, but had heard that he wanted to leave, but had been held back. Himyad al-Bahri! He called himself by another name since he had escaped the *raïs effendina*, and now thought himself more secure under his false name. I was glad to hear this, for now he could no longer claim Bin Nil to be his grandson. Barely had this hope arisen when it was killed by our guard. He walked a few steps forward and shouted to Ibn Asl:

"This is not true; this name is false. I know the old man. I have seen him before in al-Qahira and other places. He is a very well known helmsman and is called Abu al-Nil, since he knows the river as well as any."

"Abu al-Nil," Ibn Asl repeated, surprised. "Is this true? Do you really know him?"

"Absolutely. I cannot be mistaken."

"Ah, oldster, so you wanted to deceive me. You are a cheat! Do you admit that you are the helmsman, Abu al-Nil?"

"No. My name is Himyad al-Bahri. I never carried another name."

"This is a lie!" the guard insisted. "I know him for sure and can bring two more witnesses who know him."

He gave two names, and those men, being on land, were called. They instantly confirmed the guard's claim, even told the old man when and where they had seen him. I could not understand why the fact that the old man had given a false name had such an effect on Ibn Asl. In this area here and considering its conditions, it is not rare for people to change their names. If, for instance, a certain Maluf had long wanted a son and heir in vain, and his longing had at last been satisfied, he would, should he give the child the name Amal, call himself from then on, Abu Amal, Father of Amal, from the sheer joy of his finally finding his fatherhood. Of course, the old helmsman had denied having earlier carried another name. This had to be conspicuous and cause suspicion. But this was not the reason for Ibn Asl's behavior, because I now heard him say derisively:

"You have been found guilty. You claim to be someone other than you are. This must be pursued!"

"I did not lie. Maybe I am a look-alike of this Abu al-Nil. What does it matter what name I bear. Were I truly this Abu al-Nil, it would be all the same to you."

"On the other hand, I would be glad to have found this man. And since it is truly you, as these three men confirm, I am exceptionally happy. Do you have a son by the name of Bin Nil?"

"No."

"Then a grandson?"

"Neither."

"Don't deny it, oldster, or I shall force you to tell the truth! There is a young man, a crew member, by the name of Bin Nil, and if someone calls himself Abu al-Nil, then this someone must be the father or grandfather of Bin Nil!"

"So be it! But since my name isn't Abu al-Nil, but Himyad al-Bahri, and I have neither a son nor a grandson, leave me be with your Bin Nil!"

"Don't react like this, oldster!" Ibn Asl threatened. "You might regret it!"

"How so? I have no reason to fear you."

"You think that now. But if you knew . . .!"

"What? If I knew what . . .?

"That I am a very different man," it slipped from Ibn Asl's mouth.

"Another man? Then I figured right! Well then I can be even less afraid."

"You think so? It depends on who and what I am."

"Whatever you say, I am not afraid."

"You talk very confidently. I am Ibn Asl, the slaver."

"Allah! Is that true? Ibn Asl, the famous Negro catcher?"

"Yes. How do you feel now?"

Had he thought that the oldster would be shocked upon hearing this name, he was very much mistaken. The helmsman had reason to be afraid of the *raïs effendina*, having escaped him. But to be terrified of Ibn Asl, gave him, the former slave trader, no cause. This became apparent right away when, instead of being afraid, he exclaimed happily:

"Ibn Asl! This brings pleasure to my heart, provided you are not deceiving me again."

"I am telling the truth. Allah and the Prophet may witness that I am Ibn Asl."

"If you swear it like this, I believe you. And now you have no reason at all for being hostile toward me. Now I will be glad to tell you my real name."

The good oldster had no idea that he was in the process of making an enormous mistake. Had I only been able to signal to him.

"Of course, it is the one you previously denied?" Ibn Asl asked.

"Yes. I am Abu al-Nil."

"After all, then! Man, do you know what you just said?"

"Yes. I proved to you that I am not an enemy, but your friend."

"Wonder of wonders! My friend. How so?"

"Did you hear of a *dahabiyah* 'Al-Samak'?"

"Yes, the *raïs effendina* confiscated it."

"The *raïs effendina*, your greatest enemy! I was the helmsman on this ship. I was there when he searched it and discovered that the *dahabiyah* was a slave ship. He confiscated it and took the entire crew prisoner."

"You, too?"

"Yes, but I was able to escape. There was a foreign *effendi* on board . . ."

"Ah, a foreign *effendi*!" Ibn Asl interrupted him.

"Yes, this man took pity on me, gave me some money, and helped me to escape."

"Why you, precisely?"

"Because . . . I do not know."

He knew very well, but did not want to tell the infamous slaver that he had made an honest confession upon my request."

"In any case, he did it from friendship toward you. This makes you suspicious."

"Friendship? That cannot be the case, since I had never seen him before."

"But you saw him later?"

"No."

"Do not lie! You admitted being Abu al-Nil. Then you will also admit that you have a son by name of Bin Nil?"

"Not my son, but my grandson is named thus."

"Very well! Where did you see him last?"

"In Asyût."

"That is correct, very much so! Now you must only admit whose servant your grandson is."

"I do not know that. He has never been the servant of anyone."

"No? Really? Well, then he is now, and the servant of some kind of man!"

"I do not understand you. I do not comprehend. Why do you tell me this so angrily?"

"Ah, then you notice that I am angry, but do not comprehend it? Really?"

"I do not comprehend why my grandson's name can make you so angry."

Ibn Asl was convinced, as I could tell from the tone of his voice, that Abu al-Nil knew everything, which is why he enjoyed having caught the old man. He replied derisively:

"Fine, I will tell you, only to demonstrate that your pretense is of no use to you. Allah led you to me, and soon you will see your grandson and this foreign *effendi*, whose limbs, I swear to you, will rot individually from his body!"

"Allah *karim*! What did he do to you?"

"Dog, do not think you can deceive me! You are in league with him. You know everything, all his deeds, and will suffer the same fate. Do you really think I must tell you what has happened? But I neither have the time nor the desire for it now. Tie him up and throw him with the others, over there by the cabin."

"What, tie me up?" the oldster exclaimed. "I do not know anything. I was in Fashoda and . . ."

"Shut up, or you will get whipped!" Ibn Asl thundered. "I do not want to hear anything more. Later, you will learn and understand what is going to happen!"

Abu al-Nil was grabbed by several men and, despite his defense, pulled down and tied up. Then he was dragged over to us. Already, hope arose in me that the feared danger of recognition of us would pass. He seemed entirely occupied with himself and his anger toward his opponents, but then he saw me. His face assumed a very different expression, and he exclaimed:

"*Effendi*, you? Is it possible, you have also been captured?"

Ibn Asl had already walked away, but he heard these words and quickly turned again. And then it became worse. The oldster saw his grandson and cried:

"Bin Nil, my son, my child, son of my son! Oh Allah, Allah, Allah! What has happened? Why are you tied up?"

There, now he had it! The misfortune was complete. These were the results of my kindness! I must admit that, at this moment, I could not have wished more fervently than to have left this old chatterbox to his fate in Giza. The impression of his words were as I had expected. Ibn Asl did not walk over to us, but literally leaped, shouting:

"*Effendi*? Bin Nil? Allah *akbar*! What do I hear?"

"Shut up, you prattler. You bring ruin to us and yourself!" I was just able to whisper this to him, before everyone on deck had gathered about us.

"Say it again! Repeat it!" Ibn Asl demanded of the oldster. "Who are these two people?"

My warning had had its effect after all. The man did not respond. I could see that he contemplated what he should say.

"Speak! Who are they? the slaver repeated.

"Who?" Abu al-Nil asked, to gain some time.

"These two, whose names you called."

"Them? These two, here? I do not know them at all!"

"But just now you called the one *effendi* and the other your grandson, Bin Nil! I heard it myself!"

"I said these names, but did not refer to these two men."

"The Devil is telling you this! Why would you mention the *effendi* and Bin Nil, if it were not them?"

"It was just an exclamation of pain and regret. Because I talked of the *effendi* and my grandson, you had me tied up. This is why I repeated their names."

"But you said: 'Why are you tied up?' Why would you say something like this?"

"I meant myself."

"Do you think me mad, you son of a dog and grandson of a dog's son? Get the whip! We shall open his mouth!"

At that moment, a shocked shout came from the river bank.

"What a surprise, how odd, the barrels are empty!"

Ibn Asl jumped to the ship board to look down. Since I was lying down, I was unable to look down myself.

"The barrels are empty," it was repeated from below.

"Are you mad?" he shouted down. "They were all full."

"But they are empty now!"

I heard a hollow sound as if empty barrels were tossed about.

"*Mashallah* (God's wonder)!" Ibn Asl cried. "Are they empty, truly empty? Who did it? Wait, I am coming down."

I saw him disappear from the deck, but a moment later, his head appeared again to order our guard:

"Do not let these dogs talk with each other! Slap their mouths, should they dare talk!"

Then, he climbed back down. Our guard picked up a hefty piece of rope and swung it before our faces, an unmistakable sign that he would happily fulfill his orders. We therefore remained silent. Then again, I would not have known what to say to compensate for the oldster's mistake.

From the confusion of many voices, I took it that the men had gathered by the barrels. Then, it turned momentarily quiet. They had to be checking and deliberating. A while later, Ibn Asl returned, followed by all his men, so that the entire deck filled up. All eyes were on us, threatening, hateful and, if I was not totally mistaken, admiringly curious. He walked to me, kicked me, and said, his eyes flashing angrily:

"Tell the truth, you mangy jackal, or I will tear your tongue out! Where were you during the night?"

Not to answer would have been stupid. Had I only had a single hand free, I would have answered him with my fist. But to escape mistreatment, I had to talk:

"Of course, with you in the cabin."

"But you left once for the barrels."

"It could only have happened in a dream."

"Are you denying it?"

"What one did not do, one cannot deny."

"The barrels have holes!"

"I know that, too. I've never seen a barrel without holes."

He kicked me again and cried:

"Do you think you can make jokes? It was you who drilled the holes into the barrels. It could have been no one else!"

"Leave me be with your barrels! I would like to know why I should have bothered with the barrels."

"To save the *raïs effendina*. Now, my magnificent plan has come to ruin. Admit on the spot, or I will squash you with my feet!"

He lifted his leg to stomp on me. It isn't a pleasant, even honorable situation, to lie on the ground before so many eyes and be totally defenseless to all kinds of mistreatment. I had wanted to get this man, and now he had me. My situation with him was entirely different from his, had he been in my hands. He was not only a villain and a brute, but he was – nasty, utterly nasty. Did I not have any weapon against him? Is there any weapon at all against meanness, if one does not also want to be mean oneself? Were I even the most skillful fencer, I could not defend myself with a foil against a man brandishing a pitchfork. My entire self-esteem rose against the thought of trying to save myself by denial. Yes, maybe I would succeed in putting him off by cunning or gain at least some time. I needn't be ashamed of duping him. At present, though, he might gain the idea that I was afraid of him, something he was not to imagine. Fear! My situation was bad, but nowhere desperate. I did not think of being lost, but of the danger that could cost me my life, so I answered:

"Admit? Only criminals, only sinners make admissions. What I did was no sin, no crime."

"Then you admit that you did it?"

"Yes."

He stared at me, not having expected this.

"Ah, did you hear it?" he then shouted. "It was he; he admits it! Man, aren't you aware that you spoke your death sentence? Why did you make the oil run out?"

"You answered this question already yourself."

"To save the *raïs effendina*?"

"Yes. I am his friend!"

"The foreign *effendi*?"

"Yes."

"And he, you called Umar, is Bin Nil?"

"It is he."

Shocked by the frankness of my admission, he retreated a couple of paces. He was certain that everyone else would continue denying his actions, for in his opinion escape lay only in denial. He turned away from me to his men, and said:

"Did you hear it again? He admits being the foreign *effendi*. Ah, we've got him, we've got him! Allah be praised and thanked!"

Bin Nil used this moment to whisper to me:

"Oh, *effendi*, why did you admit to it? Now all is lost!"

"Not yet. Don't lose courage, and let me handle it!"

The men pressed closer to get a better look at me. Ibn Asl stepped up to me again, nodding derisively, and said:

"You are a daring fellow, a most daring one, but you do not know what it means to risk getting close to me!"

"Bah! What does that mean? I've dared greater things. Had chance not favored you, you wouldn't have found out who I am. Or do you imagine that you can ascribe it to your acumen, your smarts?"

"Vermin, you dare to disparage me?" he shouted, while he kicked me again.

"You may kick me now while I'm tied up, but let me tell you that you will pay for every kick."

"You? When? You expect to take revenge? Are you crazy?"

"I'm totally convinced of it. For how long do you expect to keep me here?"

"Until you have rotted away."

"I laugh at this. Consider that the *raïs effendina* is nearby."

"Are you relying on him? Do you hope he will save you?"

"Indeed."

"Hope till you perish! Of course, I can no longer incinerate the son of a dog, but . . .

He was interrupted. A commotion occurred alongside the ship-board, then the scout he had posted at Hagasi pushed through the men. He breathlessly reported:

"Master, there will be no petroleum fire. The *raïs effendina* is not coming up the river."

"Where from then?"

"Allah be blessed that He gave me the idea of going farther down-stream than you had ordered me. There I stood on such a high point of the bank that I could not only overlook the river, but across the trees onto the savanna. That's when I saw him come."

"Are you certain it was he?"

"Who else could it be? They were very far from me, but I saw nevertheless that they wore uniforms."

"Then it must be them. How many were there?"

"That I do not know. They walked in twos, and it was a long, long line."

"When might they arrive here?"

"They must be cautious and will therefore require more time than usual. I ran very fast, but I think they could be here in half an hour."

"Then we must leave. This dog took our oil away, which would not be of use now anyway. If we fight, we would win, but lose many of our comrades, something we must avoid. I shall come up with another clever plan to gain control of the *raïs*. On to it, men! Raise the masts and unfurl the sails! The wind is favorable and will take us quickly upstream."

Whatever was kept on land was quickly loaded. The empty petro-leum barrels were tossed into the river, then the masts went up. A *noquar* has, in addition to the main mast, a small mast forward. This vessel was actually equipped quite differently from the common *noquar* outfit. The wind began filling the sails, so we pushed off the bank and traveled upstream.

With everyone being busy, little attention had been paid to us. Our guard, too, had paid more attention to the ship's maneuver than to us. This is why we risked, ever so softly, to talk with each other. When we passed by the ship Ibn Asl had forced to land, Abu al-Nil said:

"Do you think I should call to my men, *effendi*?"

"For Allah's sake, no! You would make our situation worse and not achieve your purpose."

"But I must return to my post and cannot travel on with this terrible Ibn Asl."

"He isn't concerned whether you can, want to, or must!"

"But what is to happen to me?"

"The very same that's going to happen to us."

"What will that be?"

"Only Allah knows, not me. It is your fault alone that you find your-self in this situation."

"I was too startled and was not aware that I was not to call you by name."

"We were captives; that should have told you."

We still had the Jazirah Hassaniah to our left. On the right bank the trees grew farther apart. An open area appeared through which one could see out onto the savanna. Despite my lying down, I was able to spot a camel rider heading speedily through this opening toward the river. When he saw the ship, he straightened up like someone trying to get a better look. Then he waved his musket and hit his animal to quickly gain the river bank. At that moment, Ibn Asl stood near us, and I heard him say:

"Look! There comes Aram, sent to us as a messenger. We cannot take him on board now. We cannot stop or the *raïs effendina* will catch up with us."

He put both hands to his mouth and through this hollow mouth-piece shouted to the man, just as he came to a stop at the bank:

"*Maiyah al-Saratin, maiyah al-Saratin!*"

The man understood. He turned his camel and quickly rode away.

A *maiyah* is a swampy side arm of a river, an inlet or bay of standing water. It is the same as a resident on the Mississippi calls a bayou. In a broader sense any swamp is called a *maiyah*. *Al-Saratin* means "crayfish". The man had been directed to the "Crayfish Arm", or "Crayfish Swamp", a bay of the Nile where lots of crayfish were found and where he was to wait for the ship. He was a messenger. Whose? I had been unable to see his face clearly, yet had thought it looked vaguely familiar.

But, why should I care about the man now? I had enough to do with myself. Obviously, I was pleased to have saved the *raïs effendina*, but now I was "up the creek" myself. Could I expect help from him? Possibly, but unlikely. It was clear that he did not know exactly where to look for the "birds" that had now flown the coop. Should he find the abandoned camp, he would probably search further. And should he learn from Abu al-Nil's crew that the *noquar* had sailed upstream, he would return to his ship in Hagasi to pursue it. This would lose him precious time, with Ibn Asl gaining a head start that would be difficult to make up. The *raïs's* 'Falcon' was a fast sailing ship and far superior to the 'Lizard', but if the latter hid in a *maiyah*, the 'Falcon' would sail right past and not find it.

I could therefore not depend on the *raïs effendina*. Rescue could only be planned by me. I explained this to my two fellow-captives. Bin Nil had full confidence in me, while his grandfather was giving up all hope. He told us very briefly that, when he became separated from Bin Nil, he had found a ship destined for Fashoda. Its *raïs*, by chance knew him and took him on, later entrusting him with the position of helmsman. This morning, on their return, they were stopped by the slaver's boat. Ibn Asl' men had told them that a mighty, newly drifted-in *Umm Sufah* island had made the Nile impassable. The captain had steered the ship to shore and let the old helmsman go ahead in the slavers' boat to check out the obstruction. Instead of finding an *Umm Sufah* island, he had been captured. He now complained to all the world and Allah asking why Ibn Asl wanted to exact such revenge on us. When his grandson answered this question briefly, he moaned:

"Oh, Allah, oh heavens! Who would have thought this! Now, my years and days are no longer counted but my hours, for this slaver is going to kill us. I shall never see my folks again and find an end in a thousand terrors."

"Don't wail!" Bin Nil admonished him. "You are becoming a bother to the *effendi* with your complaints. Be quiet and allow him peace to think. He will surely find a way to free us. And then, only the two of us will be lost. You did not do anything to Ibn Asl, which is why he should not be cruel to you."

"But did you not hear what he said? He believes me to be your accomplice, and threatened me with the very same fate as yours."

The old man looked like a real egotist to me. He only thought and talked of himself, but not of his grandson, who was in much greater danger than he. I was mistaken. He was no hero, as I had seen previously in Giza, and the sudden precarious situation had totally confused him. When his grandson reproached him by saying: 'Don't you realize that you are bothering the *effendi*. Your complaints are an insult to him!" he replied, turning to me:

"Forgive me, *effendi*! I did not know what to do and say after this shocking experience. They so suddenly threw themselves on me and tied my arms and legs. This affected me so strongly that I barely recognize myself any more. I know what I owe you and want to prove my gratitude to you. Tell me what I should do."

"Don't lament, but submit quietly to your present fate! This is what I ask of you."

By now, we had left the island behind and were sailing on the open river. No ship could be seen upstream or downstream from us. Now, Ibn Asl had the two boards affixed at the pointed bow, showing the ship's name, removed, turned, and reattached. When they had first showed 'Lizard', they now read 'Karnuk'. Karnuk means "crane," in particular the crowned crane, named so for its call. On the Upper Nile, the "kar-nuk-nuk-nuk" of the crowned crane announces the approach of morning.

So, Ibn Asl had several names for his ship. Their purpose was easy to imagine. It could be expected that the *raïs effendina* would pursue the 'Lizard'. Displaying the name 'Crane', gave him a greater chance of escape. Very likely, other slaver ships employed the same ruse.

To my regret, I noticed that the 'Crane' was a very good sailing ship. To increase the ship's speed even more, Ibn Asl employed poling. Furthermore, the by-boat, attached by a rope ahead of the bow, crewed by twelve men, was rowed with all their might, with them being relieved every half hour. He wanted to gain as great a lead as was possible from the *raïs effendina's* 'Falcon'.

With the travel proceeding smoothly now, Ibn Asl found time to occupy himself with us. He came with his two officers, one of which was called first lieutenant, the other lieutenant. For some time they just stood before us without saying a word, watching us with derisive, triumphant faces, until he asked:

"Who was the man who pursued me at Wadi al-Bard?"

"It was I," I answered.

"You?" Ah, you yourself! Did you catch me?"

"Don't puff yourself up! That I could not catch up with you, you cannot attribute to yourself but the speed of your Jabal Garfah camel. You did not defeat me, but your animal defeated mine."

"Do you not think that I myself cannot defeat you, too, miserable worm that you are!"

"Try me with you being free and knife in hand; untie my hands from my back and retie them up front, not giving me a knife. Then we will fight, and it will show who the miserable worm is: you or I."

"Shut up! You were lucky. That makes you cocky. But this cockiness will soon turn to the opposite. Until now, I longed in vain to get you into my power. It finally happened, and you shall learn how a Faithful deals with a mangy Christian dog. You would be better off, had you not been born. I will . . ."

"Save your threats! I am well aware what you intend to do to me."

"Well, what?"

"First, to tear out my tongue, then my eyes, nose, and finally cut off my limbs, one after the other."

"Really, you know? Who told you?"

"Someone who experienced repeatedly my lack of fear together with my ability to escape from even the worst situations."

"Who?"

"Abd Asl, your father."

"Yes, you have escaped from him several times already. *Shaytan* protected you. But that was he, not me. You will not get away from me. Rather the heavens will collapse before I will let you slip through my hands."

"Don't imagine it. If ever there was a man who could make me feel afraid, it isn't you!"

"Dog, in a few minutes you will howl for mercy!"

"Try it!"

"Do you think I am joking?"

"No, but you merely threaten and do not have the courage to do it."

"May *Shaytan* devour you! I will show you my courage. Come here, men! You can watch how this Christian dog is tortured."

Everyone not busy gathered around. He walked to his cabin.

"*Effendi*, what's come into you!" Bin Nil said. "You are inciting him. I no longer recognize you as a cautious man. You make our situation worse!"

"No. I only want to demonstrate to him that I can teach him fear, but he not me."

Abd Asl returned. He had picked up a set of pliers, held it up, and shouted:

"First, the nails will be torn from this cursed son-of-a-bitch. First from his thumbs. Who will do it?"

"I, I, I, I!" screamed several.

A big fellow pushed back the others, reached for the pliers, and asked:

"Let me have them, master! You are aware that I know how to do it. It is not the first time I have made someone sing."

"Yes, go ahead. You have experience in it!"

The man took the pliers, positioned himself with bared teeth before me, while he alternately pinched and opened the pliers, to give me a foretaste of my forthcoming pains. I had waited for this. The fellow had extolled his ability to have caused already many to "sing" by the pain he delivered. A lesson might do him good. And should he die from it, so much the better. I quickly pulled up my knees, then "shot" my tied feet against his belly so that he was lifted up and flew headfirst over the crowd, knocking some men down in the process. He lay there as though he were dead. Blood dripped from his mouth, which I figured had come from him biting his tongue in the fall.

Everyone screamed, cursed, and threatened. Ibn Asl called for quiet and checked the victim who did not show any signs of life. He had him carried away, balled his fist against me, and grated:

"You shall pay for this, ten times, a hundred times! Now, your suffering will be worse than I had earlier determined. Hold him down so he cannot move; then off with the nails!"

Six, eight men threw themselves onto me. I did not fight back at all. One fetched the pliers that had flown far away, and got ready to proceed with the operation.

"Stop, a word first, Ibn Asl!" I shouted. "Do with me what you want. You won't hear a sound of pain. But imagine that what will happen to me will also happen to Abd Asl, your father!"

"To . . . my . . . father?" he asked, surprised.

"Yes, and not only to him, but to every one of the men who were with him."

"What do you know of my father? Where is he?"

"Out to catch me."

"This . . . is . . . true. You escaped him again. He was not able to catch you."

"Indeed. He did not catch me, but I caught him, and that in such a way that he will never again wish to meet up with me."

"*Kullu shayatin*! (by all devils)! Are you telling the truth?"

"Believe it or not. It's all the same to me."

"Where did you meet?"

"At the well."

"Which one?"

"That, I won't tell you."

"I must know!"

"I won't tell! It's my secret, for the time being."

"Untie us and I shall lead you to him. If not, he and his entire gang will be on your conscience."

"I will be glad to do it," he laughed. "You only want to save yourself by a lie."

"A lie? How could I have otherwise known that he was advancing on me."

He realized that my objection was justified, since he asked:

"They were on foot?"

"No, by camel."

"How many men?"

"Bah, do you think I will have myself questioned like a boy? It is enough for you to learn that they have all been captured and will suffer the same fate as the others."

"Then they are nearby?"

"No. We came here on fast camels."

"Why did you not stay with them?"

"They are in secure hands. Do you know someone by name of *Faqir al-Fuqara*?"

"Of course, I know him. We talked about him last night. What about him?"

"He happened to come and wanted to save them."

"Did he succeed?"

"Would I be here then? He suffered for his attempt and is now a prisoner himself. I do not understand why you are sending out men to capture me. You haven't accomplished it and will never do so."

"Allah! You are talking nonsense. You are right now my prisoner!"

"No, for you will let me go. I know that for sure."

"Before I do so, *Shaytan* will . . ."

"Stop! Don't curse and swear! You don't know what you are doing."

"You are more cunning than the fox. No one must trust you. You only imagine that we wanted to catch you, you who act as if you know everything."

"Can I also imagine that your father is the leader?"

"No. But why did you come to the Jazirah Hassaniah?"

"To negotiate with you."

"Who told you that I was there?"

"Your father. This is the best proof that I spoke with him."

"What did you want to negotiate with me?"

"The release of my prisoners."

"Why so? Do you want ransom?"

"We will talk about this later."

"I do not comprehend why you did not mention it last night."

"Then I would have had to tell you who I am, and it would have been impossible for me to save the *raïs*."

"How did you know that I was waiting for him?"

"From your father."

"This is impossible. My father would not have told you such."

"He did without him knowing."

"I do not understand how this is possible."

"You will not comprehend many things, while you continue to be after my life."

"You speak most proudly, yet you lie tied up and helpless before me!"

"Helpless! Don't be mistaken! If I haven't returned to my men within a given time, our prisoners and your father will experience the same

— 132 —

fate as those the *raïs effendina* had shot at Wadi al-Bard. Even the *Faqir al-Fuqara* will die."

A pause ensued, while he processed the impact of my statement. Then, he asked:

"How many of my men escaped from you?"

"None."

"You are lying after all, despite the certainty with which you speak, and despite the honest face you display."

"I'm telling the truth."

"And I can prove to you that you lied. Did you earlier see the camel rider coming to the river bank?"

"Yes."

"It was Aram, one of my men, who was with my father."

"Surely not at the time when I attacked your gang. He may have been dispatched somewhere, and upon his return found his comrades captured and took off quickly to report this to you."

"Can you tell me how you managed to capture my men who were sent out against you?"

"I don't mind you learning it, but I don't care to tell it myself."

"Then this old Abu al-Nil may do so."

"He doesn't know anything about it, because he wasn't there. Since I helped him escape at Giza, I have not seen him again until today, when he boarded your ship."

"Is that true?"

"Don't ask me all the time whether what I'm saying, is true! Don't you understand that it is an insult to me?"

"So! Who called himself yesterday Amm Salad from Suez and turned out to be the sought-after *effendi*? Was this not a lie?"

"No, it was a stratagem."

"You Christians do not seem to know what a lie is!"

"And you Muslims do not bother about stratagems, but rather murder right away. Thank Allah, that I passed myself off yesterday as someone else. Had I not done so, you would now carry on your conscience a hundred-fold murder. Bin Nil was present at the capture. He can tell you."

The men pressed closer. Everyone wanted to hear the interesting report and not miss a word. Since I had earlier kept the location a secret, Bin Nil was smart enough to do likewise. When he was going to talk about my listening endeavors, I forbade it. I knew everything, yet no one was able to say how I had learned it gave this issue a puzzling, secretive streak which could only be useful to me. Everyone listened breathlessly until the narrator was finished. Now, Ibn Asl exclaimed:

"Could it be believed? You killed the lion of al-Taytal?"

"As you heard."

"You did so because you did not know what you risked."

"I risked my life. What else?"

"Is that not enough? Can a man lose more than his life?"

"Yes, much, much more."

"What?"

"That which you have long since lost, your honor, your good name, God's approval and that of man."

"Man," he flew off his handle. "Do not imagine that I have suddenly become forbearing! Consider that I am presently your lord and owner! Your life rests in my hands!"

"Indeed. But with mine is linked that of your father's, the *Faqir al-Fuqara's*, and all your men."

"You came to negotiate for these men. If you let them go free, what do you ask in return?"

"First, your oath to stop with the slave hunt, and second, my freedom and, of course, that of Bin Nil's and his grandfather's."

"Would my oath be sufficient?"

"Maybe, maybe not. I may require a guaranty."

"Why do you think I would swear falsely?"

"Because I know several Muslims who swore falsely."

"Then they are not true sons of the Prophet."

"Well, I can prove to you that the *Faqir al-Fuqara* as well as your father, who is thought to be a holy *faqir*, have sworn by Allah and the beard of the Prophet and yet have lied."

"Was it you they gave that oath to?"

"Yes."

"Then they did not sin, because you are an *infidel*."

"Ah, is that how it is? So, when a Muslim swears a false oath to a Christian, it is permitted, and not considered perjury?"

"It is as if nothing had been said."

"And, saying this, you ask me to swear an oath after which I am to believe you? You caught yourself, and I will now abstain from the philanthropic proposal that I was going to make to you."

"Then we are done?"

"Not yet. I will make you another offer."

"Let me hear it."

"You set the three of us free, and I will give you your father and the *Faqir al-Fuqara*. The other captives I will turn over to the *raïs effendina*."

"What recklessness!" he laughed with derision. "This *giaur* is in our power and talks as if he can issue us orders! Why do I not raise my hand to crush you?"

"Because you cannot. If I die, so does your father, who could possibly have a worse death than mine."

"You know this with such certainty?"

"Yes. He was very incautious when he said how I was to be tortured by you. If I do not return by a certain time, he will receive the same treatment, and not just he, but each of the other prisoners. Do not waste precious time!"

"When must you be back?"

"You needn't know that. The faster you decide, the less your father will be in danger."

"I am to release three people against only two. Is that so?"

"Yes, because Abu al-Nil does not count, since he did not do anything to you."

"And how highly do you value yourself?"

"This deal has only one number: Two men for two men. The helmsman here goes along on the side."

"Is this your firm and last proposal?"

"Yes."

"Let me tell you mine then. You release all your prisoners, while I set Abu al-Nil and Bin Nil free."

"And I?"

"You stay with us."

"Thank you! Allah is great. He blessed you with such acumen that I, if I were not lying on the floor, would crawl humbly before you on my knees."

"And your wisdom is infinite. How can I set you free. Think of all the things you did against us. And there lies the man you murdered earlier."

"Murdered?"

"Yes. He still does not move."

"He is likely unconscious. Check him!"

"We do not have a *hakim* on board. But you are a foreigner, an *effendi*. All foreign *effendis* are doctors. Are you one?"

"Yes."

"Check him then."

"I'm tied up."

"If I free your hands you would try to escape."

"No."

"Who can trust you? You are strong, daring, and quick."

"Do you think I will enjoy jumping in the Nile to be eaten by crocodiles? Even if I were so audacious, I give you my word that I will not leave this ship without my fellow-captives. Release my hands! And once I've checked the man, you can tie me up again."

"Fine! But I will have my pistol in hand, and upon the least wrong move, will shoot you."

The man was carried to me and my hands released. My legs remained tied. Had I wanted to break my word, it would have been easy for me to pull a surprise which would have been to our benefit. The lifeless man before me had a knife in his belt. Pulling it out and cutting my leg ties would have taken an instant. A second one would have been sufficient to grab Ibn Asl. Although he held his pistol, he had not cocked it, didn't even have it pointed at me, but pointed it downward. Had I grabbed him and pulled him into the cabin next to us, I would have been his master and could have dictated whatever I desired. But I had given my word and had to keep it, although I was convinced that each of these men, from Ibn Asl to the last, would not have hesitated to break even the most sacred oath given to me.

"Well?" he asked, when he saw that I was done. "Did he lose consciousness?"

"Yes, he lost consciousness and will not regain it. This is what happens if one acts thoughtlessly and looks joyfully forward to pulling off the nails of a human being!"

"What? Is he dead?"

"Yes. Never again will he make a human being "sing". My kick injured or destroyed some of his organs. He bit his tongue, and, last but not least, he happened to fall in such a way that he broke his neck."

"Allah *karim*! You are his murderer!"

"Not I. It were two others, you and he, himself."

"No, it was you, for you kicked him. You will need to pay ever more by the hour. Do not think that I will release you."

"No, he must die!" called the first lieutenant.

"Die, die!" sounded twenty, thirty, fifty voices.

"Bear in mind that your father will die then, too."

"Bear in mind," he laughed fiercely, "that, until now, I have heard only you and need to hear also what Aram has to say. Probably what he will tell me will change the situation to make you tremble. But may it come as it will, you, I will not release any more."

"Then you will sacrifice your father?"

"May he die! He lived long enough. He has been after you without being able to catch you. Now, you walked into my hands on your own, and I will hold on to you and let you go only when the final sigh of your breath and the last drop of blood has drained from you. Take these three dogs away, out of my sight, down into the hold! Lock them up there and post a guard!"

We were grabbed and dragged across the deck to the hatch. There, they dropped us down the ladder without caring whether we would arrive below uninjured. It was dark down there. Once more, we were picked up and carried on, whether forward or back, I could not determine. I heard a bolt slide. It was not of iron but wood. We were dropped, a door banged shut, another bolt rattled, then I heard one of the fellows say:

"Too much talk about these dogs! It should be as fast as possible: a knife into their bellies is the best way. May Allah incinerate them! Who stays?"

"I," came a voice that sounded familiar to me.

"Fine! I will spell you. There's nothing to watch for. They are tied up, so how could they get free."

Their steps went away and it became quiet outside. I felt I was lying on a wooden floor, and listened for the sound of water to determine whether we were in the bow or the stern of the vessel. I heard nothing. Since one can hear the sound of the wake, I could assume that we lay in the bow. Our location was dry, telling me that we had not been dumped in the bilge room.

Abu al-Nil wanted to talk, but I forbade it. The main thing was to orient myself. I had to listen for everything, even the least noise. From outside came sounds of soft padding, moving away and returning. Then there was a knock on the door, so softly that it could not be heard far. We did not respond. Another knock, stronger this time, and when we still remained silent, it came softly:

"*Effendi*, can you hear me?"

"Yes," I answered.

"I purposely offered to be the guard. Will you give me away?"

"To give you away? Who are you?"

"The man you talked with yesterday at Hagasi."

"Ah, God be thanked! Unexpectedly, a lighted star had come our way. Barely noticeable as yet but, if properly addressed, it could blossom into a double star and maybe become our saving star. The man was afraid. He thought that, in anger, I might forget my word which I had given him, and talk. This worry was legitimate. If Ibn Asl learned all that the man had told me, he would face severe punishment.

If all else failed, I would rely on my strength. I would probably be able to tear the palm frond rope that tied my hands behind my back, or chafe it apart on some sharp corner or edge. The rest would have to take care of itself. However, it would be easier to use the opportunity presenting itself here. The man could not only supply us with a sharp tool, but give us also the information without which an escape would be difficult, if not impossible. I slid close to the door and asked:

"Did you hear that they wanted to tear out my nails?"

"Yes, *effendi*."

"Then you know what is intended for me, and what is still to happen."

"You will likely die."

"But then also Abd Asl with his men!"

"Ibn Asl will let his father die, only to be able to torture you."

"What do his men say to it?"

"Many are for it. But many others want you to be set free, provided our comrades whom you captured will gain their freedom as well."

"Which party is more numerous?"

"I cannot tell at the moment. But for Allah's sake, I beg you not to reveal anything you learned from me. He would simply gun me down or feed me to the crocodiles."

"I regret that I cannot save you."

"No? Allah *karim*! Do you not have mercy, being a Christian?"

"A Christian loves his life no less than a Muslim."

"But you will not be able to save it by talking!"

"There you are mistaken. You told me quite a few things I can use to my advantage."

"But you promised me to keep quiet!"

"As far as I remember, only with respect to a single item. And this promise is also invalid, since I gave it only under the condition that I would be thought to be the one I claimed to be. But that has changed. Your information is my last and most important weapon."

"Oh, Allah, oh Prophet! Then I am lost!"

He fell silent and I, too, did not add anything. First, I had to wait for the effect of my threat. It turned out much more favorable and greater than I could have expected from the brief time it took. He again knocked gently and asked:

"*Effendi*, listen, what if you could flee?"

"That would, of course, be splendid, also for you, since I wouldn't be forced to talk about you."

"But this is impossible, totally impossible. You are tied up and a guard will always be posted here. And then, if that were not enough, how do you plan to get away from the ship?"

"Do you have other concerns?"

"No, only these three, which are, in any case, more than enough."

"Oh no! These three points don't worry me at all. I need only someone to assist me."

"This would be dangerous, *effendi*."

"Not at all. Not a single person would notice or learn of it."

"What would the man have to do?"

"Two things, either is as easy and innocuous as the other. He would first need to slip me a sharp, pointed knife."

A pause ensued. He was thinking about it. Then, to my joy, he said:

"You shall get a knife."

"When?"

"As soon as we have finished our conversation. Back there stands an open crate with knives and other tools, commonly needed. And which is the second item you ask for?"

"Information, nothing else. If you give us this and the knife, you've done everything I want, and I promise not to say a word about you."

"Ask, then! I will answer, since . . . hold it, someone is coming!"

The ladder creaked. Someone was coming down, stopped at the bottom, then lit a light. I saw it gleam through the many cracks in the wall of our prison cell. Sudan's heat had dried the boards. They had shrunk and gaps had opened, several of which were wider than the heft of a knife. Instantly, I thought of the bolt. I searched for it and found it easily. It was attached to the middle of the door, about a yard long and, maybe, four inches wide. It was located between two boards and covered one of the widest cracks.

My heart jumped for joy. If I pushed the knife blade through the gap with its tip into the bolt, it could be moved from the inside. It had taken me only two or three seconds to figure this out, but then the man who had come down the ladder, stood already at the door and opened it.

It was Ibn Asl. He carried a clay lamp, shining its light into our cell. I lay on my back, seemingly with eyes closed, but kept my lids ever so slightly open to observe our prison. It was as low as a pigeon roost, two yards high, three yards wide, and a bit longer. Except for us occupants, it was completely empty; not even a hook or nail could be seen.

"Well, how do you like it here?" the slaver sneered. "Show me your fetters! I want to make sure that they are not too loose."

He set the lamp down and checked the ropes. He was satisfied. I had been tied so firmly that my blood froze at the respective places.

"Have you continued to contemplate my magnificent proposal?" he asked.

I did not answer him.

"Or do you want to tell me when the time you are expected to return has passed?"

"Precisely when I return," was my reply.

"Then it will be an eternity, because the dogs you were with will never see you again. Keep a good watch, and should these unkempt jackals talk with each other, take the whip, and slash it about their heads."

These last words had been for our guard. Ibn Asl picked up the lamp, spit at me, and bolted the door again. At the ladder, he extinguished the lamp, set it down somewhere, and climbed up. It took awhile until our ally dared knock again.

"He is gone and we are safe, *effendi*," he said. "What do you want to ask me?"

"Tell me first what kind of room we are in."

"It is the *sijn al-Bahri* (the crew's prison), where those of us deserving punishment are tied all twisted up."

"Where do you men sleep at night?"

"Down here, in this room and also in the bilge, that is if we do not carry slaves."

"Then you would need to step through the sleepers?"

"Yes."

"That is bad!"

"In the evening the crew stays at the river bank and only beds down later, usually at the same time as yesterday."

"Do you know the Maiyah al-Saratin?"

"Very well. We have often hidden there."

"Where is this arm of the Nile located?"

"On the left bank, past the village of Qawa. Its entry is so overgrown that someone, not knowing it, would never find it. And once you are inside, the ship is totally covered by hanging branches, vines, twigs, bushes, and creepers."

"That's where Aram, the camel rider, will be waiting?"

"Yes."

"When will we arrive at the *maiyah*?"

"Likely before midnight, considering the effort made to get ahead. Shortly after noon, we should pass by Muhabilah island, and by evening, Qawa."

"Can you arrange it so you will again be guard here, after we have reached the *maiyah*?"

"Easily. But, do you intend to escape from there?"

"No. This would cause you misfortune. We will only leave later, after you have gone, but it must be when the crew is still on land. Once they have bedded down down here, it will be too late. Is there a real bad character among your comrades, you dislike?"

"Oh, several."

"Can you not arrange for one of those fellows to take the watch after you?"

"If I am smart enough, I can possible do it."

"At least, try! The worse the fellow, the better I like it, since, if we succeed in fleeing, he will be punished. And now the main thing: You must be able to tell us where to find our weapons, without which I do not want to leave."

"Ibn Asl keeps them in his cabin. He considers them his trophies."

"Watch closely then, whether they will remain there or be taken to another place. I must know this positively. If you do everything to my satisfaction, I will not reveal your secret, but make you a present as well. They left us everything we carried in our pockets. This is not a good sign, but proof that they are certain to keep us captive. At the final moment, when I'm certain that our escape from the ship is going to succeed, I will leave your reward at a place you must designate now."

"If you want to make me a gift, *effendi*, there is no better place than over there behind the ladder. Some old palm frond mats lying there, below which you can hide it."

"Once we are gone be sure to get it right away, so that no one else will find it by accident."

"But how will I know when you are gone? No one is to hear or see you leaving."

"I will give you a signal. There are small long-tailed monkeys in the local woods. Did you ever hear the angry screams of such a monkey, when it is disturbed by another in its sleep?"

"Often enough."

"Fine! This is a noise that won't attract attention. But so that you know it came from me, and not from a real monkey, I shall repeat it three times, first with a longer, then with a much shorter interval. As soon as you hear it, go back on board and find your gift under the mats as planned."

"*Effendi*, I wish from the bottom of my heart to find it, on the one hand, and on the other, because it will tell me with certainty that your escape was successful. What else do you want me to do?"

"I would love to know what the camel rider is going to report. However, this will be impossible, since, by the time his report is concluded, we must already be on our way."

"Maybe, I can tell you at least some of it."

"In what way and where?"

"Down here."

"In the presence of the guard?"

"Yes, I will act as if I wanted to tell him about it. Anyway, you cannot leave right away once we land, but Aram will report right away. I will listen in. Your guard will be unable to hear the news being down here, which I will bring to him. You will hear what I tell him and learn what it's all about."

"This is a truly excellent idea! My gift will be the greater the more I am satisfied with you. I have nothing more to tell you. I know enough and don't want to disturb your conscience with the rest."

This concluded our conversation, and our ally fetched the knife for me. It was pointed and sharp, just what I needed; sharp for cutting the ropes and pointed to use it as a stabbing weapon, for I had firmly decided to kill anyone opposing us without suffering any pangs of guilt.

What luck that this man had such fear of betrayal! I was almost certain that we would be free by midnight. Our man had to keep watch for an hour and then be spelled. In the course of the afternoon, I had a thought that I best check whether the external walls of our prison had also cracks and gaps. For that, I had to get up, at which I succeeded with some effort.

I had every reason to be satisfied with my inspection. Since the ship carried no load, it did not ride deep in the water. Its outer wall, usually under water, but now above it, had been dried by the sun. The pitch had dripped from the plank joints, and by taking the knife's heft between my teeth, I was able to push enough oakum outside, producing openings at some points, large enough for a look outside. Especially come evening, this could present a great advantage. I saw the small boat still attached ahead. A small mast and sail had even been attached to support the oarsmen's efforts. This became possible only with a stiff wind, or the boat, pulling the towrope, could have easily capsized.

Ibn Asl came again toward evening to check our fetters. He seemed to consider only me dangerous, since he did not check the ropes of the others. He did not notice the knife, lying behind the old helmsman, who was squatting in the farthest corner. Once in possession of this tool, I could easily have loosened our fetters, but desisted, since I figured that Ibn Asl would come once more to check at least mine.

When he had left, I leaned against the ship's hull and looked out onto the Nile through the holes I had made. We had long since passed the Jazirah Muhabilah and should soon pass the village of Qawa. The left bank's shadows spread across the river's entire width, a sign of the setting sun. Evening came, and since I could no longer see anything outside, I lay down again.

It may have been about eight o'clock when our ally took over his watch. He spoke only briefly with us. He had not changed his mind and told us that the guard following him would deserve punishment for our escape.

"When will we arrive at the *maiyah*? I asked.

"Shortly after my watch," he replied. "This is excellent for your purposes. Right away I shall join the others going on land. Should something unexpected happen, I will warn you. By the way, your weapons lie in Ibn Asl's front cabin."

Time passed and he was spelled. We spoke softly with each other. His successor heard it, opened the door, and slung the whip inside, he had brought along for this purpose. While at it, he did not miss using plenty of "*giaurlar*" and "Christian dogs." Well, the man would soon win my recognition. Shortly thereafter, loud commands sounded above. We heard ropes being dragged across the deck; the sail was hauled in. The *maiyah* had to be close. Then, we heard the creaking of poles against the ship's hull. Then it turned brighter. A fire burned on the bank, and a man standing there, shouted: "Over here! Throw me a rope. I can tie it here to the tree."

It was thought superfluous to drop anchor, rather a rope each was tossed from bow and stern to pull the vessel close to the bank and tie it there to two trees. To accomplish this, a ladder was lowered at the bow, and several men went ashore.

The wall by which I lay faced the bank, so that I could observe what happened outside, at least as far as my vision reached. All else I had to guess. Once the ship was secure, the others, too, went on land. It could be expected that Ibn Asl would also follow, but pay us a visit beforehand. This is why I let myself slide down again. It had barely happened, when the ladder creaked, the lamp was lit, and I heard his voice:

"Well, is everything in order?"

"Everything," the guard answered. "The dogs barked with each other, then I put them to a stop with my whip."

"Right on! Give it to them!"

He opened the door, and while holding the lamp in one hand, checked my fetters with the other. Grinning, he said derisively:

"I will now talk with the men, which will decide your fate. Get ready for it! Your torture will begin tonight."

"You are talking like a child," I responded. "You cannot change my fate. It has already been decided. You won't be able to do anything to us."

He erupted into loud laughter and exclaimed:

"Fear has made you crazy! An hour from now you will sing differently."

"Today, you have experienced what happens to those wanting to make me sing."

"This happened only once; it will not succeed a second time."

He bolted the door again, extinguished the lamp, and left. I rose and looked outside. Some of the crew were cutting the rushes on the bank to make room for camping and started several more fires. Although I was unable to see them directly, I assumed this from the increased illumination and because the tree trunks did throw more than one shadow.

The time had come to free us from our fetters. With my foot, I pushed the knife out of the corner, rolled around and grasped it with one of my hands. Bin Nil put his back against mine, enabling me to slip the blade between the ropes tying his hands. I had to be careful not to cut or stab him. It was not easy, but I succeeded. Soon, his hands were free. He now took the knife to free his legs, then to free us from our ropes. All this happened so noiselessly that the guard was unable to hear it.

We then waited to see whether our ally would keep his word and come. It took half an hour before the ladder creaked and we heard his voice:

"If you could only come upstairs! There's much to hear."

"Do you want to annoy me?" our guard replied. "The Devil must have told the lieutenant to dispatch me at this time for guard duty. What is happening?"

"The *infidel effendi* truly told the truth. Our comrades have been captured; eight of them were killed by blows from musket butts."

"May Allah destroy the spawn of this *raïs effendina*! This cursed Christian *effendi* must now be done in, too. How did Aram get away? Did he not get caught?"

"He did. But the *asakir* did not tie him up tight enough. Toward morning, he was able to get free. He crept away and even took a camel. Of course, he rode straight for the Hassaniah to inform us, but arrived a few minutes too late."

"Why did he not come to our campsite?"

"Because he couldn't. He saw the *asakir* of the *raïs effendina* headed for that place. Our captured comrades will not be taken to Khartoum, as was originally planned, but to Hagasi, where the *asakir* are expected by the Christian *effendi*."

"He will never see them again, and they will be received by us in a proper manner, since I hope that Ibn Asl will try everything to rescue our companions."

"That should be obvious."

"But we must not lose any time! If only I could be up there. Don't you want to take over my watch? I gladly give you . . ."

"No way!" the other interrupted. "I just stood watch for two hours."

The ladder creaked once more. He left. He had kept his word and what he had conveyed to me was very valuable. This is why he would get the promised gift. Although he was our enemy and a bad man to boot, I had to keep my word. He was not going to call me, the Christian, a cheat.

The conversation had also provided another advantage. Opening the bolt by using the knife had to cause, if ever so slight, a noise, which could easily have alarmed the guard. Furthermore, he had stood at the door's hinge side, so that he would have been in the way when we opened the door, preventing us from fully opening it. Standing behind the door, he would have been difficult to tackle quickly and render harmless. He might have been able to shout for help.

This was all taken care of now. The man had walked several steps toward the ladder to better understand our informant, thus had unblocked the door. While they were conversing loudly, I stuck the knife's tip through the crack into the wooden bolt and pushed it back. It made a noise which the guard did not hear, however. I pushed the door open and crept outside. My companions followed. To make room for them, I had to move ahead and came to stand right behind our guard, just as he asked his comrade to take the watch for him. When our ally now left, the guard turned around and bumped into me. Instantly, my hands were around his throat. Lack of air, but maybe also the shock, caused him to collapse from my stranglehold. He was quickly tied up with his belt and got his *fez* stuffed into his mouth as a gag.

I now went cautiously up the ladder, avoiding its creaking, to reconnoiter. What I saw, pleased me enormously; the situation could not be better for us. Although I could not see the fires burning on the bank, they illuminated the area very well, even the deck. I did not see a single man on it. I then climbed back down the ladder.

Below, I took as much money from my purse as I thought appropriate and placed it under the lowermost palm frond mat. Then the three of us climbed up on the deck. We could not walk upright, of course, as we could have been spotted from land. We crept to the cabin to get our weapons, this being of greatest importance. Although it was dark in the room, we quickly found what we were looking for by our sense of touch.

"What now?" whispered Bin Nil. "It is too dangerous to climb down the shipboard ladder."

"They would have us by the scruff of our necks, faster then we could reach land with our feet," his grandfather agreed.

"But there is no other way! It would be best not to climb, but to leap down, right into their midst. They would be surprised and shocked, and before they could catch on, we would be gone."

"Will my old legs survive such a leap?"

"Don't worry!" I comforted him. "We will neither climb the ladder nor leap, but do it another way, that is, climb into the ship's boat, hanging on the river side, and row away."

"Allah, *wallah*, *tallah*! What a wonderful idea. But . . . it will not work after all."

"Why not?"

"Because the boat is attached at the stern right in the fires' illumination. We cannot get in."

"My guess is that it is hanging off the bow. It had been pulling the ship, and my guess is that they simply pulled in the tow rope, once they entered the *maiyah*. The sails had to be taken down, as well as the masts. Getting dark, they had to do so much that they likely did not take the time to bring the boat from the bow to the stern. Let's go and see!"

We crept forward to the ship's side facing the water. With our enemies gathered on the opposite side, we were able to stand up without being seen by them and look over the board. Yes, the boat was hanging from its tow rope, strong enough for a man to entrust himself sliding down. It lay in shadow. We were unable to make out whether the oars had been left. Since we could not see them on board, they must have been left in it. A light-colored object lay in the boat.

"What is that?" Bin Nil asked.

"Probably the sail, which I saw raised today during our travel. In that case, the mast will also be there, meaning that we won't have to exert ourselves rowing."

We were near the small front mast. Earlier today, I had seen there a bundle of palm frond torches, which they used hereabouts at various occasions. I crept over there where they still lay, took some, and returned to the shipboard and dropped them into the boat.

"What do you want the torches for?" Bin Nil asked.

"I will tell you later. We have talked enough and taken our time. Let's get in the boat. You climb down first, your grandfather will follow; I will be the last one."

He tossed his musket over his shoulder and climbed over the board to let himself down on the rope. At that moment I heard Ibn Asl shout, "Bring also a crock of *raki!*"

Raki is a schnapps Muslims are allowed to drink. These words told me that several, at least two men, were on their way to the deck. I turned. At that very moment, one came up the ladder, followed by a second and a third.

"Quickly, quickly!" I whispered to Abu al-Nil. "They haven't spotted us yet."

I squatted down so that they would not see me right away. But the old helmsman had to get over the board; they had to see him. The foremost one saw the oldster and therefore me, too. He instantly comprehended what was going on and screamed:

"Come, men! The prisoners are free. They are escaping!"

He came dashing over, followed by the other. I kept down, so that they could not guess what I was up to. When the first was only three paces away, I leaped up and rammed my rifle butt into his body so that he toppled back and down. The second, who was just reaching for me, I hit over the head, and he collapsed. The third was closer now. Smarter than the others, he fired his pistol at me. I leaped aside and wasn't hit. In the next second I was able to bring him down with my rifle butt.

The three fellows had screamed with the full strength of their lungs; now they lay there silently. From land the others answered. Everyone who could scream, screamed. Of course, they came running. A few moments more, and it would be too late for me. Right after the first rifle butt blow, I had turned around. Old Abu al-Nil was gone. I leapt for the shipboard, got over it, took hold of the rope, slid down in the boat, drew the knife and cut the rope – when on board Ibn Asl's voice sounded:

"Where are they? Look, look for them. They killed three of us. I do not see them. They must be in the cabin, these dogs. Get them; quickly, quickly!"

I had already pushed the boat away from the ship and gotten a hold of the rudder. The oars lay there.

"Sit down!" I demanded softly. "Ibn Asl doesn't know where we are. We must get out of sight, then he can shoot at us. Take the oars, but be silent and row properly!"

They obeyed. The boat's bow veered from the ship at a right angle. I could not steer any differently, needing to stay in the deep shadow of the *noquar*. When we were a decent distance away, I called for a halt. None of the crew were any longer on land. All of them had hurried on board to search for us. There was such a screaming and shouting that not a single word could be understood. They must have found the guard, but not us. Suddenly, it was silent. Our disappearance was inexplicable to them. They seemed to confer, for when they had earlier run hither and yon, they now stood calmly together. We were about thirty boat-lengths distance from them and could make out their figures.

"You can now imitate the monkey voice," the helmsman suggested. "We are free."

" I will dispense with the imitation," in replied, "and talk directly to Ibn Asl."

"They will hear where we are. Many of his men are holding rifles. It is dark, but should they shoot, we might get hit accidentally."

"I'll lead them astray, something you will enjoy."

Turning away from the ship, I put my hollow hands to my mouth and shouted through this megaphone, stretching the syllables: "Ibn Asl, Ibn Asl, come get us!"

The tall, dense woods surrounding us caused the words to sound as if they had come from far up the *maiyah*, with my voice nevertheless, still sounding very distinct.

"There he is, the dog, the son of a dog!" Ibn Asl screamed. "They are over there on the water! We must get our boat!"

We noticed that they were going for the boat.

"Yes, we've got it," I told him. "Make me sing now!"

"Listen, listen!" he roared angrily. "They took the boat. They are up there, maybe eighty paces from here. Shoot, shoot, you men!"

Many shots cracked westward, while we were in the south. Figuring on the mistaken direction, I now turned my face east, laughed as loud as possible, and added:

"Your shots missed! Where are you looking for us?"

This sounded as if coming from the opposite direction. They all turned and Ibn Asl ordered:

"They are not up there, but down here. Shoot there, there!"

He was obeyed, of course, without success. I turned again to the previous direction and emitted a most derisive laughter. Immediately, they all turned again.

"He is with the Devil!" Ibn Asl screamed. "I knew he was the Devil incarnate. Now, he is up there once more."

My intention to mislead them had succeeded, and we could now continue our escape without worrying about their bullets. It wasn't easy. None of us knew the *maiyah*. Where was its entry, which, as we had heard, was obscured by plant growth? I did not know, nor did the two others. We could only figure on an approximate direction.

In addition, this standing water was usually populated by crocodiles, and farther south, also by hippopotamuses. The Maiyah al-Saratin was located on the left bank of the Nile, which was all we knew. Fortunately, Abu al-Nil was very familiar with the river. I asked him:

"In which direction does the Nile flow upstream from the village of Qawa?"

"It flows north-northwest."

"Then let's try finding it. Row slowly."

I steered farther away from the ship, almost to the opposite bank, then turned to the left. We were able to glimpse stars. The sky formed a small strip which we had to follow. It became ever narrower, until it ended ahead of us. We entered the wood's canopy of leaves.

"Pull in the oars!" I advised. "We must be close to the entrance. Maybe there is an ever so slight current. Let the boat drift."

"That is dangerous," the helmsman warned. "If the current gets strong enough and we bump into something and capsize, the crocodiles will eat us.

"We will not bump into anything."

I pulled out my matches, lit a torch, and handed it to Bin Nil, for him to attach to the boat's bow. It did not matter whether Ibn Asl would see the light.

The torch light showed that we were under sunut trees, which, using our oars as measures, we found to stand two yards in the water. Of course, this could not be the entrance to the *maiyah*. We stopped at one of the trees and I tossed some leaves in the water. They moved, and were carried away. We slowly followed them, to the left of our previous direction. Now the water became deeper, so deep that we could not measure its depth with even our mast. It moved faster, but in a circular motion.

"We are moving in the wrong direction," Bin Nil insisted. "We must turn back!"

"No," his grandfather objected. "We are headed in the right direction. The water circulates here, because the Nile is flowing past outside. It is obscured by the plants. We must push through."

Through. Yes, but where? In any case, straight ahead. Trees grew on both sides. The tree crowns were covered by creepers, stretching from crown to crown, forming a plant bridge and hanging all the way down to the water. Where the bridge rose to our left, its tendrils were torn in many places. Pointing to this area, I said:

"This must be it. There, the *noquar* tore off plants when it was pushed through. Pick up the oars, and let's give it a try."

We headed for the area. The creepers hung much higher here as it had appeared earlier. We easily penetrated them, and, suddenly, the woods lay behind us, the open river before us, and the star-studded sky above us.

"Allah be thanked," sighed the helmsman. "I was getting afraid. Had we not discovered the exit, Ibn Asl might yet have reached us."

"Impossible!" I told him. "Had we not found the river, we would have gone on land, and Ibn Asl would have had great difficulty finding and capturing us there. But this is much better. We are free and on our way to the *raïs effendina*."

"Where are you going to look for him? Do you think he is still near the Jazirah Hassaniah?"

"I would need to be all-knowing to tell you this. First, we must move as quickly as possible. Which way is the wind blowing?"

"At night, mostly from the south."

We checked the barely noticeable draft along the bank and found it to our advantage. We erected the mast and raised the sail. The helmsman, being the oldest of us, was not up to exerting himself and took over my position. I, together with Bin Nil, took an oar.

"Do you want me to steer toward the middle of the river?" the oldster asked.

"No."

"Why not? We will find better wind there."

"This is correct, but we might miss the *raïs effendina*."

"You think that he might still come upstream?"

"No, but he may have his ship anchored at a bank. Wherever he is, he will post a strong watch. This is why I took the torches along. He will notice and hail us, so that we do not pass him."

"Let me ask you then to steer by my senses. I know the path the skippers are used to taking, also the spots where one can land and overlook the river."

We could not do better than leave him to his will. Had I only known where to look for the *raïs effendina*! He found the "birds" had flown the coop, and would have talked with the people of the stopped ship, and learned from them the direction in which to find his prey. I assumed that he had quickly returned with his *asakir* to Hagasi, boarded his 'Falcon', and sailed south. If this was correct, we had to meet him on the way, or he had by evening anchored at a place from where he could see every passing vessel.

Naturally, our night journey went faster than the day's upstream trip. We had three motors: the river's drop, the wind, and our oars. Unfortunately, the boat was rather large; a smaller one would have carried us faster downstream. Still, since we had left the *maiyah*, less than an hour had passed when we reached the village of Qawa. At that time, the village was the government depot on the White Nile. Substantial grain and other provisions were kept there, and every southward-heading vessel provisioned itself there, with supplies becoming ever more costly the farther one traveled south.

We stopped briefly to inquire with the *Haris al-Mishrah* (the port captain) whether the ship of the *raïs effendina* had been sighted. His answer was negative, which is why we sailed and rowed on.

A night on the Nile! What a subject for a poet! But I did not feel poetic at all. I had barely slept for several nights, and was therefore very tired, yet had to row. Bin Nil did not feel much different. I believe he rowed at times like I did, with eyes closed, half or even three-quarters asleep. Our old Abu al-Nil was just as monosyllabic as we were. He had not had the exertion we had had, which is why I guessed his silence to have a particular reason. Asking him about it, he answered:

"I am not the least tired, *effendi*. It is worry that robs me of my good mood. I am a refugee."

"Ah, you are afraid of the *raïs effendina*?"

"Of course! I was formerly arrested on the slave ship and would have been severely punished had you not let me escape. And now I am sailing straight into the hands of this stern master. I find it difficult to voice this request, *effendi*: Set me free once more! Allow me to leave the boat at the first best location!"

"Don't you want to return to your ship?"

"Before I get to it, I will be caught."

"But your are alone and without any means. You have nothing. What are you going to do?"

"Bin Nil, my grandson, will be with me."

"No," it came. "You are my father's father, and it is Allah's command that I respect and honor you. That I do! But I am now the servant of this, my *effendi*, and nothing can bring me to leave him."

"Son of my son, who would have thought this of you? Are you denying the blood flowing in your veins? Will you act against the laws dwelling in every person's chest?"

"No. My love for you and the loyalty to my *effendi* can be reconciled. You need not leave the boat. I know the *effendi*. He will protect you."

"He cannot do that."

"Do not doubt it! He can do anything he wants."

"At least I only want what I can," I commented. "Abu al-Nil, you need not be afraid. The *raïs effendina* will forgive you for what has happened in the past."

"Oh, *effendi*, if only this were true. I would thank him on my knees. I am not as bad a person as it may appear."

"I know, which is why I let you escape."

"And never again will I be seen on board of a slave trader's ship."

"That, too, I believe, which is why I will ask the *raïs effendina* to forgive you for what is past."

"*Effendi*, you drip balsam on my wound, which was caused by my conscience. Should the *raïs effendina* forgive me, I can also forgive myself. Then I need not fear anything and no one any more. I can let myself be seen by everyone and return home, without needing to think that the avenger will tear me away from my family."

"Be confident! I tell you that all will be forgiven and forgotten."

"I believe you. You saved me once before and would not take me to the *raïs effendina*, if you were convinced that it would be to my misfortune. But what should I tell him when he asks me how I got away before?"

"Do not lie to him, but tell the truth."

"Then he will be very angry at you."

"Do not believe this. Your grandson here has been of good service to him, for which gratitude demands that he follow your request for forgiveness."

This calmed him completely, breaking his silence. His heart had been lightened, which freed up also his tongue. He began telling me of his experiences. Having experienced as much as he had, there was no concern that we would run out of conversational subjects on our lonely journey.

3

The Fever Swamp

THE LIVELY CONVERSATION we maintained during our boat on our nightly downstream trip did not keep us from a careful watch. We even stopped a few times when a fantastic shadow seemed like the outline of a ship. But each time we were disappointed. Little by little, we used up all six torches which I had tossed into the boat, and so we were forced to travel without light. Toward morning the wind freshened and our speed increased. Of course, we had to take breaks from rowing, without which we would not have lasted that long. Whenever we caught a good current, we rested.

It was not yet five o'clock in the morning when we arrived at the place where the 'Lizard' had been anchored. A short distance upstream Abu al-Nil's ship had been stopped; it was gone. At Ibn Asl's former camp we went on land in the hope of finding someone. It was for naught. Now we had to sail on to Hagasi. Should I not catch the *raïs effendina* there either, we likely passed him in the night or he had returned to Khartoum. In this case, I depended on myself for the safety of the caravan.

When we approached Hagasi a faint light greeted us. The stars were beginning to fade, which told me that the light came from a ship lying at the *mishrah*. I recognized the sharp, elegant prow and the three slanted masts; it was the 'Falcon', we were looking for. The light came from a lantern at the middle mast. Of course, we headed for the vessel. However, before we had reached it, we were hailed from its deck:

"Boat, land here by the side!"

Jesting, I told Abu al-Nil to draw a bit away, as if not following the order. We had veered sideways, when the man called:

"Stop, or I'll shoot!"

Simultaneously, the ring of a small bell sounded. It was the 'Falcon's' alarm. If the deck watch gave his signal, every crew member would be ready for action inside a minute, even had he been fast asleep. I could not push the joke too far, knowing that they would otherwise start shooting at us, so I steered toward the vessel.

"Moor at portside," the watch ordered, "and stay put!"

We followed the command. Up on board it became lively and we were quickly asked:

"Whose boat is this?"

I recognized the voice of the *raïs effendina*. So that he would not identify me by my name, I told Bin Nil what reply to give in my place:

"The Lizard."

When the caller heard this answer, he shouted excitedly:

"Climb aboard at once!"

He had, of course, learned that the ship which had left the Jazirah Hassaniah just prior to his arrival there had been the "Lizard," and thought now to obtain information about it. Just then, several lanterns had been lit. Continuing my jest, I asked the old helmsman to climb the rope ladder first.

He did so without understanding my intention. When he arrived on deck, I heard the *raïs effendina* exclaim:

"This is the first one, but hold, I think I know this face! Who are you? Listen, fellow, where did we see each other before?"

Abu al-Nil was so scared by this reception that he forgot to answer.

"If I am not mistaken, your name is Abu al-Nil. Admit it on the spot!"

"Yes, *effendi*, yes!" the helmsman confirmed, fearfully.

"Wasn't it at Giza that we saw each other?"

"In Giza, yes, *effendi.*"

"Call me *amir*! From earlier times, you must know very well that I am called this! If I am not mistaken, you were the helmsman of the *dahabiyah* "al-Samak," which I confiscated earlier."

"It is I."

"I took the entire crew prisoner, except that you escaped. Welcome here and now! I am delighted to make up for what I missed before. Tie the fellow up and put him in the prison cell."

"No, no, *amir*, do not tie me up!" the oldster exclaimed. "I am not your enemy; I came of my own free will!"

"Freely? Yet my watch had to threaten to shoot you? This is a lie! Where is your ship, the 'Lizard'?"

"In the Maiyah al-Saratin."

"I do not know it. What is it doing there?"

"It was hidden there from you."

"Then its crew must have a guilty conscience. What did they want at the Jazirah Hassaniah?"

"To capture you."

"Capture . . . me?" he exclaimed. "By *Shaitan*, you are honest, exceptionally honest! Who is the *raïs* of this 'Lizard' that wants to capture me?"

"It has no *raïs.* Her master, Ibn Asl, commands it himself."

As short as this name was, it produced a strong effect.

"Ibn Asl, Ibn Asl," it came from just about every mouth, even the *raïs effendina* himself expressed his surprise.

"Did I hear right? You said Ibn Asl? So the infamous slaver is on the 'Lizard'? Now, a light is dawning on me. This son of a dog wanted to set a trap for me. Is that so? Admit it at once!"

"Yes, *amir*, you guessed it. You, together with your ship, were to be incinerated by burning petroleum."

"Allah *karim*! He made me suspicious. It was well that I took the land route. So, that's what the barrels were for – to incinerate me, my ship and all my men! I will leave right away, and you shall guide me to the Maiyah al-Saratin! As a taste of what expects you, I shall have you given the *bastonnade*. Tie his feet, Aziz, and give him twenty strokes on his soles!"

Aziz, his favorite, the young man who carried the hippopotamus whip, was ready to execute his master's commands. Abu al-Nil knew him only too well from earlier. Frightened, he lifted his hands and cried: "No *bastonnade*, no whipping, *amir*, I am innocent!"

Now, Bin Nil, his grandson, hurried up the rope ladder to tell the *amir*: "Do not have him whipped! He is my grandfather and did not lie to you."

"What, you are here, Bin Nil? How did you get here and into the company of a helmsman of slavers?"

"He never was that. He was briefly the helmsman of a slave trading ship, but never a slave hunter. My *effendi* will tell you the very same."

"Where is he, your *effendi*?"

"On the way!" I answered his question, while I jumped over the board. "Here he is!"

A general shout of happy surprise arose. The *amir* retreated a pace, stared at me for a moment, taken aback, opened his arms, and came to me, saying: "*Effendi*, you are here, you? What joy! Arrived from the lands of the Fassara! Come to my heart; let me embrace you!"

His joy was as great as it was sincere. It honored me and made me happy. His first lieutenant and lieutenant, the old *onbashi*, and many others walked up to me to shake my hand.

One man had stood apart. He now pushed his tall, lean figure with its endlessly long limbs through the crowd and called to me from afar:

"*Effendi*, oh *effendi*, my soul is full of joy, it jumps from delight, now that my eyes see you once more! I missed you, just as a beloved wife is missed by her husband. Without you, life had darkened for me like a covered forge one looks at from below, or a boot worn on the wrong foot. No one cared about me, and no one listened to my words. My bravery died away and my heroism dried up like a spot of pitch on the sleeve of my dress. But now, new pleasure overcomes me and my merits and skills will grow again and display themselves like a soap bubble inflated by the gentle breath of one's mouth."

"And then bursts!" I added, while I shook hands with him and stepped back a pace, since he was getting ready to embrace me in a most chummy way with his all too long arms. I thought them long enough to wrap themselves not just once, but twice around my body. "If no one paid attention to you, it can only have been your own fault."

This tall character was, of course, none other than Selim, my second servant, who I had left with the *raïs effendina*. I had not taken him along to the Fassara, since he did just about everything wrong and caused me one mishap after another. To my last words, he replied:

"*Effendi*, you misjudge me, as happens so often. I honestly took part in the men's worries and sufferings and, as a shining example, walked ahead of everything, which they, obviously would never be able to emulate during their entire life."

"At eating, yes!" one of them called. "Other than that, he did not do a thing. Eating, drinking, smoking, sleeping and boasting are his *forte!*"

"Shut up!" the lanky fellow thundered. "Your mouth is a spring of unpalatable water. *Effendi*, you should, for instance, have seen me yesterday when we went to the Jazirah Hassaniah to capture the slavers. My figure towered above all others, and in my heart burned the flame of battle lust which no man could withstand. When the slave hunters saw this, they ran away. We did not see them and their ship was gone. For this, the *amir* has to thank only my victorious presence."

"Don't boast already at our first meeting!" I warned him. "We need to hear other things than the oft-heard praise of fame you don't possess."

"This is true," the *amir* agreed. "Important events must have taken place which caused you to come to Hagasi instead of going to Khartoum. How come I find you in the company of the helmsman of slave traders? And where are your *asakir*?"

"They are behind and will deliver to you a group of slavers I captured."

"You caught more? Those of Ibn Asl? *Effendi*, what a lucky man you are! I have not captured any since Wadi al-Bard."

"Rejoice then, for tomorrow, if I am not totally mistaken, you will get your hands on Ibn Asl himself."

"Really, really? Where is he?"

"In the Maiyah al-Saratin, as Abu al-Nil here told you before."

"Were is this *maiyah*?"

"Upstream from the village of Qaua."

"You were there? How am I to understand this?"

"Oh, I was also in Hagasi and the Jazirah Hassaniah yesterday before you arrived. Ibn Asl had captured me."

"Cap . . . ." The word became stuck in his mouth. "*Effendi*, you are joking!"

"No."

"I assumed you to be on the western savanna, yet you are here, battling Ibn Asl, whom I tried to find in vain."

"It's easy. I will tell you. Order your people to remain quiet! It is better for us when no one in Hagasi learns what is happening and what we decide, since Ibn Asl has spies here. The local *shaykh al-Balad* is, for instance, an ally of his."

"Do you have proof?"

"Yes. He knew that Ibn Asl had set a trap for you. He even helped him by giving one of his men, who was a lookout for you here, a horse, so that he could quickly report your arrival."

"All that you know? I am most eager to hear your story. Come to my cabin. But we will tie up this old helmsman of slave traders and put him in prison."

"No, *amir*! He is a good and honest man I recommend to your goodwill. I shall explain this, too. Leave him with Bin Nil, his grandson, and order food and drink for them. We haven't enjoyed anything since yesterday."

"Then you must also be hungry? Come, you will get whatever your heart desires."

After I made sure that all the lights, except for the mast lantern, had been extinguished, we went to his magnificently appointed cabin. Aziz, his favorite, served us. Every available provision was put before us, including several bottles of wine, for the *amir* had become emancipated from the prohibition of drinking the "juice of grapes." During the meal, I recounted my story and, obviously, the *amir* listened with great attention. He was unable to remain seated, walked agitatedly back and forth, and frequently interrupted my report with the most forceful exclamations. I did not have the time to be as detailed as I would actually have liked. My narrative did not take more than five minutes. When I had finished, he wanted to hear more details, but I said:

"Not now. Time is precious. You, I and Bin Nil, must leave before daybreak."

"Where to?"

"We will take the boat I arrived in and sail some distance upstream. I will then tell you everything, together with a plan which requires your immediate company. In truth, we should not take anyone else long, but since Bin Nil and I are extremely tired from rowing, and I cannot ask you to row, two of your crew may accompany us."

"Well, then! You are very secretive. But since I know that you do not do anything without good reason, I will accommodate you. Were it not you asking, I would not do it, but rather believe that I was to be played into Ibn Asl's hands in this way."

"Change your shiny uniform, at least the outer coat, to a simpler piece. The less you are noticed upon our return, the better our plan will succeed."

He removed his coat and put on a dark *burnous*. I pocketed some snacks from the table for Bin Nil and me. Then we left.

The first, pale morning red showed when we pushed our boat away from the 'Falcon'. Two crew members rowed. I sat next to Bin Nil with the *amir* facing us. It is easily understandable that he was extremely excited. I did not let him wait for long, but presented to him the desired comprehensive report, while we slowly advanced along the left bank of the Nile. I now could answer his questions regarding my plan without incurring any problems, of which there were many. When he had finally become satisfied, we had arrived at the place where the 'Lizard' had anchored. We landed there and sat down under a tree. I ordered the two crew members to return to Hagasi by land and to let themselves be seen as little as possible. They left, but the *raïs effendina* asked surprised:

"You are becoming ever more mysterious. Are we not returning by boat?"

"I and Bin Nil, yes, but not you."

"Why not? Am I to walk, too?"

"Yes. I will tell you the reason later, but first I wish to hear your thoughts about what you think of these events."

"First of all, I am very surprised. *Effendi*, you are truly a man . . ."

"None of that!" I interrupted. "What you think of me is unimportant at this time."

"But we all owe you our lives, which is why you cannot ask . . ."

"Yes, but leave it be for the time being. I indeed ask this. Time is too precious, so that we must deal only with the most important things. Of course, your intention and hope is to catch Ibn Asl this time."

"Naturally! I swear by Allah that today or tomorrow I will . . ."

"Do not swear! Man is not the master of events. A small mistake or an insignificant chance may spoil everything. How do you think we will catch him?"

"Simple; we sail to the Maiyah al-Saratin and attack him there."

"But he isn't there any more. For two reasons, I am certain that he left the *maiyah* shortly after our escape. First, he no longer felt safe there, since I knew his hideout, and second, he had to hurry to liberate his father and his underlings. He sailed downstream after us."

"Then we need only to advance toward him to . . ."

"Miss him entirely," I broke in.

"We check every corner of the river bank!"

"Yes, and while we do this, he is already taking his men across the savanna against our *asakir*."

"He cannot do this that quickly."

"Why not? He knows that you are searching for him and that I must have met you to take you to the *maiyah*. He used the night to leave this place in order to move downstream as far as possible, landed at some hidden place, known only to him, left a few crew to guard his ship, and marched his men toward our *asakir*."

"I understand. I must quickly leave with my men to protect the caravan. You will, of course, accompany us."

"No, I won't, but, together with Bin Nil, will ride to the caravan, while you set a trap for Ibn Asl."

"Why should we not immediately move together against him?"

"Because by doing so we would not catch Ibn Asl. He is upstream from us, which puts us in the lead. He would come up from behind and find our tracks, revealing to him what our plans are. He would then fall back."

"But if he wants to rescue his father, he must follow and attack us."

"He wouldn't think of doing this. His own safety is more precious to him than his father's life and that of his men. I learned that from him and told you. Yes, he might have his slavers attack us, but would take every precaution not to fall into our hands himself. Or, what is even more likely, he would come up with some ploy that could become very dangerous to us, since we have no inkling what it is."

"So we should not move ahead of him? Should I let him do so? Then, he will attack our caravan with me arriving too late."

"Were this the case, little or nothing need be feared, since I would be with the caravan already. Therefore, be could not surprise it. But I am intent on another plan quite different. I have often achieved easily and completely by cunning what I could not have accomplished by force. You, yourself, have seen examples of that. Using such a ruse I will, with your permission, try to catch Ibn Asl. If no mistake is made, I am certain of its success."

"What do you intend to do?"

"To set a snare for him in which he will be caught. It greatly facilitates a victory if one knows the place of battle. A strategist who knows how to lure the enemy to the location where all is prepared for his reception, will likely be victorious, even with inferior numbers. If you draw him out onto the open savanna, you will not know where you will meet him and the circumstances by which the fight will take place. To avoid this, we shall determine where to await him."

"But will he come?"

"He will. Let me take care of this."

"Do you have a particular place in mind?"

"Yes, one very well suited. Of course, it must be located as close as possible in the direction from where the caravan is coming and to where Ibn Asl is moving. Jabal al-Qul is the best-suited place for my plan. Have you been there?"

"Five times. At these times, I roamed the entire area."

"I'm pleased, since I needn't covertly accompany you there to point out the locations I have in mind. There are two *maiyatan*, two swamps, connected by an inlet to the Nile. The northern one is larger and far longer than the southern one. Are you familiar with them?"

"Yes. The large *maiyah* is called Maiyah al-Humma (Swamp of Fever); I do not know the smaller one's name."

"I mean the Swamp of Fever. It winds long and narrow around the foot of a mountain. It takes over four hours to walk from one end to the other. At its middle, a bay enters far into the mountain. It is very deep, covered by *Umm Sufah*, with its banks densely overgrown by tall, thickly foliaged *gaful* trees (Balsamodendron). They attracted my attention, since I had not seen this species of *gaful* normally attain such height."

"I know them. Their exceptionally pleasant scent pervades the entire area and softens the swamp's stink. One can readily cross this place on foot; a camel rider must, however, take great care. The mountain is deeply creviced and rises almost vertically to the sky. The inlet is filled with water from the *maiyah's* arm. Between the water and the mountain is a narrow path, covered by large rocks that have tumbled down from above and make passage for camels very difficult. The path around the *maiyah's* bay has brought misfortune to many people already, which is why it it called *Darb al-Musibi* (Path of Misfortune)."

"Right on. And it will be a right and true path of misfortune for Ibn Asl."

"How do you intend to lure the man there?"

"I am sure to lure him there, but do not yet know how. It will fall into place. The "Misfortune Path" is located at the western bank. Are you also familiar with the *maiyah's* eastern bank?"

"Just as much."

"Then you will remember the dense *hagalik* woods at its southern end?"

"Yes. This woods are nearly impenetrable, with the distance between the tree trunks mostly grown over with *nabak* bushes."

"It will serve you as a hideout."

"Us? Are we to wait there for Ibn Asl?"

"Yes. Now the most important thing for you, *amir*. Remember it well! Once you return to Hagasi, you leave again right away, but talk first to the *shaykh al-Balad*."

"This dog, this traitor, I am going to punish severely!"

"Do this later. Today, be very friendly to him and give the appearance as if you were extending him your fullest trust. Tell him that you had searched for slave traders by the Hassaniah, but had not found any. You say that you had been misled by Ibn Asl, who is likely in Khartoum, and that you would quickly head there to look for him to punish him."

"Why, precisely, should I tell this to the *shaykh al-Balad*?"

"Because he's going to play an important role in my plan. He is to lay the snare for Ibn Asl, without being aware of it. He is Ibn Asl's ally, and it can be expected that Ibn Asl will secretly come himself, or send a messenger to find out where you are and what the situation is. The *shaykh* will tell him that you returned to Khartoum, which is why Ibn Asl will feel safe from you."

"From you, too?"

"Yes, because I will also talk to the *shaykh*. You will now return on foot to Hagasi and let yourself not be seen on the way, as far as that is possible. So that you wouldn't be recognized from afar, I asked you to exchange your uniform for a simpler cloak. Once you have left there, I will come sailing in with Bin Nil."

"How will you know that I have left?"

"Let this be my worry. I will be on the lookout. When I arrive with Bin Nil, I will visit the *shaykh al-Balad*. I will act as if I am just returning from the *maiyah*, and will tell him what happened up there and before, at the Jazirah Hassaniah."

"Will you tell him who you truly are?"

"Of course! He would learn it from Ibn Asl anyway. If I lied to him regarding my name, he would not believe whatever else I told him, and my plan would run the danger of misfiring. I will seemingly extend the greatest trust to him. Being the *shaykh al-Balad*, he is a person of authority for whose help I am asking. I will leave him the boat for safe-keeping and tell him that you will later pick it up."

"You come only with Bin Nil to Hagasi. He will, however, soon learn that Abu al-Nil was with you. How are you going to explain this?"

"Oh, I'll say that he fell in the water when he entered the boat during our escape. And if Ibn Asl did not catch him again, he must have been eaten by crocodiles."

"Why do you leave him with me? You could take him along."

"No. I'm short a camel. You must know that I have only two camels stabled at Hagasi."

"What are you going to say about where you will ride to?"

"To my caravan. I had left it to warn you. Now, that I heard you are safe, I can return to it. This will be a *coup* certain of success. Ibn Asl will be terribly angry that I escaped him. He will move toward our caravan to liberate our captives. When he hears that I have joined it again, he will be delighted, hoping to catch me. He will be even more inclined to attack us and, therefore, enter our trap all the more securely.

"But you do not know yet how to entrap him."

"I didn't know until now, but, presently, an idea has come to me. I will make a remark to the shaykh al-Balad that will cause Ibn Asl to come to the Jabal Arash Qul for sure. I will tell him: I spared the lives of my captives, although these rogues deserve death many times over. However, after what has happened now, I can no longer be merciful. Such vermin must be eradicated without mercy. They all wanted to torture me to death; well, then, every member of Ibn Asl's gang who has fallen into my hands will die. First will be the captives, who I am now heading for. I shall take them to Jabal Arash Qul, where I will have them tossed into the Maiyah al-Humma. When Ibn Asl hears this, he will head there immediately in order to wait for us and to save his men. Don't you agree?"

"Yes, certainly! I think you calculated correctly. But how will you force him to take a position that assures us victory?"

"Time will tell. He will be there before I am, and will have a good look at the location should he not yet know it. If his eyes are even a little open, he will arrive at the idea of setting the same trap for me which I intend to set for him. That is, he will attack from the front and back while I am on the narrow path between water and mountain. If successful, I will be lost in his opinion."

"And will you enter this trap?"

"Maybe, but, of course, only to draw him in with me and to see him perish there. You shall leave Hagasi and land at the same latitude as Jabal Arash Qul. Then, hide your ship and leave it guarded by a few men. Afterwards, march with the rest of the crew and asakir to the Maiyah al-Humma, and hide at its southern end in the hagalik woods we talked about. There, you wait for Ibn Asl's and my arrival without letting yourself be seen. It is possible that I will pay you a visit before we hit him in order to provide you with some further information. Should it not come to that, rest assured that, coming from the north, I will be on the narrow path of battle and will be attacked by Ibn Asl, coming from the south. He will, of course, find himself on the same narrow strip of land. You will advance quickly from the woods advancing toward his back. If this succeeds, he will be stuck between you and me. Unable to retreat, he must either surrender or be pushed into the *maiyah*, where he will find his inexorable grave in the deceptive *Umm Sufa* cover."

"*Effendi*, this is a very good plan. Excellent! Nevertheless, I have some serious misgivings. You have only twenty men with you!"

"Should I need more men, I'll get them from you."

"If you have time for it!"

"Maybe! Your reservation is indeed well founded."

"But you must guard the prisoners. How many men will that leave you with to fight? And, too, it is quite probable that Ibn Asl will not attack you from the south, but, rather from the north, ambushing you at the fateful place. You are trying to get him between two fires, which he will attempt also for you."

"Before you mentioned it, I was convinced of this. He will, of course set a trap for me, especially since he has more than enough time for it. Since I know this, it does not represent any danger to me. If one knows that a mine has been placed at a certain area, then one either does not go there, or causes it to explode beforehand. It can then not cause any damage. However, since I have far fewer men than you, most of whom must guard the captives, you will have to send me twenty of your men for assistance."

"And where am I to send them so that they are certain to meet up with you?"

"The men must not be seen by the enemy, but must be easily found by me. I know of a place very well suited for this purpose. I once camped there myself. It was at the northern side of Jabal Arash Qul. A very narrow dry runoff descends from the mountain. When walking upward for five minutes, the runoff widens into a small vale, overgrown with bushes."

"These are *kittr* bushes."

"Ah, you know the place?"

"Yes. I once followed the runoff, looking for potable water."

"There's none, since any precipitation drains quickly into the *mai-yah*. Whatever water remains in the little vale turns rapidly foul and unpalatable and serves only the preservation of the *kittr* bushes. I'm glad you are familiar with the runoff, which will prevent any mistake. Send the twenty men there!"

"When should they be there?"

"Not too long before I arrive, or they could possibly be discovered by Ibn Asl. If I figure it right, I should meet our caravan sometime today."

"This is impossible. The men will need five days; today is only the third."

"Consider that this Aram escaped, who last night reported what happened to Ibn Asl. After he fled, our *asakir* must be aware that he would head to Ibn Asl, which is why they would need to hurry and will require only four days instead of five. By this evening, they should therefore be only a day's trip away from here. Since I will cover at least also a full day's trip to where they are, I will most likely meet them at this distance about this time. Tomorrow morning, we leave for Jabal Arash Qul. We will not ride to it, but camp just before we reach it. Of course, I do not want the attack to take place during the night, but will save it for early morning, the day after tomorrow. I may pay you a visit at night. In any case, you can dispatch the twenty men, should I not visit you by midnight. They can walk around the *maiyah* and hide in the vale of the runoff, where I will meet with them. When I approach them, I will imitate the deep laughter of a hyena three times. I will repeat it, while I walk along the woods' edge. When the guard hears me, he should come to me and lead me to you. Now I'm finished with my instructions."

"Then I will leave for Hagasi. But before I go, *effendi*, I want to thank you for . . ."

"Nothing of that now, *amir*! If you want to have a long talk with me concerning your rescue, I don't mind, but I ask you to save this for later. We haven't got the time for it now."

"Well, then, I will leave, but, eventually, you will have to listen to the speech you just mentioned. I hope that our next meeting will be a happy and victorious one!"

He shook hands with Bin Nil and me, and left. We waited, until we were certain he had arrived in Hagasi. We then entered the boat and rowed it to the opposite bank, where we hid it in the rushes, then walked downstream until we saw Hagasi on the opposite bank.

We kept ourselves hidden so as not to be seen from across the river. The 'Falcon' was still tied up at the *mishrah*. Half an hour later, the sails were raised. It sailed toward the middle of the river and pointed its bow northward. We returned to our boat, waited a quarter of an hour, then rowed to the middle of the river where we put up the mast and hoisted our sail. The wind blew favorably, and we slowly maneuvered toward Hagasi.

Bin Nil had witnessed our conversation, thus having heard everything, no further rules of conduct were required. Just like me, he burned to compensate for what we had had to bear yesterday. Most important was now to find the *shaykh al-Balad* at home. We could not have done any better. When we approached the *mishrah*, we saw him standing by the water, looking curiously toward us. We dropped our sail, rowed ashore, climbed out, and tied up the boat. He approached us right away and said most amicably:

"*Salaam alaikum*! How come you are returning? I thought you wanted to leave with the "Lizard" for Fashoda. You could have picked up your camels upon your return."

"I thank you. It takes almost ten days sailing to get from here to Fashoda. We cannot afford such a long absence. However, we were almost forced to take one, even a much longer one."

"How so?"

He tried hard to look relaxed but could not quite control his tense expectation.

"I will tell you," I replied. "But join us a little distance from here. Important things happened which we want to tell only you about."

"You make me burst with curiosity, sir!" he said, stepping with us aside. "What important things can happen here in this little Hagasi!"

"You will be surprised when you hear. Did you know the man you rented the horses to?"

"Not very well. He said that he was one of the 'Lizard' crew, anchored at the Jazirah Hassaniah."

"Do you know what kind of ship this is?"

"A trading ship from Berber, the man told me."

"Did you ask him for its owner's name?"

"Why should I? The ship was not my concern. I am neither raïs nor port captain. Why should I trouble my memory with the names of all passing ships and their masters?"

"You are right. But I regret that you didn't do this. If so, you could have warned us, and we would not have run the danger of losing our lives."

"Your lives?" he asked, looking shocked. "Ya Allah! Were you in such danger?"

"Indeed. Do you know that the 'Lizard' is the ship of the greatest criminal and slave hunter there is. Do you know whom I am referring to?"

"I do not know if I can guess it, but I think the worst slaver is Ibn Asl, Allah may curse. But he would not risk being seen here!"

"But he was here!"

"Really, really? Allah! Had I known this, I would have summoned all the men and youngsters of Hagasi to try to catch him, and turn him over to the raïs effendina."

"Do you know the raïs of the Viceroy?"

"Of course, I know him. I talked with him barely an hour ago."

"Then he was here?" I asked, acting surprised.

"Today, here. Yesterday, at the Hassaniah."

"When we had left already! Allah be thanked! So I succeeded in rescuing him. I did not think he would be so incautious as to come. He was to be entrapped."

"Sir, you scare my veins and bones. My blood wants to curdle. To lure the *raïs effendina*, Allah may bless with a thousand favors, to his ruin. Who, who was it?"

"Ibn Asl."

"Is it possible? My tongue wants to quit working. Tell me, sir, tell me!"

"Let me ask you before I do, whether you might know me?"

"No. I never saw you before. You arrived the other day and I do not know your name."

"I am the *effendi* from the lands of Christians, a friend of the *raïs effendina*, who I . . ."

"Allah, Allah, Allah!" He interrupted me, as if uncontrollably surprised or rather frightened. You are the foreign *effendi* who has already freed that many slaves and . . ."

He stopped, recognizing that he had gone too far and said too much, since he was not supposed to know anything about me. I acted as if I had not noticed this, and said:

"So you have heard of me already? I'm glad, because now I needn't deliver a long speech which would otherwise have been necessary. You know then that I helped the *amir* a little bit to accomplish his task?"

"Only a little? *Effendi*, I know you achieved what the *amir* did not accomplish."

"Well, then you can imagine that Ibn Asl would want to take vengeance on me."

"A great revenge! I believe he hates you far more than he does the *raïs effendina*."

"This is true. I have experienced it a number of times, just as I did yesterday. I will tell you about it."

I told him of the earlier events as much as I thought necessary, but of yesterday's experience much more extensively. However, I left out that I had met the *amir*. He played as though ignorant and totally surprised, and exclaimed, when I was finished:

"Oh, Allah, oh Prophet of Prophets! Should one think such things to be possible! *Effendi*, you are a Christian, but Allah must be very well disposed toward you, or you would not have succeeded in slipping out of the hands of this bloodthirsty hyena. But where is this Abu al-Nil? He is not with you, but you said that he stood with you on the deck?"

"When he tried climbing from the deck into the boat, he fell into the water. We had no time to rescue him. If the rogues did not fish him out, he was likely eaten by crocodiles."

"What misfortune! And you arrived here just now?"

"Yes. We would have arrived earlier, had we not lost time in searching for the *raïs effendina*. We assumed that he was pursuing the 'Lizard'.

"Pursue it? How could he have arrived at that idea? He did not suspect the "Lizard." He thinks that he was fooled by Ibn Asl in Khartoum, who lured him from there by some misinformation, probably to gain time to partake in a good business venture."

"Who told you that?"

"The *amir* himself."

"Where is he now?"

"Back to Khartoum."

"This is too bad. He could have taken this captured boat along. What am I going to do with it?"

"That depends on what you intend to do now. Should you want to head for Khartoum, you can board the next ship going there, and have it towed along."

"That won't work. I can't go to Khartoum. You forget that my *asakir* are with the prisoners on the way here. I want to ride toward them."

"Then you can leave the boat here. I will send it to Khartoum. I hope you think me the kind of man you can entrust it to."

"I have no hesitation about you. You are the authority, the master of Hagasi. I would even trust you with a fortune of many thousands. I will leave the boat with you. But you needn't send it to Khartoum. Leave it here until the *raïs effendina* comes back. He can take it along."

"Will he be back soon?"

"I do not know. He did not mention it, although he has reason to. He might pursue Ibn Asl, who must be on his way to Fashoda and farther up. Ibn Asl most likely intends to get away from us. I expect him to head for Bahr al-Jabal or Bahr al-Saraf to hunt for slaves. It would be too boring and troublesome to follow him. But when he returns, we will lie in wait for him in order to take his captured slaves and settle our final account. He will then experience the same fate as his father, Abd Asl."

"What? What is awaiting him?"

"Death! I should have had these rogues shot right away, just like the *amir* did with their comrades at Wadi al-Bard. I was too kind and spared them, wanting to deliver them to him. But I've changed my mind and received the power over life and death from the *raïs effendina*."

"Did he extend such powers to you? They are usually given only by the *Khedive*."

"Yes. He received permission from the *Khedive* to temporarily assign his rights to others. In this way, less time is lost and other complications are avoided. This will achieve the purpose of bringing a quick and terrifying end to the slavers. I haven't used these assigned rights so far, but will do so now for the first time."

"You are acting right and must be praised for what you are doing, but consider the responsibility you carry."

"Bah! I would then be also responsible for the contemptible crimes these fellows will yet commit, if I let them get away. Do you take pity on them?"

"*Effendi*, what a question! The faster they are eliminated, the happier I am. I wish I could be of help to you."

"Unfortunately, you cannot. Consider what these men intend to do. They wanted to kill my *asakir* and torture me slowly to death.

Nevertheless, I spared them. But now that I have escaped a most painful death only with great difficulty, it would be literally suicidal if I did not apply the most severe punishment."

"Do you intend to judge them here in Hagasi?"

"No, they will not get to see Hagasi."

"Where? *Effendi*, do not think my asking you is simply common curiosity. My soul is so incensed by the deeds of these criminals that I would love to know if and where they will receive their just punishment."

"I am aware of your love for justice and see no reason to keep it a secret from you. Do you know the Jabal Arash Qul?"

"How could I not know it. I have been there many times."

"Also the Maiyah al-Humma, next to the mountain?"

"That, too."

"Are there many crocodiles in the *maiyah*?"

"Countless numbers! Especially the bay which protrudes deeply into the mountain, has plenty of them."

"Isn't there only a narrow trail leading around this bay?"

"Yes. On one side, the mountain's face rises steeply, while on the other spreads the floating *Umm Sufah*, below which dwell lots of crocodiles. Because of the rock debris the path is barely passable for camels. If one does not want to fall from one's camel into the maw of crocodiles, one must dismount and lead one's animal slowly and carefully along the trail."

"I am aware of it. There is no better place suited for my purpose than this bay of the Fever Swamp."

The *shaykh al-Balad* became frightened. One could see it.

"So there you want to exact your revenge? Oh, *effendi*, this will be dreadful, absolutely terrible!"

"Everyone harvests what he has sowed. And it isn't as dreadful as you think. My nails were to be pulled from my fingers. Then, each of my body's limbs were to be cut off, little by little, while I want to drop these men simply in the *Umm Sufah*, where, in a moment, they will be devoured by the crocodiles. Which death is worse, theirs or mine?"

"Yours *effendi*. But when is this to happen?"

"The day after tomorrow, an hour after the sunrise prayer, when we reach the Jabal Arash Qul and the Maiyah of Fever."

"Is this going to be the hour of death for these men?"

"Yes."

"When will you leave here, *effendi*?"

"Right now. I will get my camels."

He accompanied me to the man with whom I had left my camels and had them returned, paying only a minimal fodder charge. We led them down to the *mishrah* to water them, then back up where they were saddled. I was just tying up my camel's saddle, when Bin Nil called to me: "*Effendi*, look over there!"

He pointed toward the savanna, from where a camel rider was approaching. He was still quite a distance away, but I recognized him immediately. It was Aram, who had escaped my *asakir* and had brought the message of his men's capture to Ibn Asl. Bin Nil had also recognized him. He lifted a finger and said:

"Watch out, *effendi*!"

The *shaykh al-Balad*, standing next to us, also heard him, which is why I replied casually:

"Watch out? What for? Since you were captured you sense danger everywhere. This is a simple traveler. What else? Mount up; we must leave!"

He obeyed but gave me a surprised look. I shook hands with the *shaykh al-Balad* and said my goodbye. He bowed, and said:

"Allah *ma'ak* (God be with you)! Will I see you again after judgment day at the *maiyah*?"

"Probably. May our seeing each other again bring you a thousand blessings!"

We rode off to the west, while Aram was coming from the south. When he spotted us, he halted his animal and turned to leave. When he turned in his saddle to look back, he saw that we were leaving and stopped. Feeling safe again, he drove his animal toward the village.

"I do not understand you, *effendi*," said Bin Nil. "The rider was Aram, coming from Ibn Asl!"

"Yes. I know!"

"But you did not wait to apprehend him?"

"Think of all I have told the *shaykh*, which Ibn Asl is to learn. He will be informed by this Aram, who I'm glad to see coming. You, however, wanted to arrest him. The *shaykh* will now tell him everything I told him and convey it to Ibn Asl, who, rest assured, will then head to the Jabal Arash Qul and enter our trap."

"May Allah so provide! I hope we will not miss our *asakir*."

"We won't!"

We had been riding for some time, when I asked Bin Nil:

"Do you see the dark strip in the grass before us?"

"Yes. Tracks, but do you know whose?"

"They are Aram's tracks from yesterday. He rode along ours, which were still fresh, since he was only a few hours behind us. Our *asakir* then followed his, keeping to ours and his tracks. If we now ride along the latter we will meet our companions. Drive your animal more quickly! The sooner we meet them, the better it will be."

Our camels were rested and were glad to run. By noon we took a small rest. The tracks became subsequently fainter, but I could still make them out, while Bin Nil was no longer able to.

Considering this, we could assume that the *asakir* were also unable to make them out and had probably diverged from them. What to do? To the south was a well, called Bir Safi, the Clear Well. The Fassara guide knew it and most likely directed the caravan there. This is why we now turned south. If we kept riding as fast as before, we could make it there before sunset.

My assumption was correct. The sun stood only about three of its diameters from the horizon, when I saw trees and bushes in the distance. It was Bir Safi. Soon, we saw camels lying about and men moving. It was our caravan.

"What is Abd Asl going to say when we arrive?" Bin Nil asked.

"And the *Faqir al-Fuqara*, who wants to become the Mahdi?"

"The fellows likely believe that we have perished. May Allah destroy them! I gave the old one his life. Had I known what was awaiting us at the Jazirah Hassaniah, I wouldn't have done it."

"I hope you aren't going to lay hands on him after all?" I asked Bin Nil.

"You need not be concerned, *effendi*! This old, stinking jackal is far too disgusting for me to lay hands on him. He is safe from me!"

We had come close enough to the well so that the men there were able to recognize us.

"The *effendi*!" I heard someone shout.

"The *effendi*! And Bin Nil! The *effendi*, the *effendi*! Allah be praised and hail to us! They are coming, they are coming!" twenty voices shouted in pandemonium, with just as many men running toward us. We were forced to dismount before we reached the well. Everyone shook hands with us and all shouted at the top of their voices. I gladly let them show their excitement; their joy did not do any harm, and it was proof that I had not become a stranger in their hearts. Not even the *raïs effendina*, their superior, had been welcomed like this when he met us at Wadi al-Bard.

Of course, they wanted us to tell them all that had happened, but first, I had to hear what had happened to them. We sat down, and the old *askari* I had entrusted the command to, said:

"Everything went by the rules, *effendi*. There is only one thing we must lament. One of the captives got away: Aram. He freed himself, took a camel, and . . ."

"Followed us," Bin Nil cut in.

"This is correct. But how do you know?"

"We saw him."

"Where?"

"That I will tell you shortly," I said, "but first I want to know whether the prisoners are all well tied up."

"*Effendi*, since Aram made his getaway, none of the others will. I hope you will not charge us for his escape. When he was tied up originally, you were still present yourself!"

"Well, if that's so, then his escape was due more to a lack of vigilance than to his being insufficiently tied up. Did you not post a guard? You did form a circle around the captives, didn't you? Since he succeeded in getting away, I assume you were all asleep."

"No, *effendi*, we changed guard, but this dog must have possessed some magic to make himself invisible."

"Then his magic did not work on me and Bin Nil, since we saw him, and several times at that. But I am not angry with you. I'm even glad he got away. It could have done us harm had the opposite happened. Now, it will be of great advantage to us."

"Is that possible?"

"Very much so! We could have captured him today, had we wanted to, but instead, we let him get away, since being free he will be of greater use to us than if he were in captivity with us."

That's when old Abd Asl shouted to us with a derisive laughter:

"Do not boast! You talk such lies only to annoy us. But you cannot deceive us. Had you seen Aram, you would have captured him. Since you did not do so, you did not see him."

"Your head is the wellspring of all wisdom, you most holiest of all Muslims," I told him.

"Don't you know who he was going to?" he asked laughing.

"To Ibn Asl, your son, of course."

"Had you seen him, you would have had to be with Ibn Asl!"

"We were with him, even on his ship, and spoke with him."

"Lies, lies!"

"Watch out, or you'll get the whip. In your position one ought to strive for politeness."

Now the *Fakir al-Fuqara* sat up and said:

"You demand courtesy? Are you treating us such that we should feel obliged to offer it?"

"I treat you the way you deserve."

"I did not do anything. I was your guest, then you tied me up. This is a crime that cannot be forgiven."

"Who made you our guest? Did I use the word *dhayif* (guest) with you. Did I say *"habakak"* or *"wa sahlan,"* or *"marhaba"* (each word means "welcome") to you?"

"No, but I ate with you!"

"Then you sat away from us! You admitted that I saved your life, yet you tried to get away in order to betray us to Ibn Asl!"

"Prove it!"

"I know it, which is proof! This ingratitude got you tied up, and if you don't like it, quarrel with yourself but not with us."

"But I demand my freedom and should you not give it to me right away, I shall call Allah's curse on you!"

"Allah will change your curse into a blessing."

"And the curse of the Prophet!"

"Your Prophet does not mean anything to me!"

"You will soon think and speak differently. When you learn the power that is given to me, you will be whining for mercy!"

"For the time being you are in my power. Whatever power you may later execute, whether over your harem or your dogs, is all the same to me. Now, shut up, or the whip will come to you. I don't care to have a man shout and curse at me, who has removed himself so far from Allah and his commands that he is even able to become a traitor to the man who saved his life."

"Fine, I will be quiet, but soon the time will come – and it is close – when I shall speak. Then, millions will listen to my voice, and you will be the first to crawl in the dust before me!"

He lay down again, seeing that silence was smarter than talking. Abd Asl, however, could not arrive at the same insight, or, maybe, caution was not as important to him as the desire to learn what I had done and experienced during my absence. He likely had thought that I had ridden to my demise, but had now returned well. How could this have happened, he must be asking himself? He had to get an answer, and instead of waiting calmly to see what I would say and do, he rose and continued, using the last words of the *Faqir al-Fuqara*:

"Yes, crawl in the dust, also before me! You have no idea of the situation you are in or the dangers surrounding you. My son will be the avenger and will destroy you, like he destroyed the *raïs effendina*!"

"Yes, indeed, he did," I replied in a serious voice, while putting up a very dejected expression.

"Did he? *Al-Hamdulillah* (Allah be thanked)!" he rejoiced. "He succeeded. The enemy has been crushed and shall never rise again."

"Crushed? No, they were all incinerated."

"It succeeded, it came off! Did you hear it, you men, you friends, you faithful? It has happened! I told you, told it quietly to you. My soul was full of expectation for it to succeed. Now, the devil has burned to ashes together with his *asakir*, and the head devil, sitting here before us must tell us this. He has lost his power and must set us free. If he does not do so right away, he can expect an endless chattering of teeth!"

"Don't miscalculate!" I warned him calmly, yet he continued enthusiastically:

"Me, miscalculate! How can I be mistaken? My son, the bravest of the brave, the most feared of feared, the most terrible of terrible, has incinerated the *raïs effendina* and will now come to release us. Woe to you, should he find a single hair missing from our heads. Whatever can be imagined in pain and torture will come to you, and you shall howl like the damned, living at the deepest bottom of Hell. Free, I want to be free immediately! You have realized your impotence and seen your ridiculousness, *effendi*. Set us free and hurry off. Flee, as far as your feet and those of your camels will carry you, or else terror will consume you, like the lion over the sheep that cannot defend itself against the claws of the mighty."

"You know full well that I do not flee from a lion. You can imagine therefore that I will not flee from your terror either. May your son come; he will find out how I will receive him."

"He will incinerate you just like he did the *amir*!"

One can imagine the impression these words made on the *asakir*. Their *amir* incinerated and murdered with his soldiers. They jumped up to inundate me with questions. I demanded silence, and added:

"You shall learn everything, but let me tell you in advance that you can rest easy. The triumph of this holy *faqir* will not last long. I rode off to save the *raïs effendina*, and what I set out to do, I plan to finish, especially something so important. The *amir* is alive; he was saved."

"Allah be thanked!" it sounded from around. But Abd Asl shouted:

"He is lying! He wants to take away our joy but will not succeed at it. He begrudges us our rejoicing, but we shall continue doing so until our savior arrives. We can expect him at any moment."

"Wait till you turn black and your sinful hide bursts from the anger of disappointment!" Bin Nil called to him. "You will hear in a moment, how our *effendi* made Ibn Asl impotent and ridiculous! Listen you *asakir*, the *effendi* will speak."

All eyes turned to me. There was not a single *asakir*, as well as the prisoners, who now did not look forward with eager expectation. Just then the sun was setting, the time for the evening prayer, but no one thought to follow this duty. I told them everything up to the moment when the three of us escaped from the 'Lizard'. Up to that point, the prisoners learned everything and were even intended to, but what happened afterward I kept from them. Had they learned of the trap I was going to set Ibn Asl, they might by chance be able to wreck my plan. Although everyone pressed me to continue with my story, Bin Nil stopped their requests by saying:

"Be still now! You have heard enough for today. The *amir* is safe. we were on Ibn Asl's ship. He recognized us and took us prisoner. He had more than a hundred men, yet we escaped. When we stopped the boat not far from the 'Lizard', we could easily have shot him. We did not, but once more were merciful. However, woe to him, if we meet him again."

"But what happened when you got away from the ship?" asked another man. "What did you do then? Where is your grandfather, the helmsman, who was with you?"

"Your curiosity is even larger than your mouth, but I will satisfy it. Of course, we sailed the boat to Hagasi and rode our camels from there to here. But my grandfather stayed in Hagasi to await our return."

"And the *raïs effendina*? Where is he?"

"Also in Hagasi, to where we will deliver these prisoners."

"Why did he not dispatch more *asakir* to us?"

"Because no camels were available, you father of curiosity, and we are men enough to transport these cowardly toads. Abd Asl, however, the holiest of Muslims and ugliest of toads, may now continue rejoicing as he did earlier."

Bin Nil had done well. He had stilled their curiosity without giving away our further intentions with even a single word. It was, in any case, better, that even the *asakir* did not learn anything. An incautious remark, heard by a prisoner, could have caused us problems. The men were also glad to have me back. They had carried a great responsibility, and the old *onbashi*, with a sigh of relief, was glad when I told him that he had no responsibility anymore. The Fassara guide was just as happy, for he would have born part of the guilt for every mistake made.

I assigned the sequence of guard duty, then lay down to sleep. Bin Nil did likewise, although it was not that late. We had not slept the prior night. I was awakened early by the morning prayer, and we left shortly thereafter.

It was a hard task to get the prisoners onto the camels. They made it as hard as possible for us. In difficult cases, the whip had to be used.

Bir Safi was located straight south and being reasonably cautious, I wanted to avoid taking this direction. I kept east until noon, and only then turned south. In this way we approached Jabal Arash Qul directly from the north, while otherwise, we would have arrived from the northwest. I wanted to avoid that direction, because both the *shaykh al-Balad* and Ibn Asl knew we were traveling on this route. They might have decided to attack us out there on the savanna and not later at the *maiyah*. By traveling this way, we had taken a direction from where we would not be expected. Ibn Asl had about a hundred men, against my twenty. A fight on the open savanna could easily have proved fatal for us.

In order to be the first to see our destination, I rode far ahead of the troop. Some time, at mid-afternoon, I saw the mountain appear like a foggy spot to the south. I immediately turned and ordered the caravan to stop. It was about a mile behind me. I did this, so that none of the captives would see Jabal Arash. It was better if they did not know where they were. We lifted them from the camels and camped.

The *asakir* had no idea why we were stopping that early. It was time to inform them. Once the prisoners had been given food and drink, I led the soldiers far enough away, where none of the prisoners were able to hear us. I had them form a circle around me, and told them what was to happen today. Had I told them that each of them would receive a thousand piaster, their joy could not have been greater. Catch Ibn Asl and all of his slavers in a trap! It was a thought that excited them. Each wanted to know the task he would be assigned, the role he would have to play. I could not answer these questions, since I first had to reconnoiter, which could only happen when it was dark. Ibn Asl had to be at the mountain by now. Had I approached it by daylight, I would most likely have been noticed.

The *asakir* received orders that, by no means, should there be any talk between them about our plan. Once we were finished, we formed a circle around the captives as had been done every evening. The camels rested outside this circle, guarded by one man.

The afternoon passed without us seeing another human being. The sun set and the *asakir* prayed the *maghrib*. Evening quickly came and I could start my reconnoiter. I expected to be absent for several hours, possibly even until morning. Despite his youth, I transferred command for the caravan to Bin Nil and instructed him on how to deal with every foreseeable situation. I then mounted onto my camel and rode toward my goal.

The task I had set for myself was not an easy one. I knew the location of the *hagalik* woods where I was to find the *raïs effendina*. It is at the southern end on the eastern bank of the swamp. However, the problem was how we would meet in the woods in darkness. In addition, I had another concern. Where was Ibn Asl and his men? Most likely they were at the southern end of the swamp. But if he decided to split his men in order to entrap me in the middle, it would be much easier for him to camp on the bank in the middle of the eastern swamp. In the morning, he could then dispatch half of his men to the right and the other half to the left around the swamp. In this way he would catch me from both the front and behind. If he was camped there now, I needed to pass by him on my way to the *amir*, and, if no fires were burning, I could unexpectedly stumble onto him. But he seemed to be a friend of nightly illumination. On the two evenings at the Hassaniah and the Maiyah al-Saratin, he had had several large fires burning. However, now he thought I was still far away and did not know anything of the *amir's* presence. Thus he probably felt safe, and would likely not spend the evening in darkness. In this case, his fires would give his camp away, and I could keep my distance from it.

My camel's fast pace took me southward. The stars had come out so that I could not mistake my direction. Half an hour later, I had reached the swamp area. From now on, I had to be watchful of the deceptive ground. The Maiyah al-Humma sends several inlets into the land, making it advisable to keep far to the east.

I had ridden an hour and then another. It must have been around nine o'clock by my reckoning, when I passed a solitary tree whose outline looked familiar but was indistinct against the sky. I rode toward it. Yes, it was the *hagalik*, below which I had sought shelter from the sun on an earlier visit. At the time, I had admired its mighty shape and had impressed it on my memory. Not very far from here, just a few hundred feet to the right, the *hagalik* woods I was looking for began.

I rode across and then along its margin. It lay like a tall, dark wall to my side, sending out individual bushes like outposts, between which I had to wend my way. Nowhere did I see a fire nor smell one. Ibn Asl was certainly not around here. In a subdued voice I imitated the deep laughter of a hyena. It sounds like "ommu ommu," but still resembles laughter. There was no answer. Slowly riding on, I repeated the signal several times. Finally, after the seventh or eighth time, I heard a voice on my right:

"*Effendi?*"

"Yes," I answered, halting my camel.

"Over here!"

I rode there. A man stepped up to me, stopped before my camel and looked at me, then said:

"Yes, it is you. Dismount! I will take you to the *amir.*"

"Is it far from here?"

"Somewhat. We posted a long sentry chain, so that you would have no difficulty finding the *amir.*"

"Take me to the sentry posted closest to the *amir.* He can hold on to my camel."

While we walked next to each other, I asked him, whether they had spotted Ibn Asl with his men.

"Yes," he replied. "They arrived shortly after noon and camped at the southernmost end of the *maiyah.*"

"Did you observe them after dark?"

"The *raïs effendina* went there."

"Do they have fires?"

"I do not know. I am not aware of anything, since I was on sentry duty at the time."

We passed several more *asakir*, until one of them took my animal to hold. My guide asked me to follow him deeper into the woods, but I requested that instead he call the *amir* to come to me. I had exerted myself more than the *amir* and would likely have more to do. Therefore, I wanted to spare myself the walk through the woods with its dense undergrowth of *nabak* bushes. The man left and soon returned with the *raïs effendina.* He was very pleased to see me, especially since I hadn't been certain whether I would be coming. He greeted me with a hearty handshake, and said:

"Ibn Asl and his men are here since noon, and are camped at the end of the *maiyah.*"

"Did they light fires?"

"Six of them, in any case probably for the many mosquitos. It would be unbearable without fires by the swamp. Here, in the dense, rather dry woods we are fortunately not bothered very much."

"Did you find out what plan Ibn Asl intends to follow?"

"No, how could I?"

"I thought you were there. Did you not spy on them?"

"I was very careful! If I had gotten close enough to understand them, I could also have been seen and caught."

"But often there are signs from which one can draw conclusions. Did you not notice anything of this nature?"

"No. They sat around the fires eating and chatting. But I did not understand what they were talking about; I was not close enough for this."

"Did you see Ibn Asl?"

"Yes. He sat by the first fire that one sees upon coming from here."

"How far is it there?"

"Almost half an hour."

"I must get there. Do you want to accompany me?"

"Very much so, provided you do no ask me to sit with Ibn Asl. You are much more capable of doing this."

I had left my bright *haïk* in camp, and now left my rifles, as well. We began walking, always between bushes, first to the right and then to the left of a swampy puddle which we evaded when it gave itself away by its phosphorescent reflection. More than a quarter of an hour later, I saw the light of the first fire, then followed the others, until I counted six. Only *gaful* trees grew here and no undergrowth. The group was camped without any special arrangement, a fire here, a fire there, just as chance or notion had dictated. We stood behind a thick bush, about sixty feet from the first fire where I saw Ibn Asl sitting. He was joined by his two officers and two other men, and we could hear them talk but without understanding individual words.

"I must get closer!" I said more to myself than to the *amir*. "I must know what they are talking about."

"For Allah's sake, what has come to your mind. You would be lost. They must see you!"

"No. I have already sneaked up under much more difficult conditions. This is childsplay."

"And I tell you that you will not get me another step closer!"

"I don't even want to; I'll go alone. Straight between here and the fire stand two big trees whose trunks throw a broad shadow. If I creep on the ground along this shadow, I cannot be distinguished from it, and have the first and then the second tree as cover. The last one has a strong branch about my height, pointing in our direction. If I swing myself up onto it, I will sit, hidden by branches and leaves, at most fifteen paces from the fire and can overhear everything that is said."

"And how will you get back?"

"The same way I got there."

"No, *effendi*, I cannot allow this! I do not want you to risk your life!"

"Will I not risk it tomorrow when we fight? Will not everyone risk it then? If not now, when? And what if the fight can be avoided by my taking a risk now?"

"Do you think it possible?"

"Yes. Maybe I will learn something, which may help me decide on a plan that makes any resistance by our opponents impossible."

He reached for me trying to hold me back, but was not fast enough. I quickly stepped from behind the bush, ducked down, and crept forward in the shadows. It was no feat. In order to produce plenty of smoke to repel the mosquitos, moist branches had been ignited. This caused such a thick smoke that, at times, one could not even see through it. Since the swamp air was heavy and oppressive, it kept drifting along the ground. Taking advantage of it, I reached the first, then the second tree and was soon sitting in the branches. Only two minutes had passed since the *raïs effendina's* futile grip. I was exceptionally lucky; just when

I had found comfortable seating and pricked up my ears, I heard shouting from farther off, drawing my attention.

"The *shaykh*, the *shaykh al-Balad*!" I heard. "He is here! He has come at last."

Truly, there he was walking past the last fire, leading his camel, where he had been told where to find Ibn Asl. Discipline prevented the men from following him. He made his animal lie down and walked toward Ibn Asl's fire, where he was welcomed with visible satisfaction. I guessed its reason. He had been their spy. One of Ibn Asl's men could not have done this, for, had I seen him, I would have recognized him and become suspicious. The *shaykh*, however, would have had plenty of excuses which I would have had to believe.

"Sit down and report!" Ibn Asl asked. "Did you see them?"

"No," he said, while he sat down.

"No? Then you told me wrong. They will either come several days from now or not at all."

"They will come!" the *shaykh* insisted. "I saw their tracks."

"Once you see the tracks, you soon have the man. You should not have rested until you really saw them."

"It was too late, turning dark. The *effendi* with his Bin Nil had left very visible tracks. I followed them. They went dead straight until they suddenly turned south. He must have ridden toward Bir Safi. This morning, I kept close watch. They had to come, but did not. I waited close to noon, and since I had not seen them by this time, I assumed that they had taken a different direction. This could only be the northern one. Riding straight north, I had to come across their tracks, since they later needed to turn more to the east. And this is what happened. Evening was near when I came across their tracks, leading east."

"Naturally, straight for Jabal Arash Qul?"

"No, oddly not. If they kept riding straight from there, they would have left the *jabal* far to the south."

"Why that? This *effendi* always has a purpose, even with his smallest actions!"

"There cannot be a particular purpose here. They simply erred. No one from this area is with them. Their Fassara guide cannot know our area."

"But the *effendi* himself! From everything he told you, one can conclude that he knows the *jabal* and also the *maiyah*."

"He is a stranger, a Christian dog, from so far away, that most likely he has only been there once. It is no wonder then when an error occurs. They will eventually have turned south, after all."

"They will? I would have preferred if you had said: they did! Then I would be certain. You should have followed them further!"

"It was impossible. With evening approaching, I could no longer see their tracks. I also had to come here, since you were waiting for my report. Consider the distances I had to cover in this short time! An ordinary camel could not possibly have accomplished it. It was well that you allowed me to ride your Jabal Garfah mare. She carried me like a storm across the savanna."

So, he had ridden the slaver's famous white camel mare, the mare Ibn Asl had to thank for the success of so many of his ventures. Had she not enabled him to escape me at Wadi al-Bard, some time ago? But the camel the *shaykh* had arrived on had the color of ordinary camels. How could this be explained? Did he exchange the white mare with another *hajin* prior to his arrival here? I was quickly enlightened, when Ibn Asl asked:

"If only the *giaur* had known that my camel mare is always stabled with you when I am on my ship, since I can't take her along. He did not see her by chance?"

"No. Even had he seen her, he would not have recognized her. Whenever you leave her with me, she is tinted, so that no one knows what a famous animal I have with me. Look at her! Can she be distinguished from a common *hajin*?"

"Indeed! I would be ashamed if she actually looked like one. Just look at her build! Someone in the know sees at once the kind of animal she is. But this is a side issue. We must not talk about my camel, but of this *effendi* with his men. And yet, why must the mare lie here when she is hungry? She has traveled a long way and should eat some. Hobble her forelegs that she cannot get too far way!"

One of the men sitting with him, got up to take care of the camel. The magnificent mare could now graze. I observed her movements with almost greater attention than I expended on listening to her master. This camel, ah, it had to become mine! I would rather let Ibn Asl escape than to let this mare get away!

Ibn Asl was visibly disappointed by the results the *shaykh al-Balad* had delivered. He continued:

"Since you do not know the place where the caravan with the captives is camped, we cannot go ahead with our plan. That's just too bad! Twenty of these *asakir* dogs! And we are five times greater in numbers! How easy it would have been to surround them on the open savanna!"

There, I heard it! I had figured right. How well it was that I had taken the detour north, east, and finally to the south. Had we kept to the straight route, Ibn Asl would have attacked us tonight before we even reached Jabal Arash Qul.

The *shaykh* responded to the accusation:

"It probably serves us well that this did not happen. You know the *effendi*. He is watchful and does not miss anything. It would have been impossible to surprise him."

"He would, however, have been surrounded by a hundred men! Consider that! He would have had to surrender without mercy, being unable to raise a hand."

"Do not believe this! He, surrender? You know him even better than I do. I am convinced you should doubt your own words. There would surely have been a fight. Figure that every *askari* would have killed at least one of us, and you must count more for the *effendi*. I am also certain that the *giaur* would immediately have turned on you."

"He would not have seen me. I know what I owe myself. I pay my men well, for which they must fight. My safety is much too important that they could expect me to partake in a fight. This is not cowardice but calculation and caution by me. Would you expect me to put myself where the bullets whistle by? But should they come, they will be ours, leaving them unable to fire a shot."

"Then do not make your preparations too late. The *effendi* said that he would arrive at Jabal Arash Qul one hour after the prayer of sunrise, and it is certain that he will do as he said. This is why the group you intend to send north must leave here by midnight, at the latest."

"I will send them off even earlier. Then, you are convinced that my people, hiding in the runoff, will not be noticed?"

"Yes. If one walks for just a few minutes up this runoff, it widens and is filled there with *kittr* bushes, offering good cover. If, at daybreak, a man climbs up on a rock outcropping, he can see the caravan's approach. Once it has passed, one can follow it slowly while being unnoticed, until it arrives on the trail between the steep walls of the *jabal* and the *maiyah's* crocodiles. Then, the group hiding in the runoff will be behind the caravan, while our other men are at the ready in front of them. Just when the prisoners are to be thrown into the swamp, I, the leader of the first group, will fire a shot. The result will not be in doubt. The *effendi* will realize that he is surrounded by a superior number and that resistance would be pure madness. He will surrender. To facilitate this, you should accept conditions you do not need to keep later."

This was excellent! The *shaykh al-Balad* intended to head for the same runoff, where I planned to be, ready for the ambush. The trap to be set for me was exactly the same one I would set for them. How good it was that I had crept up on them against the *amir's* will."

"How many men will you assign to me?" the *shaykh* asked.

"How many do you need?"

"Half of your one hundred would be just right, but I will not need them, I can make do with fewer."

"I will give you forty, which leaves me sixty. You head out an hour before midnight, about an hour from now. Is it necessary that we stay in contact?"

"No. It would be difficult to maintain anyway. It would need to be done around the long *maiyah*, which would take far too much time. Our plan is so simple. As soon as there is daylight, you occupy the southern end of the bay. The caravan will come from the north, with me following it. As soon as you hear my first shot, it is time. How fortunate it was that the *effendi* came too late to Hagasi! The *raïs effendina* had just left. Had they met, the *amir* would have stayed, and we would have had to watch your father and the captives be thrown into the swamp. This takes care of everything. I will try to sleep a little, being tired from the long ride. Wake me up when my group is ready to leave."

He lay down, and I could then leave, it being obvious that nothing of importance could still be overheard. I used the moment when another smoke cloud descended between my tree and the fire, swung down, lay down on the ground, and quickly crept away. I was not noticed on my return to the *amir*, who was still standing at the same spot behind the bush where I had left him.

"*Effendi*, I trembled for you!" he said. "This kind of recklessness can cost you your life."

"Oh no! You will hear right now the exceptional benefits it brought me. I now know these people's plan."

I told him what I had overheard. When I was finished, he whispered excitedly to me:

"They are entering the trap, they will, *effendi*! But by what cunning will you get the *shaykh* with his forty men in front of you, instead of him following you?"

"No cunning will help there. I must take them prisoner."

"This is dangerous since it cannot be accomplished without an attack and resistance."

"It's not dangerous. I occupy the place before he arrives with his men. They either must surrender or get killed to the last man."

"But you have only twenty *asakir* with you."

"As it is, I will, of course, need them all to guard our prisoners. Can you give me forty men to take along?"

"Gladly."

"You still have enough then. At daybreak, Ibn Asl will occupy the narrow passage. You follow him. Leaving the prisoners under a good guard, I will come from the north, which brings our opponents between us. I am now telling you the same the *shaykh* said earlier: 'When you hear the first shot, it's time'."

"Well, then I will throw myself on the enemy."

"But let me urge you about one thing: I heard that Ibn Asl never participates in a fight. He will probably stay back here, too. Take care that he doesn't escape. Rather dispatch a small group of maybe ten men to keep a watch on him and not let him get away."

"I will do my best. When do you want the forty men?"

"Right away! Go back and get them ready. I will soon follow you."

"You do not want to return with me right away? Why not?"

"Because I want to capture the slaver's white Jabal Garfah mare for myself."

"Leave it be! You could spoil everything. If you are caught, all will be given away."

"Catch me? Bah!"

"But once they notice her missing, they will figure on a thief and conclude that there are people around. It will cause suspicion."

"They will think that the mare was poorly tied up and walked away and can easily be found by tomorrow. Aside from the great value of this camel, I have another important reason to seize her. Should Ibn Asl not partake in the fight, he can, despite all caution, escape from you. If he then has the mare, no one can catch him. If I have her, I will catch him, no matter what he tries to do."

"This is correct, but I am still afraid that you will be noticed."

He continued to oppose me for a brief time and then left. I crept in an arc around the fires. The *hajin* stood in the dark by a bush, nibbling its leaves. It let me approach easily. Ibn Asl did not know how to train such an animal. It should have taken flight on my approach, or at least snorted. I untied its forelegs, slung the leading rope from the halter and led it away. It followed willingly as if it were mine. Taking a detour, I returned to my earlier position, then walked toward the *hagalik* woods, where the *raïs effendina* waited greatly excited to see me. The forty men were ready.

"Allah! It worked," he said. "*Effendi*, you are a very dangerous camel thief. You should get life in prison!"

"Pardon me, high representative of Egyptian justice, I steal only from thieves and robbers!" I laughed. "I will leave right away. Are these men equipped with enough material to tie up forty men?"

"They have everything. We brought it from the ship."

"Then, farewell, and tomorrow a victorious, happy wiedersehn!"

"May Allah so provide!"

"Don't let Ibn Asl escape!" I warned him once more. Then, we left, with one of the *askari* leading my camel, while another took the white *hajin* by its halter.

I first headed for the solitary *hagalik*, then took the same direction back that I had come. Because we were walking, we advanced much more slowly than before. Several hours passed before we reached the northern end of the swamp. We then walked around its western border. Eventually, we saw the dark, compact mass of the mountain rise before us. I called on my memory, so as not to miss the runoff. Twice, I failed, but then found it after all.

The first task now was to hide the two camels, which we could not take with us. I led them a sufficient distance away, staked them down and left a guard with them. Then, we walked up the runoff until we reached the little valley.

Its walls were not very steep. Thirty men had to climb up and spread out. They received orders to remain totally quiet until I initiated the attack. They were to take cover behind boulders, so that they could defend and protect themselves from bullets should the enemy resist. If one of our opponents should come climbing up while it was still dark, two or three men were to get him by his throat so that he could not scream and then take care of him with a knife stab.

With the remaining ten, I walked a short distance back and then climbed partly up one side of the runoff's slope. We sat down there and waited to let the *shaykh al-Balad* with his group pass, so we could then follow them.

He had wanted to leave by eleven o'clock at night, and we had begun our walk shortly after ten o'clock. Most likely, we would have to wait only an hour, but it actually took much, much longer. They arrived shortly before daybreak. He had not hurried, knowing that my caravan would arrive only an hour past daybreak. We heard them walk past us, after which we climbed quietly down and followed them. Near the entry to the valley, we stopped. Of course, the slavers thought they were alone and talked loudly with each other. They found places between and around the bushes and demonstrated by their lively laughter that they were in a very good, victorious mood.

When it came to jolliness, the *shaykh*, despite his rank he ought to actually maintain, was ahead of everyone. He joked in high spirits and spoke of the booty they would take including its distribution. I learned later that he had been promised plenty for his participation. The good man had speculated wrongly and got something very different.

Daylight was coming, when I heard him say that he intended to have a look for the morning red. I thought he would climb the valley's inside wall, but instead he came toward us.

"Bend down!" I whispered to my men, while I did so quickly myself. I didn't want the *shaykh* spotting us too soon. He came toward us, walking slowly. When he almost bumped into me, I rose before him and took him with two hands by his throat.

"Tie up only his hands, not the feet!" I ordered the *asakir*. They complied.

I did not squeeze his throat so hard that he lost consciousness but threatened him, whispering in his ear:

"A sound from you, and my knife will enter your heart! If you promise to be quiet, nod!"

He nodded. I did not expect any resistance from him. Fright was sufficiently powerful, and it showed later that he was a coward who was good only for betrayal but not for a fight. He had assumed the leadership of the forty slavers, convinced that he would not find any resistance from us.

I left eight men where we stood. Two accompanied me with the *shaykh* up the runoff to a point where our voices could not be heard in the valley. The two *asakir* held him on each side. With my knife in hand, I let him feel its point against his chest, while asking him:

"Do you know me?"

"Yes. You . . . are the . . . *effendi*," he stammered. "Why do you treat me like an enemy? Did you not tell me that you respect my authority?"

"And you believed this! Oh, you, the greatest and topmost of all blockheads! Only a brainless fellow like you could have thought you could deceive me. But while you were convinced you were cheating on me, I tripped you up."

"You are mistaken, by Allah, utterly mistaken! I came as your friend, your benefactor and admirer."

"And the forty men you brought along, are also my admirers, benefactors, and friends?"

"Yes. I gathered them in the surroundings of Hagasi and led them here to help you against your enemies."

"Against my prisoners, you wanted to say! I don't need any help against them. And why did you hide here?"

"Only to wait for you. I do not understand how you can think that these men are connected with Ibn Asl!"

"Shut up!" I told him. "Your duplicity is obvious. As of today, it has come to an end. I saw through you the moment we met. You had no inkling that I was deceiving you. You lent Ibn Asl your horse. That gave you away. When I arrived with Bin Nil in the boat, I had earlier met the *raïs effendina* on his ship and had reported to him about you. He was then just as friendly to you as to me. We did this to lure Ibn Asl here through you. We accomplished it since your stupidity is almost greater than your wickedness. Now, Ibn Asl is here, but the *raïs effendina* is, too. He will capture Ibn Asl just like I did you. We will surround him and his sixty men on the rocky trail, just as you had wanted to do to us. Yesterday, without you knowing, I sat near you by your fire and heard everything you reported and also what was discussed afterward."

"This is impossible!" he shouted, without thinking that his words constituted an admission.

"I shall prove it to you. You arrived on the tinted camel mare. She lay down. Ibn Asl ordered one of the two men who sat there, in addition to you and his officers, to get her to rise and to hobble her forelegs, so that she could feed. Was she then not missed?"

"Yes. She was gone; she must have gotten lost."

"No, she didn't get lost; I took her. I shall prove this to you in a moment."

Turning to one of the *asakir*, I asked him: "Can you ride a camel?"

"Quite well, *effendi*," came the reply.

"Your comrades are camped with the prisoners north of the *maiyah*. Get them quickly! Go down the runoff, turn left, until you meet a sentry at some distance, who I left with the two camels. If you don't find them right away, you can shout. Once there, mount the slaver's Jabal Garfah mare and ride straight east, past the *maiyah's* end. By then, day will have come, and you will see my tracks which will take you exactly north to the camp. Hurry up, and get the others to be just as quick!"

The man left while I continued speaking with the *shaykh*:

"You just heard where our camp is located. You wanted to find it yesterday, so that you could attack us on the open savanna. But I suspected this and took a detour. While you looked for me in the west, I was long since north of here. That an honest man is always smarter and wiser than a criminal, you cannot and do not want to believe until it is demonstrated to you to your detriment. You've heard enough now. Do you still deny everything?"

"*Effendi*, how many *asakir* are with you here?" the coward asked.

"More than enough to finish you off. We arrived here an hour before you and occupied the heights, as you noticed, and also the entry to the valley, so that not a single one of you would escape. You, their leader, has been captured. If you command your men to surrender and hand over their weapons, I will exert my influence with the *amir* for a milder punishment."

"Ya Allah! Hand over our weapons. Surrender! Forty men!"

"Yes, obviously, this sounds different than earlier, when you so victoriously distributed the booty already. Answer my question! I don't have time. Say yes, and you will at least keep your lives. Say no, and we will gun you all down!"

"*Effendi*, be kind, be merciful! Let me see how many men you have."

"You don't believe me? I do not lie; that ought to be enough for you."

"Oh, you are smart! Whatever you cannot achieve by force, you try to accomplish by cunning. It will be the same here, because . . . oh, Allah, oh Muhammad! It is happening! There it goes!"

Wild shouting had erupted in the valley. Shots were fired; then it was suddenly still.

"There's proof of my words' truth," I told him. "Come! Your body will serve as my shield. Should someone take a shot at me, the bullet will hit you. Remember that!"

I pulled him along up the runoff. At the entry to the valley stood the eight *asakir* with their muskets at the ready. Daylight was coming, and it was possible to see sufficiently. At these latitudes, day comes as quickly as night.

"What happened, why the shots?" I asked.

"With daylight breaking," I was told, "some fellows tried to climb the valley slopes. Our men higher up forbade it, and when they were not obeyed, they fired."

"What's the situation inside? It became quickly quiet."

"The slavers hid under the bushes."

"There you see the courage of your heroes," I told the *shaykh*. "Come with me inside, but give me the least reason, and you'll get the knife!"

The knife was in my right hand, so I grabbed him by his neck with the left and pushed him ahead of me into the valley. Upon my signal, the nine *asakir* followed.

"Have a look up there and notice the muskets!" I demanded of the *shaykh*.

The *asakir* had found cover behind boulders or built-up stone embankments. One could not see anything of them, except their musket muzzles that pointed downward from all sides. A look at the bushes almost caused me to laugh, although my situation was not entirely safe. One of the fellows could easily have taken a shot at me, but none had the courage. As it was, they did not even know yet who had surrounded them. They had only seen the musket muzzles and had immediately taken cover. As if the bushes could have protected them! Here an arm, an elbow, there a shoe, or a bare foot peeked from the greenery. All lay still; none dared move.

"Where are your heroes?" I asked the *shaykh*. "Order them to show and defend themselves!"

"The *effendi*, the foreign *effendi*!", it now sounded from the bushes.

"I give you only a minute," I continued. "If you haven't ordered them by then to hand over their weapons, you will get the knife blade to its handle into your body."

"Will I be pardoned?" he asked.

"I promise you leniency. You cannot ask for more. Pardon is up to the *raïs effendina*. Be quick before the minute is over!"

He turned back and forth under my grip. When I raised the knife, ready to stab, he screamed from fright:

"Let me off, *effendi*! I will do what you ask."

"There will be no letting you off. You are my prisoner. Order your men to come here singly to hand over their weapons so they can be tied up, just as you will be. If one makes the slightest suspicious move, the people up there will shoot him. Now, hurry up, time's running out!"

Fear for his life caused him to give the order. His men obeyed in that one after another crept from below the bushes. A quarter of an hour later, all were disarmed and tied up. The first act of today's drama had played out according to my expectation, something we all could be satisfied with.

We now had to await the arrival of Bin Nil with the caravan. I walked down the runoff and sat down outside. Almost an hour passed until I saw them coming. Bin Nil rode side by side with the messenger. When they saw me, they began to gallop in order to arrive before the caravan did.

"*Effendi*, we were concerned for you," the faithful youngster said when he made his animal kneel down next to me and jumped from the saddle. "When you did not return by morning, we thought you might have had an accident. Did the enemy fall into your hands?"

"Yes. Are your prisoners aware of this?"

"No. Your messenger spoke quietly to me. But they saw the Jabal Garfah mare, and figured that it had been taken from Ibn Asl, their master. They concluded from it that an event had occurred which, while not dangerous, must have been rather unwelcome. Where are the men you captured?"

"They are up there in the valley. We will take your prisoners there, as well, but leave the camels down here under guard of some men."

When the caravan arrived, the prisoners were taken from their camel mounts. We left their feet free, so that they could walk up the runoff to the valley. One could see that the sight of the camel mare had filled them with concern. They looked searchingly around and exchanged questions and answers. Only the *Faqir al-Fuqara* and Abd Asl appeared as though they had not noticed anything and felt secure.

"*Effendi*," The *Faqir al-Fuqara* asked, "why are we being brought here? What is to happen here?"

"A pleasant surprise," I replied.

"Are you mocking us? It seems that we can never expect anything pleasant from you. I came into your power through the fault of one of the greatest devils, and although I did not do anything to you, you drag me around like a wild animal. You are neither my master nor owner of my rights. I demand that you untie me and give me a camel, as you promised, so that I can go home."

"Where is your home?"

"At present in Khartoum."

"Then be patient for a little while longer. You will ride in the company of many of your friends there."

"I do not care for company. I came alone and want to leave alone. You must let me go, for you have no power over me."

"And none at all over us!" Abd Asl insisted. "Where does the *raïs effendina* get permission to assign you his rights? And if he were allowed to do this, why are you dragging us in all sorts of directions across the savanna? I demand to be taken to Khartoum!"

"Your wish will soon be fulfilled," I told him.

"But when? Today, we had to take a detour to arrive here. Do you think this is wise? Should you meet my son, a real possibility, you will surely be lost."

"I have met him repeatedly without being lost."

"You were lucky, something you will perhaps not experience again. Should you cross his path once more, you will be judged by Allah. You know how many warriors my son has. Here, on the savanna, you will be unable to resist him. He will squash your small bunch! The Prophet cannot possibly accept that a Christian thinks himself superior to us, without being punished. His avenging sword is already flaring over your head. Who knows at what moment it will hit and shatter you!"

"I will show you over whom it is flaring. Follow me up here!"

The camels had their saddles taken off and were now grazing. Three *asakir* remained with them. The other soldiers took the prisoners into their midst and led them after me up the runoff. Imagine how shocked the newcomers were when, arriving in the valley, they saw forty of their comrades lying tied up on the ground. Abd Asl cried out angrily and shouted such abuse and insults that Bin Nil applied the whip to silence him. The others remained quiet. All of them had their feet tied up again and were put with the others.

I was able to leave now. The twenty men that had accompanied me to the Fassara *duar*, remained to guard the prisoners and the camels; the forty the *raïs effendina* had assigned me yesterday, accompanied me. Bin Nil was to command the former group, but he asked so fervently to join me that I gave him permission to do so. I thought that I could entrust command of this group to the Fassara guide and the old *askari onbashi*, something he had done before. A surprise was out of the question, and since the prisoners were all well tied, there was no reason why twenty *asakir*, whose faithfulness was without doubt, would require a special representative to supervise them. They might also have felt insulted by it.

It had been determined that I would arrive at Jabal Arash Qul one hour after sunrise. When we now left, it was a bit later, which could not be of any disadvantage. I urgently impressed on the *asakir*, who stayed behind, to maintain a good watch. For specific situations, I issued certain rules of conduct and was now convinced that no irregularity, no mistake, could happen. It was unthinkable that I could have committed a mistake in so doing, yet found out later that I had been guilty of too great a trust.

While I had yesterday kept to the eastern side of the *maiyah*, we now marched north on its western side. Here, the space between the *maiyah* and the mountain was the width of a quarter hour's walk, but various bays and peninsulas reduced or enlarged this width from time to time. The mountain was bare on top and greenery grew only at its foot. The farther we proceeded the higher the mountain loomed and the steeper became its walls. And the *maiyah* came ever closer to it.

After we had walked for some time, the swamp closed in from the right, so that in places we could only walk in twos. Ahead, individual *gaful* trees appeared, indicating that we were approaching the place where we could expect meeting Ibn Asl and his men. When I drew Bin Nil's attention to this, who walked next to me, he said: "Shall we not stop, *effendi*? One of us should creep ahead to reconnoiter where the slavers are?"

"That's superfluous in bright daylight."

"But you have spied before by day!"

"Because the terrain allowed for it. But here the space to move is too narrow. In any case, Ibn Asl has posted a sentry, who must only watch the narrow trail to spot a spy coming. No, we will simply march on."

"But then we walk smack into their hands!"

"That's what I want! They will not shoot at us right away, but hail us. Ibn Asl wants me alive and will have given orders not to shoot me. If I therefore walk ahead, you will be safe. Stay behind a bit with the others, and let me go about thirty paces ahead of you. When I stop, you also stop, until I order you to come."

"Sadly, I must obey you. I would rather stay by your side with the decision that close at hand."

"Not yet. Ibn Asl will not show himself until we are amidst the actual narrows, which we haven't reached yet."

"But if the *raïs effendina* is not in position yet?"

"That doesn't pose any danger to us. We would drive Ibn Asl toward him. There's nothing to fear for us, since we have no enemy behind us. There's only one thing to fear, which is that Ibn Asl escapes."

We continued our walk. I went ahead by myself with the others following at the requested distance. When I had passed the first *gaful* trees, the narrowing path turned sharply to the right with the bay of the swamp beginning here.

Coming from the left, it penetrated far into the mountain, which rose steeply and formed, if I may express it this way, a hollow cone, on whose walls no human foot could possibly find traction. To my left lay the swamp, completely covered by *Umm Sufah*, between which, open, oily-shining water spaces stared like oozing witches' eyes at me. Higher up, rocks and boulders had broken off, tumbled down, and were now littering the trail. Many were covered by moist mosses or with rotting, stinking plant remains, through and over which my slipping feet proceeded only with caution.

Whoever was attacked here from the front and rear simultaneously, could not possibly defend himself and had to surrender. To the right, the steep rock walls offered no escape and to the left was the yawning swamp, from whose rushes and *Umm Sufa* stared the repulsive heads of numerous crocodiles. It was a place filled with terror and ruin. So, I alone was to be spared here, to be saved for even more awful pains. But my *asakir* were to be pushed into the swamp, thrown in, a meal for saurians, of which there were plenty. It seemed they made their living by the stronger devouring the weaker.

Would it be inhuman if I made it the slavers' same fate? How much blood was already on their hands! How many thousands and thousands of Negroes had been made unhappy by them! It seemed to me that it would not be too harsh a punishment tossing them into the *maiyah*, but rather a just one. As you did to me, so I do to you. This is the law of the desert, just like that of the prairie, the savanna, the pampas, and the llanos of South America, and if . . . but I could not finish this thought, for not far from me sounded a loud, preemptory voice:

"Hold it! Not a step more or we will shoot!"

I stopped and looked closely ahead. Behind two *gaful* trees standing next to each other, with several boulders in front of them, three men had to be hiding, for I saw as many musket barrels pointing at me – a fatal situation, for it took only the squeeze of a finger and deadly lead would enter my body.

"Who are you?" I asked, acting as if I were facing only one opponent.

"I am an old acquaintance of yours. Do you want to see me?" came the answer.

"Naturally!"

"Put your weapons down; then I will step out!"

"Would I be such a fool?"

I leaped for the next tree, behind whose trunk I found good cover. The men before me had to be in some quandary. They had arrived in time there and had waited for a signal from the *shaykh al-Balad*. But I had come too close to them. No way could they let me come closer or even pass, since they were supposed to show themselves only after that signaling shot of the *shaykh's*. What to do now? To gain some time by small talk? It almost seemed the only way, for the speaker replied:

"If we want, we can easily force you, but you shall learn in a peaceful way what we ask of you."

"Tell me, then."

"Not like this. Leave your weapons and walk to the boulder between us! I will do the same."

"Fine, I will come. But if I see any weapon, even the smallest knife, you will end up in a place from which you will not return!"

I stuck my revolvers in my pant's pockets, leaned the rifle to the tree trunk and put my knife next to it. I could have left the revolvers, too, since I was totally sure of what I was doing. A look back told me that my men had stopped. The foremost ones, including Bin Nil, stood around a corner behind some bushes. While I could see them, the fellow I was talking with, could not. I knew who he was. I had recognized him by his voice. It was Ibn Asl's first-lieutenant. But why didn't Ibn Asl talk to me himself?

"You did not expect me here, did you?"

"Yes and no," I answered calmly. "I knew that you expected me here. But I also say 'no,' because I thought Ibn Asl would address me, not you."

"Allah, you knew that we would expect you here?"

"Bah! I know even more; I know it all. You are waiting now for a signal the *shaykh al-Balad* is to give you. A shot from his musket will tell you the beginning of hostilities?"

"Allah is all-knowing. He hears, sees and knows all. But how can you know of the *shaykh* and his intention?"

"You will learn how. Call Ibn Asl!"

"He is not here."

"I know that he is here."

"You know it? Then your famous all-knowing is not so remarkable as you want to make us believe. If you knew where Ibn Asl presently is, you would show yourself far less confidently than you do now!"

The words gave me pause to think. Had I only left Bin Nil with the prisoners! I figured right away that Ibn Asl had changed his plan as far as it concerned his person. He likely did not trust the *shaykh* to have sufficient prudence, and had assigned command here to his two officers. He must have gone to the northern end of the *maiyah* to take the forty slavers from behind me, relieving the shaykh. Fortunately, he had come too late. We had captured these men already. If I told myself that, he alone could not have liberated them but needed to have other men along, or some unforeseen coincidence to turn events in his favor. In any case, his capture was not as certain as we had thought until now. Of course, I did not let on my concern, but replied with a lofty smile:

"You needn't tell me where he is. I know he is here by the *maiyah*. If he isn't there ahead with his sixty men, he went for the forty, which were to wait for me in the valley at the end of the runoff."

"*Ya latif* – my goodness! He knows of the runoff!" exclaimed the first-lieutenant. "Who told you?"

"I know: that's enough. I told you already that I know everything. You nincompoops should finally tell yourselves that you cannot deceive me, or set a trap for me. The trap here, I set, not you."

"You? This trap?" he laughed derisively. "I do not want to claim that Allah blinded you, since you could see only me so far. But let me tell you that you are surrounded with your twenty *asakir*. You earlier called us numbskulls, yet never in my life have I come across a greater blockhead than you!"

"Really? Are you going to prove this to me, you numbskull of numbskulls?"

"The proof is easy. Was it not the greatest foolishness there is, to tell the *shaykh al-Balad* that you intended to take your captives here and throw them to the crocodiles?"

"A foolishness this was supposed to be? Man, I could cry from pity for you. It wasn't foolishness, but smart calculation, which shows to be right on at this very moment."

I now told him how I had begun it and what I had achieved. He now clapped his hands and exclaimed:

"Oh, Allah, oh Muhammad! That . . . that . . .one should believe?"

"Even if you cannot believe it, you will! Where is the shaykh with his forty men? Why does he not give the agreed upon signal? Why does he not shoot?"

"He will come; he will surely come yet. Even if he would not come, you could not triumph. You have only twenty men, but we are more than sixty and will . . ."

"Nothing you will, nothing at all! You can't do anything else but surrender to our mercy."

"Do you think us mad?"

"Since you entered my trap so willingly and inconsiderately, I think it is you who is mad. But your question proceeds from a very wrong condition. You think your rear is free, which isn't the case at all, since behind you now stands the raïs effendina with his asakir."

"The . . . raïs . . . effen . . . dina?" he stammered. You are lying!"

"I'm telling the truth. And I have neither twenty men, but many, many more. At first, I had only twenty, but as I told you, last night the raïs effendina assigned more asakir to me. I demand herewith that you surrender your weapons! Should you refuse, what will happen to you is what you wanted to do to us: we will throw you to the crocodiles."

"Effendi, what has happened to your mind? You want to get me through lies . . ."

"Be quiet, and do not insult me!" I interrupted him sternly. "I'll show you kindness by proving the truth of my words in order to prevent useless blood shedding. Raïs effendina! Amir!"

I called these two titles across the swamp's bay by putting my hollow hands to my mouth.

"Here we are, *effendi*, here!" it came back, and from much closer than I had thought.

"Well?" I asked the first-lieutenant. "Can you hear that the *amir* isn't standing more than two hundred paces behind you?"

"Who was it?"

"Who else is it supposed to be? My shout told him that I am here, after which he will now advance. I advise you to surrender. You shall also get to see my men."

I turned and waved. That's when Bin Nil with his forty *asakir* broke from behind the bushes and advanced. The men held their muskets at the ready. Although they had to walk one behind the other, since the trail arced, there was no need to point their guns forward, but their bullets would fly across the bay into the slavers. When the first-lieutenant saw my men coming, he shouted:

"Oh Allah! These are almost a hundred men! I will not let myself be caught by them. *Effendi*, I will leave, I will!":

He leaped for the trees behind which he had earlier hidden to pick up his musket, and ran back, followed by the two others who had accompanied him. We advanced a short distance after them to where I found sufficient cover for us. I did not think we would see any fighting, yet I positioned my men in such a way that they were hidden behind boulders, trees, and bushes.

I now waited for what would happen. I was ready, but had to find out first what was going to happen on the *amir's* side. The first-lieutenant had received a healthy shock. Misled by the long line of my men, he had thought them more numerous than they actually were. It suited me fine. The more superior he thought us to be, the larger had to be his worry and thus his willingness to surrender.

Then I heard loud voices on the bay's other side, but was unable to understand what was said. A shot cracked, another, a third and a fourth. Men shouted. Then it turned quiet again. A quarter hour passed, after which a man came walking around the trail's curvature, wearing the *amir's askari* uniform. Knowing him, I stepped from behind the tree trunk. There could be no deceit. When he saw me, he hurried toward me.

"The slavers let you pass?" I hopefully asked.

"Yes, *effendi*, they had to; they surrendered their weapons," he replied.

"God be thanked! But shots were fired?"

"The *amir* wanted to tell them that we were serious. Four of them were shot; only then did their officers ask for mercy. You are to come with your men to help tie the hands of the captives."

Following this request, we marched forward and soon came across the first enemies. The ones I could see still held their muskets, but gave no sign that they would use them against us.

"*Effendi!*" I heard the *amir's* voice.

"Here I am," I responded.

"Our opponents have surrendered. Their hands are to be tied behind their backs, then they must form a single line and march along the narrow path to the runoff. Let none escape!"

With the narrowness of the trail, this was the only way. Often, only two men could stand side-by-side. The ropes that tied them, just as the seized weapons, had to be handed from one man to another. When I was done and the *amir* reported the same, we began to move, my *asakir* first, then the captives, followed by the *amir* with his men. Once the trail widened, we had the slavers double up with the *asakir* marching by their side, their weapons ready to prevent possible escapes. Later, we could continue even more comfortably, which is why the *amir* joined me to talk. Of course, he was just as delighted as me about the success of our enterprise, and just as annoyed at not having captured Ibn Asl.

"Where is he?"

"Didn't his first-lieutenant tell you?"

"He admitted that he had gone to the runoff. He seems to have arrived at this thought only this morning. Maybe, we can still catch him."

"Hardly, provided he has not been captured already."

"By our guards at the runoff's valley?"

"No, but by the camel guards. Before he reached the valley, he had to pass by these men."

"How many are they?"

"When I was there, I thought three sufficient, but when I left, I ordered two additional ones to join the three."

"That was enough. It would have been impossible for Ibn Asl to accomplish anything against five men."

"Not by force, but how about by cunning?"

"What ploy could he use?"

"Hmm! Do all your *asakir* know him?"

"No."

"Then we can expect him to pose as someone else. If he is believed, he could cause us some major damage."

"This is true. Let's hurry!"

"Shall I not go ahead? The sooner one of us arrives there, the easier it will be to make up for a mistake that might have happened."

"Yes, hurry on and take your Bin Nil along upon whom you can rely. We will follow as quickly as possible."

Unfortunately, it became apparent that my concern had not been unfounded. When I arrived with Bin Nil at the northern face of the mountain and saw the grazing camels, I immediately realized that not all was in order. Next to where the camels grazed stood five guards, and inside this semicircle, where the runoff entered the mountain, a group of men was gathered that ought not to have been there. Something improper had clearly happened. Of the five men two lay on the ground, while the other three were bent over, busying themselves with the prone men. When these three saw us coming, they jumped up and stood there awaiting our arrival. They were the Fassara guide and the old *askari* whom I had assigned command to, together with another soldier. Already from afar I noticed that they were uncommonly embarrassed.

"What happened here?" I asked. "What's the reason for these two lying on the ground, unmoving?"

"They are . . . injured, *effendi*," the *onbashi* replied.

'"By whom?"

"By a stranger."

"How was that possible? Did you not know the man?"

"No. I never saw him, and this one," – with that he pointed to the soldier – "who stood guard with the others, did not know him."

"And the other guards?"

"Whether they knew the man, I do not know. I cannot ask them, since they are unconscious."

"But they are two, and together with this soldier, make three. I had ordered five to stay with the camels!"

"*Effendi*, now there are five here," said the oldster, while he lowered his eyes.

"Five!" I said angrily. "There's now a total of ten soldiers here, meaning there are only ten instead of fifteen with the prisoners. What kind of mess is this! If you do not follow my orders better, it is no wonder that such things happen. You are the oldest of the *asakir*, but had I assigned command to a child, my orders would have been followed more conscientiously. And these two men are supposed to be only injured?"

"I think so, *effendi*. I hope that they are only unconscious and will soon come to again."

"Did you try to revive them?"

"For an hour, but despite our efforts, we have not been able to revive them."

"I'm certain of that. Just look at their faces! They look bad. Let's have a look."

I knelt down to check the injured men, who lay in a puddle of blood. One of them had been shot in the back of the head, the other in the chest. Not even their jackets had been opened. They were dead.

"Man," I angrily snapped at the old man, "don't you have eyes! These two died immediately from the bullets they received. Now, I want to hear how this misfortune could have possibly happened?"

"*Effendi*, ask him; he was present." He pointed at the soldier.

"Talk!" I demanded.

"Sir," he began hesitantly, "I am not guilty; believe me! The three of us had just relieved the guards, when . . ."

"You three?" I cut in. "So, despite my orders, there were still only three guards after the relief?"

"Yes, but it was none of my doing."

"I know that, since it wasn't for you to decide this. Go on!"

"The three of us had just relieved the guards, when we saw a man walking around the swamp across the savanna. He hurried straight for us, but when he spotted us stopped as if frightened. He then approached us more slowly."

"Was he armed?"

"Yes. I stood closest to him and hailed him. He obeyed, stopped, and approached us only after I gave him permission to do so."

"That was a mistake. You either should not have permitted him to come close, or should have taken him captive."

"We wanted to do the latter, which is why we permitted him to walk up to us."

"Did he ask who you were?"

"Yes."

"And you answered?"

"Yes. There was no reason not to tell him that we were *asakir* of the *raïs effendina*."

"But there was reason; very much so! You committed an unforgivable foolishness. He wanted to find out, who he was dealing with to adjust his answers and requests for information. Can't you see that? He was smarter than you! By all means, I must learn exactly what happened, every word that was said, possibly even the sequence of questions and answers. Therefore, remember well and provide honest information. Only by doing so will I be able to forgive you, something you haven't actually earned. So, his first question was?"

"Who we were. I told him. He then wanted to know where our comrades were. I did not want to tell him, after which he said that he was a friend of the *amir*."

"And you believed it?"

"Not right away. I was cautious, *effendi*, and told him to his face that he was lying. But then he started to speak very proudly. He claimed to be a messenger of Khartoum's governor, dispatched to the *raïs effendina* with some urgent and most important orders."

"The governor of Khartoum cannot order the *amir!*"

"I did not know that. He presented himself as a high officer, a *Mir Alay* (colonel) and spoke with such a commanding voice that we had to believe him."

"Had to? When a dog barks at you instead of submissively whining, do you then think him to be a lion? But, go on! In any case, he asked for just about everything?"

"Yes. He knew also you and spoke so well of you that our mistrust completely faded. He wanted to know where you were, where the prisoners were, in short, we had to tell him all, everything."

"That the prisoners are kept up there in the valley?"

"Yes. We had to tell him that the forty men had fallen into our hands that morning."

"So he learned also that the *raïs effendina* is here at the *maiyah* and how many *asakir* he has with him?"

"That, too."

"Did you tell him also how we intended to catch Ibn Asl?"

"He inquired especially and urgently about this."

"Well, then the right fellows were standing there in front of him. He could not have wished them to be more stupid or gullible! Where were your heads and your thoughts? It seems you have told this stranger everything, all of it, instead of arresting him, and keeping everything from him until my return, as was your duty! What did he look like?"

"He wore a white *haïk, effendi.*"

"His build?"

"He was not tall, but broadly built."

"His face?"

"Covered by a full black beard."

"I thought so. Do you know, you son, grandson, and great-grand-son of foolishness who you were talking with and who you divulged important information to? It was Ibn Asl, the infamous slaver, the leader of our enemies in person!"

"Ya Allah! Is it possible?"

"Of course! Everything is possible with you, even the most impossible rashness, as you just confirmed. What did he do after you provided him with such beautiful and extensive information?"

"He demanded to talk with the man you had assigned command here."

"Well! Do you know what should have been done then?"

"What, *effendi*? I thought I had not made any mistakes."

"Had you acted correctly, it would look very differently here. Had one of you stayed here with the camels, the other two should have demanded that he surrender his weapons, and taken him in their midst to lead him to the commander. Did you do this?"

"No."

"And why not?"

"Because he ordered that one of us should go and get the commander."

"And who went?"

"I did."

"Which saved your life! Three appeared too dangerous for him, which is why he sent one away to be able to deal with the remaining two that much easier. Keep talking!"

"I left. I still had some suspicion, and when I stood between the high banks of the runoff, I stopped to think whether it would be better to take him along right away. While I thought about this, I heard two shots in quick succession. The sound was near the camels. I ran back as fast as possible and saw the man mount the white camel. My two comrades were lying on the ground. As you said earlier: He had shot them."

"Did you not attempt to shoot him?"

"Of course! I immediately fired for his head, but unfortunately the bullet missed. Then, he moved very fast and was soon so far away that my second bullet would not have reached him."

"In what direction did he ride?"

"Where he had come from."

"To the east, then?"

"Yes, he disappeared behind the swamp."

"And then?"

"Then the *onbashi* came. He had also heard the shots. I told him what had happened. He then posted five guards here, and we tried to revive the two men before you arrived, but were not successful."

"Yes, every numbskull corrects his mistakes only when it is too late. You bear the guilt for the death of your comrades and the escape of the slave hunter. I do not want to judge you, but leave it to the *raïs effendina*. Rather I will try to undo your foolishness, although I am certain that this will be impossible. Quickly! Help me saddle Bin Nil's and my camels; they are the fastest. We will pursue Ibn Asl. But you, old man, return now to the prisoners. Since you left only ten guards with them, a second accident could easily be added to the first. Report to the *raïs effendina* that I will most likely not be gone long."

Two minutes later we sat in the saddle and rode for the swamp, behind its eastern end, as we had been told, but Ibn Asl had disappeared.

At Wadi al-Bard, when Bin Nil and I had pursued the slaver on his white camel, we had ridden the same animals we were riding today. At that time, we had not been able to catch up with the white Jabal Garfah mare. Then, as now, she was superior to our animals. For good reason, one will ask why I did not make an attempt to apprehend Ibn Asl. As it was, I did not want to rely on the insufficient speed of our camels, but on my cunning. While we at first rode slowly side-by-side, Bin Nil had that same thought when he asked:

"*Effendi*, do you really expect to catch Ibn Asl? Remember when we pursued him at Wadi al-Bard! We rode the fastest *hujun* the raïs *effendina* was able to get for us, and yet, Ibn Asl disappeared on his white camel like a shooting star behind the horizon."

"That is correct, but I do not want to pursue him, but want him to run into my open arms. I believe that he is still around."

Saying this, I pointed to the savanna north of us.

"Then he would be the greatest fool I could imagine."

"Oh, no. You have seen that my calculations, even when bolder than normal, are usually correct."

"That is true. But will the present one be also?"

"Ibn Asl wallowed in the flush of victory; the greater will now be his disappointment. When he heard what has happened, or what was about to happen, he did not dare enter the valley above the runoff to get to his captured men. He realized that he had lost and had to save himself by fleeing. However, he could escape only by using his camel's speed. The mare had disappeared the evening before, but he now found it grazing with ours. This gave him the idea to regain ownership of it, in which he succeeded by fooling the guards. On the back of this incomparable animal he knows himself safe from any pursuit, since no other rider can catch up with him. For this reason, he needn't be rash fleeing, but do what is closest to his heart, next to his own safety, which is to find out what happened to his men. It is possible that they might not have fallen into our hands. In that case, he would not need to flee, but could become quite dangerous for us. He will spy on our return. When our group appears from between the swamp and the mountain, then turn around the latter for the runoff, a secret observer will see immediately what the situation is."

"But there cannot be a secret observer, since no one can hide there."

"You are mistaken. The open savanna offers very good hiding spots, precisely because it is so open. One has to guess trying to find a spy behind a bush or tree, but tell me with certainty the point where I can find a man hiding on the savanna."

"You are generally correct, but Ibn Asl has a white camel that would give him away."

"You do not take into consideration that it has been tinted."

"Yes, I forgot. But he wears a white *haïk*, which one can easily spot."

"He will take it off."

"But there is still an objection you will not be able to refute. If he wants to observe us, he must come close enough to see us clearly, at which time we can see him, too."

"I saw a ship's telescope on the "Lizard." Ibn Asl took it along, as I saw last night when I observed him by the fire. Using it, he will be able to observe us from a distance too great for our eyes. He must have had this spy glass hanging around his neck. Unfortunately, I did not think of asking the soldier about it. This is what I imagine: He rode a good distance away, then returned close enough to the runoff, from where he can observe through his telescope. He has dismounted there, made his camel lie down, then kept his spy glass pointed in the direction from where our group is coming."

"But then he could also see the two of us now, *effendi*."

"Indeed, but that doesn't matter. He doesn't know what we intend to do. The question now is, where will he will ride to, or rather flee, once he has observed us."

"Upstream on the Nile, where his ship is moored."

"I think so, too. Down here, he must figure that all is lost. He is alone and has no men to liberate his compatriots. He finds his only salvation in his fast disappearance. He will first head for his ship, then take it, or his much faster camel, to Fashoda, where friends and allies await him. There, and in the area of Fanakama, he can hire new men to continue his shameful trade. From there, it is apparent that he will ride south in the direction of Hagasi, from where he came. I base my plan on this, and ask you to assist me in its execution."

"I shall gladly do everything you wish me to do, *effendi*. Just give me your orders!"

"If he really does what I expect him to do, I can just about imagine where he presently is. Our group comes out from between the *maiyah* and the mountain, then will turn to the left. Opposite this area, Ibn Asl must find his position, if he wants to see clearly. I also know the width of his hiding spot, as well as its length. It is a matter of his telescope's range. Where the length crosses the width, there I will find him."

"I do not understand this, and ask you to explain it."

"That isn't necessary. You need not understand me so completely, since you will not be looking for him. Rather I will. I shall circle around him, so that he does not become suspicious, then approach him from behind and flush him out. He will flee in a southerly direction. You will now head there to a spot which he will likely pass. You and your animal lie down, so that he cannot see you until it is too late. Once he is close enough, you aim for his camel and shoot it."

"Why not him?"

"No matter how evil he is, he is still a human being. And although his camel is precious, it is only an animal. It will fall; he will jump up to flee. You quickly get into your saddle, after which we've got him between us, with you ahead of him and me behind. He will have to surrender."

"He will shoot at us."

"Not a chance! I will take care that he won't. If he really wanted to, my bullet would get him before he is able to trigger his musket. I hope you understood?"

"Yes. But where is the spot to post myself; where you expect him to pass? I am eager to learn how you will determine this on the open savanna?"

"It is easier than you imagine."

"Really, *effendi*? He will ride south, yes, but you cannot know how far east or west he will head."

"If I don't know it yet, I will figure it out. He cannot go too far east, since this amounts to a detour and would bring him too close to the Nile, where he might be seen. He will therefore keep as far as possible to the west. But there, the swamp sends a long, narrow arm into the savanna, he cannot cross, and must detour around. He will, I am convinced, come close to the end of this arm of the swamp, where you will expect him."

"Is this far from here?"

"Not at all. We are now at the northern end of the swamp. Look southeast, where you will see a dark line at the horizon."

"I see it, *effendi*."

"These are the bushes, marking this arm of the swamp. Where the line ends on the left, the swamp ends, and that is where you will wait."

"Then I know what to do. I am to go there immediately, right?"

"Yes. But make no mistake! Aim well, so that you don't miss."

"You know that I do not shoot badly, *effendi*."

We parted. He rode south, while I rode north on the savanna. If Ibn Asl lay in wait about where I expected him, he had to see me and question the reason for my ride. Most likely, he would figure that it was aimed at him, but I did not think him smart enough to trust me to make the calculation I had. I kept more to the west so as not to come too close to him. Had he become aware of my intention now, he would have fled, and I could not have driven him toward Bin Nil.

Once I was sufficiently distant from the mountain, as far as I thought his telescope would reach, and figured that I was at the same height as he, I then kept more to the east, but only little by little, so that my intention would not become obvious to him.

At that, I figured that his intention was to head to the place where our *asakir* had to appear. I was greatly interested to learn whether my calculations had been up in the air or not. To ride onto the savanna to catch a man, who wasn't even there, would have annoyed me and also shamed me a little.

Luckily, I was to escape at least this embarrassment, for I suddenly spotted some movement in the grass ahead of me. I saw a camel lying on the ground. A man jumped into its saddle with the animal leaping up and running off.

So, it had been him, after all. He had lain precisely where I had guessed him to be. Now he "shot" away straight ahead of me. Turning in his saddle, he swung his musket derisively over his head, just like he had done when he escaped me at Wadi al-Bard. I could not, or rather did not want to shoot. I might still have reached him, but the distance was just too great to be sure that my bullet would reach him.

I noticed that he did not flee in the direction I had expected him to, but rather kept more to the right as if he wanted to head straight for the runoff. The reason did not remain hidden for long. Just then, our *asakir* came marching with their captives. He headed straight for them in order to see as much as possible. He wasn't at all concerned about me.

I was certain that he would risk approaching them only beyond their shooting range. Then, he needed to turn to the left to get past the swamp. Despite the short time that had passed, he had already gained a considerable lead and now even stopped to better observe. This is how much he relied on his animal's speed. I used this to get closer to him, not by riding straight for him, but turning more to the *maiyah*. Of course, I could not cut him off this way, but at least reduce the distance between us and, maybe, get to fire a shot.

The *asakir* saw him, also me, and guessed that he was an enemy. They started screaming aloud, and he responded likewise. Then he turned to look for me. He realized that I intended to cut him off and again drove his animal on, now heading obliquely in my direction. What a magnificent camel this Jabal Garfah mare was! I did not get to fire a shot. While I drove my camel to top speed by hitting it, it did its best, but to keep up with the mare, or even to catch up to her, was impossible.

To my satisfaction, Ibn Asl now headed straight toward Bin Nil. I veered even farther to the left causing him to keep more to the right, in order to push him to the end of the swamp's afore mentioned tongue. This required drawing his attention as much as possible away from the direction ahead, so that he would not spot Bin Nil too early. For this reason, I began shouting some of the worst swear words, in short, making a racket that could be heard far across the savanna. He turned to look back a few time and answered with loud laughter. This noise also served the purpose of warning Bin Nil of our approach.

We rode so fast that the bushes, behind which I knew Bin Nil was hiding, seemed to come "flying" toward us. The slaver was still twelve hundred, a thousand, then only eight, then six hundred paces away. He did not quite trust the swampy area, for he veered more to the left to avoid it. He had come within four, then three hundred paces, and was still veering farther away from Bin Nil. Doing this, he would pass so far from the young man that he would be unable to shoot at him.

That's when I saw him come running from behind the bushes, musket in hand, straight into the savanna toward Ibn Asl, who, of course, saw him, too, and became suspicious. He turned sideways, however his camel had such momentum that it still ran straight ahead before being able to turn. Right then, Bin Nil stopped, aimed and fired. I saw the smoke from his musket, heard the shot, and saw the mare halting in mid-stride, as if she had received a blow from the front. But then she gathered herself and "flew," driven by blows from her rider's musket, as if she had been fired from a canon. Now, Bin Nil's second shot cracked, but without hitting her. Ibn Asl raced past the swamp's tongue – he had escaped us. A few seconds later I arrived with Bin Nil and stopped there.

"Effendi," he called, "I could not help it. I hit the camel. Did you see it? It stopped temporarily in mid-stride."

"I saw it," I told him. Your first shot hit home, but not the second."

"It was also well-aimed."

"But triggered too late!

"From surprise, effendi. Should one not be surprised, knowing that one has hit home, yet the animal runs off uninjured? I know that I hit her. She must drop shortly. I aimed for her chest."

"Let's see if we can find any blood."

We followed the tracks for some distance without finding a single red drop. By now, the rider was disappearing at the southern horizon, something that could not have happened that fast had the camel been badly injured.

"Maybe, it was a glancing shot that touched only its hide," I said.

"No, *effendi*. I am so sure, that I could swear by Allah, the Prophet and all *Khulafa'* that I hit its chest. Consider that the distance was only fifty, at most sixty paces. How would a glancing shot have been possible?"

"From excitement. But I don't think this possible either. A glancing shot would not have given the camel such a backward jolt. You must have hit it full on. Let's have a look around. Maybe the bullet was deflected by something."

The spot where it had happened was easily found; the camel had torn the ground there with its toes. We searched in the grass, and there, something metallic shone. I picked it up, and, indeed, it was the flattened bullet from Bin Nil's musket."

"How sad, what a shame!" he exclaimed. "It must have hit and been flattened by a hard item."

"So it seems!" I confirmed. "I had noticed earlier that the camel's chest straps were adorned with small tiles and large buttons. The bullet must have hit one of them. You can see now how much better it would have been had you quickly fired a second time."

"Forgive me, *effendi*! I was truly shocked when I did not see the animal fall."

"Don't be angry about this good shot, but rather about the one you did not fire fast enough."

Regret slowly disappeared from his face. He brought his camel from behind the bushes where he had hidden it. We mounted up and rode for the runoff. Already from afar, we saw our men being very busy there. The earlier captives had been brought from the valley and were joined with the news ones. They sat in the grass of the open savanna, with only their hands tied and surrounded by numerous guards. Nearby, the *asakir* were camped. Not far from them, the *amir* had settled with his officers. Behind these groups grazed the camels. The *asakir* were clearly enjoying themselves. They had won without any of them being injured, and had made an excellent catch that would bring them rich reward money. As for the prisoners, they were much quieter. When I arrived, they threw me grim, hateful looks, and when I dismounted near them, I heard old Abd Asl say to his neighbor:

"For all this we have to thank this mangy *giaur*, this stinking dog. May Allah tear him apart and toss him to the wind."

I did not pay attention to his words. The *raïs effendina* rose, came toward me, and told me:

"I learned everything while you were away and shall severely punish the guilty. There, they lie."

He pointed to a place I had not yet paid attention to. There lay the old *askari*, the *onbashi* I had assigned command to, and the soldier who had been so forthcoming with Ibn Asl and let him get away. Both had been tied up. He continued: "I was told that you and Bin Nil were chasing after Ibn Asl. Who was the rider you were pursuing when we arrived? I saw him, but could not make out his face."

"Ibn Asl."

I told him the events while we sat down, joining his officers. When I had finished, he stroked his beard contemplatively and said to my delight, not with the expected angry expression:

"Had we caught him, we would have been spared plenty of effort and exertion. I cannot rest until I have got this rogue in my power. I shall not let him catch his breath, but hound him until he collapses before my feet. This man alone is more dangerous than all his men together. It would have been fortunate, a triumph, a satisfaction, had we caught him, but I do not want to complain, and, for the time being, will remain satisfied. Look at the captives and count them! One hundred sixty slavers! Has ever a capture like this been made, *effendi*?"

"At least, I have not heard of anything like this."

"Yes, it has not happened before. I am known now. From now on my name will be mentioned by such scum bags with twice the awe, for which I have to thank you."

"You are giving me more credit than I deserve! I was able to support you a little, but only because chance favored me."

"You call this 'little'? Who captured the slavers in Wadi al-Bard and freed the Fassara women? You! Who then captured the sixty slavers at the well on the savanna? You! Who must I thank for my not being incinerated with all the men on my ship? You! And who delivered today's catch to me? You again! And you cannot speak of chance at all. What you call nothing is but the result of your smarts, your boldness, your precise calculations, which almost never fail you. Thus, the honor I am going to earn is not mine, but yours. But you shall learn that I am deeply grateful to you. However, you can gain my greatest gratitude if you would fulfill a request of mine."

"What is that?"

"When must you return to your homeland?"

"Whenever I like."

"Then, for the time being, stay with me! I want to tell you something, make you a promise: If you help me catch this Ibn Asl, I am prepared to . . ."

"Hold it, no promises!" I interrupted him. "You allowed me to see you as my friend, and I proved to you that I am yours. There is no dealing, no promising, no price and no reward between friends. I have time. Why should I not make it available to you? I started the game with Ibn Asl. Why should I not take it to its end? The question of slavery is of the greatest interest to me. Why then should I not occupy myself practically with it, and take advantage of the opportunity which you offer me? That which I wanted to do earlier and, in addition, can achieve best by staying with you, I shall do."

"Until we have caught this dog!"

"Yes, until he has been rendered harmless."

"I thank you, *effendi*! Only now am I certain that I will catch him. Where do you think he can now be found? Where will he turn to today?"

I explained the reason for my views, about which I had earlier already talked with Bin Nil. He listened attentively, and, when I was finished, said:

"I agree completely with you. He went first to his ship, then will go to Fashoda to look up his friends, who are waiting for him there. What should we do?"

"We must go after him."

"Of course! But, regrettably, I must first get to Khartoum to bring the prisoners there. Then, I must gather provisions and ammunition for a longer travel, since it is possible that we will pursue Ibn Asl far into the south, into the swamp areas of the Nile arms. This will take several days. Consider, too, that it will take me a week upstream to reach Fashoda. Arriving after such a length of time, it is assured that Ibn Asl will be gone already."

"Could you not use a government steamer in Khartoum which, taking you in tow, would get you to Fashoda much faster?"

"If one of these small *waburat* (plural of wabut) happens to be there, I will indeed requisition it. But even then would Ibn Asl have left town before my arrival."

"Then we follow him, that's easy."

"Not as easy for me than for you. If you perhaps were to reach Fashoda earlier, you then could make inquiries and preparations, so that I would not be delayed upon my arrival. Then we could go after him right away."

"I have also thought of that and have already made a plan, which I want to present to you. Our views match and our intentions meet in a most happy way. I shall travel ahead."

"*Al-Hamdulillah*! My heart beats easier now. You could not have given me better proof of your friendship than by this valuable service. I accept it gratefully and shall provide you with everything necessary. But how do you intend to travel such a distance?"

"Excluding yours, which is the better sailing ship, all others, stopping at night, need a full eleven days, even longer with an unfavorable wind. We ought not waste that much time if we want to catch Ibn Asl."

"But he takes just as long."

"Do you think he will travel on his "Lizard?" Certainly not! He must fear your 'Falcon'. I am totally convinced that he will ride. He can't do any better with the matchless camel he has."

"I agree. Then you intend to ride, too?"

"Yes, provided I can get two good camels."

"But you have one, even two of the same quality. Or are you no longer satisfied with them?"

"They are truly excellent animals. Consider, though, the distance they have traveled, yet are still as fresh as the day I got them. Of course, they were treated very well and rested at the Fassara for some time. But you had requisitioned them. Don't you need to return them?"

"It is entirely up to me. If the Viceroy needs them, that's enough for their owner. You can safely keep them."

"Fine. Then I'm certain that Ibn Asl won't gain too much of a lead."

"How about it, do you want to ride alone?"

"It would indeed be the best. A companion would only be a hindrance. This is why I think that . . ."

I was interrupted, which I had expected. Bin Nil had been allowed to sit with us and had heard everything. He now cut into my talk:

"Not everyone is a hindrance, *effendi*! There is one, who is willing to give his life for you, and who will run after you, if you do not take him along. You have two camels of equal speed. If I ride one of them, you will not be held back. And if I am no great help in danger, you will nevertheless have a servant in me, who is at least useful with basic help. I implore you: take me along! Will you reject your Bin Nil?"

"I would take you along, were I not thinking of your grandfather, Abu al-Nil."

"Does he prevent you from allowing me to come along?"

"Well, do you want to part from him again, after you found yourselves so unexpectedly and happily?"

"Bin Nil will need to part with him only for a short time," the *raïs effendina* said. "Sailing from the Jazirah Hassaniah here, I recognized what a useful helmsman this Abu al-Nil is. I have forgiven him whatever happened earlier and am prepared to hire him. This means, he will come with me to Fashoda to be united there with his grandson."

Old Abu al-Nil, as well as Selim, the bragster, had not come with us to Jabal Arash Qul, but had remained on board ship. For his words, Bin Nil almost embraced the *amir* from joy. He effusively thanked the *amir*, and if I did not want to appear less friendly than the *amir*, I had to promise to take him along, something I had intended anyway. Despite his youth, Bin Nil was more reliable than many another, and to undertake such a long ride alone in a foreign country, isn't everybody's choice. Thus it was agreed that we would stick together as before.

Once this had been concluded, the *raïs effendina* said:

"I know that you would like to depart right away, but you will have to accompany me to the ship first. I want to give you a few items on board to take along, and you will also find fresh provisions and ammunition, better than the poor leftovers you get here."

"However, I would then be very pleased if we don't delay any further, *amir*."

"We will march off the moment I have executed several acts of justice."

"Do you intend to hold court here?"

"Yes."

"About whom?"

I shuddered at the thought, remembering Wadi al-Bard and the slavers, whom he had executed there on first sight.

"First, the two *asakir* over there," he replied. "They deserve death."

"Death?" I asked shocked of this severity. "Their small offenses aren't serious crimes that one punishes with death!"

"Disobedience, especially when it has such consequences, is punishable by death, at least by me."

"The other, ordered only to stand guard, is, in any case, not as punishable."

"He is just as much! He revealed everything without permission. He is guilty of his comrades' death as well as Ibn Asl's escape. Consider the kinds of men I have under me! They can be ruled only with firmness."

"Using leniency, I got along with them just fine!"

"For a short time, yes, that is possible. But soon they would become too much for you. My *asakir* know me, and these two miscreants know exactly what is expected of them."

"Then it's really death?"

"Yes, I will have them executed now."

Maybe he was right, maybe not, but I could not force myself to think such severity warranted. I pitied the two poor devils, did not change my mind, and kept talking to him until he finally relented, and said:

"Fine, I will make the lives of these two fellows a gift to you. They may walk away, never to be seen by me again."

"Hold it, *amir*! This is not what I meant. Whatever one does, one ought to do completely and correctly. If you spare them from punishment and chase them away, this isn't a full pardon."

"Am I to even keep them in my service?"

"Yes, especially that."

"Especially? Is your asking for their lives nothing special?"

I laughed, offered him my hand, and said:

"Shake hands; they'll remain with you. You aren't a stern barbarian, although you want to appear like one. Let me tell you that obedience from love is worth a thousand times more than from fear. I know you better than you think, and know very well that your *asakir* love you despite your severity."

"So? You learned that?" he asked pleased, while an almost sunny smile crossed his face.

"Not just once, but often. So, *amir*, will you grant my wish?"

"You will see and hear it right away."

He ordered the two men to be untied and brought to him. When they stood before us, one could see from their hangdog looks that they expected the most severe punishment. He told them:

"I was going to have you shot, you sons of disobedience, but this *effendi* requested mercy for you, and when I granted his wish, he then demanded that I keep you. I granted this, too! Kneel before him, you dogs, and thank him in the dust! His compassionate hand caught you before the gate of death and returned you to life."

They truly threw themselves down before me and kissed my hands, two Muslims a Christian! After they left and sat again with their comrades, I saw the looks of these otherwise so insensitive men directed at me with an expression of loving gratefulness. I insist again and again that love, Christian love, is the greatest power in Heaven and on Earth, and that there is not a single human being whose heart will not open to it sooner or later!

"I am actually glad to have granted you your wish," said the *raïs effendina*, "for this gives me the certainty that you will let me act now at my discretion. Nevertheless, let me tell you beforehand that my gratitude and friendship, as great as both are, cannot cause me to grant you a second, similar request. I urge you, therefore, not to put me into a predicament! Bring the *Faqir al-Fuqara*!"

The man was brought. His hands tied, he stood between two *asakir* guards. He looked defiantly at the *amir*, who contemptuously looked him up and down, then asked:

"What is your name?"

"I am called the *Faqir al-Fuqara*," was his reply.

"I asked for your name, not what you are called! Answer!"

"*Faqir al-Fuqara*," he repeated defiantly.

"Aziz, open his mouth!"

Recall that Aziz, the *amir's* favorite, was the young man who knew how to apply the hippopotamus whip with such expertise. He was sitting with the soldiers. Upon his master's call, he jumped up, came to us, pulled the whip from his belt, then snapped it five, six times so quickly over the man's back, that the punished man was not even able to make a single move to avert them. But then, he turned, spit in Aziz's face, and screamed, while his dusky Negro face contorted into an angry grimace.

"Dog, you dared to whip me, me, the holiest of holies, the *Faqir al-Fuqara*, before whom millions will kneel to . . ."

"Aziz," the *amir* interrupted this diatribe with a thundering voice, "the *bastonnade!*"

The *Faqir* quickly turned to him, shouting:

"What? The *bastonnade* for me? Did Allah turn that far from you that you are capable of the ungodliness to whip his favorite . . ."

"Aziz, a gag!" the *amir* once more interrupted.

The *asakir* who had accompanied me to the Fassara, and had all too frequently been annoyed by this man, were pleased that he had finally found his master. They came closer and took care that the *amir's* orders were quickly executed. The *Faqir* was pulled down, and when he opened his mouth to scream and curse, a corner of his garb was stuck into his mouth as a gag. His struggle was in vain; so many hands held him down that he was eventually unable to move. He was then put on his belly. Several men sat on his upper thighs, his arms, his body, and held his head. Others lifted his calves to bring his bare foot soles to a horizontal position.

"How many blows, *amir*?" Aziz asked.

"Twenty each," came the reply.

The forty strokes were conscientiously counted, and when the last one had hit, the two feet formed a swollen, burst, and bloody mess. Then, the gag was removed and he was let go. He rose groaning to a sitting position and looked at the *amir* with an expression one could not readily read from his now bloodshot eyes.

"Once more: What is your name?" the *raïs effendina* asked.

"Muhammad Ahmad," he gurgled.

"Had you said this right away, you would have been spared the *bastonnade*. I demand obedience. Calling yourself the *Faqir al-Fuqara* does not impress me in the least. This *effendi* saved your life by killing the lion, yet you thanked him with ingratitude. You wanted to betray my *asakir* to Ibn Asl. I should actually kill you, but I despise you and do not want to honor you by being judged by me. Drag this grandson of ingratitude to the swamp and leave him there by its bank. There, he may tell vermin like himself of the Mahdi he wants to become and drink stinking water until his feet will permit him to stagger home across the savanna!"

This order was executed. Two men took hold of the *Faqir al-Fuqara* and dragged him to the swamp. Should he truly become a ruler of the faithful, at least within a certain area, with what feelings will he remember this not very honorable episode of his life?

I did not think of putting in a good word for him. I thought that he richly deserved this punishment. However, with this last event today's tribunal was not finished yet, for the *amir* ordered to fetch old Abd Asl.

This man had earlier wished for Allah to tear me apart and toss me to the wind. Now, he might want to speak differently. At least, that's what I thought, although he came walking firmly toward us with a stubborn face. I thought of the cave at Ma'abdah, where I had seen him for the first time. How pious and honorable he had appeared to me there. And then, how I got to know him as a very different person. The following day, he was after my life, and since then until today had pursued me with diabolical hostility. One ought to honor age, but a man who commits and revels in the worst crimes, although he stands already with one foot in the grave, is doubly punishable. The *amir* must have thought and felt the same, for his looks rested on the old man with an expression of revulsion and disgust, when he said most sternly:

"I looked for you for a long time, you holiest of *fuqara*. You always escaped me, but now I will judge you."

"I demand another judge!" Abd Asl answered.

"There is none who would judge you severely enough. Be it me or another, none can punish you the way you deserve! Your foul deeds count in the hundreds; you enslaved thousands of human beings, brought them death or the impoverishment of their tribal members. How many villages did you burn, their inhabitants murdered? And with all that, you displayed the face of a saint, sounded the prayers of an honorable man, and presented yourself as a worshipped *marabut*. This role has come to an end, and I am going to send you where you belong, to Hell."

"You do not have the right to kill me," the old man cried.

"Many, lots of men have had this right and still do! That they did not do it, is a great sin, for they gave you the time for ever new misdeeds. I neither want to, nor must, commit the same sin. I have the sacred duty to eliminate you, so that your mind finally stops giving birth to bloody deed after bloody deed. I judge you, and the judgment is death!"

These words sounded like hammer blows. Had the old man hoped until now to go free – and he assuredly did so – he now had to give it up. Yet he tried one more means, while he put on his most pious, honorable face, and threatened:

"Still, I am a saint, a *marabut*. If you lay hands on me, I will curse you. Then, all the faithful will avoid you, and you shall become like the hyena of the desert that is pursued and must eat carrion until it dies from hunger."

"Keep cursing! The curse of a monster like you will turn to a blessing. Your threat will not save you; it is ridiculous. You must and will die! But how? There is no death that does you justice. You and your son wanted to tear off this *effendi's* tongue and every limb individually. I should actually have you die this way, but you shall be killed by your likes. You are a monster, and monsters will devour you. I shall have you thrown to the crocodiles in the *maiyah*."

"Oh, Allah!" the old man cried. "You cannot do this! Spare me, *raïs effendina*!"

"Spare you? Think back! This *effendi* spared you, this Bin Nil gave you your life, and yet, again and again, you tried to take theirs. You are a devil, whose nature it is to repay charity with misdeed. My judgment stays: You will be thrown to the crocodiles!"

The *amir* had been totally serious. Nevertheless, Abd Asl looked at him searchingly, as if the *amir* might actually be of different mind.

However, when he recognized from the stoney features of his judge that he had made a firm, indisputable decision, he began howling.

"This is not possible; it is inhuman!"

"Shut up! You are being done right. When did you ever act humanely? Woe to him who does harm! This is my motto by which you shall die. And your son will perish likewise. Tie up his feet, then take him to the swamp! His friend, the great *Faqir al-Fuqara*, may witness how he is devoured by the crocodiles."

"Mercy, mercy! One more word!" the old man wailed, when he was seized.

"What? the *amir* asked, giving a signal to wait. But instead of talking to the *amir*, he turned to me:

"*Effendi*, you are a Christian. You must not permit me to die such a terrible death. Ask for my freedom; have me pardoned! I know that the *amir* listens to you."

"You do not deserve it," I responded, convinced that the *amir* would not meet my request.

"Must I deserve it? Are your teachings not those of love, mercy, and compassion? You told me so in Asyût."

"Yes, and after I had explained it to you, you lured me underground, where I was to perish miserably!"

"Do not think of this now, but only of the commandments of your faith, so that your Jesus, once he becomes your judge, will have mercy on you."

"Shut up!" the *amir* commanded, who might get the idea that I would yet be moved to intercede on Abd Asl's behalf. "The *effendi* cannot do anything for you, for I will not listen to his voice. Tie him up!"

The old man fought with tied hands and feet against the execution of this order. In doing so, he roared not like a human being, but like a wild animal. One can imagine that this scene by no means found my approval. The monster deserved death, and while it should be, it was not necessary to throw him to the crocodiles. This could be stopped; at least this I wanted to prevent.

A thought occurred to me. I remembered the cave guide at Ma'abdah I had promised to search for his missing brother. What I had learned since then suggested that Abd Asl knew of his fate. This is why I demanded now: "Let him off for the moment! I must speak to him."

I was obeyed and the old man called to me:

"I thank you, *effendi*! This is help when I most needed it. You have decided to speak for me?"

"Maybe. Answer me some questions!"

"Ask, *effendi*! If I can give you information, and I will do so."

"You know Bin Wasak, the guide at the Ma'abdah cave?"

"Yes. You saw me talking with him."

"Did you also know Hafiz Sikhar, his brother?"

"Him, too," he nodded.

"Do you know his present whereabouts?"

Instead of answering, he looked at me searchingly for awhile, then asked: "Why do you want to know this?"

"I am looking for Hafiz; I want to return him to his brother."

"Yes, I can tell you where he is. I will tell you, provided all the prisoners here are set free."

"Man, are you mad!" the *raïs effendina* exclaimed. "This is a request only a madman could make."

"But I said it, and will hold to it."

"Tell me then, *effendi*, what it is about this missing Hafiz Sikhar?" the *amir* asked.

"He traveled to Khartoum to collect a large amount of money from the merchant, Baryad al-Amin. He did receive this money, but since then has disappeared. At the time, Ibn Asl was in business with this merchant. He was poor, but after Hafiz Sikhar's disappearance, he suddenly turned rich and entered the slave trade."

"Then he murdered Hafiz Sikhar and took his money," the *amir* suggested.

"No, Hafiz Sikhar was not murdered!" Abd Asl shouted. "I will tell you where he lives, if you will set us free."

"That cannot be. But from friendship for this *effendi*, I shall make you a proposal. You tell him the place where the missing man lives, and I will not have you thrown to the crocodiles. You will be shot."

That is when the old man broke into a malicious laughter and replied:

"How merciful you are, oh, *amir*! Do you think that death by a bullet is not death? I want to live, to live! And if that will not be, you will not learn my secret. To shorten my death throes by at most two seconds, you demand the freedom of this Hafiz Sikhar, whom my son should actually have killed. This price it too great, much too great!"

"Well, then, take him away, at last!"

Ibn Asl's feet were also tied and he was carried away to the swamp. He remained rather quiet while this was done. We, too, were quiet. No one in camp spoke a word, until several shouts, some miserable whining, and finally a scream sounded from the swamp that went through bone and marrow. It was the end of the old man. When the men who had carried him off, returned, one of them said:

"At first, he acted as if he were strong and fearless, but when he saw the beasts lying there, he began howling. The devils of the swamp tore him immediately apart."

I shuddered. And yet, I felt as if even this punishment had not been too harsh. The *raïs effendina* said to me:

"Too bad that it happened so fast. He deserved a much, much longer death struggle, but, unfortunately, we must leave. Will you be angry with me, *effendi*, for not agreeing to your demand?"

"No, I could not hold this against you, since, what he demanded, was truly mad. He and all others free? And, in the end, he would have lied to me after all. But I had at least one result. Until now, I had not had the least trace of the missing man. But the old man let himself be carried away when he said, 'this Hafiz Sikhar, my son should have killed'. I now know from whom I can obtain more information, and that is Ibn Asl, who robbed the missing man. Do you know the merchant Baryad al-Amin in Khartoum?"

"Yes. I have seen him often."

"Is he honest or not?"

"Honesty itself could not act differently than he."

"I love to hear this. The Ma'abdah guide described him also as an honorable man, however, there were some points in the man's story that still require clarification. If he carries a mask, I shall tear it from his face once I am in Khartoum, which, unfortunately, will not happen that soon. When will we leave here?"

"We can so right now."

"Are you finished with the tribunal?"

"Yes. It was actually only for the old one, who had to be rendered harmless, in any case. This had to happen here, and I was able to do it, being fortunate enough to have the power. Once in Khartoum, I will not have time to occupy myself at length with the fate of these men. I must hand them over to the local courts, where it could well have happened that Abd Asl might have gotten away for a hefty sum of money."

"One ought to think that, especially in a case like this, the bribing of judges would not be possible."

"Yes, one should think so, and, concerning myself, I would not have had the legitimacy of my judgment bought for millions. But I once heard that there is a Christian country whose goddess of justice is represented as a blind woman . . ."

"That was a heathen country, Greece."

"Whether heathen or Christian, or Muslim, it is all the same. And it is the same here. Have you heard of the *mudir* of Fashoda?"

"Yes. His name is Ali Effendi al-Kurdi. He is also known widely by his gruesome put-down of the military revolt in Kassala."

"There, he applied too much justice; later not enough. It was a shame! Under his system in Fashoda, there was a strict ban on the slave trade, when, in fact, nothing of this ban was visible. The slavers openly frequented his home. For each slave, he was secretly paid a head tax, for which the slavers found protection from the law. I knew them all, but could not apprehend them. Whenever I came to put the noose to one of these bandits, it was cut by al-Kurdi. If the highest representative of a province, the *mudir*, does this, what can one expect from the lower and lowermost officials? Fashoda had become the departure point for all slave hunts. The slavers gathered there to make their preparations, and when I said even a word about it, I was either laughed at or shouted at by the *mudir*. I could no longer permit this to happen. I went directly to the Viceroy, told him about it, presented him proof, and the success manifested itself. Ali Effendi al-Kurdi was deposed and a new *mudir* installed."

"Will he be more just than the previous one?"

"Yes. I am convinced. I know him. It is me he has to thank for his position. I proposed him, and am very glad that the Viceroy followed my recommendation. The new *mudir's* name is Ali Effendi, and has always been called Abu Khamsah (Father of Five- Hundred) by his subjects."

"What circumstance must he thank for this name?"

"A very commendable habit of his that gained him great respect. He is totally inaccessible to bribery and other weaknesses of this kind and, when in court, is used to dictate five hundred blows to anyone he has found guilty. Since he distributes this gift with the same generosity to poor and rich, the lowly and distinguished, he is mightily feared by everyone, and I trust him to soon establish a clean environment in Fashoda. He is my friend, and I asked you in part to accompany me to the ship to give you a letter of recommendation for him, so that you will find the necessary support while I am still absent."

Of course, such a letter would be most welcome, since it would facilitate much and make possible things that otherwise would have been difficult if not impossible.

In the course of this serious and low-voiced conversation, we had both kept a serious face. This seemed to have raised the belief in the captives that the tribunal was not over yet and that we were still talking about the punishment of the rest. The two slaver officers assumed this, and it appeared to worry them quite a bit, for the first-lieutenant sent a guard to us, asking whether he could talk with us, that he had some important information. Of course, this was permitted. When two *asakir* brought him, and the *raïs effendina* asked what he had to say, he answered:

"You had the judgment on Abd Asl executed, oh, *amir*. Will you now also judge us?"

"Do you, by chance, expect me to let you get away?"

"No. We know you. We are in your hands and cannot hope to get off unpunished. But we ask for your mercy and to do with us as you please, but not to throw us to the crocodiles. How can the archangel Jibra'il (Gabriel) find our bones on the day of resurrection, if they were crushed and devoured by these monsters?"

"You villain! Now, in your fear of death, you call on the promises of the Qur'an. Did you also consider the religious commandments when you committed your misdeeds?"

"*Amir*, the capture of slaves has been permitted for centuries. What is religion's influence here when this permission was abolished by people."

"And what is Islam's business with your bones? If they burn in a crocodile's belly, they need not burn later in Hell. You should therefore be grateful to me, if I have you follow Abd Asl right away."

"For Allah's sake, please do not! I shall prove to you that I am not as evil as you think, and do not deserve such a death."

"So? I would like to know, how you, the leader of these mad dogs, want to present such proof?"

"Allow me to do so. I heard earlier that this *effendi* was inquiring about a missing man. If I provide information about him, will you then spare me from the crocodiles?"

"No, because you will come up with some lie, just to save yourself."

"No, *amir*. Allah knows that I will speak the truth! Take me along and keep me prisoner until you have convinced yourself. Should you find that I lied to you, you may feed me to the crocodiles, or should you be so pleased, devise an even more horrible death."

"I cannot promise you anything beforehand. We shall check the veracity of your words. Should we find them to be true, I may decide not to have you devoured. Do you know where this Hafiz Sikhar is?"

"Yes, but I do not know the area or the village."

"What? You know his whereabouts, but neither the area nor the village? Man, you are talking nonsense!"

"It is truly so, *amir*."

"Did you possibly talk with Ibn Asl or his father about it? Did they include you in this secret?"

"No. These two never communicated with us so trustingly, but I once heard them speak about this Hafiz Sikhar. They were unaware that I was nearby."

"What did they say about him?"

"I do not recall the individual words, but remember the overall content. You will learn it now. In earlier times, Ibn Asl was poor and became rich only through Hafiz Sikhar. He took a large sum of money from him and shared it with someone else."

"Who is the other?"

"I do not know this. I could not deduce it from what I heard. Neither his name nor his position was named. Ibn Asl wanted to kill Hafiz Sikhar, to eliminate the witness of the theft from the world, but the other did not agree. With the stolen money they undertook a *ghasuah* (Slave Hunt), and to render Hafiz Sikhar harmless, they took him along and sold him to the chief of a savage tribe deep in the south."

"What tribe was it?"

"That is what I do not know, *amir*. You now learned everything I can provide. Will you now have the kindness to fulfill my request?"

"Ask the *effendi*, whose business this is. He may be inclined to intercede on your behalf."

The prisoner followed his direction, asking me to intercede for him. Wanting to use his fear of death or rather of crocodiles for my purposes, I told him therefore:

"Whether I will do something for you depends very much on your further honesty. Have you heard the name Baryad al-Amin?"

"Yes. He is a merchant in Khartoum. You earlier asked Abd Asl about him."

"Does Ibn Asl still have business connections with him?"

"No. At least I am not aware of any."

"That's taken care of, then. But let's go on: Does Ibn Asl carry lots of money on him?"

"Yes, almost his entire fortune. He was going on a slave hunt, larger than any before. But where, remained a secret even to me. He treated this venture very secretly. Where it was to go, I was only to learn in Fashoda."

"Were you going to stay there for long?"

"Until we were finished gathering our supplies."

"I saw that your ship, the "Lizard," was empty. Was it to be loaded in Fashoda with the necessary trade goods?"

"Yes. Also the other ships."

"What? More ships were to be equipped?"

"Yes. But how many I was not told."

"Ibn Asl must have very confidential business friends. Do you know them?"

"He customarily remains very cautious and discrete even with his closest subordinates. He never let me in on his friendships and connections. This is why I know only of a single man in Fashoda, of whom I can say assuredly that he is in contact with. His name is Ibn Mawlay; he is the major of the Arnoutlar, who are stationed in Fashoda."

"That's enough. Only one more thing: Where did you leave your ship, before you came here?"

"It lies in the Nile's right arm at the Jazirah Muhabilah. Ten men were left to guard it."

"Enough! I see that you are telling the truth, and am satisfied with you."

"I thank you, *effendi*! Will you now have the kindness to intercede for me with the *amir*?"

The *amir* now answered in my place:

"Since you did not lie to us, I promise that you will be safe from the crocodiles, but nothing else. Woe to him who does harm! All of you cannot go unpunished. That is good enough!"

The first lieutenant returned to his place, calmed, at least for the time being. Now preparations were made for our departure. My inquiries had been successful, but they were of a nature that I told myself that it would be exceptionally difficult, if not impossible, to track down the Ma'abdah guide's brother. There was only a single person from whom I could learn the whereabouts of this unfortunate man – Ibn Asl himself. And provided I could catch him, it was doubtful whether I would be able to extract the desired information from him. In this matter, too, I had to rely on my lucky star.

The 'Falcon' was moored on the left bank of the Nile at the same height as the swamp. To get there, required a walk of about two hours, something the prisoners could easily do. Their accommodation would be under deck. Since our camels could not be loaded, too, they were to be taken by land to Khartoum, for which ten or twelve *asakir* sufficed. It was shortly after noon when we left. The *amir* had taken the lead of the group, while I, on my camel, purposely brought up the rear. I did this because of the *Faqir al-Fuqara*. He lay helpless by the swamp, exposed to the myriad of mosquitos, hungry and thirsty. I felt pity for him, although he did not deserve it. I did not want to let go of my water bag, which is why I had picked up another when no one was looking, and had hung it from my saddle. It was still half full.

When the last of the men were gone for some distance, I left, too, but not to follow them, but instead rode to the *maiyah*. I did not know where the *Faqir al-Fuqara* was, but it was most likely near where Abd Asl had been thrown into the swamp. I could not miss the spot since distinct tracks led to it. The *Faqir* had not been carried, but dragged across the grass.

I found him lying next to an ugly *osher* bush, not far from the swamp's bank. There, the swamp was covered by stinking green water plants, in and on which rested giant crocodiles. These were the grave-diggers, also the graves of Abd Asl.

When the *Faqir* heard me coming, he turned his head toward me, and stared at me with his bloodshot eyes. His dark face was crossed by an almost feral grimace. Several syllables escaped rattling from his lips, most likely curses I did not understand. His hands were still tied, and his mangled foot soles were covered by insects, increasing his pain. I dismounted and cut the strings, so that his hands were free now. I then put the water bag next to him and added a few provisions I had taken from my saddlebag. It was enough for several days. He observed me doing this without saying a word.

"Here's something for you so that you don't pine away," I said. "I cannot do more for you."

He only answered with a poisonous hiss.

"Do you have a wish?"

He remained silent.

"No? Then farewell! Two hours from here, straight east, flows the Nile. You can get there before your provisions run out."

I mounted up again. Just when my camel began its stride, grateful words came from behind:

"Allah may curse you. Fear my revenge, fear revenge!"

I soon caught up with my group and joined the *amir* in the lead. There was no need for us to remain with the group. It was unlikely for a problem to occur, which is why we rode ahead to get to the ship faster. Arriving there, we entered the *amir's* cabin, where he wrote the promised letter of recommendation. He then put a small bag in my hand, saying:

"You will encounter expenses in Fashoda on my behalf. Use this money as if it were your property. I will not take any back."

When the soldiers with the prisoners arrived, I did not concern myself with anything but the preparations for our forthcoming ride. We were richly furnished with everything necessary and said our goodbyes shortly following the afternoon prayer, since we hoped to still cover a good distance that day.

The *amir* took my lion hide along to Khartoum, there to have it prepared for me to pick up later. Our way did not take us along the Nile, whose bends we chose to avoid. Rather we took the open plain providing faster progress. We were not worried at all about what we might experience along the way.

4

The Father of Five-Hundred

TWO PEOPLE, ALONE in the wide desert. The sun burns so hard that one feels like being roasted and so, as not to be blinded, one must pull the *haïk's* hood down over one's face. There is nothing to talk about; all has been said. Besides, the tongue lies so heavily in one's dry mouth that even were there conversational material, one would rather keep silent. Ahead, behind, to the left and right, there's nothing but sand! The camels walk their pace, mechanically, like wound-up machines. They do not possess the temperament of the noble horse, which expresses to the rider that it enjoys life with him, but also suffers with him. The master can be at one with his horse, but never with the camel, were it even the most precious *hajin*. This is demonstrated already by the way he sits on the former versus the latter.

The horseman embraces the body of his steed with his legs; his thighs fit well, by which he makes true the saga of the Centaur. The embrace puts the limbs, the muscles and nerves of a man into close contact with those of the horse. The animal feels the intentions of its rider before he has consciously indicated them. It will love him, dare with him, "fly" with him, and will consciously even enter into death with him.

The camel is very different. Sitting in the saddle on a high hump, the rider touches the animal only when he crosses his feet over its neck. There is little contact, no external and therefore no internal union. Sitting so high on it, he leaves it behind in spiritual understanding. When it is good-natured, it obeys the rider like a slave without showing the least trace of individuality; but when it is malicious and stubborn, which most of them are, it is in continuous warfare with him, tiring him and eventually filling him with aversion, if not loathing. Real love for its master will rarely be found in a camel.

This is what makes a solitary ride through the desert even lonelier. One feels a living creature beneath, yet cannot occupy oneself with it. The horse, by neighing, snorting, or the movement of its ears and the tail, and various modulations of its gait, reveals its feelings; it "talks" with the rider, communicates with him. The camel plods steadily ahead, carries its master for days and weeks, but still will not get to know him.

Thus, a ride through the wasteland becomes a real pain, and one greets the smallest break, which some favorable circumstance has sent, with delight.

Our two *hujun* belonged to the kind of docile camels. Once we had mounted up, they began to run like hell, and kept running and running at the same speed without any refusal, without stopping, and without demonstrating the least trace of independent will. This was terribly boring; finally, one loses one's own will, falling mentally asleep, retaining nothing but the bleak awareness of being carried on an endlessly straight line across the sand.

Suddenly, a sharp scream woke me from the mental limpness I had sunk into. Bin Nil, too, was startled and looked up into the sky from where the scream had come.

"*Shâhîn!*" he said, pointing skyward, then relapsing again. Yes, it was a *shâhîn*, a falcon, whose scream we had heard. It circled high above us. The appearance of this bird did not seem at all noteworthy to Bin Nil, but I had instantly regained full energy.

"Watch out, someone's coming!" I said.

Bin Nil rose once more and looked around. When he did not spot anyone within his range of sight, he said:

"Did the sun rob me of my vision. I do not see anyone, *effendi*."

"Me either, but, rest assured, we will soon meet people. A falcon kills only living prey; it never eats carrion. Being here in the desert, which supports no living being, it must be following a caravan."

"Or it got lost, or is simply traveling."

"A falcon here, getting lost? No. Let's watch what the bird will do."

We kept the bird in our sight. It still hovered above, watching us. Then, we heard another scream, with a second falcon flying in from the west, joining the first. Together, they circled several times above us, then flew away in the direction they had come from.

"They must have been a male and a female?" Bin Nil suggested.

"Yes," I answered, while I halted my camel and reached for my telescope to follow the birds' flight. "Stop, too! It's always good to know what is going on."

"But you cannot know anything hereabouts before it comes into your sight."

"But I've seen it already, that is, the falcons. They flew straight west; I still see them clearly. Now, they are circling again." After I had observed the birds for maybe two minutes, I continued: "They are still circling, but keep drifting southward. I conclude from this that a caravan is traveling over there. It comes from the north, moving to the south, and that so slowly that I guess it includes people on foot."

"How do you know that it moves slowly?"

"The falcons hover above the caravan. Their speed corresponds with that of people."

"*Effendi*, you truly know how to magically produce images from thoughts. Will we meet these people?"

"Yes, provided we purposely don't want to miss them. They are so far away that a walking man would need an hour to get there."

"W'Allah! How can you know this so accurately? The falcons cannot have told you this!"

"Who else but them? I know how fast a falcon flies. I also know how long these two took to get there from here. It is easy to calculate the distance from these two values."

"Is it possible to observe these people without being seen by them?"

"Indeed, it is – through my spy glass. Let's head over there. We'll spot them in a quarter of an hour."

Our tiredness had vanished. The falcon's scream had awakened us. We turned southwest and while maintaining this direction, I pointedly kept the falcons in my telescope's sight. I did this to estimate our distance so as not to approach the caravan too closely that we could be spotted by its people with bare eyes. The ground was level here, so that we were unable to hide. We expected the character of the desert to change only toward evening, at which time we planned to arrive at the Nid al-Nil, a long, in places very broad, but shallow lake, which held plenty of water at this time. I had heard that this Nid al-Nil held water, even at the driest time of the year, and that it actually never dried out. It even provided hippopotamuses with a place to live. I had not previously imagined these animals lived that far north.

After about a quarter of an hour, the falcons appeared so close in my telescope, that I thought it wise to stop and now pointed it toward the horizon. At first, I tried to spot the caravan with my bare eyes but was unsuccessful. However, through the spy glass I saw a long line of animals and people riding and walking. I had not been mistaken. When I had seen enough, I handed the telescope to Bin Nil. He had to search for some time until he finally located the caravan, after which he observed it long enough to finally say:

"*Effendi*, you were right. It is a caravan. I would not have guessed it even with the falcons showing up. They are twenty-five riders and fifty-four men on foot. What kind of caravan could it be? One does not walk the desert. Could it be a slave caravan?"

"Almost unthinkable! Where would slaves come from here? And a slave caravan at the White Nile, moving north to south is, in any case, most peculiar. The opposite direction is the usual one, with the slavers getting their goods in the south, then moving them northward."

"What kind of country would these people come from?"

"The lands of the Takalah. But wait! Saying this name, I remember that the Takalah, although they are Muslims, have the reprehensible custom of selling their children."

"Allah! What sin and shame! Who would sell his son or daughter for money? These Takalah must surely be Negroes!"

"They are not quite black, and one ought not think them to be inferior or incapable people. When Egypt conquered the Sudan, the Takalah resisted the longest. They are brave warriors and became famous for their fight against the Egyptians. The country is marked by its rich copper mines and the hospitality its residents extend to all foreigners entering their area. The latter ought not to lead someone astray and expect great friendliness beyond their hospitality. They are ruled by a 'Mek' (derived from Arabic Malik – King), whose right is to sell all those subjects of his, who disobey him into slavery or, for whatever reason, have become unpopular with him. Prisoners of war, if they are not butchered, as ancient custom prescribes, can also be sold."

"Then it is quite possible that this caravan is composed of such people. Do you think we must fear anything from them if we should meet them?"

"Likely not. Neither has reason to quarrel with the other."

"Shall we head over there?"

"No. Although we needn't shy away from them, there's no reason to seek them out. We want to reach the Nid al-Nil before evening to camp there. Should they show up, well, so be it, but there is no reason to pay them a visit."

We veered south once more. Happily, the monotony of the ride had been broken, and the expectation whether we met the caravan or not, prevented us from returning to the condition of inward contemplation that had earlier enveloped us.

The afternoon passed and toward evening we noticed that we were approaching our destination. The southern horizon which, until now, had looked hazy against the sky, now stood out starkly, and since this dark line ahead could not possibly be a mountain range, we decided it was most likely a forest.

We reached the lake at a place where it was narrow. The Nid al-Nil's waters stood low here against its high banks, thus almost never providing sustenance. The incline on both sides was so steep that we couldn't possibly cross it with our camels. This required us to ride along the shore until we found a suitable spot for passing.

The Nid al-Nil is a shallow lake which holds plenty of water in the charif, the rainy season, but was now, at the place we had arrived at, totally dry. A quarter of an hour later the banks became shallower, forming a maiyah, or rather a kind of lake whose water was so clear that it could not really be called a swamp. It was so wide that the opposite shore was invisible. On our side it was covered by tall trees.

Not being able to cross, we had to ride on. Soon, the lake curved to the left, then turned into a narrow arm of standing water that connected it with a second, larger lake. The water here could not be very deep, since numerous, well-crowned trees rose from it. At any rate, this part would likely dry out completely even before the onset of the dry season. It should not be difficult to cross, which is why I decided to make camp here.

We dismounted and let our camels drink the rather clean water. We then tied them to the bushes growing under the trees along the bank, so they were able to eat the juicy twigs and leaves. When, later, we were occupied collecting dry branches for our fire to protect us against the always present mosquitos by the water, we saw the caravan, which we had observed earlier, approaching. The men riding in the lead, among them a veritable goliath, observed us from afar. Then the giant rode toward us, looked at us glowering, and rode to the bushes in order to look between and over them. He then asked without greeting:

"What are you doing here at the Mahada ed Dill?"

The name means 'Ford of Shadow'. We had thus found the right place to cross the Nid al-Nil. It is always a bad sign in the Orient when one does not greet the other. The man didn't make a trusting impression, which is why I responded curtly:

"We are resting, as you can see."

"Will you stay for the night?"

"This depends on whether we like it here and whether we will not be disturbed."

"Are you alone?"

"Don't ask us, but use your eyes!"

"The merits of politeness were seemingly not taught you."

"I do possess them, but am used to displaying them only if I am also treated politely. You failed to greet us."

"I do not know you. Tell me who you are!"

"Only when I have learned your name and position."

"I stand higher than you, which is why you must answer me first. Know that I am Shadid, the bravest warrior of the king of the Takalah!"

"And I am the *mudir* of Jarabub. I hope you know this place!"

How this name occurred to me, I could then say just as little as I can today.

The place is known because the most famous Muslim order of modern history was founded there, but no *mudir* exists there and never has. I assumed this title to impress the Takalah. Who and what I was, I neither wanted nor should tell him for obvious reasons. An untruth can be considered a lesser crime versus a truthfulness, turning oneself not only into a suicide victim, but risking the well-being, even the life of others.

"I never heard of this place," he replied dismissively. "Your *mudîrîyah* has likely been gnawed to bits by termites."

"May Allah forgive you your ignorance! Did you never hear of Sidi Sinussi?"

"May Allah drive a hole through you! How can you insult a faithful with this question? Everyone living on this Earth knows that Sidi Sinussi is the greatest prophet preaching Islam's word. Do you know those places called Siwa and Farafra?"

"Of course!"

"They shine like the stars to all places on Earth, for located there are the universities where the students and disciples of Sidi Sinussi are educated."

"You know this, yet don't know Jarabub, shining even brighter? Yes, Sidi Sinussi resides in Jarabub, while only his schools are in Siwa and Farafra, still, all three places are part of my *mudirieh*. From them shines the purest light of Islam from which the shadows of all heresies must give way. My house and that of the Sidi are joined by a single door. We live under one roof and drink from the same bag. Tell me now who stands higher, you or I? Woe to him, who refuses to greet me! To him, like the blasphemer, will happen that which the hundred-and-fourth Sura speaks: 'He will be thrown into *al-Hutama*' (epithet for Hell). *Al-Hutama* is Allah's fire which he bangs together over the evildoer'. Keep boasting now, oh Shadid, who is nothing but the servant of a man!"

Hearing this, he made his camel kneel down before me, dismounted, bowed deeply, and said:

"Let the sun of forgiveness rise over me, oh *mudir*. I had no way of knowing that you are the friend and companion of this holy Sinussi. Your order will encompass the entire world, and before your might all men will bow, now alive and who will yet live. How must I call your young companion?"

"His years number few, but the merits of his mind have made him famous already. He was educated at the university of Farafra and travels with me to make the splendor of our order shine also in these lands. He is a *khatib* (Muslim preacher). Call him this!"

This would have been something for Selim, the boaster, who would surely have given a brilliant speech overflowing with self-adulation. But Bin Nil said only, however, in a most dignified voice:

"You offended us only not knowing us. We forgive you."

That he, as a Muslim, confirmed the untruthfulness I had spoken, was a sign how much he loved me. The Takalah was visibly embarrassed. I saw that he would have liked to camp near us, but found it not compatible with the respect he thought due us. He looked back to his caravan, which had stopped behind, and said:

"We wanted to stay at this place until tomorrow, but must now look for another, not daring to camp near such holy men."

"Before Allah all men are equal. I permit you to rest here with us," I said.

"I thank you, oh *mudir*, and assure you that my people will be very reverent listeners of your speeches."

"Do not think that we will preach to you. Everything in its time and proper place. The word may only flow from one's mouth when the inner spirit is powerful."

Naturally, I would not think of acting as the Muslim preacher here. I simply wanted to impress the man, nothing more. And I succeeded, as the totally changed behavior of the Takalah proved. Yet despite his deep deference to me, he filled me with such disgust that I would have loved to wish him far away. His features were regular, with his voice strong and pleasant. Still, I was unable to account for why he was so off-putting.

He waved to his people to come closer. We had not been mistaken; there were as many people as we had counted. Likewise we were now able to differentiate the sex of the members, something we had been unable to do through the telescope. Half of those walking were actually females, but all, as we noticed only now, had their hands tied to a long rope. They were prisoners.

The riders drove them on. Shadid shouted some words after which we were greeted with great deference. After the men had dismounted, they first took care of their animals, then led the prisoners to the water to drink. Afterward, the captives had to lie down close to us without being untied. From the way in which they obeyed, one could see that they had totally resigned themselves to their fate.

What caught my eye was that there wasn't the least difference in appearance between the prisoners and their captors. They seemed to come from the same stock. They were not black, but a blackish-brown. The males' beards were light and their hair not frizzy but straight. The leader assigned five of his men the special task of watching the prisoners, and told the others:

"Open your eyes, you people, and see here two men whose prayers may open the heavens for you. Here sits the famous and holy *mudir* of Jarabub, a supreme leader of the Sinussi who lives with Sidi Sinussi in the same house. Next to him, you see a pious young man, to whom, despite his youth, is given the gift of spreading the pure teachings of the Qur'an. Bow to them, and do not annoy them with ill-considered words."

This last admonishment could also be construed as: "Be smart and cautious, and do not give away what evil fellows we are by thoughtless talk!" They crossed their arms at their chests, then bowed almost to the ground. Afterward, they settled so close to us – although they did not bother us – that they had to understand everything we were talking about. They took their provisions from their bags to eat, however, the prisoners received nothing. I therefore asked Shadid:

"Don't you think the others are also hungry?"

"I am not concerned if they go hungry," he replied. "They get to eat and drink once a day. Should they be hungry now, they can sleep. They are *ariqa* and have already gotten more today than they should expect. They could drink here."

"Water from the lake, while you took it from your bags?"

"For *ariqa* water is water. If they do not like it, I cannot help it."

"So, they are slaves. Where did you buy them?"

"Buy them? Oh *mudir*, how can the saints who know heaven be so inexperienced on Earth? A Takalah never buys *ariqa* but 'makes' them."

"Then these slaves are tribal members of yours?"

"Naturally!"

"What did they do to have been made *ariqa*?"

"What they did? Actually nothing. The Mek needs money, which is why he is selling them."

"Can he sell every one of his subjects?"

"All those that are disobedient or, for some reason, do not please him any more. Every father has his children, every man his wives, and every powerful leader can sell those he lords over."

"What would you say if the Mek were to also sell you?"

"I would have to resign myself to it," then added so softly that only I could understand it: "But I would not accept it and would throttle him."

That he thought me to be a saint did not prevent him from trusting me with this truth. Either even a high-ranking Sinussi did not count much with him, as he earlier seemed to imply, or nothing at all was sacred to him. That the latter was the case, showed right away, when I asked him:

"Did you sell *ariqa* before?"

"Often. These here include a wife and two daughters of mine."

"Why are you selling them?"

"Because I took another wife, and because it is better that one is paid for daughters than having to feed them."

He said this with a totally incomprehensible lack of feeling and in a voice quite obviously expressing not only his own, but the opinion of all human beings, as well.

"Did they submit willingly?" I inquired.

"What were they going to do to prevent it? They pleaded and cried, but what is the meaning of a woman's tears? Women do not have a soul and can therefore not enter Heaven."

"Where are you taking these slaves?"

"To Fashoda to a man who regularly takes my *ariqa*."

He had intended to give me a different answer, maybe a more precise one, but had cut himself short, seemingly not trusting me all the way.

"Have you often been to Fashoda?" I continued.

"I travel there every six months to sell *ariqa*. Where will your present journey take you, oh *mudir*?"

"First to Makhadat al-Kalb where I will cross the White Nile to visit and preach to the people of the Fungi."

"Will you also go to Fashoda?"

"Not now, maybe later."

By now the sun had touched the horizon, meaning the time for the *mihrab* prayer had come.

The men, who had sat nearby, even the tied-together prisoners, rose to their knees, with all eyes on me. It is the duty of the most distinguished to speak the prayer with the others joining in only at certain places. This was a critical moment for me. I had often prayed with Muslims, but, of course, not aloud and not to Allah or the Prophet. But now to prescribe to these many people the various bows and to lead the prayer, the Fathha, the prescribed Qur'an verses, the greeting to Muhammad and the archangel – this was impossible, and would have been a very great sin. Bin Nil extracted me from this predicament by saying:

"*Mudir*, you always spoke only the three prayers of the day and left the two evening prayers to me. Allow me to do this today, as well?"

"Yes, oh *khatib*, you favorite of the Prophet, lead the prayer," I replied. "Your words take the same path as mine and shall reach the same destination to where every prayer is directed, as if coming from my own mouth."

When the *mihrab* had been spoken, I ate with Bin Nil. While doing so, the Takalah turned their faces toward the lake so that they would not see me eating, as courtesy prescribes it to be done for a distinguished or pious man. Since I kept silent afterward, Shadid did not dare talk to me. The others, too, kept totally silent, thinking me and my young preacher to be deeply immersed in pious thoughts which they ought not disturb.

Then the moon rose, throwing the shadows of the tree crowns upon us. To my right lay the sterile, merciless desert; on the water to my left shone the tiny elfin bodies, the blossoms of those forever restless plants that are not rooted in the soil and therefore continuously change their location. They are especially plentiful on Lake Chad. There, the residents of Bornu and Baghirmi sing a paddling song, a most sweet tune, which demonstrates clearly that these peoples, too, are rich in poetry. The song, freely translated, would read like this:

"Homeless drifts the Fanna
Above the rippling waves,
When on the lake, gigantic large
The Talha's shadow rests.
He spread the nets
In bright moonlight,
Sang into the silent night
Dreaming to be alone, he might.
Then rushing from the waters
So lovely, ghostly pale;
He stopped the boat from its advance
Was never seen again.
Now, homeless drifts the Fanna
Above the rippling waves,
When on the lake, gigantic large
The Talha's shadow rests."

Instead of being immersed in the depth of Islam, I thought, when seeing the bright blooms of the 'homeless Fanna', of this song and its location, where by night lions, elephants, rhinoceroses and hippopotamuses, the giants of the animal kingdom, meet peacefully at its shore; peaceful except for the fear of succumbing to their mighty opponent, the lion. Suddenly, a Takalah broke the silence by pointing out to the desert, calling:

"A man, a rider. Who might this be?"

Someone came riding directly toward the 'Ford of Shadow'. He had to know it well. He appeared to come from the northeast, that is from the Nile, while our direction had been more to the northwest. His bright *burnous* reflected the moonlight. He had to see our burning fires. That he approached without hesitation led one to conclude much. Only when he had come very close did he halt his camel and offered greetings:

"May Allah give you a hundred thousand of such nights. Allow me to rest with you?"

Since I and Bin Nil kept silent, Shadid, the Takalah's leader, replied:

"Dismount and sit down. You are welcome."

The man hopped from his saddle, let his camel go to the water, and stepped to the fire to sit between Shadid and Bin Nil. Since the prisoners were not lying by the fire, but more in the shadows, he had not been able to see them clearly, but now noticed that they were tied to a rope. Immediately, his face assumed a noticeably satisfied expression, and his voice sounded relieved, when he said:

"Allah sent me at the right time to the 'Ford of Shadow'. Am I correct that these captives are members of the Takalah people?"

"Yes," the leader replied.

"Then, Shadid, the highest servant of the king, must also be here. Who of you is he?"

"I am. But who are you that you know my name?"

"I am a Bin Baqqara and live at the *mishrah* Umm Oshrin (Mother of Twenty). I am friends with a man you know, too – Ibn Asl."

"Is your acquaintance connected with your presence here?"

"Yes, I was sent to you as his messenger."

"He sent you to me? Not to where I live, but here to this place where it is very doubtful where and when I could be found? There must be an extraordinary reason!"

"There is! However, he was quite certain that I would find you here. He said that you leave your lands twice annually to go to Fashoda, and that you undertake these trips at specific times."

"This is true."

"He knows the days of your departure and arrival very well and can therefore easily figure where you will be on a given day. He said that I could be certain to meet you tomorrow or the day after at the ford."

"He was off by a day, because I left a day earlier this time. What is the message you are bringing?"

"It is a warning. You are not to approach the Nile too closely and, this time, you are not to deliver the *ariqa* directly to Fashoda, but rather hide them nearby. Then you are to go to Ibn Mulai, the *sangak* of the *Arnautlar*, to tell him where they can be found."

"Why these conditions?"

"Because there is a foreign *effendi* who roams this area in order to catch slave traders and deliver them to the *raïs effendina*."

"May Allah destroy this dog!"

"On top of this, he is a Christian!"

"Then Allah may not destroy him, but keep him for all eternity in the most terrible corner of Hell. Why does this Christian dog bother with slave traders?"

"I am to tell you that most likely he is presently on a sailing ship belonging to the *raïs effendina* which is on the Nile sailing to Fashoda. Since these people oftentimes go on land, they could easily discover and apprehend you, should you come too close to the river. This is why Ibn Asl sent me to warn you."

"This was not necessary. The Viceroy's laws are none of my concern. I serve my King. Our laws permit the sale of people. When I act according to them, no one can do anything to me. Furthermore, I have a mighty protector in Ali Effendi al-Kurdi, the *mudir* of Fashoda, who has plenty of times snatched a catch from under his nose. What do we need to fear then? I shall not change my usual direction of travel, especially not because of a cursed Christian. Rather, I would be pleased to come across him, if only to crush him between my fists."

He rubbed his enormous hands together, at which time the expression of his otherwise not unpleasant features had taken on a very different one. One can easily imagine the interest with which I witnessed this conversation. At the same time, I was pleased to hear that neither Shadid nor the messenger knew of the recent dismissal of the *mudir* Ali Effendi al-Kurdi. I was just as glad to learn that the *sangak* of the *Arnautlar* was truly the one the first lieutenant of the slavers had named as such. I now was certain to whom I had to turn. Shadid's words demonstrated great self-confidence. I liked this, for, the safer he felt, the more he worked into my hands. Still, I had no presentiment of all I was yet to hear. The messenger cautioned against the man's self-confidence by warning him:

"Do not feel so safe! Do you think Ibn Asl would have sent me, were he not convinced that it is necessary? This Christian *effendi* is supposed to be much more dangerous than the *raïs effendina* himself."

Now, Shadid rose, stretched his mighty body in length and breadth, and called:

"Rather be quiet and look at me! Do I look like I must fear anyone, and even less a Christian? I can knock down five or ten such dogs at a time!"

"Yes, you are strong, Ibn Asl told me so, but he was nevertheless of the opinion that this Christian is just as strong, maybe even stronger than you."

"Stronger than me? How can Ibn Asl insult me like this? I have never been vanquished by any man!"

"He did not intend to insult you, but did not refer only to the physical strength but also to that strength, or the advantage, a cunning man has over his opponent. This *giaur* is said to be the epitome of deceitfulness. He is able to deduce everything, even the most secret, and always causes those setting a trap for him to fall into it themselves. Ibn Asl has told me some. He did not have much time, but the little he told me about this Christian should urge you to be very cautious."

"Then, tell me about it! I want to hear with my own ears why a faithful Muslim should fear an *infidel* dog."

He sat down again with the messenger now telling about our adventures. Although, this was done only in outlines. When the messenger had finished the Takalah commented:

"This dog really seems to be most dangerous. I must beware of him. But since he does not know me, or anything about me, I need not fear him."

"How can you say that he does not know anything of you? He captured Ibn Asl's men. What if he succeeds in getting one of these men to talk?"

"That is true."

"Even if he did not know anything about you, he would still stop you, when you meet him with *ariqaariqa*."

"I would defeat him!"

"Maybe, yes, if he would attack you openly. But you heard how cautious and cunning he is. Avoid him as much as you can."

"Fine, I will do so, but not because I am afraid, but because Ibn Asl wants me to. Where is Ibn Asl now?"

"It was yesterday afternoon when he arrived on his camel mare at the *mishrah* Umm Oshrin. I left shortly afterward to come here. From that you can figure that he will already be far beyond Makhadat al-Kalb by tonight."

"Is he riding all the way to Fashoda?"

"Yes."

"Since all his men were captured, where is he going to get new ones for the slave hunt?"

"He wants to hire Shilluk and Nuer, maybe also Dinka, as he finds the opportunity. But this must be soon, because the *raïs effendina* is after him. He will hide in Fashoda, since he wants to wait for you. And I just remembered: he asked that you take good care of, and watch especially, one slave. I am to tell you that he is the one he asked for six months ago on your previous trip."

"Hafiz Sikhar? There he is, the first on the rope."

"It is most important to Ibn Asl to have this man returned. You are to guard him carefully."

"I shall keep an eye on him and remain cautious. But Ibn Asl forgot the main thing. He did not let me know that which is most important. What if I meet this Christian *effendi*? I do not know him and could easily succumb to his cunning, if not to his strength. Ibn Asl saw him, even talked with him, so how could he forget to give me a description of this dog through you?"

"Allah! What a messenger I am!" the man exclaimed, while he hit his forehead with his hand. "Not he, but I forgot it. He gave me a very clear description, and then added another name, Bin Nil."

"Woe to me! I reached involuntarily for my revolver, for the conversation was taking an unpleasant turn. If the man recalled the description correctly, I would be given away. Bin Nil had the same idea and gave me a concerned, searching look.

"Bin Nil?" Shadid asked. "Who is he?"

"A young man, who, although he is a Muslim, stands always by the side of this *effendi*. May Allah tear him apart. Never does one see the one without the other. This is why Ibn Asl gave me a description of the two."

"Tell me then!"

"This Bin Nil is about eighteen years old and does not wear a beard. He is of slender build, but is very strong. His hair and eyes are dark, his cheeks full. His last known dress consisted of . . ."

He stopped, looked surprised at Bin Nil, and exclaimed:

"What surprise! The description I was given for this disloyal Muslim fits precisely this youngster, sitting next to me."

"You must be mistaken or it is a coincidence."

"But I tell you, it fits exactly!"

"This is possible because you did not get to see this Bin Nil. Thousands of young men have dark hair and eyes, slender build and full cheeks. But this young man is beyond a shadow of doubt, for he is a famous *khatib* of the sacred order of Sidi Sinussi."

The messenger crossed his arms before his chest, bowed to Bin Nil, and said:

"Then I must be mistaken. I did not want to insult this pious *khatib*, Allah may bless."

Thank God! The smaller half of danger had passed. But what was going to happen to the other greater hurdle? To learn this did not take long, for Shadid said:

"This Bin Nil is anyway a secondary matter. The main thing is the description of the *effendi*. Give it to me as exactly as possible."

Silently, I wished it to turn out as inexact as possible. Unfortunately this wasn't the case. Ibn Asl had impressed my description most thoroughly on his messenger. Barely had my figure, my face and part of my garb been described, the speaker stopped once more, as he had done giving Bin Nil's description. He stopped, stared at me stunned and continued:

"Allah is great! Should one imagine it possible? There sits in person the one I am describing. It is him, it is him! No doubt is possible!"

One can imagine the excitement these words raised. Everyone stared at me, even the captives raised their heads, with one of them calling:

"Al-Hamdulillah! Maybe I will be saved now!"

Fortunately, no one paid attention to these words, although they had been directed to me exclusively. Only I had taken note of them, since I had occupied myself for some time already with the man who had spoken them. He had been called Hafiz Sikhar by Shadid, which was the name of the man I was searching for, that is the Ma'abdah guide's missing brother. Was he the one? Ibn Asl had conveyed through this messenger that he should be exceptionally well guarded. He had to be important. I was much more inclined to think that I had found the missing man here, although much spoke against it. However, my belief had been strengthened by the exclamation I had just heard. He had understood the messenger's story. He must think me to be an enterprising and fearless man, and, that if I were the feared foreign effendi, only the intention to liberate the captives could have led me here. This is why his incautious lips spoke the words that he might now be saved. Of course, I had no time any more to pay attention to him, but had to dedicate myself to the danger to my physical and spiritual self.

A brief look to Bin Nil calmed me. He looked not at all scared, but his face displayed such a superior smile, as if he were assuredly the one I had called him, a khatib, and was now puzzled by the possibility of being thought someone else. I could rely on him and needn't worry at all about his behavior.

Concerning myself, I looked at the messenger questioningly with-out saying a word. I acted as if I were incapable of understanding what he had said. Shadid kept looking from him to me. He had been con-vinced that I matched the description, but the dignified calm I main-tained confused him.

"What are you saying?" he asked the messenger. "This man, sitting here to my right, is supposed to be the *infidel effendi*?"

"Yes, it is he! He cannot be anyone else."

"You are again mistaken. This holy man is the *mudir* of Jarabub, the confidante and best friend of Sidi Sinussi."

"Is this true? Can you prove it?" the messenger asked.

"He told me so himself."

"He himself, he told you!" the Baqqara Arab laughed. "If you were not told by another, safe man, your proof is poorly founded. Did I not tell you that the *giaur* has often assumed a different name?"

"Allah! So I heard. Should . . ."

He looked at me with eyes in which trust and mistrust fought for victory. I replied with a firm, puzzled look, asking:

"What does this man say? Is he talking about me?"

"Of course, he means you!" Shadid answered. "Did you not understand?"

"Had I understood him, I would think him to be mad, but rather assume to have heard wrongly."

"He claims that you are the Christian *effendi*, he talked about."

"May Allah be merciful to him! Did he truly say this? His mind must be sick. He should immerse some cloth in water and wrap it around his head to make the fever disappear."

"I am not ill. I know what I am saying!" the Baqqara exclaimed. "One can err with one person, but with two together it is impossible. The young man matches Bin Nil exactly and the other the *effendi*. It is them! What kind of camels do they ride? Ibn Asl said that they have gray *hujun*."

"This is correct," Shadid replied.

"Right! So this is more proof that I am not mistaken. Don't let yourself be fooled, oh Shadid! Check it carefully!"

Shadid had become doubly suspicious. He said to me:

"You heard what he says. I hold deference to your holiness, but I do not have proof for it being true. I ask you therefore to help me trust you."

"So you really mistrust me?" I asked seemingly surprised. "I am to prove that I am who I am! Tell me where we are!"

"Well, here by the Machada al-Dill."

"And where is this *effendi*, as Ibn Asl said himself?"

"Sailing on the Nile."

"Can I therefore be him?"

"What Ibn Asl said was only an assumption. If only one of you matched the descriptions, an error is possible, but since you both match, it looks bad for you. If you are this *effendi*, I must kill you."

"But I am not the one!"

"That has not been proved. Do you carry some kind of proof, telling the truth?"

"I am the sole and best proof."

"Then I must arrest you and take you to Ibn Asl."

"You will not do this, since our sacred work would suffer from it."

"If you do not enable me to believe in this sacred work, I cannot take it into account."

"You will take it into account, as I am convinced that you are aware of the power and secrets my order possesses. I would make them apply to you."

The area's population is possessed by the starkest superstition, which is why these words produced the salutary effect I had intended. Shadid found himself in difficult straits. Were I the *effendi*, he had to kill or at least arrest me. But were I truly the Sinussi I pretended to be, I not only was a holy man but also a magician, who, to avenge himself, could bring all kinds of good and bad spirits into being. He was terribly afraid of these, my magical powers. However, the messenger kept stirring him up more and more by making further remarks against me, so that he finally told me:

"I do not know what to do. I do not want to mistrust you, and yet you cannot legitimize yourself. However, there are two ways by which you can remove my doubts. Will you agree to them?"

"Speak first!"

"You heard that this *effendi* is supposed to be a very strong man. Fight me and prove that you have the strength he is supposed to have."

This was, of course, some craftiness and cleverness that would not earn him a prize. The good man could not imagine that a strong man could put on an act. I would have instantly agreed to his request had I not to maintain the honor of my assumed spiritual position. I, therefore, replied:

"You are saying that I could legitimize myself in two ways, first by dueling you. But we journey to preach, not to fight. Compare your figure with mine. Were I to fight you, I would certainly be defeated."

"Not everything depends on one's build."

"Yes," the slaver's messenger agreed. "As I was told by Ibn Asl, the foreign *effendi* does not have the build of a giant, yet has the physical strength no other, not a single one, can match. If you are this *giaur* you could likely overcome Shadid. If you do not overcome him, then this is proof that you are not this *effendi*."

"So it is," Shadid nodded. "Should your conscience be clean, wrestle with me. If you do not, I assume that you are afraid to give yourself away by your strength. Decide, therefore!"

True to the role I was to play, I did rise, but said concerned:

"If it were heard in Jarabub that I wrestled with you and was overcome, the respect I must demand would largely be lost."

Now, my crafty Bin Nil came smartly to my aid, saying:

"Who would divulge it, oh *mudir*? None of the men here are likely to ever come to our homeland, and you can rest totally assured of my discretion."

"Did you hear?" Shadid said. "Should I overcome you, your honor will not suffer. Your concern has thus become unfounded, and I challenge you once more to decide."

"Well, then. Let it happen. What are the requirements for the fight?"

"We take off our upper garments and hug each other. The one who lifts the other from his position and drops him down is the victor. Are you agreed?"

"Yes, I don't mind." I replied, while we removed our *hâka*.

Of course, I did not intend to have myself thrown, but if I offered too little resistance, this would have made him suspicious. In all honesty, I would have liked to measure myself in earnest against this goliath to learn whether I would be able to wrestle him down. Unfortunately, I could not do this.

We stood at the ready. He stepped toward me and put his mighty arms around me, I putting mine around him. He now tried to lift me. I resisted as a strong man would. Twice did he lift my feet, however, every time I was able to gain the ground again. On the third try, he gathered his entire strength, lifted me, and while he kept his left arm around my chest, grabbed my thighs with his right hand, so that he now held me horizontally, then laid me on the ground. While I let it happen, I gained the conviction that I could have done likewise, had I only wanted to.

"He is not weak," my opponent said, "but has some good strength, but it is not exceptional."

"I knew that I would be overcome," I commented, while I got up. "I can't possibly be a match for a man like you. I have lost."

At that, I acted as if the exertion had taken all my breath away.

"Yes, twice you were able to reach the ground again, but for that your chest is now heaving as if you had been running for some time. You are no giant. You passed the first test. Now, we will do the second."

"What is it?"

"Supposedly, there are Christians who know the Qur'an, but no *giaur* can know it by heart as a Muslim can. I am certain that if one preaches the *Sura al-Kuiffar* to an *infidel*, he will not be able to repeat it correctly. Do you know it?"

"Yes."

"Can you also say it without making a mistake?"

"Maybe, if you recite it correctly and clearly."

I had no need to have it recited, for I knew it by heart. It is the hundred-and-ninth *Sura* and is supposed to have been revealed to Muhammad, when some Arabs demanded that he honor their gods for a year, after which they would just as long pray to his God. It is very short, only a few lines long, but its peculiar wording makes it even difficult for an Arab to recite it without making mistakes. It is especially used when there is suspicion of drunkenness, since it is virtually impossible for a drunk to finish it without stumbling. Shadid took the same for granted when applied to a Christian.

"Let's see," he said with a superior smile. "I shall recite it for you. By the way, you gave yourself away already by asking me to speak it for you. A good Sinussi, especially a *mudir*, an outstanding member of this sacred brotherhood, must be able to recite this *Sura* without hearing it first."

He put himself into position, lowered his head, folded his hands, and began:

"In the name of the all-compassionate God! Speak: Oh, you unbelievers, I do not worship that which you worship, and you do not worship what I do not worship, and I shall never worship that which you do not worship, and you shall worship . . . not worship that which I not . . . that I worship, for you you have my religion, and I . . I . . I have . . . I have no . . no .. no . . ."

He halted, realizing that he had lost his way. Not taking the wrong sentence structure into account, he had twice used the word "not" and once the word "my" although they are not included in the *Sura*.

"Well!" I smiled. "Are you no Muslim or are you drunk?"

"I am neither!" he exclaimed angrily. "This *Sura* is truly the most difficult there is, but you being a Sinussi ought to be able to say it without losing your way."

"If I misspeak only once, you shall receive everything I own!"

"Really? I take you by your word. By the way, you need not make me this promise, for should you make the least mistake, I will take you to be a Christian, the foreign *effendi*. Then, your life is forfeited, and everything you carry is my property, as well."

"But will you be able to judge whether I make a mistake or not? Just now, you weren't able to speak the *Sura* yourself, and what one wants to assess, one must know and understand oneself."

"I know the *Sura*, even if I cannot say it without losing my way. Speak, then!"

I complied by reciting it so fast that his ears were unlikely to be able to follow:

"In the name of the all-compassionate God! Speak: Oh, you unbelievers, I do not worship that which you worship, and you do not what I worship, and I shall never worship that which you worship, and you shall never worship that which I worship. You have your religion and I have mine."

In its English translation this Sura sounds pompous, but it is different in Arabic. The conjugation of the word "*ihtarama*" (to worship), is so peculiar that it truly is difficult not to confuse the affirmation with the negation, and the first person singular with the second person plural. When I had finished, Shadid said:

"Truly, he can, and so quickly and without the least chance of getting lost. He cannot be an *infidel*!"

"But," the messenger butted in, "I recall Ibn Asl saying that the *infidel effendi* knows the Arabic language and the Qur'an so well, as if he were born here and has studied with the best *ustath* (professor at a Muslim university) in al-Qahira. Beware! Do not judge too quickly, you could easily be mistaken!"

"Do you think so? How else should I test him?"

This sounded dangerous for me. The messenger was of the firm opinion that I was the *effendi*. Through his influence, the good opinion Shadid now seemed to have gained of me could easily be reversed.

It was advisable not to wait for this, which is why, acting angrily, I said:

"More tests? I won't go for this! Do you know what a *mudir* from Jarabub represents? Nevertheless, I condescended not only to wrestle with you but also to recite the *Sura al-Kuiffar*. This is more than enough. Am I to humiliate myself even more before you? No! Whoever insults a *mudir* of the Sinussi and a *khatib* of this pious brotherhood in this way, cannot expect to see the faces of such people for any length of time. We were hospitable to you and allowed you to camp near us, so we shall now leave this place, turn our backs to you, to . . ."

"No, you may not!" the messenger exclaimed, interrupting me. "We will not let you leave!"

"No?" I asked, while I looked down on him. "How do you want to prevent us from leaving?"

"I will use force!"

"You want to lay hands on us, men of Allah's?"

"Yes. Sit down!"

He reached for me to push me down. I, however, stepped back a pace, and thundered at him:

"Hold it, incautious one! Shall I hurl the curse on you from which your body will dry up and your soul pine away? Should you wish to try whether *Lani* Allah (Allah's curse) has been handed to us or not, I don't mind, but let me tell you that your life will end in terror and perpetual horror. Whoever wishes to hold us back may try. Whose hands dare touch us?"

I looked around. All remained silent, standing or sitting unmoving, frightened not only by my words, but more so by the tone of my voice. I went to the bushes and untied my camel. Bin Nil did likewise. We mounted up and drove the animals into the water. No one thought to prevent us or ask us to stay. Not a word was said; no shout of goodbye followed us. I was glad of it.

As I had guessed, the water was not deep at this place, reaching not even to the camels' bellies. Some bushes grew on the opposite bank, giving way to grass at least as far as the moisture of the Nid al-Nil penetrated.

Once I thought that we could no longer be seen, I turned left toward the lake. Until now, Bin Nil had remained quiet, but now said:

"You are riding east, *effendi*, when our direction should be to the south! Why do you diverge from it?"

"For two reasons. First, we do not want the Takalah to see our tracks. Had we ridden to where the grass ends and the sand begins, they would have found our tracks in the latter, but not in the grass, which will have risen again by morning. With water nearby and dew falling, the grass that's been trampled by the camels will right itself from the moisture a few hours later."

"Do you suspect the Takalah to pursue us?"

"Not only do I suspect it, but know it for certain. They will want to recapture Hafiz Sikhar."

"Hafiz Sikhar? Yes, this name was mentioned, I recall. It is the name of the brother of the guide at Ma'abdah. Do you think he is here with the Takalah?"

"I am convinced of it."

"And you want to liberate him?"

"Yes. This is the second reason for turning eastward to the lake."

"Allah! This will be another adventure. *Effendi*, whoever rides with you will not fall short on experiences, even dangers. I almost became worried for us when they guessed who we were. Why did you lower yourself and have yourself tested?"

"Because it was smartest. Would Shadid know for certain that I am the Christian *effendi*, he would not go to Fashoda, even send a fast messenger there to warn Ibn Asl and the *sangak* of the *Arnautlar*. Our ride to Fashoda would be unsuccessful, be for nothing. We heard plenty, something Shadid knows just as well as we."

"This is true, *effendi*. So, now we ride eastward to mislead the Takalah, but then turn south?"

"No. We ride back on this side of the lake shore until we arrive at the narrow, steep drop, across which we cannot take our camels. Then, you will stay there with the camels, and I will clamber across to get Hafiz Sikhar."

"What do you want with him?"

"We must take him along to Fashoda."

"That requires another camel!"

"I will take one from the Takalah."

"Hmm! To untie Hafiz Sikhar without anyone noticing, then spend precious time to steal a camel, this is too much for one."

"I wouldn't mind having you with me were it not necessary for one of us to stay with the camels because of wild animals."

"Do you believe there are some hereabouts?"

"Where there is water, there is life, and where there is life, carnivores are found."

"Do you believe I can defend the camels against lions? Should you answer this with a 'yes', I will be most grateful for the trust you are showing me, but I do not think that I could meet it. You know that I am not afraid, but to kill a lion takes more than mere fearlessness. Upon your return, you would find me and the animals torn apart. This is why it is better you take me along."

He was right, which is why I was willing to accede to his wish. It was correct that I could encounter a situation where a helper would be good to have.

As I described earlier, the place where we had arrived at, the Nid al-Nil, had a narrow, waterless gully. We had turned to the right there and had come upon two bays of the Nid al-Nil, only then arriving at the ford. To get there, we had ridden along the northern shore. Now, we rode back along the southern banks of the first bay and then the second one, in order to arrive at the dry gully, which was exactly opposite the place where we had arrived at the Nid al-Nil. With the moon shining, the path caused no difficulty. Still, I would have preferred darkness. My intentions were such that moonlight could pose a danger to me.

We halted, dismounted, and tied the camels to tree trunks. I would have liked to leave the rifles here, but we could have come across a larger carnivore, against which knives and revolvers would be useless, which is why we took them along.

Then we climbed down on our side and up the other and followed the same direction by which we had reached the ford upon our arrival. Of course, we proceeded more slowly than before when we had ridden camels.

Nearing the ford, we noticed that no fires were burning any more. I was glad for it and it told me that the Takalah were sleeping. I left Bin Nil waiting under a tree and sneaked on alone. About a hundred paces from camp, I lay down, in order to creep the rest of the way.

The moon was already low and produced shadows across the camp, which was very useful to me. However, the Takalah had posted a guard for the slaves. He was slowly walking back and forth next to them. Although I did not see him, I heard his soft footsteps. Before I could undertake anything directly, I had to orient myself well. I, therefore, circled around the entire camp. I found everything the way we had left it. The prisoners were lying where they had before with the others likewise. To get to the man I thought to be Hafiz Sikhar, I had to render the guard harmless. The saddles lay in two piles next to each other. Some camels lay on the ground, others stood, their forelegs hobbled, facing the water next to bushes or in the grass to eat. I could now proceed based on this information. I returned to Bin Nil to fetch him. He crept with me as close as possible as his lack of practice advised. Then, he had to sneak around the camp to the opposite side, where the camels were. I pointed out a tree behind which he was to hide and wait for me. Then I crept towards the prisoners.

When I was at most ten paces away from them, I stopped to listen. They all seemed to be asleep, which was no wonder, being so poorly treated, provided with so little water, and having to walk for days under the burning sun. There was no movement. Only the guard was still pacing back and forth in the same direction. I approached him as close as possible, let him pass, jumped up, took him from behind by his throat with my left hand, and gave him a blow to the head with my right fist. He spread his arms and sank down. No conspicuous noise was made. I cautiously loosened my left grip. He remained still, being unconscious. I lifted him up and carried him to Bin Nil to guard. When I happened to cross a spot of moonlight, the light momentarily fell on his face. To my surprise I noticed that it was no Takalah, but the Baqqara Arab, the messenger Ibn Asl had dispatched. This pleased me for several reasons.

"Who are you bringing?" Bin Nil asked softly, when I arrived at his place. "Is it Hafiz Sikhar?"

"Not yet. It is the Baqqara who the Takalah made the guard of the prisoners."

"He treated us poorly and must be silenced. Shall I knife him?"

"No. We will take him with us. He is Ibn Asl's ally. Therefore, it is our duty to deliver him to the *raïs effendina*."

"We would do even better to knife him."

"But then Shadid can readily tell who was here. But if we take him along, he will be suspected of having freed Hafiz Sikhar and taken him along."

"That is true, *effendi*. But that will require his saddle and his camel."

"That's not necessary. The more camels and saddles we take, the greater will be the suspicion against him. It will look like he has exchanged his poor property for a better one. Let me handle it. We can take our time, the Takalah are sound asleep."

The Baqqara was tied up and gagged. Then I crept again to the prisoners. Hafiz Sikhar had been the first on the rope, something very advantageous to me. I had taken notice of where he lay and found the place easily. Still tied to the rope, the prisoners lay in a circle. They slept like the dead. Only one wasn't asleep, precisely the one I was looking for. When I had come close with my head to his and touched him softly with a finger, he whispered:

"*Effendi*, is it you?"

"Yes."

"Allah! I waited for you. My heart pounded from worry that you might not be the one from whom I could expect rescue."

The circle of prisoners was such that their feet were turned inward with their heads outward. Since I was, of course, outside the circle, my head was against his, which is why he could not see me. I raised my chest, pushed my face over his and whispered:

"What's your name?"

"Hafiz Sikhar from Ma'abdah."

"What is your brother's name?"

"Bin Wasak."

"Then you are truly the one I'm looking for. Greetings from your brother."

"Oh, Heaven, oh, Allah! What . . .!"

"Psst, quiet! Not so loud! Are the people next to you asleep?"

"As soundly as you could wish."

"Lie still then, I will set you free."

I checked with my fingers as to how he was tied up and how he was tied to the rope. A few cuts with my knife and he was free. Should he try to rise, he could easily wake up one of his neighbors. To prevent this, I took him under his arms and pulled him from the circle, slowly and carefully, so that he did not bump into his neighbors to the left and right. Then, he had to creep behind me to Bin Nil. Arriving there, he immediately wanted to indulge in expressions of thanks, but I cut him off:

"Quiet now! You can talk later as much as you like. Now we must hurry."

I checked the Arab. He was just coming to. He tried to shout and tear his fetters, but succeeded at neither. The fetters held fast, and what was supposed to be a scream for help, came only as a softly wheezing groan through his nose. Bin Nil put his knife on his chest and threatened:

"Another noise and I will stab you in your chest!"

That helped. The Baqqara remained still and no longer moved until we had him secure later.

"A couple of camels, now, *effendi*," Bin Nil suggested. "One for each."

"We need three," I answered. "We need more water now for which we need an animal to carry it. We also need to take a few bags, since we have only two."

"Permit me to select the camels, *effendi*. I am familiar with our animals," said Hafiz Sikhar. "I will select the best."

Before I could hold him back, he had slipped away, leaving us to nothing else but to wait for his return. Of course, I was very unhappy about his departure. He could wreck everything. Fortunately, this was not the case. About a quarter of an hour later that seemed to me like an hour, he returned and said:

"I am done, *effendi*. We can leave."

"Done with what?"

"Little by little, I carried three saddles, also three bags, across the gully. Did you not see it?"

"No. You must have been very careful."

"That was necessary. And the three best camels are also ready. We can go."

"Did you notice whether one of the sleepers woke up?"

"They are all asleep. Come, you can follow me confidently."

"First, take the knife and musket I took from the Baqqara. You will need weapons now."

I tossed the Baqqara over my shoulder. Hafiz Sikhar led us to the ford, where he had tied up the three camels. We could not mount up since they would have screamed. Bin Nil and Hafiz led the animals, while I carried the Baqqara. This is how we entered the water that reached up to my belt.

Arriving on the other side, I removed the Baqqara's foot ties so that he could walk. While the camels were standing, we put the saddles loosely on them, something they accepted calmly. Then we walked along the southern bank of the larger of the lake's bays. Each of us led an animal, I also the Baqqara, while Bin Nil and Hafiz carried the water bags.

When we had covered a sufficient distance, we stopped to properly saddle the camels. They could become noisy now, since they could no longer be heard by the Takalah. For this they had to kneel down. I mounted up and put the Baqqara crosswise before me. When the two others were seated, we hurried off, along the other lake, then to the left, where we had left our animals.

Would we still find them? Yes, they were still there. We dismounted and tied up the acquisitioned camels nearby, after we had relieved them from their saddles. Then we camped under a tree to which the Baqqara was tied. I took the gag from his mouth and asked him:

"Bin Baqqara, do you now know with certainty who I am?"

He did not answer.

"I know that you aren't deaf, and I'm used to getting an answer when I ask a question. If your mouth remains closed, it can easily be opened by the whip. Therefore answer!"

"Yes, I know!" he angrily exploded. "You are the *effendi* and your companion is Bin Nil."

"But the *effendi* is supposed to possess enormous physical strength, and I was overcome by Shadid?"

"You pretended. I knew it."

"But I was able to say the *Sura al-Kuiffar* without becoming hung up. How can I then be the Christian *effendi*?"

"You can do everything."

"Not everything, but much. For instance, I can easily snatch a Baqqara Arab from a bunch of Takalah to take him to Fashoda to deliver him there to the *raïs effendina* for punishment."

"Why should I be punished? I did not do anything."

"You have even less brains than a crocodile has feathers. I will make sure, though, that you shall get some lessons. The *raïs effendina* . . ."

"I am not afraid of him," he interrupted me derisively.

"I know very well why. You think the *mudir* of Fashoda will support you against him."

He admitted to this, if not directly, then indirectly by answering:

"What is an *effendi* against a *mudir*. What power does an *effendi* have?"

"Only a numbskull, who has not learned anything, doesn't know anything, and doesn't understand anything, can ask this. Your head resembles a runny egg, of which only the shell remains. Let me tell you that the great princes, the Sultan's sons, are called *effendi*. Ministers call themselves *effendi*, and also the Viceroy of Egypt likes it to be called *effendi*. But what is the *mudir* of Fashoda against these mighty lords? Do you actually know this *mudir*?"

"Yes."

"Tell me his name then."

"He, too, is an *effendi*. His name is Ali Effendi al-Kurdi."

"This is not true."

"How can you call me a liar, you, a foreigner, who does not know this country and its conditions!"

"It seems that I know it better than you after all, because Fashoda's *mudir* is called by another name. Might you know the name Ali Effendi Abu Hamsah Miah?"

"Yes."

"Listen, then. The famous general Musah Pasha, following requests by the *raïs effendina*, has been in Fashoda to discharge al-Kurdi and appoint Abu Hamsah Miah. Al-Kurdi was taken to Khartoum as a prisoner. This was at the instigation of the *raïs effendina*. Now deny that the latter isn't as powerful as your disloyal and traitorous *mudir* al-Kurdi."

He remained silent. In any case, he had to be frightened by what I had told him. I continued:

"Now you know how much you can rely on your al-Kurdi. He is no longer able to protect marked criminals. These days he would thank Allah for having someone to speak for him. When I turn you over to the *raïs effendina*, he will take you to the new *mudir*, where you will experience why he carries his name most rightfully. By this I mean that the 'Father of Five-hundred' will, as an introduction, issue five hundred blows to you immediately."

"To me, a free Arab?"

"To you, the messenger of a slave hunter! What or who else you are otherwise isn't my concern."

"Then let me tell you that you will be subject to the revenge of all Baqqara tribes. If I am beaten, this will be worse than being killed. Take note of this!"

"Your tribes, were there even a hundred or a thousand, cannot do anything to me. They have as little power over me as they can now protect you. Nevertheless, while I do not fear them at all, I am prepared to set you free tomorrow on one condition."

"Which is?"

"You tell me the truth about how you got to know Ibn Asl, and answer all other questions about him that I ask you."

"I will not do this."

"We are done then. Just remember, that I promised to reward you with your freedom, but since you did not want to talk, the 'Father of Five-hundred' will later open your mouth."

At that, Hafiz Sikhar remarked:

"*Effendi*, if you want to learn of the malice of Ibn Asl, I am the right man to give you an example of it."

"I will indeed ask you for it. But before you do, you ought to learn a bit about me, for . . ."

"Oh, *effendi*," he interrupted, "I know you already. I have heard plenty about you from the Baqqara, when he and Shadid talked earlier about you. I lay nearby and heard everything. I had no idea that you knew my brother, but I felt as if Allah had sent me a voice that secretly told me: this *effendi* has already freed so many; if the man sitting there is one and the same, then he must have come to rescue me, as well. This is why I was so thoughtless to call my name and to call out words of hope. Had Shadid heard them, I would have fared badly."

"It was good that you said your name. Only by doing so was my attention drawn to you, and now you are free. By the way, later, in Fashoda, you would also have gained your freedom. It was my intention to draw the *mudir's* attention to your group. You know me somewhat from this Baqqara's stories to which I have little to add. I came to Ma'abdah to visit the famous crocodile cave. Your brother took me into it, then made the hand of a female mummy a gift to . . ."

"The hand of a female mummy?" he cut in. "Describe it to me."

When I had followed his request, he exclaimed:

"*Effendi*, you must have done him some great service!"

"Not at all."

"No? Well, then you must have left a good impression like no other before. It is the hand of a pharaoh's daughter, an Egyptian princess. I know the value my brother placed on it and am very glad that you succeeded so quickly in gaining his favor."

"This goodwill is mutual, I can assure you. I carry the hand with me and can show it to you as soon as it is daylight. It is in my saddle bag. When your brother heard that I was going to Khartoum, he told me of your disappearance for which he had no explanation, and asked me to search for you."

"Had he not done this before?"

"Of course, he had made a real effort to find you, unfortunately in vain. While he did, it appeared to me that he had committed a big mistake by extending too much trust to the merchant Baryad al-Amin. This man should have not learned that a search was on for you. I am highly suspicious that he is connected with your sudden disappearance."

"Naturally! Of course!" Hafiz Sikhar exclaimed. "It is he who delivered me into Ibn Asl's hands."

"Ah, I thought so. When your brother told me of him, some of it did not sound quite right to me. Although Baryad carried the nickname al-Amin, 'the Honest', he did not appear to me to be very honest. He claimed to have paid you all that money, but insisted that he did not know much more about you. It sounded impossible to me. Right away,

I thought of keeping a close watch on this man. I intended to observe him covertly and to investigate him. Unfortunately, travel events pushed me in different directions so that I haven't made it to Khartoum to this day."

"Lucky for me! Had you not met us today, I would never have tasted freedom again."

"This assumption is likely misleading. Ibn Asl was involved in Baryad al-Amin's business. When I learned this, I immediately guessed that your whereabouts or fate could be learned from him. There were other reasons to pursue this man. This had to succeed sooner or later, following which he would have had to confess what had happened to you."

"Still, Allah be praised that I myself can tell it to you now. I never believed that such a mishap could happen to me, and I really do not know how I deserved it."

"Concerning the latter, all men, including you and I, are sinners. We live only by Allah's compassion. Every event we call a misfortune, we richly deserve, yet Allah ordains that this misfortune, if we let it act upon us in the right way, will turn out to be our salvation and blessing. Don't speak therefore of earning it! It was a trial, sent by Allah, to, maybe, purify your heart, and direct your spirit in and upward."

He did not reply and a long pause ensued. Then he took my hand and said, while he squeezed it heartily:

"*Effendi*, your words are exactly right. In my misery, I quarreled with Allah. I cursed my life and all of humanity. At times better and brighter thoughts came but I closed my heart to them. But now that I enter life once more and my spirit trembles from joy, when you speak of purification and the direction of the spirit from the inside to the above, I am overcome as if by a bright lightning bolt giving me the insight that you are right. Who and what I have been before, I will tell you later. Today, I suddenly stand here like a new man, without having had any presentiment of it. Yes, I did not suffer in vain. Allah be praised for it!"

"I am truly glad to hear such words from you. You lost months and years of your life, but in their place found inner treasures whose value isn't transient like time. And whatever in material wealth was taken from you, I hope to be able to return to you in the future."

"You?" he asked wonderingly. "Are you so rich, *effendi?*"

"Oh, no. I'm even poor. But I know that Ibn Asl carries lots of money. If I catch him before he has spent it, he will have to replace all losses to you and your brother."

"It does not take Ibn Asl for this. He is not as secure as Baryad al-Amin is."

"Then, he, too, profited from the crime?"

"Of course! Baryad was poor, but good. My brother knew this and gave him the money he needed to establish his business in Khartoum. Some time later, he lend him an even greater sum for the enlargement of his business. When the time came to repay these amounts, I traveled to Khartoum to have them paid to me. I met Baryad al-Amin. He had become a different man. He had engaged an assistant by the name of Ibn Asl, who had drawn his attention to the profitability of the slave trade. He lusted for the riches to be gained by it; avarice had entered his heart. The slave trade, however, if it was to be conducted like a business, required lots of money. Having to pay me what he owed me, would not have left him enough for the slave trade. That is when the Devil whispered to him: Do not give it to him, or even better, hand it to him, demand a receipt, then take it again. He obeyed this devilish voice. I had no idea about it. I was warmly welcomed, was handed the money, and confirmed its receipt. For a few days longer I lived with him. The day before my departure I said my goodbyes to other acquaintances in Khartoum. The *dahabiyah* I intended to travel downstream with was to leave by early morning. I went to bed early and was awakened by a blow to my head. When I woke up, it was only to lose consciousness again right away. When I came to I felt rocking motions under me. Was I on a ship? No, because only a small boat would rock like this but no ship. I opened my eyes; it was dark. I wanted to get up to move about, but found I was tied up. I shouted aloud for help, but only to hear a threatening voice close by telling me that I would be whipped, if I did not remain quiet."

"You must have been on a camel?"

"Yes. It was night, but I could not see any stars. When daylight came, I saw that I lay in a *tachtirwan*, a woman's sedan chair, which was carried by a camel. I was covered by heavy blankets. Imagine, they had dressed me in woman's clothes, had even put multiple veils over my face, as I later found out. In case we were stopped, I was to look like a woman. As you know, no one must concern oneself with the passenger of a *tachtirwan*. They stopped in late morning. The camel was made to kneel and I was taken from the *tachtirwan*. We were out on the savanna. Five men accompanied me. I did not know four of them, but the fourth I knew very well. He was Ibn Asl."

"What? He risked being seen by you?"

"Oh, he risked much more. He had the nerve to tell me every-thing. Without this truly incomparable impudence and his presence at the time, I would not have known how everything had happened even today. Laughing, he told me that they needed my money for slave hunts, that he and Baryad al-Amin were business partners and would share the profits from the hunts. He himself had been for killing me, but Baryad had been too weak to permit it, since he was grateful to my brother. But since I had to be rendered harmless, they wanted to make sure that I would never again meet someone I knew and also would never return. What was meant by it, I only learned at the end of this journey, when we arrived in the lands of the Takalah, and I was handed over to the Mek of these people as a slave. He did not have to pay for me, but had to make sure that no one knowing me would ever see me. I still heard Ibn Asl concluding a contract with the Mek. He was to supply slaves to Fashoda twice a year on specific dates, to be paid immediately with certain goods. Then I was taken away."

"Where to?"

"To a terrible place, which I left only on the day of my transport to Fashoda where I was to be returned to Ibn Asl. Do you know of the famous copper mines of the Takalah?"

"Indeed, I know of them."

"Well, I was taken to such a pit and chained to work there. From that day on, I never saw the sun again. When I was recently released from the chains, someone with little mercy told me that I was to be taken to where I was to die."

"How come to die?"

"At the previous slave transport, Ibn Asl had asked for my return. He fell out with Baryad al-Amin and was conducting business on his own account. He no longer needed to heed his former business associate's wishes and thought himself more secure if I were no longer alive. Although he could have told the Mek to kill me, he did not trust him enough to do so. This is why he demanded my surrender, synonymous with my death. Am I to tell you what all I suffered and endured? Not now, maybe some time later on. And shall I now tell you the joy I delight in, being certain to have escaped slavery and certain death? I see an angel in you, sent by Allah, whom I . . ."

"Don't talk like this" I interrupted. "Allah ordained it. He alone you must thank. Do you feel strong enough for the ride to Fashoda?"

"Yes. I would have had to walk the desert anyway. The hard work steeled my muscles. You need not be concerned for me. When will we be in Fashoda?"

"I hope to make it in four days."

"And Ibn Asl is there?"

"Most likely."

"Woe to him, then! I shall avenge myself. I shall not let the *mudir* get him, but I . . ."

"Allow me to interrupt! Do not rack your brains with the thought on how to avenge yourself. You aren't the only one to settle an account with him. I will tell you about it. Let's rest now. We have a long ride ahead, and I think that you, especially, have need for rest."

"Me, sleep? *Effendi*, what a thought! Someone who was dead and has been returned to life is supposed to think at the moment of his awakening of sleep? No, no! Even if I wanted to, I could not. But you go ahead and sleep. I will sit here quietly, without moving, and taste my blessedness, see the firmament, Allah's Heaven above me, and feel thousands of stars arise in me."

"Well then, I see indeed that you would much rather stay awake then go asleep. Do so, then, but wake the two of us before daybreak, not later, so that we can keep an eye on the Takalah. And watch this Baqqara well, that he doesn't get away."

"*Effendi*, rest assured of this. He is Ibn Asl's envoy, my devil. Whoever comes from this man cannot expect leniency and compassion. I would rather kill myself than give him his freedom."

After what he had suffered, I was, of course, certain that I could not find a better guard for the Baqqara. I therefore lay down, wrapped myself into my *haïk* and fell asleep worry-free. He was very conscientious, for when he woke me and Bin Nil, morning had not come yet; the stars were just beginning to fade.

While I had fallen asleep, a thought had occurred to me, which I now put into action. I wanted to spy on the Takalah to learn what to expect from them next. It might be possible to do it by land but would be highly dangerous. It had to take place on water. But how? Even were there a boat available, we could not have used it. It had to be a raft, but one that did not draw attention. It could not look artificial, but had to have a natural appearance. I decided to build a small floating island, something not too difficult to accomplish with plenty of building material available. To select it, Bin Nil and I went closer to the lake.

Arriving there, I found the bristly-haired shoots and feathery leaves of numerous ambag trees growing. Ambag makes excellent material for rafts. The wood is so light that a raft carrying three men can easily be carried by one. Since, over time, water enters the spongy pith, eventually sinking the raft, such a vehicle is, of course, unsuited for a longer trip. However, I could not find anything better designed for my purpose. It is, by the way, a peculiarity of the ambag that it always grows in the vicinity of papyrus stalks.

Next to it grew a kind of tough, grassy Andropogon giganteus, also Hibiscus cannabinus, both very well suited to connect the three-to-four-meter-long ambag trunks. To make the raft appear like an island, we placed tall *umm sufah* bundles on its outside. Some hefty branches, to which we tied rushes, served as oars. This work was so easy and fast that we were finished and had the raft afloat before full daylight had come. The contraption carried Bin Nil and me easily. Hafiz Sikhar had to stay with the camels and the Baqqara.

When daylight had broken, I was delighted to find that the grass on our yesterday's tracks had righted itself fully. The place where we had slept lay well hidden behind some bushes, assuring me that the Takalah, should they be looking for us, would discover it only by sheer chance.

We entered the raft and first rowed it across the smaller lake, which one could actually call a pond. When we entered the larger one, we had to be cautious while approaching the Takalah's camp. We rowed the raft so slowly that it appeared driven by the morning breeze. Someone paying close attention would not even notice that it moved. The oars, too, were not noticeable; we had covered them very well with *umm sufah* bundles.

The Takalah seemed to be a very sleepy group. We closed in on the camp, yet did not hear the least noise coming from it. Bright daylight had by now arrived. Still, we risked rowing to the lake's end, where the Nid al-Nil suddenly narrowed, forming the 'Ford of Shadow', where we landed. Had we disembarked here, we could have reached the camp in fifty or sixty paces. Discounting the various animal voices, it was so quiet as if no human being were around. We peered through the rushes – no one was visible. Just when I was about to get up to take a better look, it suddenly became noisy and lively. I heard a startled voice call:

"Wake up, you sleepers. A misfortune has happened!"

There was a moment of quiet, which was quickly followed by the chaos of many voices. Men were running in all directions and returning. They shouted, screamed, cursed, asked and answered. It was difficult to differentiate between which individuals said what. I could only discern that Hafiz Sikhar's escape, the Baqqara's absence, and the three missing camels were talked about. Everyone seemed to be of a different opinion, wanting to bring their's to the fore. The racket caused by the men could only be compared to that made by sparrow brains, which was eventually terminated by the head sparrow, that is Shadid, who shouted in a stentorian voice:

"Shut up, you prattlers! Do not talk stupidly. Let us check this odd situation with shrewdness and in quiet."

Well, I was interested in knowing what result these people's shrewdness would produce. The Baqqara was gone; they called for him, but he did not show up. Hafiz Sikhar was gone; he was called, but did not return. Three camels were gone; they searched for them, but did not find them. Since these two men and three animals had disappeared together, they were of the opinion that they had also left together. However, since camels are not known to kidnap people, but that usually the opposite is the case, it was thought that the camels had been taken by the two missing men. One of the two had been free, the other a captive, tied up. The latter could not have left without the help of the former, accordingly the Baqqara must have untied Hafiz Sikhar to free him and take him away with the help of the camels.

"This traitor, this dog!" Shadid screamed angrily. "This is why he offered himself to keep watch."

"Maybe, he came with the intention of freeing Hafiz Sikhar," another commented.

"Of course!" another agreed. "Whatever he said was all lies, all storytelling."

"He was a rogue," a fourth insisted; the two Sinussi were good people."

"They were even saintly men!" screamed a fifth. "How we insulted the pious and learned *mudir*, and that for such a scoundrel. The *mudir* will call down Allah's wrath."

"He has done so already," a sixth voice clamored, "which is why Allah sent us this heavy loss. Had we believed these holy men, this misfortune would not have happened."

"My water bag is missing!" another shouted suddenly.

"Look and see whether other things are missing!" Shadid ordered.

"My water bag is also missing!" shouted another.

"Mine, too; also my camel!"

"My camel is gone, too, just like yours, oh Shadid!" someone shouted from farther away.

"What?" the leader asked. "My camel is missing, my expensive Abu Havas *hadjin*?"

"Yes. We gathered all the animals. Look! You can see that precisely the three best camels are gone."

"Oh, Allah, oh, Hell, oh, Devil! Ruin onto this accursed Baqqara! We must find his tracks."

"Yes, run, search, you men!" Shadid ordered. "Search in all directions, on ours and the opposite side of the ford. Only three or four stay to guard the slaves!"

The men immediately obeyed his command, which is why it suddenly turned quiet.

"*Effendi*," Bin Nil sniggered, "had we known this, we could have taken the captives and all the camels. We were far too cautious."

"Yes, we could have taken everything. But why should we have struggled with it, when Shadid will bring all to Fashoda anyway. Everything turned out in our favor. Now, I'm curious as to whether they will change their erroneous assumption when they are finished with their search."

"Oh, no, these people seem to be blind."

He was correct. The men who had dispersed in every direction, returned. The result was that no one had found anything. From the north of the lake, the direction the Baqqara claimed to live, the *mishrah* Umm Oshrin, to where he would have headed, there were no tracks to be found. He had to have ridden south. However those, who had searched in that direction, insisted that no tracks were discovered there either. This is why Shadid now waded across the ford to search himself. After some time he returned, ranting, raving, and cursing, to declare:

"There is truly nothing to be found. What will the Mek and Ibn Asl say when I must tell them that this Hafiz Sikhar has escaped? Oh, Allah, how will we be received by these two?"

Now, one of the men, who had to be the smartest, commented:

"No tracks disappear in such a short time; think about this, oh Shadid!"

"What are you saying?'" Shadid asked.

"Where there are no tracks, no camel has passed. If there are no tracks all around, then the Baqqara has not left, but is hiding somewhere with Hafiz Sikhar and the camels. You must admit that he acted very astutely. The piousness and holiness of the two Sinussi were in his way. He thought them to be dangerous to him, which is why he accused them and came up with a story to render them harmless. Was this not smart of him?"

"Very cunning indeed."

"Well, then you must trust him to have acted just as smartly later. He had to tell himself that we would discover his tracks, which is why he made none and stayed in the vicinity to wait until we are gone."

"Allah *akbar*! I did not think of that. You might very well be right. Go ahead, men, and let us search for them! Check everywhere, up and down, right and left, and on both sides of the water!"

Now things became bit less than comfortable for us. If we stayed on the raft, there was a slight chance of being given away. Then, too, we had heard enough, which is why we pushed off and rowed back, but so slowly that someone watching for minutes could only then notice that our island was moving. And that they would pay such close attention was unlikely. There were several real rush-covered islands drifting in the lake which made ours less conspicuous.

We saw several Takalah crossing the ford again, searching both banks. If they extended their search also to the other lake, where our camp was located, they might discover it after all. But we did not have to worry at all that this would happen. Should we be discovered, it could only be by a few men, which we need not fear. Before they could bring the others, we would be long gone and in a safe place. But I preferred if we weren't discovered at all. It fit my plan very well that the story of the foreign *effendi* would not be believed. This would change, however, the moment they recognized that the Baqqara had not acted untrustworthy, but had been abducted together with Hafiz Sikhar and the camels.

Our travel across the larger lake proceeded very slowly. However, when we had entered the smaller one, we were out of the Takalahs' sight and could row faster. We soon arrived at our campsite and disembarked. We had been gone for a long time, which is why Hafiz Sikhar had become concerned for us. He was glad to see us return. We told him what we had seen and heard, after which I climbed a nearby tree whose dense foliage covered me completely, but still permitted a view in all directions.

After some time I saw two Takalah on the northern shore, looking around. They could not cross and were therefore no danger. But soon thereafter three others approached on our side. They walked from bush to bush and tree to tree, looking behind every possible cover. If they continued for another two minutes in this direction, they would discover us. I quickly slid down the tree, left our campsite and walked a short distance toward them without letting myself be seen. I found some dense shrubbery, covered to its top by thorny vines. Expecting them to pass by, I crept inside.

It did not take long for them to come. They first looked into some nearby bushes, then turned to my hiding place.

"It is for nothing," one of them said. "They are not over here. Let us turn back."

"Only a few steps more to the corner over there where the *subakh* stands!" came the reply.

Oh my! I had just been sitting on this *subakh*, and behind that corner was our campsite. Now, they were only five paces away from my bushes. I reached for its branches and moved them as if an animal were rising, and tried to imitate that hiss and growl a carnivore emits when disturbed in its rest. I rolled my tongue, making a rather low sound, breathed noisily through my nose, then let go a short, hoarse scream. Upon hearing it, the men reacted fearfully:

"The lion has woken up. Allah protect us from the 'Killer of Herds'!"

I had often tried to imitate the roar of a lion on lonely rides. The human vocal apparatus is incapable to reproduce it correctly, however, some similarity can be achieved. This was also the case here. The three terrified Takalah recoiled when they heard me.

"A lion, a lion!" one of them screamed. "Oh, Allah, oh, protector, oh, preserver of life, protect us from . . ."

I was unable to hear the completion of this sentence, since the fellow, who ranted in this way, had run away so fast that I could no longer hear his last words. His two companions, equipped with faster legs, had gotten even ahead of him. Now I heard Bin Nil's laughing voice coming from our corner:

"*Effendi*, they will not come back! What all you accomplish! Now, you have even turned into a lion. The angry growl and hiss were excellent. It sounded exactly as if a lion had been disturbed in his sleep. But the following roar sounded less real. One could hear that it did not come from a lion's throat."

"Because you knew who the lion was."

"Yes. But it sounded very natural to the Takalah. They will beware of checking the *subakh* and our corner. When you left and crept into the bushes over there, I was afraid that this was precisely what would give us away. I did not know that you were going to play the 'Lord with the big Head'. But I am happy now that you did. How did you arrive at this great idea, *effendi*?"

"It is that one gets the right thought in the right situation: entirely unexpected and without much searching."

I had returned and saw that Bin Nil had his knife in hand. Upon my questioning look, he explained:

"When the Takalah came closer, I told the Baqqara that I would stab him, should he make the least noise. They are gone now. Shall we leave?"

"No. I want them to leave first."

"But we will lose precious time waiting. You know how quickly we want to get to Fashoda."

"We will recover this loss of time on our good camels. I must figure out how we should ride so that the Takalah will not come across our tracks. Since they expect a lion to be in the vicinity, they will not delay by the ford much longer. They will expect the carnivore to use the ford as a game pass. I will keep an eye them."

To do this, I once more climbed the tree, this time taking my telescope along. Using it, I was able to look across the lake, however, the trees and bushes at the shore behind which the caravan was camped, prevented me from observing the men's activities.

About half an hour later, I noticed some movement by the ford, then saw the group appearing from the trees on the shore's opposite side and turn south toward the desert. A group of camel riders was in the lead, another brought up the rear, with the captives walking in the middle. I followed the caravan until it had disappeared over the horizon. With no particular purpose, I happened to point the telescope north and then east, and spotted some moving dots in the latter direction. Were they animals or people? They were coming closer, yet not directly toward us. They were headed in a more southwesterly direction, which is why they had to meet the caravan south of us. Even through the spy glass the figures were too small for me to determine who or what they were. Then they became smaller and smaller until I was no longer able to see them. So, I decided to climb down from the tree.

Last night I had been unable to clearly distinguish Hafiz Sikhar's features. Now, by day, I saw that he looked very similar to his brother. He asked me to show him the mummy hand, and when I followed his request, he said that he was familiar with it, and that it was truly the hand of a pharaoh's daughter, as he had said. I now opened my waterproof belt, took out the two letters his brother had given me in Asyût, and said:

"Bin Wasak gave me these letters, when I lived in the Pasha's palace in Asyût. He told me to open them upon my arrival in Khartoum."

"Then they are your property," Hafiz responded, while he took a look at them. "Put them away and open them when you get to Khartoum."

"I would rather you open them now. At the time, I believed that I would travel directly to Khartoum, your bother thinking likewise. But it turned out differently. I had to ride to the Fassaras' homeland. In the meantime, a not inconsiderable time has elapsed, and who knows what important content the letters hold. It might be better to know it."

"Open them, then!"

"No, you do it. I am not in Khartoum yet."

"Then I will. They could contain something that might be of advantage to us."

He opened the envelopes. Each contained a recommendation letter and remittances to a Khartoum establishment.

"Did my brother know you before you came to Ma'abdah?" Hafiz Sikhar asked.

"No."

He looked at me for a long time, his eyes shining moistly, when he asked:

"This, this my brother did for me, and I thought he had totally given up on me. These remittances tell me more than you can imagine. Their amounts are huge. Earlier he must have tried all kinds of things to discover my whereabouts. He saw you for the first time and handed you such letters! You must have appeared a very honest and trustworthy man, considering that you are a Christian and were a total stranger to him. What would you have done with that much money?"

"Given it to you, as soon as I found you. Pocket the recommendations and remittance; they are yours! We shall remain together until you can return to your brother. Should I have need of something, I will tell you."

"Fine. Under this condition, I shall keep the papers. But where am I to put them not having a pocket?"

It was true. He did not have a single pocket, since he, now a rich man, wore only a rather tattered loin cloth.

"You will get pockets in a moment," I told him. "This Baqqara is of the same build as you are. You will change clothing. You take his and he will take yours."

"I dare you!" the Baqqara snapped at me. "I am a free Bin Arab and will not go naked."

"Earlier, he was a captive and you were free, which is why he went naked and you wore clothing. Now, you have been captured and he is free. Consequently, you will also change your clothing."

"I will not allow it."

"Bin Nil, cut some switches for a *bastonnade*!"

"Beat me?" the Baqqara screamed. "The *bastonnade* for me? Who gives you the right?"

"The Viceroy. I stand here in place of the *raïs effendina*. Even if this were not the case, I would do as I please. You are an ally of my mortal enemy. Last night, you spoke and acted against me. By what right, I ask you, just as you asked me for mine? By the right of the stronger – the laws of the desert and savanna. I advise you: if you care for the soles of your feet, submit freely to my order! I offered you freedom for open admission, but you did not accept my proposition. Therefore you must blame yourself if its consequences do not meet your pleasure. Off with his habit!"

Bin Nil wanted to remove the Baqqara's *haïk*, against which he fought. I became serious. He was put on his belly in front of the tree and had to lift his calves from the knees upward. They were tied to the trunk so that he could not move. Now, Hafiz Sikhar sat on his back so that he had to stay put, and Bin Nil cut a finger-thick twig from a bush. Upon the first blow the punished man screamed loudly; on the second, he whimpered.

"Stop, stop, *effendi*. I will obey. No free Arab can endure this *bastonnade*."

"You could have saved yourself. Let the two blows be a lesson to you."

He was untied, after which the clothing exchange proceeded easily. We then made ready to leave. There was enough water for people.

For the camels we filled the water bags from the Nid al-Nil. After that we mounted up and left the place, where I could never have imagined finding Hafiz Sikhar, the long-missing brother of my friend, the guide of Ma'abdah.

The Takalah were not to see our tracks, as I mentioned, which is why I let them get ahead of us. At first, we followed theirs, later to diverge from them. After we had ridden for approximately a quarter of an hour, we saw another set of tracks coming from the left. They had to originate from the creatures I had seen through my telescope as small dots on the eastern horizon. Here now was the place where they had met the tracks of the Takalah.

"Who might they be?" Bin Nil wondered. "These are very small imprints."

I dismounted and asked him to do likewise, so that he would learn to identify tracks. What he learned from me could later be of use to him. On first sight, I knew what they were, but I asked him:

"Have a close look at these tracks! What kind of animal may have made them?"

"They must have been donkeys?" he said, looking questioningly at me.

"Yes, donkeys," I nodded satisfied. "And how many?"

"Four or five."

"No, only three. If one wants to know the number of animals, one must look for the total number of impressions of a certain foot. Whoever counts all hoof prints, will miscount. For instance, let's take the right foreleg. You can recognize the imprint from several marks, mainly that it points more to the outside, that is to the right, and is more convex than the inside, the left. Observe then the variety of impressions of these right-side fore-hooves, and you will arrive at the number of animals. Now, what were the donkeys carrying? Riders or loads? Or did one of them not carry anything?"

"How can one know this?"

"By the depth of the impressions, by the regularity of the walk and by other signs provided more by chance. The heavier an animal is loaded, the deeper its hooves indent the sand. A pack animal will usually step lighter in front than in back. A riding animal has a less regular walk than a pack animal, since it is more dependent on the will of its rider, while a pack animal calmly walks its pace. Come along the tracks for some instance and you will notice that every donkey will have trotted for a time on the right, then the left, and also in the middle. This rarely, if ever, happens with pack animals, meaning they were ridden. What kind of riders might they have been?"

"How can I know that? I did not see them, and since they sat in saddles they left no tracks of their own."

"Yet, nothing is easier than that. Only a certain kind of people ride donkeys."

"Do you mean these were *tujjâr*?"

"Yes. Only *tujjâr* use donkeys here. So, that much we know. Where they came from is of no interest to us, but where they are headed is what we want to know, since they are ahead of us, and we may catch up with them."

"Can you also read this from their tracks?"

"No, at least not now, since their tracks join those of the Takalah here. Let's go on."

We took our camels by their holders and walked on. The two others stayed in their saddles and followed. After some time, the tracks broadened into a wide, trampled place, then continued on in their earlier narrowness.

"Here, the *tujjâr* caught up with the Takalah," I explained, "and the Takalah stopped for awhile to welcome and question the traders. Maybe, this wide trampled spot tells us even more. Let me have a closer look."

It appeared to me as if the majority of the Takalah had not waited, but had continued their ride almost without interruption. I counted and compared the individual imprints, found even the tracks made by several human feet, and explained to the others:

"Only five Takalah stopped; the others rode on. Those five talked for some time with the *tujjâr*, who dismounted from their donkeys. Then both groups followed the others. They halted here to greet and question each other."

"Will the Takalah not be hostile to the *tujjâr*?" Bin Nil asked.

"At this time there's no indication of any ill-will. However, considering what happened, the Takalah must not be in a very good mood, which is why the *tujjâr*, provided there are no other reasons, should have reason to be cautious. Let's walk on some distance before mounting up again."

I was just turning forward when Bin Nil pointed in this direction, saying:

"Look ahead, *effendi*, there, to the left of the tracks, sits a hyena."

"And next to it, two more lie in the sand," Hafiz Sikhar added.

I shaded my eyes with my hand in order to see better. Suspecting disaster, I exclaimed instantly:

"These are no hyenas but people! I hope the five Takalah did not pounce on the traders! Let's get over there quickly!"

We hurried on, the two of us in a trot with the two riders following. The one Bin Nil had thought to be a hyena from a distance, had his back turned to us. It was no surprise that my young companion had erred across such a distance. The man had planted his elbows on his knees and held his head as if he had a headache. When he heard the noise of our approach, he turned his head toward us. Seeing us, he made an effort to get up, but failed. With our two camel riders being a few paces ahead of us, he first spotted the Baqqara. His face took on an expression of fright, and he shouted:

"I am lost! This is Amr al-Makashaf, the *shaykh* of the Baqqara!"

I had heard this name a few times before. It was that of a Baqqara chief known as being exceptionally warlike and violent. At the time, he had played his role within a narrow range, but later stepped far beyond it. He was a relative of the Mahdi. On April 6, 1882, the *mudir* of Sannaar sent a wire to the Vice-governor, which said: "The Baqqara, Shaykh Amr al-Makashaf, a cousin of the Mahdi, is approaching my city with several thousand Baqqara warriors and plans to conquer it for the Mahdi. Send help as quickly as possible!" So, this man was presently my prisoner. It made me wonder that a *shaykh* had passed himself off as a messenger. His relationship to Ibn Asl could not be a mere acquaintance, but had to be a much stronger connection. This was confirmed by his response, for barely had he heard the man's words that he called dismissively:

"You are mistaken. Although I am a member of the Baqqara, I am not their *shaykh*."

"Why do you deny it?" the trader asked. "How often have I been with you? You know me and are well aware that I know you."

"Be quiet! You talk nonsense. I see that you are injured. Fever may distort your words."

As he said this, he looked at me with deep concern which convinced me that he was not truthful. He wanted to be seen as an ordinary man so that, as much as possible, he would receive mild treatment in Fashoda. However, the trader stuck to his conviction by insisting:

"I do not know the reason why you deny yourself. Yes, I am injured, but fever has not overtaken me yet, and I know what I am saying. We did not do anything to these slave-trading Takalah, and I beg you for Allah's sake not to think that I am an opponent of people who catch slaves. Spare me, oh *shaykh*!"

I now asked him:

"Why do you find this explanation necessary? Are you implying that this *shaykh* Amr al-Makashaf is also a slave hunter?"

Until now, the man had not paid any attention to me. He looked at me surprised and replied:

"How can you ask me such a question? You are in the company of the *shaykh* and must know even better than I that he is a friend and a customer of Ibn Asl's, the famous slave hunter."

"This is not true. It is a lie!" the Baqqara exclaimed. "I am not at all the one you think I am!"

"Be quiet!" I demanded. "I know very well what to think of you, and your effort to confuse my judgment is for naught. You are much too stupid to deceive me."

Turning to the trader, I continued:

"I am not with him. I am a foreigner, not a Muslim, but a Christian. Look closer at this *shaykh*! Haven't you noticed that he doesn't carry any weapons? Haven't you yet noticed the rope with which he is tied to the camel?"

Until now, the man had held his head by his two hands. He now lifted it to look closer at the *shaykh*, then cried in surprise:

"Allah does wonders! He is tied up. Did you fight him and take him prisoner?"

"You shall learn soon enough. First of all, I want to check you and your two companions, who lie there like the dead."

"They are dead. They were shot. You can see the large puddle of blood they lie in."

"Did they also shoot at you?"

"No. I was the first they laid hands on. They hit me with the musket butts on the head. When I came to again, I found my companions dead. We were robbed of everything, even our donkeys."

"Not the animals. The donkeys will still be around somewhere. I shall find them. But first, show me your head."

It was badly swollen, but fortunately for the injured man, there was no break. Whoever had hit him, had done so with the flat of the butt, not its sharp side. The other two men were clearly dead, shot through the chest. I took off their head scarves to apply a wet compress to the living man's head. It did him so much good that he could rise and now speak with less of an effort. He still seemed to be afraid of the *shaykh*, which is why I reassured him:

"You are with friends. This chief of the Baqqara can do you no harm, although he is a friend of the Takalah, who attacked you. He joined them at the Nid al-Nil. I will tell you again that you have no reason to fear him. Might you have heard of the *raïs effendina*?"

"Yes, sir."

"Well, I am a friend of his and took this Baqqara prisoner in order to take him to the *raïs effendina* in Fashoda. Rest assured that you can speak openly with me. Where did you come from, and where were you headed?"

"We were in Dar Famaka, where we sold our merchandise and received only *at-tabr* for it. We then crossed the White Nile to ride to Bahr al-Arab, where we intended to exchange our *at-tabr* for ostrich feathers, which we would plan to carry to Khartoum. We would have been assured a good profit had the Takalah not robbed us here. I am now poorer than before. May Allah curse them!"

At-tabr is gold, which is found in the area talked about. It comes in the form of grains or dust found in small leaves in the Alluvium. In this area *at-tabr* serves almost as the sole means of exchange, while the otherwise everywhere acceptable Maria-Theresia-thaler are little liked. For better handling of it, it is often melted into rings or into very small quantities in the form of a cheap coin tied into cloth or leather pieces.

"I presume that at the outset you were not treated with hostility by the Takalah?"

"True, they were even very friendly," the man replied. "When we met them, their leader had the caravan proceed until we could no longer see it. He stayed back with four other men to question us. He did this in such a way that it was impossible to mistrust him, then permitted us to join them. We rode on, following the caravan, but when we reached this place here, I was suddenly clubbed. And you know the rest."

"Did you mention the *at-tabr* you carried?"

"Yes. They asked us how we were going to pay for the ostrich feathers, which prompted me to mention the gold dust."

"You should never have done this. You see the fruit your excessive trust bore. The five Takalah became greedy for your gold dust, and so that they did not have to share it with their comrades, they let the caravan get out of sight, and then attacked you. For the same reason, they left you everything else. Otherwise they would have taken everything down to your bare bodies. This would have given the robbery away and they would have had to share. This is why they did not take your donkeys, but chased them off, as I can see from their tracks."

"Why did they not leave them here? Why did they make the unnecessary effort of driving them so far away that one could not see them anymore?"

"Out of caution. The effort wasn't as superfluous as you think. You three lay flat on the ground and therefore could not be seen from afar. Had they left the donkeys standing with you, they could have been spotted from afar and drawn someone's attention who would have discovered the murders. While you aren't dead, you would have perished, had we not come along and found you. And this only because we purposefully followed the Takalah's tracks."

"What must be done now, sir? We must follow the murderers. I want to avenge myself and take the loot back."

"You will get back what they took from you. I promise you that. However, this does not require pursuit of the caravan or any fighting. And do you think in your condition you are capable of doing battle with them? I will now look for the donkeys, and then you can join us."

"Where are you headed?"

"To Fashoda, as I told you already. The Takalah are also going there, but since they have the slaves who are walking, we shall arrive before them and immediately upon their arrival, we will have them received by the *mudir's* police."

The donkey tracks led straight out into the distance, one animal following the other. After a quarter of an hour, I found them lying next to each other, their saddles still on their backs. I mounted up on one of them in order to ride back. The two others followed willingly without any need to lead them.

We buried the dead as well as possible. Then the injured man was put onto the camel that had carried the water bags, and we rode on. The three donkeys, carrying only the water bags, trotted easily after us.

We were about thirty miles from Fashoda. Had I been alone with Bin Nil, we would have covered the distance in two days in a fast ride, but under the present conditions this was impossible. Hafiz Sikhar had been for too long cooped up in the copper mine. He would have been strong enough to walk, but now it showed that the fast ride and the swaying on camel-back, strained him more than he had expected. The trader constantly cooled his head with water, but it still hurt so badly with every step of his camel, that we were forced to slow down. We no longer followed the tracks of the Takalah, but kept far to their east. Then we overtook them during the first morning, finally arriving in the morning of the fourth day near Fashoda. Fashoda is nothing but a large village of huts, which, only because of the walls surrounding the government buildings, the military barracks, and the *mudir's* dwelling, looks rather impressive from the outside. However, this good impression quickly vanishes once one enters the place.

Cannons are placed on the walls, reinforced at night by numerous guards, a somewhat unnecessary precaution against the rebellious Shilluk.

The government buildings are surrounded by miserable houses and numerous *tukul*, which are erected on a brick platform. The many earlier devastations by fires, led to the prohibition of building these poor huts entirely of straw. These *tukul* were in part inhabited by Shilluk and soldiers, inclusive of their wives and children. The streets and lanes, provided one should use these terms, consisted of holes, dirty puddles, garbage piles, and hills of mud. In order to keep from getting stuck, one had to negotiate between, through and across them like a tightrope performer.

Fashoda is a place of exile, just as Jabal Gasan and Fassoql were earlier. However, the number of criminals never increases very much, with newcomers quickly perishing from the unhealthy climate.

Since this place is the last fortified border post on the White Nile, it has a garrison of almost a thousand soldiers. These are black foot soldiers and a number of *Arnautlar* commanded by a *sangak*. Because of their insubordination and violence, these *Arnautlar* are exceptionally hard to control. That their *sangak* is a secret ally of Ibn Asl, has been mentioned already.

Do not think that we entered the town without a thought; that would have been irresponsible. I had to assume that Ibn Asl had already arrived. The Turk, Murad Nassyr with his sister, the *muza'bir* and the *mukkadam* of the holy Qadiriyya, my vengeful enemies, would likely be around. Added to this was that I had to beware of the leader of the *Arnautlar*, who would have been told everything about me by the afore mentioned people. They knew me personally, which is why I could not let myself be seen by them if I wanted to achieve my purpose. This is also why I said that we arrived near, but not in Fashoda.

We made sure not to approach the town too closely, but halted about an hour before at a location well suited for a temporary hiding place. This was a woods of *sunut*, *hegelik*, and other tall trees, among whose trunks grew *kittr* and *vabaq* bushes, tightly interwoven by *Cyssus quadrangularis* vines. There, we took cover at a place where we could only have been detected by pure chance.

It was my intention to send a messenger to the *mudir*. I would have preferred to send Bin Nil, something I could not risk, since he was also known to some of the afore mentioned persons in Fashoda. This is why I entrusted Hafiz Sikhar with the message and handed him a letter of recommendation from the *raïs effendina* to take along. Of course, I instructed him very well on how to conduct himself and what he should say. We waited for four hours after he had left. When he returned, it was in the company of a man wearing the dress of a common man. I had expected that the 'Father of Five-hundred' would send one of his trusted officials but learned to my surprise that this simply-dressed individual was the *mudir* himself. The severe man characterized himself right at the moment of our meeting.

"You had to wait for a long time, *effendi*," said Hafiz Sikhar. "This high sir is . . ."

"Silence!" the other thundered at him. "I treated you kindly since I took pity on you for your sad fate, but do not think that because of it I am the likes of you. How dare you introduce me to the *effendi*! And how dare you have the audacity to apologize to him for having to wait! Am I a dog, who must be ready when he's whistled for, you rascal?"

Well, I thought silently, this will be something! Here is the 'Father of Five-hundred' himself. If he conducts himself like this with us, how then will he deal with criminals?

Now he turned to me and studied me curiously, whereby one could not detect the least friendly expression. I had stood up, took his questioning look calmly, and said:

"Who are you? Ali Effendi himself?"

"Ali Effendi?" he responded sternly. "Do you not know how to address a *mudir*?"

"I do know and shall comply with the duty of courtesy as soon as I am speaking to a *mudir*."

"This is the case now, for I am the *mudir* of Fashoda."

An Oriental would have crossed his arms and bent toward the earth, but I only lowered my head, offered my hand, and said in a polite voice:

"May Allah give you a thousand years, oh *mudir*! I am glad to see your face, which is that of a just man under whose administration this province will rise and shall be cleaned of its rabble."

He hesitated and did not shake my hand, gave me a surprised look, and replied:

"From what I read and hear about you, you are quite a competent fellow, and yet do not seem to be a friend of great compliments."

"Every man has his own ways and must be taken accordingly, oh *mudir*."

"That means I must also take my servants according to their ways. May Allah have mercy! I would not get far this way! You Christians are peculiar people, so I shall take you indeed as you are, that is both very brave and very rude! Let us sit down."

I smiled to myself having been called rude by him, the personification of rudeness. We sat down. He pulled out a matchbox and a leather bag of cigarettes, lit one, without offering me one, blew its smoke contentedly through his nose, put the cigarettes and matches for future use within comfortable reach next to himself, and began:

"So, you are a servant of the *raïs effendina*. Where and how did he actually get to know you?"

"Whether he got to know me or I got to know him makes a difference, about which we needn't occupy ourselves with now; but when you think that I am his servant, you are sorely mistaken."

"Well, then, he calls you a friend in his letter, but I know this. It is just a formality and is part of the recommendation. You are a courageous, even a daring man, and you also do not seem to be stupid. But as a Christian you will never become the friend of a Muslim."

"Why not? If I respect and love a person so much that I find him worthy of my friendship, the fact that he is a Muslim does not prevent me from offering him my friendship."

"Ah!" he exhaled. "Then you extended it to him, not he to you?"

"Whoever spoke the first word, is a mute point. It is sufficient and must also suffice you that we are real friends. If you do not want to believe it, it makes no difference to me."

"What? You are indifferent as to whether the *mudir* of Fashoda believes you or not? I have not met an man like this before!"

"There is a motto in my fatherland, which says: As you do unto me, so I do unto you. I like to follow it."

"This is much, too much! Listen, if someone else dared to say this, by Allah, I would have him given five hundred on the spot!"

"Yes, this is the usual application, which is why you are called Abu Khamsa Miah. But I am safe from receiving this most dear present of love."

"Safe? Do not believe this! If I wanted, who or what would prevent me from having you given five hundred?"

"My nationality and my consul."

"I don't give a damn for them."

"Well, then how about this one? You would certainly give a damn."

Saying this, I held my fist very close to his nose such that he quickly pulled his face back, exclaiming:

"Man, you want to hit me?"

"Not as long as you don't want to hit. But, we have jested long enough now and shall talk about necessary items. We are . . ."

"Who determines here what to talk about, you or I?" he interrupted.

"I do, because you are visiting me. If you do not care to follow me, you can leave. I can get around this area and the world without you."

He looked, no, he literally stared at me, tossed his cigarette stub away, and shouted:

"Allah is great, no, he is greater, no, he is much greater, he is the greatest, but you are the greatest boor I have ever come across! What a pleasure it would be if I could have five hundred counted on you! But I think I will yet get to it."

"And I hope then to prove to you that my bullet would enter your head before you would have completed issuing the respective order."

"May the Devil devour you! I believe the best way to get on with you is by courtesy."

He once more lit a cigarette. I replied:

"Then begin with by also allowing me to also smoke a cigarette."

I took one, lit it, and quickly added, when I saw him getting angry again:

"This was your duty earlier when you lit the first one. You omitted it, yet admonished me to be polite. What am I to think of you? It's all the same to me, whether you are coarse or friendly to me. I am not asking for the least favor from you. I rather came to help you fulfill your duty. Same for same, this is the law of the desert: Life for life, blood for blood, and – rudeness for rudeness. Get to know me and you will think differently of me. You even refused to shake my hand. I have spoken with higher, more upstanding men than you, and yet was treated politely by every single one of them."

He again tossed the just-lit cigarette away, balled his fist, and wanted to angrily break out but controlled himself. The angry wrinkles of his faces smoothened, his look became softer and softer, but then his anger suddenly returned. He threw a furious look around, pointed at the *shaykh* Amr al-Makashaf, lying on the ground, and barked at him:

"I see you are tied up. Are you the Baqqara who delivered Ibn Asl's message to the Nid al-Nil?"

"Yes," the man admitted.

"You dog, you seven-times son of a dog, you consort with slavers? I will have five hundred given to you, five hundred as assuredly as I have five fingers on each hand. You will get one hundred a week, then can go to wherever you like to tell how you enjoyed your visit with Abu Hamsah Miah. Unfortunately, I cannot behead you, you rotten bastard, since you have only been found guilty of this messenger service. But have no worry, each individual blow of the five hundred will keep flickering in your mind until the Devil will light you a whole raft of fireworks in Hell."

With this explosion his anger seemed to have abated, for suddenly he now turned to me with a most pleasant face, at last shook my hand, and said:

"*Effendi*, you must be present when this dog gets whipped. It will refresh your soul and strengthen your heart, clear your mind, and lighten your spirit. Oh, there is no greater joy than to hear these violators of our good and just laws howl, moan and whimper! But now, tell me what has happened since the *raïs effendina* got to know you, or, he added, correcting himself with a smile, how you got to know him!"

"This would turn into a long story which, to listen to, would take much time."

"It is part of my function to hear this report, and I have always time for the fulfillment of my duties."

"Permit me then to have Bin Nil tell it."

"Why not yourself?"

"When he is finished, you will understand my reason, without me having to tell you."

"Fine, then he may speak."

Bin Nil began.

I reached into the cigarette pouch and took a second one. Then, I stretched out, put my hands behind my back and let Bin Nil talk. He did this briefly but extensively enough. From every one of his words, one could hear how much and honestly he loved me. The *mudir* might have heard already some of Hafiz Sikhar's story, and some more must have been mentioned in the recommendation letter of the *raïs effendina*. But now, he heard matters he had no idea would take his full attention and interest. From time to time, he expressed his feelings in the most vivid and original terms. When Bin Nil was finished, he reached for the match box and the cigarette pouch, shook both their contents on me, and exclaimed:

"Smoke, smoke, *effendi*, keep on smoking! You earned it, yes, by Allah and the Prophet, you've earned it! And when you come to me, you shall get even more – an entire full carton, although they are scandalously expensive, yes, shamefully expensive!"

"How much do you pay?" I asked, curious about the price of cigarettes, which somehow must have strayed into southern Sudan.

"An entire piaster per piece."

"That's expensive. Did you not bargain the price down?"

"Haggle?" he asked grimly. "I would not think of it! I am not used to haggling; I pay honestly, full and equal: every piaster one blow. When the fellow had received fifty blows, he ran away, left me the goods and declared crying that he had been paid in full and waived all rights for the rest. Smoke, therefore, *effendi*, and enjoy it. You are a devil of a man, and the *raïs effendina* must be delighted to know you. You Christians are actually not that bad, and I believe now that he truly considers you his friend. I am *mudir*, which is, by Allah, nothing little, but let me make amends for my earlier straightforwardness. However, for that you must also do me a favor, which you cannot deny me."

"But I don't yet know whether I am able to accommodate your wish."

"You can!"

"Well, in that case – yes."

He now squeezed both my hands and exclaimed happily:

"*Hamdulillah*! That means blows, blows, five or six thousand blows or more! You must catch Ibn Asl, but not for the *raïs effendina*, but for me."

"Fine!"

"And this fat Turk by the name of Murad Nassyr."

"All right."

"And the *muza'bir* and the most dear *mukkadam* of the holy Qadiriyya."

"Also these two," I nodded.

"I thank you, I thank you! There will be a festivity like I never experienced. I will hang them all, but before that, each will get his well-counted five hundred onto the soles of his feet, also the Turk's sister, yes, by Allah, she, too!"

"She is a girl, oh, *mudir*! What crime do you want to charge her with?"

"The greatest there is. She wanted to marry Ibn Asl, the slaver."

"Wanted? Not at all! She had to. This marriage is no more than the seal of a business connection."

"Don't try to tell me!" he eagerly demanded. "Here, no one seals anything but me alone, and I always seal it with five hundred. But you must catch all of them for me, you promised."

"I will keep my word. However, I needn't catch one, since he's already in your hands, the *sangak* of your *Arnautlar*."

"Ibn Mulai? To this day he has earned my trust. Do you really think he knows Ibn Asl?"

"I'm convinced of it."

"Then, he will also get his five hundred . . ."

He stopped; a thought seemed to have occurred to him. He considered it, then continued:

"So he is the addressee! This is why I wracked my brain and tried so hard in vain! *Effendi*, I almost believe you are right, and that I gave my trust to an unworthy man."

"I could swear that this Ibn Mulai is an ally of the slavers."

"It is most likely, for the letter's passages that were obscure to me, fit only him, as I realize now."

"May I know what letter you are referring to?"

"Yes, you even must know. Yesterday, my men caught a Nuer Negro at the Bringhi *saribah*. He looked suspicious to them. When they checked him over, they found a letter in his mop of hair. The man tore free, trying to get away, when they shot him dead. This morning they delivered this letter to me. It is from the Saribah Aliab, located up there at Bahr al-Jabal. Whoever was to receive it, was to read it, and then forward it to Ibn Asl."

"Ah! Might this be Ibn Asl's *saribah*?"

"That I don't know, since I've only been here for a short time."

"I almost think so. May I see and read this letter?"

"Yes, of course, *effendi*. I'm just having a thought, a wonderful thought. The *Arnaut* must get this letter."

"You're right! This way we convict him easily. But who is to deliver it to him?"

"You."

"I? I mustn't be seen by the *sangak*, nor in Fashoda, as yet."

"Why not? The ones you want to hide from have not arrived yet."

"But if one of them comes and goes covertly?"

"That is impossible. Day and night guards stand by the river bank. You pass yourself off as the messenger from the Saribah Aliab. If he keeps the letter, he is guilty, and I will have him whipped until he admits everything. We will then learn from him how to capture the others."

"But I am no Negro. Even if I colored myself, my facial features would reveal that I am no Nuer. Is the messenger mentioned in the letter?"

"Not a word."

"It might then be possible, however, it seems better that another trustworthy man deliver the letter."

"And I don't care to assign someone else to this task. First, it is so dangerous, only a courageous man can do it, and secondly, it is not merely a question of delivering the letter, but that the *Arnaut* must then be sounded out by the messenger. You alone can accomplish this."

I should not have agreed to this plan. It not only sounded impractical to me, but even dangerous. It was proven later that I was correct. But before I even had met the *mudir*, he had, because of his love for justice, sounded already simpatico to me, and that he expressed such trust so quickly after our rather unfriendly introduction, flattered me. Dear, foolish vanity clouded my sight, and I tackled a matter that could not be messed up, but I would do with great probability. "Me alone" could only accomplish it! Was I then not obligated to him and myself to prove that he did not have a mistaken impression of me? I replied:

"Fine, I'll do it. Where and when will I get the letter?"

"Where and when you like."

"Where does the *Arnaut* live?"

"He occupies a house next to the barracks. Do you want to pick up the letter, or shall I have it sent to you?"

"No pickup. I must not let myself be seen by day. However, if I come after dark and have to see you first, time will pass that I need otherwise. But don't send it either, since this would require a messenger to come here, where I want to stay hidden. I shall have Hafiz Sikhar accompany you back. I can entrust the letter to him."

"He shall get it. I will also send some fresh provisions with him."

"Until we can enter town, we have sufficient provisions. I have a greater need for a new, fitting suit. I have probably been described to the *Arnaut*, when my mode of dress was likely mentioned, too. He would recognize me immediately, which is why I must dress differently. I also cannot take my weapons along."

"But everyone here is armed."

"Then send me an old, long musket, an old knife, and an old pistol. I'm not certain yet who I will impersonate, certainly not a rich or high-ranking man. This is why dress and arms must be as simple as possible."

"Your wish will be accommodated. But what will the others do while you are in town?"

"They will wait here."

"Why that? They can come to me. When it has turned dark, no one will see them. And once you are finished with the *Arnaut*, you also come straight to me."

"But remember, it is to remain a secret who we are and what we intend to do. If I pose as a slave hunter I can impossibly live with you."

"Your concern is invalid. At first, we are only dealing with the *Arnaut* with whom you will be done today. Thereafter, you have no more reason to remain hidden. No, you will reside at my place. I am looking forward to it and can tell you that I will have much, very much to talk with you about. I want to inquire of you about the conditions and facilities of the Occident, and much more. I don't want to leave you stuck here in the woods. You also have the prisoner, this dog of a Baqqara with you. Why should you bother with him? You take him along, and while you go to the *Arnaut*, the others will bring him to me. I will have him locked up, and as soon as you come, I will give you the pleasure of being present when he gets the first one hundred."

"As you like, *mudir*. You are lord here, and I shall do what you consider right. But how will we get across the river?"

"As soon as it turns dark, I shall post two discreet servants near the bank. You turn the camels over to one of them, and he will take them to a reliable Shilluk for care-taking. The other will row you to town and will point the way to me. When you then come to me from the *Arnaut*, we can discuss everything else in greater detail. I have stayed longer here than I expected and must return now. I left secretly in disguise, and some of my people will become concerned and raise a racket when I return too late."

"Then the only matter left are the Takalah. I suppose you will take them into custody?"

"Allah! What a question! Of course, they will be. The slaves get their freedom and the others their punishment, the five murderers even death. Imagine that each will get five hundred blows, and calculate how many this makes in total. Fashoda will not have seen that much fun before. What a warning example this will make for the entire Egyptian Sudan! Delight for the just and trembling for all unjust! I am very grateful to you, *effendi*, for it is only you who put me in the position to set such an example. I did not expect something like this. I was mistaken about you, which you must not hold against me. When do you think the Takalah will arrive?"

"Not before the day after tomorrow, but then at any time."

"They will be received as is called for. But this friend of theirs here, shall taste the *bastonnade* before. I will have him beaten so that his howls will be heard all the way in al-Qahira and up there at Amin Pasha."

He had risen, and gave the *shaykh* a kick so that he tumbled sideways. He then left with Hafiz Sikhar, but returned a few moments later, to say:

"I will not take any cigarettes back with me. Smoke and enjoy them. For the time being, keep the pouch and matchbox as a memento of mine. May Allah protect you until we see you this evening!"

Of course, I shared the cigarettes with Bin Nil. For awhile we sat silently smoking. Once the *mudir* had left, I no longer considered the enterprise I had obligated myself to as smart and began to regret my agreement. Unfortunately, I could no longer back out of it. The Baqqara moved from side to side. The *mudir's* kick had hit him such that he was in pain. Might he have earlier been of the opinion that he would be spared, being a *shaykh*, he now recognized that this was not the case. He realized that he was sure of getting the five hundred: five hundred blows to the foot soles! And after that, locked up for five weeks in who knew what kind of hole! He was scared stiff; one could see it from the expression on his face. He began to contemplate how he might escape this disaster and arrived at the conclusion that this could only happen through me. He had to try to win me over. This line of thought became obvious when he turned to me with a proposal:

"*Effendi*, may I talk to you?"

During our ride, I had given him scant attention, and even now acted as if I had not heard him.

"*Effendi*, I must tell you something."

"Be quiet!" I told him, although I figured that what he wanted to say, would be of interest to me. He fell silent for awhile but soon started anew:

"You will regret if you do not let me talk. What I have to tell you is important to you."

"I don't care to hear anything. You want to get off the five hundred, a subject, which, obviously is of great importance to your foot soles."

"But I offer you much in return."

"What is it?" I relented.

"Information about the Saribah Aliab you earlier talked about. I heard everything and it should be welcome to you to be informed of its local conditions."

"That is indeed the case. Are these conditions known to you?"

"Maybe? Certainly! Very well even."

"Whose *saribah* is it?"

"Should I truly answer this question? Do you think I will do this without a return favor?"

"Yes, I imagine that you will gladly sell these secrets for fifty or sixty blows."

"No, no, *effendi*, not the *bastonnade*! Ask the *mudir* to get me off the five hundred, and I will tell you everything I know about the Saribah Aliab."

"You will not know much."

"Not much? I know everything. I have been there myself."

"For what purpose? At what occasion?"

"I can tell you this only, if you promise to speak for me with the *mudir*. Also, whatever I am going to tell you, must not harm me."

"I can make you this promise. But whether the former will be successful, I doubt very much."

"I do not doubt it. I heard what is being told about you and what the *mudir* thinks of you. He thinks so highly of you that your intercession will certainly be successful."

"You are probably mistaken, but I promise to put in a good word for you. But let me tell you this. I will not see myself being cheated. If you think you will escape the *bastonnade* by some sheer story telling, you are mightily mistaken. What do you know about the *saribah*?"

"It is Ibn Asl's."

"I thought so. That which I want to learn now shall in no way, as I promised, harm you; tell me honestly then: did you participate in the slave hunt?"

"Yes, *effendi*. But you must keep this from the *mudir*."

"I don't think I can pass over this matter in silence, but I promise you that under no circumstance will it be charged to you. I can put myself into your position. Being a Muslim you thought slavery permitted and its prohibition an interference in your age-old hereditary rights."

"So it is, *effendi*, so it is! Imagine, *effendi*, that we Baqqara live only by our herds, and that a single plague among them, can easily destroy us. Thus, it was the slave trade which, in such cases, gave us the means to live, not to go hungry, until our herds had recovered. We gave the slavers our warriors as *asakir* and for every captured slave received a certain payment. This payment was made in slaves, charged cheaply, while we resold them for a much higher price. This made us a welcome profit."

"And you not only assigned your warriors, but went yourself?"

"Yes. We traveled to the Saribah Aliab, from where the hunt took place."

"Who commands there when Ibn Asl is absent?"

"A sergeant by the name of Bin Ifram. A bullet got him a stiff leg, which is why he can no longer partake in the hunt. But at the settlement, he is very good, and since Ibn Asl can rely on him, he entrusted him with the command."

"I know enough for now. But it is quite likely that I will later want to hear more from you."

"Later? I hope that the *mudir* will set me free upon your intercession, and I can return to my people."

"I think so, too. But you know what we intend to do. It is possible that Ibn Asl is no longer here, in which case we must follow him. In any case, this Saribah Aliab is his destination, and since you know it so well, you will need to be our guide."

"Allah may prevent this! What are my people to think if I stay away for months? And must I be your guide against Ibn Asl, who is my friend and trusted me so highly?"

"This is a concern that need not occupy us presently. I spoke of this only as a possibility, and do not consider it likely. Let's be quiet now and wait calmly for what is to happen!"

"Calmly," he sighed. "Yes, you can be calm, but I . . I . . . ."

He had been correct. His information was of great importance to us, since we now knew where we would find Ibn Asl for certain. But first, I hoped that he was still in Fashoda.

After about three hours, Hafiz Sikhar returned heavily loaded with a suit, the asked-for weapons, two fried chickens, some other meat, cakes, and a full bottle of *raki*. We ate, also gave the Baqqara his share, like he had been fully equal to us on the ride, except for his freedom, of course.

By four o'clock afternoon had arrived. It would take us an hour to get to the Nile. By six o'clock it turned dark, which is why we got ready to leave our cover. I had picked it with the best of intention, but sensed now that this was probably for naught. An hour later, we left. I had changed my clothes and, in my new habit and sunburned face as well as hands, looked like a veritable slave hunter. However, my face itself could not be modified; it might give me away.

Hafiz Sikhar had had the place by the river bank described by the *mudir*. This was where we were to meet the two waiting servants. The *mudir* had also advised me to be highly alert when dealing with the *Arnautlar's sangak*, he being a rather strong and violent man.

Of course, I had read the letter thoroughly and gained the conviction that it had been written by the Saribah Aliab's sergeant. It was not sealed, but had been glued together by some kind of dough, enabling me to close it again so that, at least by night, it was difficult to see that it had been opened.

It turned dark before we reached the river bank. We found the servants, one of which took the camels, and led them away; the other put our saddle bags into the boat and rowed us across the Nile to town. I must mention that the trader was still with us, his three donkeys staying with the camels.

After we disembarked on the opposite bank, the servant led us first to the barracks where he pointed out the *Arnaut's* house. He then took the others to the *mudir's* house. My task, which I did not see as easy, was about to begin.

As far as I could see in the darkness, the building's ground floor had only two small embrasure-like windows, with a narrow, low door between them, which was clad in iron sheeting. There did not seem to be a door handle or a lock. On the door, I felt a small, about two-inch, protruding lever, by which one could lift the bolt on the inside. I tried this and felt the handle rise, yet the door would still not open. There had to be another bolt. I knocked. Shortly thereafter I heard steps, then a voice asked:

"Who is outside?"

"A messenger to the *sangak* from Bahr al-Jabal."

"Come back later. He is not here."

"I am unfamiliar with this area. Let me in! I will wait for him to return."

Silence! the man seemed to consider, then said:

"Stay put! I will check."

He left. After some time I again heard steps and another voice asked:

"Is your message that important?"

"Yes. I have a letter."

"Give it to me! I will open the hatch."

"I cannot do this. I can hand the letter only to Ibn Mulai, the *sangak* of the *Arnautlar*."

"Come in then."

A heavy iron bolt rattled, and then the door opened. I looked into a narrow hallway illuminated by an oil lamp. The man holding it wore the dress of the *Arnautlar*. The weaponry he carried, even inside the house, consisted of two pistols, two daggers, and a scimitar. Two dark eyes flashed questioningly at me from his nasty face, while he demanded in an ill-tempered voice:

"In with you! Why do you come by night? Could you not have come earlier!"

"No one can come before he has arrived. I must get away again tonight. It was ordered to immediately hand over this letter."

"You use a very curt tone, fellow. I am an *Arnaut* and my knives are never holding fast. Understood? Follow me!"

I had entered, and he bolted the door after me. Muskets hung on the walls to my left and right, giving the small space the appearance of a guardroom. Opposite the entrance was a second, open door, which he led me through. Behind was a larger room from whose ceiling hung a four-armed clay candelabra that illuminated the room only sparsely with its smoking oil flames.

Each of the four walls had a door; there were no windows. Below the candelabra lay a reed mat, on which squatted four wild characters who looked to me unfriendly but also curiously. They were rolling dice. My guide squatted down with them to continue the interrupted game while throwing me a few words:

"You wait here until our master returns. But keep your mouth shut and do not bother us, or we will do it for you!"

One can imagine that I was not very thrilled about my situation. I found myself in a location which most likely was the meeting place of every one of my mortal enemies. I was behind ironclad doors and guarded by five fellows belonging to the wildest rabble of troops one can imagine. The poor weapons at my disposal made me literally defenseless, requiring me to rely solely on my bodily strength should the need arise. I had given my own weapons, my suit, the watch, in short my entire property to Bin Nil for safekeeping.

That these *Arnautlar* were immensely coarse I heard from every word they spoke. Their expressions were larded with curses, and with every throw of the dice they quarreled and repeatedly became so excited that I often thought that they would leave the decision to their knives or pistols. I was not paid any attention, which pleased me very much. In this way time passed, one half hour after another. Since I had no watch, I did not know how late it was, but I must have sat at least three full hours in this cave until there was a thunderous knock at the door.

"The *sangak*!" the *Arnaut*, seemingly the sergeant, called. It was he who had opened the door for me when my request was reported to him by one of the others.

He rose to open the door for his superior. His comrades, too, got up, but left the dice lying on the floor. The *sangak* could see what they had been doing.

The bolt was moved twice, and then I heard a soft voice. The sergeant reported my presence, after which they entered, the *sangak*, of course, being the first. There are human faces that possess a deceiving resemblance to certain animal types, with the respective person then having usually the outstanding characteristics of that animal. When I saw the *sangak's* face, I involuntarily thought of a bull who, with horns lowered and malicious looking eyes, was ready to attack. He gave me only a brief look, then said:

"Come!"

He walked through the door the sergeant pushed open for him with me following. We were in the dark. He opened another door to the right from where some light penetrated and shouted with a booming bass voice:

"Hey, watch out! When I came, I thought I saw some fellow in front of the entrance listening. Climb over the rear wall and walk in two units to the left and right around the building. He disappeared when he heard me coming. Should he return, arrest him and bring him to me!"

He then turned to the left, where we entered a well-lit room, apparently a *semalük* (reception room). An upholstered bench wrapped around three walls with a rug in the middle. He stopped on the rug, turned to me, and asked:

"You have a letter?"

"Yes. From the sergeant Bin Ifram."

"Give it to me!"

I handed him the letter. He kept it in his hand without opening it, gave me a searching look, and asked:

"Your name?"

"Iskander Patras."

I chose this Greek name for my European features, and because there were many Levantines among the soldiers stationed in the Sudan, as well as hang-around civilian, people of Greek descent.

"A Greek," he said. "Where from?"

"I was born in al-Qahira by Greek parents."

"Christian?"

"Yes."

"Doesn't matter to me. What are you doing at the Saribah Aliab?"

"I am an interpreter. I've roamed the area for some time and understand the local dialects."

"That makes you money without needing to smell powder," he remarked disdainfully. "Let's see what this Bin Ifram has to tell me."

Only now did he look at the letter. My heart hammered. The room was well lighted.

If he saw that it had been opened, I could expect the worst. Fortunately, his curiosity was greater than his circumspection. He tore the envelope open, making me feel better. Turned away from me he read, pocketed the letter, turned back, and asked:

"Do you know the letter's content?"

"The sergeant did not tell me."

"But you know who is to get it?"

"You, I suppose!"

"I am to give it to your master, Ibn Asl. The sergeant seemed not to have great confidence in you that he kept this from you."

"Were this true, he would not have sent me to Fashoda."

"Hmm! But he certainly must think you to be a chatterbox. How did you travel?"

"To Lake No in a small boat. There, I met a *noquar* from Diakin on the way to Khartoum who took me along."

"When did it arrive here?"

"Just past sunset."

"Odd! I was up by the river and did not see a *noquar*!"

"They did not want me to come in here," I quickly cut in to divert him from this dangerous thought. "I waited three hours for you."

"You must be hungry then. You will get to eat and while doing so, tell me of the *saribah*."

He stepped outside, waving me to sit down. Had he rather waved for me to leave! I knew enough now that he knew of the *saribah* and the sergeant and therefore stood without doubt in relationship with Ibn Asl. I had to submit and leave what was to come to my good fortune.

His last words, of course, caused me that feeling of scratching oneself behind the ear. I was to eat and at the same time tell him about the *saribah*. To eat, well, I wasn't the least afraid of that. I could do him this pleasure as he liked, but to talk, oh, this tiresome talking! What did I know of the *saribah*? The Baqqara *shaykh* had wanted to describe it to me. Had I only not prevented him from doing so! But this, too, would not have sufficed. This *Arnaut* could put a hundred questions to me for whose answers I would have needed to have been there.

A short while later the *sangak* returned with a lit pipe in his mouth. He was followed by an *Arnaut* carrying a huge bone on a board from which dangled a few meat scraps, thee remains of a beef hind quarter. They looked as if dogs had quarreled over them. The man placed the board in the middle of the rug and left, while the *sangak* ordered:

"Sit down and enjoy!"

I could obey him with respect to the sitting, but the second half of his order wasn't as easy to execute. Nevertheless, I tried by pulling out my knife to attack the bone. While I first looked it over from all sides to determine from which direction and means I could best get at its sinewy appendages, the *Arnaut* asked me:

"Since when were you at the *saribah*?"

"For two years," I replied, while I worked with all my might to remove a digestible scrap.

"Who hired you?"

"Ibn Asl himself at the *mishrah* Umm Oshrin. Amr al-Makashef, the *shaykh* of the Baqqara, had, at some occasion, recommended me highly."

"He did? That speaks for you. The *shaykh* is a reliable acquaintance of ours. How is the sergeant?"

"Not well. The wound on his leg came open."

"Allah! That means he might die. What did you do while Ibn Asl was that long absent?"

"The men trained very well, but I was not there."

"No? You, as the interpreter, are needed at the *saribah*! Where were you?"

"An interpreter has better uses for his time. I was with the black people of the Rohl and Shur, preparing for a good catch. I had some nice success. The sergeant assigned me a similar task."

"Now? Where are you being sent?"

"To the Takalah."

"But that is in the opposite direction! However, twice a year we get slaves from there. But do you dare visit these people?"

"Dare? I have been there several times. The Mek means me well, and his confidant, you know, too. I mean Shadid, who has become a good friend of mine."

"What? You know Shadid, the strong one, and are even his friend? Then you are indeed a very useful man for us. For how long will you stay here?"

"I cannot remain long. The *noquar* I want to travel with to Matariah island, will leave here before midnight."

"Eat quickly then that you do not miss it. But watch out for the ship of the *raïs effendina* on your trip, and especially avoid a Christian dog, a foreign *effendi*, who is making the area unsafe from here to Khartoum."

"A Christian? I'm also a Christian and have no reason to avoid him."

"You have every reason! He is an ally of the *raïs effendina* and seems to be after our people. Apparently, you have not heard of him, which is why I must tell you about him."

I was glad for the turn in the conversation. I had succeeded in gaining the trust of the *Arnaut*, who believed my stories. I had also managed to prompt him to ask me to eat faster and leave so that I would not miss the departure of my ship. Now, he wanted to talk himself, and I was removed from the danger of being asked things I did not know anything about. Could it get any better? No! Until this very moment luck had been on my side, but now it suddenly turned its back to me.

There was a big ruckus at the entrance of the building. Voices screamed; doors were opened and shut; then an *Arnaut* entered to report:

"Sir, we have the fellow who was listening outside."

"Bring him in!"

"When we caught him, the pious master with his friend happened to arrive. They wanted to see you and seemed to know him."

The man left again. A terrible presentiment occurred to me. A pious master was coming? Hmm! And who was the stranger they had apprehended, who was known by the pious one? Not my Bin Nil, I hoped? It was possible that, due to my long absence, concern for me had driven him here and –

The door opened and, well, they brought in Bin Nil, the poor devil.

I had risen and stepped into a corner, where I could not immediately be seen from the door. Four or five men had grabbed Bin Nil, with eight or nine following. Behind them entered – the *mukkadam* of the holy Qadiriyya and the *muza'bir*. Both had been after our lives in vain so far, but now it looked bad for us. What to do?

Five *Arnautlar* were holding Bin Nil. He could not get free; there were nine others, plus the *sangak*, the *muza'bir* and the *mukkadam*. I needed to tackle a total of twelve men if I wanted to get out. Outside, in the other rooms, there had to be more *Arnautlar*. Then there were the iron doors, my lack of knowledge of the building's interior and the uselessness of my weapons. While I weighed all this in a single moment, I knew what I had to do.

"Who are you, dog?" the *sangak* snarled at Bin Nil. "Why are you hanging around my house?"

Bin Nil had not yet seen me. He may have thought to rescue himself by a simple lie, for he answered:

"Sir, I did not mean anything bad. I am a crew member on a ship that is anchored here and . . ."

"A lie, a lie!" the *mukkadam* cut in. "Don't believe him, *sangak*! We know him."

"So? Then tell me who he is!"

"Sir, our heart beats most joyfully, and you will be surprised. We have caught the friend and companion of our fiercest opponent, Allah may curse."

"What opponent?"

"The *effendi*, the Christian dog! This young man is the Bin Nil, we told you about. Bin Nil, the faithful companion of the *effendi*. Where one is, there is also the other, and since we found Bin Nil here, then we can safely expect his master to be also in Fashoda."

"Is it possible? This is supposed to be Bin Nil?" the *sangak* exclaimed doubtfully.

"Yes, yes! We are not mistaken; we know him well. Have him whipped until he tells us where his master is!"

"That isn't necessary," I said while I stepped from the corner. I can tell you myself where I am."

The impression these words made, were totally different from what I had expected. I was going to surrender without a fight, thinking resistance to be nonsense. I rather figured on better circumstances later. I had thought they would immediately throw themselves onto me to tear me down, however, the exact opposite happened.

"The *effendi*, the *effendi* himself!" the *muza'bir* screamed. "He is right among us! May Allah protect us! Oh, Allah, Allah!"

The startled men stood there like marble figures. Some of them gaped, and none made a move to subdue me. I had to make use of this. Two leaps took me to Bin Nil. I tore him free and tossed him out the door, so that the *Arnautlar* holding him tumbled left and right. Punching for an opening, I rushed after him and got out. Behind me, they had taken hold of themselves.

"Out, *Arnautlar*, out!" the mighty bass voice of the *sangak* shouted. "Stop the fugitives, hold them!"

Bin Nil had fallen in front of the door and had not yet risen. I stumbled over him. Opposite us, the door was pushed open, hitting my head. *Arnautlar* came rushing out. Behind us pushed the others. My eyes were dancing; I had been hit at a sensitive spot. I felt myself being grabbed. I fought ten, twenty hands, kicked and hit, jerked my feet left and right, back and forth – all in vain. We were subdued and dragged into the reception room, where we were tied up.

It is impossible to describe this scene. I boiled from the effort, Bin Nil did likewise. The *Arnautlar*, too, stood panting and wheezing around us. The *sangak* pushed them apart, so that he could get to us, twirled his long mustache left and right, and shouting derisively and triumphantly:

"What a Day! What happy hour! What surprise! Did my ears hear right? Yes, this man would not have tried to escape, were he not the one described."

"Bah!" I responded. "I admitted that it was I."

"After all! And what impudence, what insolence to even admit it! Lift the fellows up and stand them by the wall! I must get a closer look at them."

His order was followed. When we now leaned like display pieces against the wall, the *sangak* put himself before me and first recited everything, item by item, he had heard from me, as if he wanted to incite revenge on himself. He finally said:

"What do you want from me? You did not come here without some purpose."

"Indeed, I did not."

"Answer, then! What were you up to against me?"

"I may tell you later, but not now."

That is when he turned to the *mukkadam* and the *muza'bir*, saying:

"This most cursed of the *giaurlar* is even worse and more dangerous than you described him to me. Imagine, he came to me earlier, calling himself Iskander Patras, and claimed to be the interpreter at the Saribah Aliab. He delivered a letter he most likely wrote himself, and now the question is, what had he in mind with it?"

"Some evil, for sure," the *mukkadam* commented. "If he is not going to tell you, have him beaten until he admits to it."

"I shall do that at once."

"Then you hand him over to us. We will take him to Ibn Asl, where he will find the fate that was repeatedly promised him."

"Yes," I cut in. "My limbs are to be torn one by one from my body. But there's still time for that. To learn what I wanted from you, oh *sangak*, you need not have me whipped. You heard that I was going to tell you. I came here to warn you of Ibn Asl and his people."

"What warning!" he laughed derisively. "Are you mad?"

"Then the *mudir* must be, too, for it is he who sent me to you."

"He? A lie, a threefold lie!"

"Ask Bin Nil, my companion. We live with the *mudir*, and he sent me to talk with you about Ibn Asl."

I saw that he became frightened, the way he changed color.

"Dog, tell the truth!" he demanded of Bin Nil. "Where do you live?"

"With the *mudir*," he replied.

"Did he talk about me?"

"Yes, as my *effendi* said already."

"You have talked this over; you lie!"

"Think what you want, but let me extend my row of deeds, you recited earlier, by one more. You will have learned from Ibn Asl that Amr al-Makashef, the *shaykh* of the Baqqara, was sent into the desert. We captured this *shaykh*, took him to Fashoda, and handed him over to the *mudir*. This was done before I came to you. The *shaykh* is now in prison and will get the famous 'five hundred', if not worse."

"Man, what damage you do us! I would love to crush you."

"You will leave that be, for if I haven't returned to the *mudir* by midnight, you will be locked up. Rest assured of this!"

"Don't believe him! He lies to save himself!" the *mukkadam* warned.

"I will know within a few minutes where I am at."

With these words, the *sangak* stepped outside. When he returned, he withdrew with the *mukkadam* and the *muza'bir* to the farthest corner, where they negotiated very animatedly. They did this until an *Arnaut* entered.

"Well?" the *sangak* asked aloud.

"The *shaykh* of the Baqqara lies in chains in prison. I saw him," the man reported.

"Put the prisoners down again, then, all of you leave!"

We were laid flat on the floor once more. The three stood quarreling in a corner. We were unable to understand what they were saying, but saw their very vivid gestures and expressions. Finally, they stepped outside. Before doing so the *sangak* came over to me and said:

"You arranged this nicely, but it will not help you after all. We shall not see each other again. May *Shaytan* devour you, you dogs!"

He spit at us and left. For a short time we lay alone in the room. What was I to do? To admonish my good Bin Nil, because his worry had driven him to commit this stupidity? I wouldn't think of it, and it would not have changed our situation anyway. He started himself by saying in a choked voice:

"*Effendi*, I was very rash, something you cannot forgive me. Pour your anger over me. I would prefer this to the silence that depresses my soul."

"I'm not angry at you," I told him. "You only brought harm to yourself, not to me."

"No, also to you. Had I not come and been caught, you would now be free and be able to return to us."

"You are mistaken. I would also have been recognized without your presence."

"But you, by yourself, could have more easily escaped than the two of us."

"Hardly. With the situation as it was, escape together with you would not have been any more difficult than if I had been alone."

"If this is truly your opinion, then I am at least calmed with respect to your anger, not, however, for what is awaiting us. They will surely kill us. In no way can we hope to escape these people who carry such fierce hate for us."

"I'm still hopeful, and won't give up. I have found myself in much worse situations without giving up courage, and you, too, when you were stuck all alone in the deep well at Asyût to starve miserably, had less reason than now to expect rescue. I am convinced that nothing will happen to us here in Fashoda. They will take us to where Ibn Asl is. We simply must wait. I am glad I don't have my weapons and other property with me. They would have taken it, and should we be able to escape, would have lost all. How about your belongings?"

"I do not have anything. I left the musket and pistols with the *mudir*, and since he was not to learn of my intentions, I had to get away unobserved, I had only my knife with me, which alone was taken."

Four men entered, carrying long and wide raffia mats and ropes. We were gagged, our eyes were covered up, then we were wrapped in the mats with the ropes wound around. Thus, we formed two stiff rolls that were picked up and carried off. Our heads stuck from the rolls, so that we, at least, did not suffer want of air. Of course, we were unable to see where we were being taken. I felt as if it was across dirt piles and mud holes. Then I heard water splashing and we were put onto some hard flooring.

"Off now, quickly and cautiously!" I heard a commanding voice.

I heard the noise of oars engaging water. We had to be in a boat. Deep silence ruled around us, only from time to time broken by a whispering voice whose words I was unable to understand. Later, when we had left Fashoda behind, they spoke louder, but nothing that would have told us about our destination. Whatever I understood were only brief commands concerning the rowing and the use of a rudder.

A long, long time passed. How many hours, I was unable to guess. When we finally landed, I felt as if an entire day had passed.

"Who is there?" called someone, the voice coming from higher up, it seemed.

"Men of the *sangak*," came the answer.

"Is Ibn Asl here?"

"No, but come on up!"

A little time passed during which we were talked about. Also now I was unable to understand anything, but sounds of happy surprise became mixed with whispers. Then we were tied to ropes to pull us up. We were dropped hard, then unwrapped from our covers. Our gags and blinds were removed, and I could see that we lay on deck of a ship. About twenty men surrounded us. I could clearly see their faces with the moon shining brightly.

That meant that the rowing had not even taken all night, but only until early morning. It was still dark. Of course, it was no wonder that time had become so distorted for me.

The one standing closest to me was Murad Nassyr, the fat Turk, I was supposed to travel with to become his associate in the slave trade. Seeing his outline standing before me, I had to think of the farewell words he had shouted to me in Korosko. They had been threatening enough, still, I had much less respect for this fat Turk than for his allies, who possessed more energy and were much more dangerous than he. He spoke with a man, who had to be one of those, who had transported us to the ship. I heard him ask:

"Where are the muza'bir and the mukkadam? Why did they not come along right away?"

"They left Fashoda by land to go to the Dinka, where Ibn Asl is. They intend to inform him of the capture of these two men."

"They may not find him there any more. I expect him with the hired Dinka at any moment. Should he arrive before those two return, we must stay here for their sake, and lose precious time."

These words showed that Murad Nassyr did not possess an excess of smarts. It was a mistake to talk in my presence that Ibn Asl had hired a group of Dinka for the slave hunt. He had been forced to do this, since we had captured all his men. Murad Nassyr now turned to me, asking viciously:

"You still know me, you dog? Do your thoughts reach back far enough to recognize who I am?"

Since I did not reply, he continued:

"Remember Korosko and the words I left you with."

When I now did not say anything either, he added:

"I threatened you then that, should I see you again, I would crush you. Now, that I have seen you once more, prepare yourself for death. You are lost and will not find any mercy from us."

He may have thought that I would now respond. When it did not happen, he kicked me, and barked at me:

"Open your mouth, you dirty toad! Or did fear cause you to become mute?"

Now I laughed aloud and replied:

"Fear? Of you? My dear fat one, don't let yourself be laughed about. No one is scared of you, me the least. While you can devour *pilaf* with mutton tail, you can't me!"

"Dog, you even deride me. I shall double your pains for it."

"Leave me be! You play such a ridiculous role with your threats that one can only laugh about you. You remember me from Algiers and must therefore know that your boasting will not impress me. Go, lie down and sleep; this is in any case better than trying to scare me."

He gave me another kick, shouting:

"I will remember that! I know that you were told the pains you will suffer. They will only be made more terrible than you imagined. Do not think that you will escape again this time. I will guard you myself and will not let you out of my sight until Ibn Asl returns. Pick the dogs up and follow me with them!"

He went to the fore deck. We were carried after him to some kind of cabin. One of two doors next to each other were opened, as I was able to see. We entered a kind of living room, where he now checked our fetters. This was done by the light of a lamp. When he was convinced that we were well tied and could not escape, he issued the necessary orders for our accommodation.

The room we were in had no wooden walls, but rather resembled a tent. Poles had been put across the ship's bow with mats placed on top. It was a sun roof from which several canvas sheets, walls, that is, hung down. The front wall consisted of two pieces, making them the previously mentioned 'doors'. A canvas sheet across the room separated it into two parts. We found ourselves in the right one. From the part to the left I heard female voices, which let me assume that the Turk's sister with her servants was accommodated there. On the far end of the contraption hung another curtain that had been raised. Behind it was a bow space, about six by four feet, where various kinds of baggage and junk was kept. The latter stuff was now removed to make room for us. Strong iron pegs were nailed into the deck to which we were tied, a not unnecessary caution, for should we be able to come free of our fetters, we only needed to lift the matting that formed the ceiling to climb over board.

When we had been fastened down in this manner, Murad Nassyr said:

"You cannot move any more. Now try to escape me. Ibn Asl will be back by this afternoon, then your fate will be determined. I live right next to you and can hear every word. If I hear the least thing I do not like, you will get the whip. May Allah now give you a pleasant rest and even nicer dreams."

He spoke this derisively, then left with his men. We saw light through the thin canvas behind which his shadow moved. This told us what he was doing. He lifted the side canvas and disappeared behind it. We heard whispers and recognized his voice and that of a female, who, as I had guessed, and subsequently learned, was his sister.

He soon returned to his room and sat down. A little while later another shadow showed on the canvas. His sister had entered. They whispered to each other, after which he rose and walked out onto the deck.

This had barely happened, when another female figure stepped from the side partition. She approached the canvas, behind which we lay, lifted it a bit, and said softly:

"*Effendi*, where are you?"

"Here," I replied. "Who are you?"

"I am Fatma, whom you know."

So it was Fatma, the favorite servant of the Turk's sister. What was the purpose of her contact? Surely not a bad one.

"What do you want from me?" I asked.

"My mistress sends me. She heard from the master that you were captured and will be tortured to death. This hurts her heart."

"May Allah bless her for her compassion."

"Yes, she is a good person. She wants to rescue you."

"*Hamdulillah*! In what way?"

"Unfortunately, she cannot do much, but whatever she can, she will. When her hair began to vanish, you returned the pride of her head. She has not forgotten this. She wants to thank you for it, and I am to ask you to tell me a wish you might have."

"Where is she?"

"Outside, on deck. She talked her brother into stepping outside so that I can talk with you."

"But what if he suddenly returns and sees what you are doing?"

"She intends to keep him outside until I give her the signal that I have completed my task."

"This is well. Quickly, bring me a sharp knife."

She left, brought the knife, and tried to hand it to me.

"I cannot hold it with my hands being tied. You must show me the love to cut me loose."

"Allah, what are you asking of me! My hands tremble from fear, but I will do it anyway, you being the benefactor of my mistress."

Indeed, I felt her hands tremble when she cut the rope. I now took the knife, squeezed her hand, and said:

"I thank you, Fatma, you loveliest of daughters. May Allah bless you for it! Do you know how many men are on the ship?"

"Twenty and then some. They lie outside sleeping."

"Where are the men who brought us? Did they return to Fashoda?"

"No. They are lying with our men."

"Then their boat is still hanging by the ship?"

"Yes."

"This is what I wanted to know. You can leave now and need not give the signal, because your mistress will find out in a few minutes that you did your task well. We will probably see each other again. I will then thank you more thoroughly than I can now."

She withdrew.

"What delight, *effendi*," Bin Nil said. "You were right. One should never give up hope. We are saved, provided we are not stopped."

"Stopped? If I am in free possession of my limbs and have a knife in hand, I won't be stopped by twenty plus men. Rest assured of that. It is as if we were free already."

With my hands free, it was no problem cutting the rope holding my feet and severing me from the peg. I did the same for Bin Nil. We stood up. I lifted the mat that was forming the roof and looked outside.

The moon still shone. We were moored on the right side of the river. Not far from the ship I saw the fantastic shadows of three side-by-side standing candelabra euphorbias which, later, would serve as a distinctive feature for me. On deck lay the sleeping men. The Turk stood with his sister back by the steering wheel. Both were looking over the board at the water. The boat must be hanging on the riverside. The ship was tied down with a bow and a quarter anchor. The chain for the former hung from a strong iron ring, attached to the inner bow board, that was our prison.

"Everything looks good," I said. "We climb on this chain over board. No one will pay any attention to us. Once we are in the water, we will swim to the boat."

I pushed the mat above our head fully aside and silently vaulted over the board to climb down the chain on the outside. Bin Nil followed. It was no problem getting down. Our getting wet only pleased us in this climate.

Of course, we swam, without making splashing sounds, as close as possible to the ship's hull, so that we could not be seen from above. The boat we were looking for, hung on the water's side of the ship. There was now the question of whether the oars had been left in it. When we got there, we were delighted to find them inside, so we climbed in.

"Let's get away quickly, *effendi*!" Bin Nil urged. "Being free, let's not dally here for a moment."

He sat down on the bench and to push the boat away, he put the oar against the ship's hull. It was then we were noticed.

"The *effendi* is free!" Murad screamed. He is getting away. He is down there in the boat. Come, men, pursue them. Two thousand, three thousand piaster to the one who brings him back to me!"

"Ten thousand piaster to the one who will catch me!" I laughed in response. Then, I engaged the oars with Bin Nil following suit, and our boat 'flew' downstream as if shot from a bow. Obviously, we had been transported upstream, which is why we had to head in the opposite direction to return to Fashoda. It was not much later that we were no longer able to see the ship.

Bin Nil was an excellent rower. I, too, had learned to use oars, which is why we were not concerned that we would be caught. A quarter of an hour later, we reduced our effort since there was no need for such speed.

It must have been about ten in the evening, when we were captured at the *sangak's* place. A look at the sky told me that it had to be about three in the morning. With one hour on the ship, the travel from Fashoda to it must have taken four hours, a time that had appeared like eternity to me. Traveling downstream being faster, I figured that it would take us three hours to Fashoda, arriving there by six o'clock.

One can easily imagine the mood we were in. Bin Nil rejoiced from time to time. I remained quiet, but my joy was no less than his. And who did we have to thank for our rescue? To the dissolution of a simple, well-known salt, by which I had once moistened the bare spot on the head of the Turk's sister. At that time, I had not imagined that this cure would later save me from such a plight. The sister was a good and grateful girl after all. I resolved to try everything to prevent her from becoming Ibn Asl's wife.

Upon daybreak we had come close enough to Fashoda to see it in the distance. A small sailboat was cruising back and forth across the river, crewed by a single man. When he noticed us, he headed toward us, dropped his sail, and asked:

"Where do you come from?"

"From up there," I answered, pointing backward. "We want to get to Fashoda."

"Who are you?"

"Why do you ask? Are you an official of the *mudir*?"

"No. But I am looking for a foreign *effendi* and a young man by name of Bin Nil, who both disappeared last night without a trace. The *mudir* is searching for them. Since you are two, and I do not know you, but the description fits, I believe that I found the missing men."

"Do you know the *sangak* of the *Arnautlar*?"

"I have seen him, but never talked to him."

"Do you hate or love him?"

"Sir, this is a dangerous question. Since I am expecting neither good nor bad from him, I will answer to it. I do not hate, nor love him, but am indifferent toward him, although he has much influence and power."

"I can now also be honest, although I have actually no reason, to keep the truth from you. We are the ones you are looking for."

"Really? Is it true?" he asked pleased. "*Hamdulillah!* Then it is me who will earn the rich reward!"

"What reward?"

"The hundred piaster, the *mudir* is going to pay for finding you."

"You shall get them, although he would have seen us again without you."

"Would he?" he asked disappointed. "Allah! Then I will not get the money."

"He will give it to you. Ask for it!"

"No way, *effendi!* Instead of the piaster I would receive five hundred blows."

"You shall get the money. I give you my word. And should he refuse, I will give it to you. But I do this with the condition that you take us to the *mudir*, without us being seen by the *sangak* or any of his *Arnautlar*."

He looked wonderingly at me and asked:

"*Effendi*, did these *Arnautlar* make you disappear?"

"I cannot answer your question, since I don't know you."

"Oh, you can trust me. I am a poor fisherman and take what I catch only to the *mudir's* kitchen, where I am paid for it, while I do not get anything from the *sangak*."

"Where do you live?"

"Here, just outside the town. You can see my hut on the left bank over there. It stands far away from the other huts and houses."

I told him what had happened to us, then continued:

"If the *sangak* learns that we returned, he may find time to flee before the order to apprehend him can be given."

"*Effendi*, I would be surprised at what I am hearing here, if I did not know what a violent man the *sangak* is. If this is so, you are right. You must not be spotted getting to the *mudir*. I will take you to my hut where you can wait until I meet the *mudir*, whom I will tell whatever you order me."

"Fine, I am agreed."

"But you must not follow me in your boat, which would be too conspicuous. It must not be seen that I have two men with me, for people would know right away that it is you. Climb into my boat. First, I will row you alone to my hut, then pick up Bin Nil, who can wait here on the bank until I return."

I jumped into his boat and was taken to his hut, at the outermost town limits. His wife, a Negress, was home, and was told to keep us hidden and not let anyone into the hut. He then went for Bin Nil. When this was done and he had received detailed instructions from me, he went to the *mudir*.

It took almost an hour for him to return. He brought different clothing, a female dress for Bin Nil, and a eunuch's one for me. I had to blacken my face. I would have been less recognizable in woman's clothing than in those of a harem's guard, but my figure did not fit this masquerade.

When we had changed, we once more entered his boat, and the fisherman rowed us closer to town, after he had ordered his wife to keep silent.

Bin Nil was heavily covered with a veil over his face that made him resemble a woman. He found the disguise extremely funny and kept giggling, less about himself than the black face my beard did not fit.

When we disembarked, no one was around. Maybe it was coincidence, because so many people were on the lookout for us to earn the one hundred piaster. We reached the government building without being observed by anyone. An official waiting there, took us to the *mudir*, who had made sure that no one inside came across us.

He sat smoking on his silken divan. When we entered, his serious, even stern face greeted us with a happy smile. Yes, it looked, as if he had to make an effort not to laugh aloud.

"Allah does wonders!" he exclaimed. "Who has ever seen a Negro, a guard of women, with such a beard. Were you recognized, *effendi*?"

"No. We were not seen by anyone."

"That is well. Sit down and take the pipes I made ready for you. But you will wait outside the door to find out whether I will give you the money or not!"

These words were addressed to the fisherman, who did not immediately obey the order, but asked entreatingly:

"Forgive my boldness, oh *mudir*, and allow me to . . ."

"Silence! Or you shall get instantly five hundred!" the *mudir*, thundering, cut him off. "Out with you!"

Bin Nil and I had sat down next to the *mudir* and lit our pipes, after which I had to tell what had happened. During my report, the town administrator's features did not change, nor did he say a word. When I was finished, he still kept silent for a while, but then spoke, not like I had expected, but rather softly and very calmly. But precisely from this quiet one could guess on the size of the anger he was forcefully suppressing.

"Yesterday," he said, "when you told me that this son-of-a-bitch was an ally of the slavers, I did not believe it. You now demonstrated the truth of your words. He will . . ."

He stopped in mid-sentence and looked down. He was outraged and deeply excited and did not find it commensurate with his dignity to let us know his feelings. A little while later he clapped his hands. A servant entered and received an order:

"Go, see the *sangak* of the *Arnautlar* and tell him that I wish to speak to him. It concerns a secret. He is not to tell anyone who he is going to see. It must be clear to you when you convey this information, that only he will hear it. Before you go, send me Abu Khabdat (Father of Beatings)."

The man left, and shortly thereafter a black, exceptionally robust fellow entered, who crossed his hands before his chest and bowed almost to the floor.

"There's work coming up," the *mudir* told him, while his thumb pointed over his back to a door. The 'Father of Beatings' bowed once more, then walked out backwards. When we were alone, the *mudir* said:

"Do you know why the *sangak* is being asked to come secretly?"

"I can imagine why. For your safety."

"Allah! You guessed it!" he exclaimed in surprise.

"This wasn't difficult. I know the *Arnautlar* well enough. They are extremely hard to keep in line. When you sentence the *sangak* and his men hear of it, you can expect a revolt."

"So it is! He is to get his punishment without anyone knowing. When you did not return yesterday, I sent for him. He had me told that no one had visited him. Later, I went to him myself and was told the same. Then I learned that Bin Nil had also disappeared and immediately issued the order to search for you everywhere. This dog tried to lead me by the nose. He is aiding and abetting the slave trade, a traitor and murderer. You shall see and hear what I plan to say and do to him. Step over there in the other room, where you will find everything you need. You shall hear the *sangak's* statement and enter at the right moment."

He had pointed to another door. We followed his request and entered a room where I found all my property. There was also everything to remove my black coloration, which I, of course, did quickly. Then I changed my clothing. Bin Nil kept wearing his woman's clothing, since his actual suit was still with the fisherman. I had just finished chang-ing when I heard steps. The *sangak* entered the *mudir's* room. We were able to hear everything, for what I had called a door, was simply a rug-covered opening.

"You had me called, oh *mudir*," I heard the *Arnaut's* voice.

"Yes, secretly. Who else knows of you coming here?"

"No one."

"Sit down!" the *mudir* told him. "Have you found any trace of the missing men?"

"Nothing, so far."

"This is bad! I will not rest until I have found them."

"I, too, did everything possible. All my *Arnautlar* have gone search-ing, although I do not understand how I can demand of them, being right believers, to search for the stinking tracks of a Christian."

"I want this Christian; that should be enough for you and them. Did you check thoroughly at your place?"

"Yes, but in vain."

"Odd! The *effendi* went to you and his companions heard clearly that he knocked at your door."

"That may well be. The door was opened, but no one was there. Later, the guard noticed that some strange characters were slinking about the door. Who knows for what purpose the Christian came and why he so suddenly disappeared?"

"He told me his purpose. There was no reason for him to disappear. However, there was good reason for some local people to make him disappear."

"Then I advise you to ask these people!"

"I did, but they deny knowing anything."

"Give them five hundred and they will confess!"

"Since you advise me to do so, I shall have it done, and you will be present for it."

"I thank you, my lord! You know that I love justice and am always glad to be present when you exercise it on those who have sinned against it. It will be my pleasure to hear the howls of these dogs. But let me ask you now for the secret, the reason you had me come."

"You shall hear it right away. Yes, it is a secret, whose solution is very dear to my heart, and you are the right man to help me with it. Might you know a *muza'bir*, a pickpocket from al-Qahira?"

"No."

"Then you might know a certain Abd al-Barak, *mukkadam* of the holy Qadiriyya?"

"Him neither."

"These two men are presently in Fashoda. I must find them, they being allies of the slaver Ibn Asl."

"Shall I search for them? If they are truly here, I will find them for certain."

"They are here. They were still seen last night. Supposedly, they knocked on your door."

"Allah! What might they have wanted from me? It must be a mistake. Such people would not be mad enough to risk coming to me."

"There are madmen, who are sometimes of a clear mind. One more question. Did you ever talk with a Turk by the name of Murad Nassyr?"

"Never. What's the matter with him?"

"Later, about him. I must only ask you about one other person, a Takalah by name of Shadid."

"I do not know him. How come you are asking me so many unknown names?"

"I do so to facilitate your discovery of the secret. I did already some advance work for you, but you are to finish the matter. About four rowing hours upstream, a ship is moored, belonging to Ibn Asl."

"Allah, Allah!"

Until now the *sangak* had answered quickly and uninhibited. This last exclamation revealed that he was frightened.

"On this ship," the *mudir* continued, "is the Turk, I asked you about. He has a sister along who is to become Ibn Asl's wife."

"Who do you know this from?" the *Arnaut* asked subdued.

"Later, later! First, you should know that Ibn Asl is presently with the Dinka in order to hire a number of warriors for a slave hunt. This ship has been under observation, and this morning it was noticed that a boat landed next to it carrying two round packages. The packages were carried on board. Might you know the content of these packages?"

"How could I?"

"Then try to. This is the secret I wish so very much to be revealed. You are smart, very smart, and I think that you will have no difficulty discovering it."

In the course of this conversation, I had pushed the rug aside a bit in order to observe the two. The *mudir* sat with his face turned toward us, the *sangak* had his back toward us. I thought the right moment had come and whispered to Bin Nil:

"Step in quietly and stand by the door!"

I pushed him in and saw a smile of satisfaction cross the *mudir's* face when he saw my disguised companion. In any case, the *sangak* did not appear to be very comfortable. At this moment, he seemed to ponder what to make of the *mudir*, for it took him awhile before he answered:

"I shall find out, sir. I will leave at once to find this ship. The packages must still be there."

"Maybe not. But it doesn't really matter. I only wish to learn their content. This is very important for me, so important that I have a reward for you if you can discover this secret, the magnitude of which you have no idea."

"*Mudir*, I am the most faithful of your servants," the *Arnaut* assured him, flattered.

"Yes, you are the most faithful of all. This is why I have chosen a woman for you as proof of my benevolence, no *houri* of paradise can be compared to her."

"A woman?" the *sangak* exclaimed surprised and disappointed.

"Yes, a woman; a model of beauty and virtue, an example of loveliness. So that you recognize the great treasure you are about to receive, you shall see this angel of angels now. Come closer, you, the beautiful one, and reveal your face, so that this brave *Arnaut*, enthralled by the sparkle of your eyes and the wonder of your soul, will sink down before your feet!"

He waved to Bin Nil, who slowly came closer. The *sangak* jumped up. He had a wife. That he was being offered a second one struck him as strange. And especially being asked to have a look at her was something not customary. Eyes wide, he stared at the deeply veiled figure, and said:

"A woman, truly a woman! What a surprise! Has she already been the wife of another, or is she still a girl? What is her color? White or black?"

"Find the answer yourself! Look and be surprised."

The *mudir* got up and removed the veil. The result was very much what I had expected. The *Arnaut* let go an inarticulate, hoarse scream of fear.

"Well, how do you like her? Aren't you delighted?" the *mudir* asked, while he purposely assumed a position such that the *sangak*, who had turned around, had to turn his back again toward me.

I used this opportunity to also enter unnoticed by the culprit. He did not reply. His face had turned pale, and he seemed unable to move.

"You must be speechless from joy," the *mudir* mocked. "If this happens upon seeing one package, imagine how great will be your happiness when you see the other. Have a look behind you!"

The *Arnaut* obeyed mechanically. When he saw me, he instantly regained his composure.

"By Hell!" he screamed. "I have been toyed with, but that will not continue. *Shaytan* destroy you three!"

He turned for the door to make his getaway, but I blocked his exit.

"Off with you, dog!" he hissed. "You are repugnant to me!"

"Maybe this is why you told me last night that we would not see each other again," I responded. "But I was convinced that I would see you once more in order to settle my account with you."

"Off! Step aside, or I will make room!"

He pulled his knife making ready to stab. That's when I struck his elbow from below and he dropped it. I took hold of him, lifted him and threw him to the floor such that I thought he had broken his neck. His eyes were open, but he did not move.

"Allah, Allah!" the *mudir* exclaimed. "This is how you deal with this giant! This is what the *raïs effendina* reported, and which I did not want to believe. Is he dead?"

"No," I replied. "He will move in a minute, very suddenly, to . . ."

I did not continue, for what I had expected happened. Suddenly, the *sangak* reached for his belt and pulled out a pistol aiming it at me, at which time he half-raised his body. His immobility had been a feint. Bin Nil, standing behind him, bent down, and grabbed the hand holding the pistol; simultaneously, he kicked him in the belly so that he dropped down again and lost the pistol. He wanted to get up so he could continue his defense, however, the kick had disabled him. Halfway up, he held his fist toward me and uttered a curse impossible to repeat.

"Leave him be!" the *mudir* ordered. "The crook isn't worth being touched by you. *Effendi*, you heard what I told my 'Father of Beatings'. Once, an order has been issued, then care has been taken to make sure that the respective person is secured. You need not expend any more effort on him."

He clapped his hands. With this signal, two Blacks stepped in, took the *sangak* on both sides and pulled him off the floor. The *Arnaut* saw the 'Father of Beatings' and guessed what awaited him.

"Do you want me beaten?" he roared at the *mudir*.

"I only intend to follow your own suggestion," he responded. "Earlier, you gave me excellent advise for the *bastonnade*, which will now be applied to you."

"Do you know what this means?"

"Only that a dog will be beaten."

"But this dog has teeth! A small signal from me and my *Arnautlar* will attack you! You do not know me yet!"

"I know you exactly. I earlier told you the names of your friends. This makes it unnecessary for me to tell you your list of sins. If you think that I do not know you yet, I know you that much better than you know me. I am called Abu Hamsah Miah. You will get five hundred!"

"Five hundred!" the *Arnaut* screamed. "That will cost you your life!"

"Do not threaten me! Beg Allah that he guide you safely across the 'Bridge of Death', so that you do not tumble into the fires of *Jihanna*!"

The *Arnaut* started, gave the *mudir* an indescribable look, and asked haltingly:

"Bridge . . of . . Death! Then . . you . . plan to . . whip me . . to death?"

"You will get five hundred and will not be seen again. This is what I told the 'Father of Beatings', and what I have said will be done!"

"Not yet, not yet! I still have arms and hands to fight and tear you apart!"

He tried to get free of the two Blacks in order to throw himself onto the *mudir*, but the assistants of the 'Father of Five-hundred' were experienced. They pushed him down, held him, and in the blink of a moment attached a leather strap around the top of his head and chin by which the lower jaw was pulled tight against the upper, so that he could no longer move it or scream. Then, they carried him out.

"He gets what he deserves," commented the merciless town administrator. "We will join as witnesses."

"Not I," I replied. "I do not care to be present at this event."

"Do you have weak nerves? An administrator cannot have them if he wants to clear a path for justice. I am not forcing you to be present. Wait here for my return."

"Wait a moment, *mudir*. I must tell you something important."

"What?"

"Entrust me with a group of *asakir* and some fast boats. We must hurry to capture Ibn Asl's ship, or he will escape us."

"Fine by me, but because of the *Arnautlar*, who are not to see you, you must wait a few hours. If they spot you and miss the *sangak*, they will establish the connection. I am here only too short a time to be strong enough against them. It wasn't the *mudir* who commanded here in the past, but the *Arnautlar*. They governed by the fear they imparted. I shall tame them, but it does not work as fast as I would like."

"But how will you arrange for me to leave with troops without the *Arnautlar* noticing?"

"I will send them downstream to collect taxes, which they will be delighted to do. Let me issue the order right away."

He walked through the door from which the *sangak* had been removed. I walked out the other door where the fisherman still waited, Bin Nil's suit over his arm. I took from him for my companion to change. Afterwards, we sat down once more to smoke and to await the *mudir's* return.

While sitting there silently, we clearly heard the blows falling rhythmically in the room next door. At first, they were accompanied by groans which, little by little, turned fainter to finally stop. It is impossible to describe my feelings, as I heard this. I could have hated the *mudir*, yet had to realize that the application of his iron fist was appropriate here.

When he returned, he sat down with us and lit a pipe. Nothing was said. His head turned sideways, he listen to the noise of the smacks that put my teeth on edge. Finally, the door opened and the 'Father of Beatings' stuck his head in to report:

"Five hundred!"

"And the *sangak*?" the *mudir* asked.

"Will not be seen again, my lord."

"Off with him!"

The Black's head withdrew, and I asked:

"Then the *Arnaut* is dead?"

"Yes."

"Where will he be buried?"

"In the belly of crocodiles. They do not talk. Now, it's the Baqqara's turn. I sent for him and I promised to have him whipped in your presence. This time you will attend?"

"No, thank you."

"It isn't as bad as you think, *effendi*. Only when the respective fellow is not to be seen again, is it that he will he be beaten to death. The Baqqara will get his blows in five installments. Then he can return to his tribe."

"Still, I ask your permission to be absent."

"I cannot force you. Listen, it started already!" The beating could be heard again. Since no one spoke, I involuntarily counted. How long did it take, how infinitely long, until the 'Father of Beatings' reported his one hundred? And those had been given to a free Baqqara, a relative of the later Mahdi! He was taken back to prison and would get the remaining four hundred in four weekly installments.

I now reminded the *mudir* of the fisherman still waiting for his hundred piaster. He had him enter and asked him:

"Do you expect to receive the award I had announced?"

"If your kindness permits me to entertain this hope, I shall do so, my lord," the man replied humbly.

"My kindness doesn't allow you anything. You have nothing to hope for."

"But I brought you the *effendi* and Bin Nil!"

"They would have come without you. I give you a choice: Either you say that you were paid or you get five hundred. What do you prefer?"

"Lord, I have been paid!"

"Then you can go."

The 'Father of Five hundred' was a friend of justice to the extent of being inhuman. To pull out his purse did not seem to be part of his passions! Even the best man has his weaknesses! The fisherman turned to leave, but in the entranceway turned his head again to ask me:

"*Effendi*, will you keep your word? I am a poor man."

"What is it? What word are you to keep?" the *mudir* asked me.

"I promised him the hundred piaster," I replied, reaching for my wallet.

"And you want to give them here? What are you thinking? You are my guest and do not pay anything. Did you not hear that he was paid?"

"I heard but did not see it. Permit me to give them to him!"

"No! If you insist, he will get them from me. But I have no money. Taxes are paid in the form of animals and fruit, which is why I can pay him only in this way. He may go to my shepherd and ask for three sheep. Now, off with him!"

When I checked the following day, I learned to my satisfaction that the man had truly received the sheep. He now seemed to be sure of it, for he thanked me with three deep bows while his face shone from joy.

He had barely gone when it was reported that the *Arnautlar* had left. Their destination was the area of Kuek. Woe to the poor people from whom these soldiers were to collect taxes! Not only were these to be paid, but the people had to provide also for the *Arnautlar's* provisions, which they determined themselves. One can imagine the injustices occurring there. Once the residents hear that the taxing soldiers are coming, they usually take flight with wives, children, and their few belongings and return only when the soldiers are gone.

Now, a number of sail boats were procured for fifty well-armed *asakir*. Of course, I joined this delayed expedition with Bin Nil. When we left, it was already past noon. Toward five o'clock we arrived at the three candelabra euphorbias but the ship was gone.

I went ashore to check there and found the tracks of many people who had boarded the ship. They had all been barefoot. Their number was impossible to determine, but I was able to guess the time of their embarkation rather precisely. The imprints were at least five hours old, which meant the ship could no longer be caught and we had to return to Fashoda without having achieved anything.

After this setback, I hoped at least for some other success: the apprehension of the five Takalah, who had attacked the three traders and had killed two of them. The third one had fortunately recovered.

Shadid, their leader, knew the *sangak* of the *Arnautlar*. It could be expected that he would hide near Fashoda and then send a messenger to the *Arnaut*. Since this messenger would obviously go directly to the *sangak's* home, it would be best to wait for him there and arrest him. This is why I asked the *mudir's* permission to move to this home together with Bin Nil and the surviving trader. This was readily granted. Hafiz Sikhar, who we had liberated from the Takalah, also moved in with us, not wanting to become separated from me. A few soldiers were assigned to our service. They were to guard the entrance and receive orders to bring anyone asking for the *sangak* immediately to me.

It was late evening when we moved in. The next day passed without the messenger showing up. But barely had the third day broken, when we heard knocking outside. The expected messenger had arrived. He was brought in and was taken aback to see me instead of the *sangak*. I told him that I was indeed the foreign *effendi*, and in no way the *mudir* of Jarabub, and even less, a Sinussi. I also told him that I was the one who had kidnapped Hafiz Sikhar and the *shaykh* of the Baqqara. This made him even more fearful and unwilling to talk. I threatened him with the *bastonnade* and when even this did not help, I had preparations made to use the whip on him. Seeing this, he was ready to tell me the place where Shadid was hiding with his caravan. It was the same woods, about an hour's distance from Fashoda, where we had also waited for the return of our messenger. When I reported this to the *mudir*, he made fifty soldiers of his garrison available to me – no *Arnautlar* – in order to take the members of the caravan prisoner. We marched off, taking the messenger along to lead us to the respective location, which he had been unable to describe exactly. He had to walk between Bin Nil and Hafiz Sikhar, who made it clear to him that should he make any attempt to betray us, he would be killed.

Caution made us take a detour. We could assume that Shadid would watch the direction from Fashoda and notice our approach, should we come straight for him. We therefore approached in an arc arriving at the woods from the south instead of the east.

Coming closer, we approached slowly, under the trees. Now it turned out that the messenger, because we had arrived from a different direction, was unable to find his comrades' camp. We therefore halted, and I went to reconnoiter.

Chance took me quickly to the right place. Well hidden behind trees, I was able to observe the caravan. The people were camped at a place that was very advantageous for us. It was surrounded by bushes on two sides, permitting an unobserved approach. I went to get my soldiers and posted them behind the bushes. After this was done, I had some fun by returning the short distance alone, then openly approaching the caravan from the other side. When the Takalah saw and recognized me, they jumped up in surprise.

"The Sinussi, the Sinussi, the *mudir* of Jarabub!" they shouted.

I conducted myself so fearlessly as if there had been no differences between us, and greeted them.

"You are here, in the area of Fashoda?" Shadid asked grimly. "How did you get here?"

"On my camel."

"Where is your companion, the young *khatib* of the Sinussi?"

"Nearby."

"What are you doing in Fashoda? You look suspicious to me. Why did you not tell us that you were headed for Fashoda?"

"Because you asked us only where we came from, but not for the destination of our journey."

"Did you just now arrive in the woods?"

"No. We arrived earlier. We live in town with the *sangak* of the Arnautlar, or rather in his house."

"With him? You are aware that I know him. I sent a messenger to him. Is he home?"

"Not any more. He is now either in Heaven or in Hell."

"Allah w' Allah! He died?"

"Yes, yesterday."

"From what illness?"

"From the *bastonnade*."

"Oh, Allah, oh, Muhammad, oh, Prophet! Are you telling me that he was beaten to death?"

"Indeed."

"A *sangak* of the *Arnautlar* beaten to death! This can only have been done on the order of the *mudir*, who was his patron and friend."

"The previous one, yes, but not the present one."

"Is there another now?"

"Yes. Ali Effendi al-Kurdi was dismissed since he aided the slave trade. Although the new *mudir's* name is also Ali Effendi, he is an entirely different man. He routs out the slavers and is called Abu Hamsah Miah, since he has every slaver he catches given five hundred blows."

"May Allah stand by us! All our calculations are ruined. Our messenger should long have returned, and I am afraid for him. If the *mudir* catches him, he will have to admit to the purpose for which he came to Fashoda."

"No harm done there."

"None? You just said that every slaver will get five hundred blows, and we are here to sell slaves."

"But you did not hunt for them, rather they are the property of your Mek, who sent them with you to Fashoda. You must follow your lord's commands. Then, according to the rules of your tribe, making slaves is the king's prerogative, and the *mudir* cannot take this away. He therefore cannot punish you, but can forbid you to sell the slaves."

"Allah be thanked. These words relieve my heart. I need not be as concerned for myself as you for yourself."

"I, concerned? How so?"

"You are not the one you claimed to be. Only when you were gone, several of your statements seemed suspicious to me, and the longer I thought about them, the more certain it appeared to me that you are not from Jarabub. You are now once again in my hands, and I insist on learning the truth. Do not lie to me again, or I know the means to extract the truth from you!"

"Bah! What does it matter to you to know who I am!"

"It very much matters to me, because due to my credulity and my rash trust in you, I told you things that no one is to know. What if you are this cursed foreign *effendi*?"

"Hmm! That's true, but you can't change that anymore."

"Not change it?" he asked, looking at me stunned. "What is that to mean?"

"It means that I am indeed this 'cursed' foreign *effendi*."

"Dog! You dare tell me this?"

"Why not? I see no risk. I shall tell you even more. After we left you, the Baqqara disappeared, together with a slave by the name of Hafiz Sikhar."

"So it was."

"I freed this Hafiz Sikhar while you were asleep, cutting him off the rope. And I took the Baqqara captive to have him punished in Fashoda. He has been sentenced to five hundred blows of which he has received already one hundred."

"How dare you tell me this!" Shadid exclaimed, reaching with both hands in an effort to get a hold of me. But he dropped them again, totally perplexed by my apparent boldness. I continued unswervingly:

"What you told me about the *sangak* was, of course, to his detriment. I brought charges against him, after which he received the *bastonnade* from which he died."

"So, you are guilty of his death! And you even take pride in it! This will be punished on the spot! I will squash you with my fists!"

He now wanted to grab me for real. I stepped back, warning him:

"Don't you dare touch me! At the Nid al-Nil I let myself be overcome by you only as a feint; if it gets serious, you will end up with the shorter stick!"

"I am serious, totally serious! Show me now the shorter end of the stick!" he screamed, forcing himself onto me.

"Bin Nil, come!" I shouted, while I evaded the giant Takalah by quick turns. He vehemently tried to catch me, paying neither attention to what I had said, nor what now happened. He had eyes only for me. He heard the screams of his people, but thought they applied to his fight with me. I backed off in such a way that he kept his back turned to his men. In the process, a tree root tripped him, which allowed me to get a hold of him and to drop him completely. He wanted to get up, but I held him down until Bin Nil arrived with some *asakir* to tie him up.

He gnashed his teeth in anger. His eyes were bloodshot. But, he still had only me on his mind and screamed hoarsely:

"Dog, you dare try to tie me up! The *sangak's* death will hit you tenfold."

"Did you suddenly turn blind?" I asked. "Have a look around to see what has happened. Who's going to free you? Your men, by chance?"

The Takalah had been completely taken by surprise. Of course, our attack had not been directed at the roped-together slaves, who, obviously, had no inclination to take part in the brief struggle. The warriors had not been prepared for an attack, so that they were quickly wrestled to the ground and disarmed. They now formed a tight group, surrounded by the soldiers with their guns at the ready. When Shadid saw this, he screamed:

"Soldiers – here! We have been attacked! Liar, traitor, cheat! I thought you were alone in the woods."

"That was very unwise of you. You will now follow me to the *mudir* in Fashoda!"

"What am I to do there? You just assured me that he cannot touch me."

"With respect to your selling slaves, he indeed cannot do anything against you. However, there is another weighty reason that caused me to surprise you here. Are there perhaps one or several among you carrying gold dust from Dar Famaka?"

"Gold dust? From Famaka? We were never in that area," he replied, though becoming visibly embarrassed.

"Oh, one can possess *at-tabr* from there without ever having been in the area. One can have acquired it by barter, but also by theft or robbery."

"What are you trying to say? I do not understand you."

"I am telling you that, in my opinion, five of you are carrying such dust."

He became frightened, kept silent for awhile, then insisted:

"I do not know anything about it."

"Then I know more than you and shall point out those five. Did you not meet north of the Nid al-Nil five traders riding donkeys?"

"No," he said in a strangled voice.

"Don't lie! You greeted them and sounded them out. Then you had the caravan proceed while you stayed back with four of your men in order to murder the traders. And for this murder you have now been arrested."

Turning to his men, I continued:

"Your leader deceived you. You must admit that you came across the three traders. Shadid learned that they carried much gold dust and decided to take it from them. He sent you ahead and kept only four men with him, using their assistance to attack the traders. The five took the gold dust, and kept the robbery from you, so that they did not have to share the gold dust. Was that comradely? Could not every one of you have demanded his share? You know who the four were who stayed back with your leader, and I call on you to point them out to me. Only the perpetrators will be punished; the others can return unhindered to their homeland. But if you keep silent, you will share in the blame. Think about it!"

Shadid tried to guard against my words by shouting commandingly:

"We are no robbers, no murderers! We did not kill any trader and do not have any gold dust. My men are courageous Takalah, and none will lower himself to answer you, the *infidel*."

The Takalah had become restless before. They had grumbled with each other, and the innocent had been in the process to separate themselves from the guilty. I had very well noticed this. But now, they had given up, not moving or saying anything. I had taken the rescued trader along and had forbidden him to let himself to be seen at the outset. He still stood behind the bushes from where I now called him. Before he even reached me, he raised his voice, saying:

"*Effendi*, all five of them are here. I recognize them at once"

He pointed at Shadid and four others, who I had right away tied up. We checked their pockets but did not find anything. I now had their camels pointed out to me in order to search the blankets, saddles, and saddle bags. This proved successful. Each had hidden his share very cleverly, but all was discovered. Only now did the innocent think the time ripe for one of them to declare:

"*Effendi*, Allah knows that we are innocent. Demand whichever oath; we are willing to give it. We do not know anything of this deed. We were deceived."

"I believe you and repeat my assurance that nothing is going to happen to you. Although I must take you to the *mudir*, he will not hold you. Only should you refuse to come will you be punished."

I had good reason to search here in the woods for the gold dust and not later in Fashoda. It could be expected that, should the *mudir* get his hands on the dust, part of it would become stuck there, maybe even all. I wanted to prevent this out of consideration for the poor trader. I took the man aside when we made ready to depart and asked him:

"Do you know the families of your two murdered companions?"

"Of course I know them. We three are closely related and have always traveled together. You found the dust, *effendi*. What will happen to it? Do you remember your graciousness telling me that I would probably gain possession of my property again?"

"Yes, I do. I think you are an honest man who will not cheat your relatives. Here's the dust. You know where your three donkeys are. Go get them and take off, so that nothing will be taken from you!"

He held the five small parcels in his hands, looking soon at them, then at me, then asked in a voice trembling from joy:

"Is it possible? You really mean it? I am to get everything? You do not want to keep anything for yourself?"

"No. I have no right, and even if I did, I wouldn't keep anything!"

"Oh, *effendi*, there are five packages; take at least one, take two!"

He held them up to me.

"I repeat that I will not take any."

"But how am I to repay you for your generosity? I know that the *mudir* will be very angry at you."

"Let him be; I don't mind. Just take care that he not get a hold of you."

"Oh, he will not get to see me, I shall run, run right now, and not stop until I am far, very far from Fashoda. May Allah bless you! You are a Christian, *effendi*; would it only be that all Muslims be such Christians."

He pulled my hand to his lips, then hurried away. He did not care to march back with us, and I did not take offense at his actions.

Our departure encountered some difficulties with Shadid fighting against having to come along or to have himself carried off. Although he was tied, he possessed such unusual physical strength that he caused us difficulties even in this condition. Only Bin Nil's whip made him come to his senses. Thereafter, we freed his feet and tied him to a camel's tail. If he did not want to be dragged, he had to walk whether he liked it or not.

His four accomplices were smart enough to be more compliant. The others followed willingly as they had promised.

Our group caused quite a stir when we arrived in Fashoda. Old and young came running after us until we disappeared behind the gate of the *mudir's* building.

When I reported to the 'Father of Five hundred', his first question was for the gold dust, as I had expected. How he flared up, and how he looked at me when I told him who I had given it to. He became coarse, very coarse, and honored me with various names which I have no desire to quote. He ran around his room gesticulating, and when he finally stopped, he snarled at me:

"I shall have this trader brought back. He must still be where you left your camels and donkeys. I will have him arrested; I will lock him up; he will get the whip. I must get the gold dust; I must. Do you understand!"

"But if the man is gone?"

"Then I will have him pursued, even if I must send my entire garrison after him."

"And if this is also in vain?"

"Then I will chase you to the Devil; do you hear?"

"Will that get you the gold?"

"No, unfortunately, no! But I will at least get some revenge! I just recalled the five Takalah. Woe to them if I cannot retrieve the gold dust.! They will suffer for it, suffer a lot!"

With that, his anger was diverted from me to people more deserving than myself. He ordered the entire group, guilty and innocent, to be locked up and to be guarded most closely. He sent men off to return the trader with his gold. I retired to my assigned room and did not let myself be seen until he had me called toward evening. He was still very much excited and growled at me:

"He is gone, this dog, across all mountains, and with him the gold dust that might have gone into the government cashier's office. No one was able to find out where he went. He picked up the donkeys and disappeared like a drop falling into water. May Allah destroy him! But I will get some compensation. What I have missed in gold dust, the Takalah will get in more beating. This will refresh my heart and calm my soul. I sent for these dogs to have them brought here. I will hold court now, and you must join as a witness. Come!"

He took me down to the courtyard where all Takalah were lined up under military guard. Bin Nil and Hafiz Sikhar were already present. In a corner stood a framework whose sides were connected by broad belts and narrow straps with buckles. Next to it lay a pile of finger-thick rods with the 'Father of Beating' sitting nearby. This explained to me the friendly purpose of this framework. A large audience occupied half of the courtyard.

It is superfluous to describe the court proceedings. Shadid with his four accomplices were sentenced to "five hundred blows and not to be seen again". The others were acquitted, but as tribal members of murderers were assigned ten blows each across the board, not excluding the slaves. In no way did the latter want to return home, where they were certain to be sold again. They asked me for advice, and I suggested they talk to the *raïs effendina*, whose arrival was expected shortly. He would need people for the apprehension of the slavers, and since the Takalah were famous for being brave men, I was certain that he would hire them.

When the judge's decision had been made the 'Father of Beatings' began his work. The Takalah were, one after the other, buckled onto the framework with each receiving his ten blows. The necessary work was performed so methodically, and the delinquents took their ten blows with such simple heroism, that watching it became almost amusing entertainment. But when the first murderer was buckled on, I left. There is a difference between ten and five hundred blows!

Against expectations, the *raïs effendina* had been delayed in Khartoum and again on the way. He was so late that he arrived on the sixth day of my stay in Fashoda. He took on the Takalah and equipped his ship with ammunition and fresh provisions. Then we began the journey by which we expected with certainty to achieve our goal. Unfortunately, Ibn Asl's six day head start could not be made up as easily and quickly as we had wished.

5

The Saribah Aliab

SAILING UPSTREAM ON the White Nile to where the Sobat river enters is facilitated by a good northern wind which arises regularly at daybreak. Then it fills the sails nicely and only goes to sleep by evening, to begin its work again the following morning. But once the Sobat has been reached, the wind on the Nile fades, or it cannot be used very well, due to the river's numerous bends. Only when the Nile flows in a suitable direction are sails used. In between, a ship must be pulled or poled forward. This is hard and cumbersome work. If the banks are firm and dry for the men pulling, everyone is happy. But if there are swamps, where the men would sink in, row boats must then pull ships upstream. But even this is not possible when the river's surface is covered for some distance with *umm sufah*, impossible to row through. Then, only poling will do. It often takes an entire day to bring a vessel through a single *umm sufah* field. Once through, one sails across an open distance only to arrive at an even longer and more dense place of reeds.

The river banks' scenery has also changed. Now, the Nile is no longer the river passing through a desert, its moisture allowing only the nearby area to support rich vegetation. Its many major and minor arms penetrate a wide, low-lying, swampy and often densely wooded area.

Here, fever rules and biting flies become a terrible plague. Giant crocodiles by the hundreds lie in the mud. Hippopotamuses graze on the
river's bottom, and numerous larger and smaller carnivores populate
the dense, often impenetrable forests. One can travel for days without
enjoying a single open view. The water is almost unpalatable. Game
rots within hours; provisions spoil, and one could doubt that people can
live here. Yet they do. Entire tribes and peoples, elsewhere often strictly
separated, are closely mixed yet maintain their characteristic traits.

These people, in no way, are the lords of the 'Black Continent'. They
are all more or less of dark color – Negroes – the much-sought game
of slave hunters.

Thus, a White arrives and befriends a Negro tribe. By cunning or
for a paltry payment, he is ceded an area on which he establishes a
settlement, called a *saribah*. In possession of greater knowledge and
superior weaponry, his initial friendliness soon turns to unfriendliness.
The Blacks now fear him, where earlier they loved him.

He hires other Whites to come, the scum of various areas and social
strata of the Orient. They come with muskets and powder. They bait
the Blacks with poor-quality cotton cloth, brandy, tobacco, and glass
beads. But they truly come for ivory, white in the form of elephant tusks
and black in human shape.

The chief of the black tribe and his people are won over by the
promise of a share of the booty. Then the predatory raid begins. The
white participants call themselves *asakir*. They are officers, lieutenants
and common *asakir*, who risk the least and take the lion's share of the
raid's profits. The Blacks aren't soldiers and must carry out the hard-
est tasks, serve as scouts, expose themselves to the greatest dangers,
and be the foremost in attacks. They receive as much or as little as the
wretched advances give to them. These are usually offset by the shares
of booty paid them or even end in debt.

With larger and better organized hunting parties, there are also
black soldiers who are, however, always at a disadvantage against
the Whites. The owner of a *saribah* pays the wages from the booty,

consisting of humans or cattle. The black *asakir* are given the old or sick slaves, and cows which are of no use to them.

And how is such a *ghasuah*, such a slave hunt, organized and executed? Well, very much in the way a burglar performs his venture, enriching himself with others' goods and sooner or later ending in prison. However, the slave hunter is a bit worse since he 'steals' human beings and destroys and depopulates entire villages. And while he 'makes' a hundred slaves, he kills as many old people and children, who are of no use to him.

Three weeks had passed since we had left Fashoda, and had reached the Rohl river's confluence at Bahr al-Jabal. With everything taken into consideration, we were satisfied with our travel. The 'Falcon' was built for speed; it obeyed the wind, the draw-rope and the poles much better than a cumbersome *noquar*, and slipped more easily than such a vessel through the many reed beds we had to cut through. Its furnishings provided more comfort than those of a slave ship. Our provisions had kept well. We caught fish, hunted daily for game, had good medical supplies and mosquito nets for everyone. Our state of health was therefore rather good.

Unfortunately, we had experienced a small collision that had held us up for three full days. We were also short a pilot familiar with the area. The actual helmsman of the 'Falcon', the old Abu al-Nil, knew the river only to Lake No. After we had turned into Bahr al-Jabal, we found ourselves almost totally ignorant of the river's condition, which, when considering our task, we needed to be just as familiar with as Ibn Asl.

We were looking for the Saribah Aliab? Where was it?

Several of our men had claimed that they could easily find it, but it showed that they had taken on too much. We were presently moored where the Aliab area began. The Nuer Negroes living here called themselves the Aliab, however, a Saribah Aliab could simply not be found anywhere. At times, we met a lone Negro boatman and inquired with him, but without success.

The ship's complement consisted of the crew, the hired Takalah, and one hundred soldiers under the command of a captain. If Ibn Asl's group was just as strong, we were still not afraid.

Here, at the confluence of the Rohl river, the Nile was very wide. The sun burned down with no wooded bank offering shade. There were only reeds and nothing but reeds. The crew had had to exert itself by poling and was very tired. We had therefore dropped anchor to rest and let the worst heat pass. This being too boring for me, I took our small boat to shoot something edible. I was considered the game provider for the ship since I was usually ahead with the boat in order to hunt.

As usual, I was accompanied by Bin Nil. I gladly took him along, since one cannot always be ready to shoot when pulling oars. Sometimes, the little Djangeh boy asked me to take him along and I permitted this, from time to time. He enjoyed himself in a childlike manner with everything I shot. As mentioned previously, this boy and his sister had been enslaved from their Djangeh tribe and taken to Cairo where they were forced to work for the *mukkadam*. Every evening they had to turn in the money they had earned, yet were starved and beaten. I had freed them from slavery and taken them on the 'Falcon', where they still were. Appropriate to their strength, they were kept occupied, well fed, and treated lovingly. Since they owed me their freedom, it was no wonder that they expressed particular affection to me. We had the intention to return them to their tribe, but had not yet found the opportunity to do so.

The time for hunting was not favorable. The heat was too great and animal life seemed exhausted into stupor. To survive the heat without harm, we had to moisten our heads and chests from time to time. This is how we slipped upstream for about an hour between the *umm sufah* islands, when Bin Nil thought it advisable to turn back. However, I did not want to return without some game and stood up in the boat for a better look. That is when I saw upstream an object moving toward us. White on top and dark below, it could from a distance, be taken for a large aquatic bird with dark body and white head and neck. I quickly sat down again so that I would not be seen and asked Bin Nil to hold the boat at a reed island where we were hidden behind the tall reed stalks.

I readied my rifle to take a shot at the bird, no matter its species.

A little while later, we heard quickly approaching splashing. I took aim. The bird appeared, right in my line of fire. Oh God, I almost pressed the trigger. It was not a bird but a man, a Black. The Negro sat in a small, dark-colored canoe and was dressed in a vest-like canvas cover, leaving his well-muscled arms free. A white cloth was wrapped around his head. This is why, sitting in his canoe, he had resembled a bird with a white head and neck, seen from the front. He passed without seeing us.

"A man, a Negro," Bin Nil whispered. "Shall we go after him?"

"Of course! Maybe, we shall learn something about the Saribah Aliab. Go pull! He paddles fast; we must catch up with him."

Bin Nil engaged the oars. We 'shot' from behind the reed island, following in the wake of the Black. As mentioned before, Bin Nil was a capable oarsman. We closed so fast on the Negro that he soon heard the noise. He turned, saw us, became afraid, and began to paddle hard, wanting to flee. This was suspicious.

We no longer could get any closer. Bin Nil and I traded places, therefore. Being stronger than he, I took the oars and Bin Nil the rudder. The oars bent under my pressure.

"We are catching him, *effendi*, we are catching up! Keep on going!" he urged me on.

A minute later, he told me that the distance had been halved. But right after this he shouted:

"He wants to escape sideways into the reed islands."

"Take my rife and fire the right barrel! But make sure not to hit him!"

The shot cracked and almost simultaneously I heard a scream ahead. Bin Nil kept the rifle aimed and told me with my back facing forward:

"He's stopping. He sees me ready to fire another shot. He is afraid and has pulled in his paddle."

"Let me take the rudder again! I want to talk to him."

We traded places. The Negro had put his paddle inside his canoe and was waiting. His not unpleasant face expressed half fear and half defiance.

"To which people or tribe do you belong?"

"I am a Bongo," he replied.

"Where are you going?"

"To Fashoda. I want to become a soldier, and heard that *asakir* are needed there."

"This is quite true. You will likely be accepted."

"Do you think so, master? Do you know this town?"

"Yes. I am coming from there."

He was going to say something, swallowed it, but then opened his mouth after all, to say:

"Do you know the *sangak* of the *Arnautlar*?"

"Very well."

"Is he still alive?"

"Why should he be dead?"

"Because . . because . . because . . .!"

He faltered. I took the rudder in my right, the rifle in my left hand, and told him sternly:

"Fellow, you are lying. You are not a Bongo, for then you would be a more brownish color; but instead you are deep black. Also, a Bongo never has his forehead tattooed like you. We must get to know each other better. Down there our ship is moored. You can't see it from here. Paddle slowly ahead of us; we will follow. If you try to escape, I will send a bullet through your head."

The man realized that resistance was useless, put his paddle into the water and moved slowly downstream. We followed at the same pace. When we arrived at the 'Falcon', we tied up our boat and he his canoe, after which we climbed on board. He did this with the expression of a man conscious of his innocence, but I could not help noticing his worried looks. In no way was he as unconcerned as he wanted to appear. The *raïs effendina*, called *amir* by his subordinates, asked why I had brought him aboard. I told him. Looking at the Negro, he said:

"He looks harmless. Why should he claim to be a Bongo, if he isn't one?"

"For some reason which we will be certain to find out. Look at his face. His tattoos are very peculiar. There's a vertical stripe in the middle of his forehead from which lines extend to both sides, consisting of dots that are drawn in arcs to the parting of his hair and to his temples. If I'm not mistaken, it is the Dinka who tattoo themselves in this way, but never the Bongo. He lied to me for a reason. That he wants to become a soldier isn't true, and asking me for the *sangak* of the *Arnautlar* has increased my suspicion. I think he is a messenger someone has dispatched to the *sangak*."

"Might this be Ibn Asl?"

"It's either him or another slave trader."

"If this is true, this Black would be of great value to us. Let's have a few words with him."

He demanded the Negro to tell the truth and should he not comply, threatened him with severe punishment. Still, he received the very same answers I had gotten earlier. Now the man was checked. Nothing was found on him, although the search included even his hair, which, except for a small tuft on the top of his head had been shorn smooth, something also found with Dinka tribes. And nothing was found in his canoe either.

What to do? The suspicion I felt about this Negro was well-founded, I was certain of that. But unable to prove anything, we had no right to hold him. When he was told that he could continue his trip, I asked him whether he knew where the Saribah Aliab was located. At that, his questioning look went over the ship, the *amir* and myself, and he replied:

"Yes, I know."

His look had been very telling. I concluded from it that the Black knew the vessel he was on and who he was talking to. If I wasn't mistaken, he must have been made aware of us, but by whom? It could only have been by Ibn Asl. From this, I concluded that his statements had to be taken with a grain of salt.

"Well, where is it located?"

"Up there," he said, while he pointed upstream of the main channel, "in the area called Bahita, four days' travel from here."

"What kind of people live there?"

"A tribe of the Shur."

His answers came slowly. One could see and hear that he thought about each word before he spoke. In doing so, he did not possess the necessary control of his face to suppress an expression of complacent cunning. Internally, he delighted in his belief that he was putting us on. I acted as if I believed him and asked:

"Are you certain? Have you been there?"

"I was there," he insisted, entering the trap I set him with my last question.

"So, then you are sure of what you are saying! But how come it isn't the Shur but the Tuitsh who live in this area?"

"The Tuitsh?" he said embarrassed. "They do not live there."

"Oh, yes! They dwell on the right bank of the river, while the Kytsh have their huts on the left bank. The Shur's area is much farther west. And, supposedly, the distance is only four days travel? You have said this to get us to sail for Bahita. But I know the correct distance. We would not make Bahita, even with a favorable wind in under twenty-five days. You were incautious. Your lie was too crude, too evident."

"I am not lying, *effendi*," he tried to assure me.

"*Effendi*? You apply this title to me. Then you know me?"

His embarrassment increased, but he replied quickly:

"I address every noble White in this way."

"Then you see me as a nobleman, yet still think to be smarter than me? You are mistaken. You want to lead us astray, but we will beware of following your untruths."

"Sir," he exclaimed, "I did not tell you anything but the truth."

"Of all you said, only one thing is true which is that you know the *saribah*. You don't want us to find it, which is why you indicated the wrong direction. I will take the opposite for the truth. The *saribah* isn't located on the main channel but on a side arm of the Nile, not in Bahr al-Jabal, but in the Rohl, you came paddling down. Tell me who owns the *saribah*. Since you were there, you must know."

"It belongs . . . belongs . . .," he stammered embarrassed . . . to a White, whose name I forgot."

"Better say that you don't want to admit to this name, because you don't want to be seen as knowing its owner. His name is Ibn Asl. Do you remember the name now?"

"Yes," he admitted hesitantly.

"Fine! So you know this man. You were at his place. You are one of the Dinka he hired down by the White Nile. He sent you with a message to the *sangak* of the *Arnautlar* in Fashoda, and warned you that you might come across us on your way. He described our ship, the *raïs effendina*, and me, and told you how to act should you get to speak to us. Will you be so cheeky to deny this?"

His intellect was insufficient to realize that I had arrived at my assertion by some simple, obvious logic. He looked at me shocked, then at the deck, and remained silent.

"Answer!" I demanded sternly.

"It is not the way you think," he tried to assure me. "I am a Bongo and want to go to Fashoda to become a soldier. I told you so already and cannot say anything else."

The man's doggedness could have put me in a predicament, had something unexpected not happened at this moment. The Djangeh boy, who had been asleep, had woken up and with his sister was approaching our group that had formed around the *amir* and the Negro. When he saw the Black, he stopped petrified, stared at him with wide open eyes, then screamed aloud:

"Agadi, *Aba-charang*!"

This was not Arabic, but the dialect of the siblings' tribe. They meant: 'Agadi, my father's brother', meaning 'my uncle'. The man had not noticed the children, but when he heard himself called, he quickly turned toward them. He recognized them and they hurried to him. His surprise was so great that he let himself be embraced without offering any resistance. They wept, no, they howled from joy and climbed up on him. That is when his paralysis broke into a shrill shout of delight. He embraced them, danced with them across the entire deck, at which he hollered words I did not understand. They were not Arabic, but of the Dinka language, of which I knew only scant words and expressions. After some time he calmed down and sat down with them. They conducted a colorful and very lively conversation that must have lasted half an hour.

Of course, we did not disturb them and quietly awaited the result of this conversation. Once he had learned everything, he got up and approached me, his eyes beaming happily. He made a deep, deferential bow and said, now in Arabic:

"*Effendi*, forgive me! I did not know of the children's' presence and what you did for them. You are a good, a very good master, and not an evil man as I thought earlier."

"Ah, then you knew me after all?"

"Yes. When I met you up there on the river, I did not know who you were, but when we arrived at the ship, I knew who I was facing."

"So I guessed right earlier that we were described to you?"

"Yes, and that so precisely that I am surprised that I did not recognize you right away. Ibn Asl did this."

"You are one of his warriors?"

"Yes, I am a Djangeh, he hired. I am even their leader."

"You are to bring a message to Fashoda?"

"So it is. A letter to the *sangak* of the *Arnautlar* by the name of Ibn Mulawa."

"We did not find the message. You must have hidden it very well. Where is it?"

"*Effendi*, I gave Ibn Asl my word to hand it only to the *sangak*."

"You are an honest man, but Ibn Asl is a villain who will likely cheat you."

"Cheat me? Why?"

"You are the Djangeh warriors' leader. As such, it is impossible that he would let you be away from them. If he nevertheless sent you off, it must be assumed that he has some dishonest intentions for your people. Was there not someone else, a White, he could have dispatched? Your men are meant to be leaderless. Do you understand?"

Contemplating, he looked down grimly, then said:

"Ibn Asl said that this was great proof of his trust. He cannot plan anything terrible against my Djangeh. He needs them to hunt slaves."

"This is true. He will hunt slaves with their help, but what will happen when he no longer needs them? What if he does not pay them their wages but makes them slaves?"

He looked at me shocked and needed time to consider such a behavior possible. Then he exclaimed:

"*Effendi*, is something like this possible?"

"Trust any, even the worst depravity to Ibn Asl. And what kind of people are with him? Ask your young relatives, the boy and the girl!"

"They told me everything, everything. You saved them. You have saved many other slaves already. You know everything beforehand. Your eye looks ahead to what will only happen later. Should you also see correctly here? Then, woe to Ibn Asl! If I could only find out whether you are right."

"This is easy to find out. In any case, it is written in the letter. Give it to me."

"But . . but . .!"

His honesty made him resist to hand the asked-for item to us. He fought with himself. At last, concern for his people caused him to make the decision:

"*Effendi*, one must not only be honest but also astute. If Ibn Asl plans something evil against us, my honesty will be of no help."

"Then tell me where you keep the letter."

I was curious to learn the hiding place, since we had him and his canoe searched thoroughly without finding anything. He replied:

"The letter is in a small clay vessel attached to the bottom of my canoe."

The light canoe was pulled on board. At its keel, a small, vial-like clay bottle was attached, its opening sealed with sap. We cut it off and broke it. Its content was the looked-for sheet of paper. The *amir* took it to read it, but shook his head, looked at it again, once more shook his head, then asked me:

"Do you understand Persian, *effendi*?"

"Yes. But how would Ibn Asl come to this language? And the *sangak*, who would need to be able to read the message, must know it also. Is the letter truly written in Persian? Give it to me!"

He handed it to me. I looked at the writing, written with ink and pen, but it was neither Arabic nor Persian. Although I was able to read the words, they were totally incomprehensible. I then got the idea that Ibn Asl had most likely used a precautionary means, so that the letter, should it fall in the wrong hands, could not be read.

As one knows, Arabic is written from right to left. I therefore tried to read from left to right and, *voilà*, it worked. The letter read:

"I am sending you Agadi, the leader of the Dinka warriors. I told him that we would move against the Rohl to make them slaves. However, my drive is against the Gohk, something he must not learn since they belong to the Dinka people. Send me right away fifty or more *asakir*, who must be white. They should wait for me at the Saribah Aliab. When I return from my slave drive, I shall make the hundred-fifty Dinka warriors also slaves with the help of the Whites. Then I need not pay them and will even get money for them. I sent their leader away, so that they will obey only me and assign you the task of making certain that he does not return. I heard that the Christian *effendi* paid you a visit. I was unable to see you since he escaped, following which we had to leave very quickly. Knowing your cleverness, I am convinced that his escape will not harm you. He knows nothing of the Saribah Aliab, which is why he will not find us, as much as he may search. And should he, after all, come across this Dinka Agadi, I have instructed him in how to mislead him."

This was the letter's content with no address nor signature. I read it to the *amir*. The Djangeh heard it, and when I had finished, he asked:

"Who is the Dinka mentioned in the letter?"

"You, yourself, and by the Dinka warriors he means your men. Do you have one-hundred-fifty men?"

"Yes. We are to move against the Rohl to make them slaves."

"But you heard that the drive is not intended against them but against the Gohk."

"These are our brothers. I will not permit it."

"You are no longer there and cannot prevent it. With you gone, your men must obey Ibn Asl, and he will tell them that you had agreed to the drive against the Gohk. Once your men return, they will be enslaved and sold instead of being paid. And you, well, you will die in Fashoda, should you go there and deliver this letter."

He looked at me unbelieving. He, the Negro, the heathen, was unable to comprehend such evilness. I came to his help by explaining briefly to him what I knew of Ibn Asl, which was more than enough to demonstrate to the man into what kind of hands he had fallen. When I was finished, he exclaimed:

"*Effendi*, permit me to leave the ship. I must leave immediately for the *saribah* to warn my men and to avenge myself on Ibn Asl!"

Rashly, he turned from me, but I held him back by his arm, telling him:

"Stay! Although you can go whenever you wish, for you are free and no longer our prisoner, I advise you to remain with us. You will not be able to change anything and would face certain death."

"I shall kill Ibn Asl, but he not me!"

"You don't know him. Just think what you are against him! And would you still find him at the *saribah*?"

"No, because he was going to leave right away for the *ghasuah*. I must go after him. I will learn the direction he took at the *saribah*."

"You are mistaken. You would be taken prisoner there and murdered. You alone cannot do anything, nothing at all. This is why I advise you to stay with us. With us you will get faster to the *saribah* than by paddling your canoe. And we will protect you. We will go after Ibn Asl and take him and all the Whites prisoner. Then, your Djangeh will be saved."

"You are right *effendi*. With your permission I will stay. Who would have thought this! You were described to us as the worst enemy of black people, and I was glad to accept the task of deceiving you were we to meet. Now, the enemies have become friends and the friends enemies. I told you a wrong direction. You were supposed to sail upstream on the Bahr al-Jabal, but now I will guide you up the Rohl to take you to the Saribah Aliab."

"How far is it from here?"

"We will likely need five to six days."

"Are you familiar with the *saribah's* surrounding?"

"Of course! It is situated on the river's right bank that is, on the left side when we arrive there."

"Are there mountains?"

"No. The area is totally flat. There is nothing but forest. The *saribah* is surrounded by a thorn hedge no man can penetrate. When Ibn Asl established it, he had many trees cut down which are still lying there. New trees have grown up between them together with bushes and vines, which have made the thicket surrounding the saribah a wall, no one can get through."

"But only on three sides. The river side must be open?"

"It is closed as well, except for the entrance which can be barricaded with beams and thorn branches."

"Then this *saribah* is a veritable fortress!"

"Yes. Ibn Asl said that only ten men are needed to easily defend it against several hundred."

"If the latter have no smarts, yes. How's the inside constructed?"

"It is a large, square place on which about twenty round *tokuls* made of reeds and mud have been built. They are very strong. Ibn Asl occupies one of the *tokuls*; two hold provisions, and in the rest the *asakir* live."

"Of course, Ibn Asl's present visitors live also in one of these huts. You did see these people, didn't you?"

"All of them. They were on the ship that took us to the *saribah*. There was a White by by name of Abd al-Barak . . ."

"This is the *mukkadam* of the holy Qadiriyya, from whose hands I freed your brother's children. Go on!"

"Another was called *muza'bir*, and a third was a Turk, a very big man. He was accompanied by his sister, who was served by two white and two black girls."

"Do you know why this Turkish woman came?"

"To become the wife of Ibn Asl."

"The wedding was to be celebrated at the *saribah*. Do you know whether it took place already?"

"No. They wanted to wait until the return from the slave drive."

"Do you know who and how many are participating in it?"

"Everyone, except for the Turk, who did not want to leave his sister, and ten *asakir*, commanded by an old, lame sergeant. But *effendi*, I could tell you all this on the way. Why lose time by staying here? Don't you see that the wind is rippling the Nile's waters?"

"You are correct, we must weigh anchor. But it was well that we stayed for some time. Otherwise, we would have already sailed up Bahr al-Jabal and have never met you."

The anchor was raised, the sails set into the wind, after which the 'Falcon' diverted from its previous course turning to the right into the Rohl river.

This tributary was not as wide as the Bahr al-Jabal, but carried enough water to support even larger ships than ours. I mentioned before that there was nothing but reeds in this area. Until evening, we kept cruising between *umm sufah* islands. Then, the banks showed bushes once more, tree growth returned, and soon there was forest to our left and right – dense, closed forest. The river became free of reeds and it was easier to get ahead. With the sky being clear, the stars became visible after sunset. We were able to see for a great distance, enabling us to sail through the night.

The next few days, luck was with us so that we were able to sail exceptionally fast and arrived at our destination earlier than expected. By evening of the fourth day the Djangeh told us that the *saribah* was so close that we would arrive there in an hour. We had to halt and moored at the right bank of the river.

The question was now what to do. Should we, tomorrow, in bright daylight, arrive at the *saribah*? This was not advisable, since its entrance was easily defended. Despite its ridiculously small number, the garrison could give us trouble. Then, it was not certain whether Ibn Asl had left the settlement already; there could easily have been a reason for delay. Therefore, I thought it advisable to reconnoiter that evening, to which the *amir* agreed. He would have loved to take part in it, but considered it his duty to remain on board.

I needed two men with experience on the water and therefore picked Bin Nil and his grandfather, Abu al-Nil. Of course, the Djangeh had to accompany us, since he knew the precise location of the *saribah*. It may have been close to nine o'clock when we pushed off from the ship.

Bin Nil and his grandfather rowed. I took the rudder, while the Djangeh squatted down in the boat's bow. The stars twinkled in the sky with the water reflecting their images. Half an hour later, we could expect the moon to rise.

At first, we kept in the middle of the river. After half an hour's rowing we were closing in on the *saribah*. So, we steered to the bank to find cover in the shadow of trees. Although the Djangeh assured us that no guard would be posted at the entrance, now, when only ten men occupied the place, we could expect the sergeant to be more cautious. Our approach had to be such that we would not be spotted by a guard.

The stars were turning paler now with the moon rising, although it could not yet be seen, still hidden behind the forest which, while we quietly slipped past, resembled a dark wall with not a single, small opening. The Djangeh commanded our boat, indicating in the softest voice how to row and to steer. The oars were moved and dipped so carefully into the water that they made no audible noise. At last, the Negro whispered:

"Here is the *mishrah*, where we must moor."

"Not by the *mishrah* itself, but before, next to a tree!" I corrected him.

A *mishrah* is a landing place. Our boat should not get there, since it would be seen by a guard, possibly posted nearby. Just then, we spotted a gap in the dense forest, about twenty paces wide. This was the *saribah's* landing place. Narrowing from the water to the top of the bank, it ended at the boards and thorny branches which barred the *saribah's* entrance.

I steered the boat to the bank and near a tree that was half-submerged in the water. The Djangeh rose in the bow to tie it to the tree. However, in the shadows, we missed seeing a long and strong root, invisible in the water, the boat brushed against and tilted. The Djangeh lost his balance, fell into the water and shouted most fearfully, knowing that crocodiles populated the river nearby. He went under, rose, and was grabbed by his arm by Bin Nil. A short distance upstream were some sand and mud banks, from where a dark mass was rapidly coming toward us. The Djangeh, looking fearfully around, shouted:

"A crocodile, a crocodile! Get me into the boat!"

He was indeed in great danger. I jumped from my position at the rudder and took him by the other arm – a jerk of mine and Bin Nil's, and the threatened man toppled into the boat, which swaying, threatening to capsize. Already, the board was dipping into the water, when, lucky for us, the crocodile bumped its head against the tilted side, righting the boat. Bin Nil slapped an oar on its snout, causing it to disappear below the surface.

Now, the boat was tied to the tree, after which we remained there quietly for at least ten minutes to listen. When nothing moved, we assumed that the Negro's scream and shouts had not been heard. I got ready to step from the boat.

"Not you alone!" Bin Nil whispered. "Take me along, *effendi!*"

Having made such noise, I thought it better not to be alone, and gave my assent. We climbed from the boat where the forest grew to the water and the *mishrah.* I did not take a rifle along, but only a knife and my two revolvers.

Once we stepped on solid ground, we squatted down to listen once more for some time. Deep silence ruled, and nothing suspicious could be heard. Just then the moon rose above the trees shining its light across the open space of the *mishrah* and enabling us to look it over. It lay so brightly illuminated before us that we would not have missed even a mouse hurrying across. We rose to walk up the bank and check how the entrance to the *saribah* had been closed. It consisted of strong poles, connected by a dense thorn weave with a height of at least twelve feet.

"There's no way to get through, *effendi,*" Bin Nil whispered. "We must return."

"It wasn't my intention to enter the *saribah,*" I replied just as softly. "Let's see whether these poles have been rammed into the earth. These people must have a comfortable entrance. If this entanglement is as solid as it looks, I assume that there is some kind of gap somewhere else."

I bent down to check the base of the poles, when, next to me, I heard Bin Nil's scream. I wanted to rise but received a blow to my head and lost consciousness.

When I came to again, I was tied with ropes like an Egyptian mummy is with cloth strips, and lying in a *tokul.* A fire burned, whose smoke escaped through an opening in the roof. Next to me lay Bin Nil, tied up like myself. When he noticed my eyes opening, he said:

"Allah be thanked that you woke up! I thought you were dead, *effendi.*"

My head hurt. It flickered before my eyes, and my ears hummed like a swarm of bees. Seeing that we were alone, I replied:

"Did they also club you?"

"No."

"Tell me then what happened and how we got here. We must be in one of the *saribah's tokuls*.

"Unfortunately, yes. We are here despite you saying that it wasn't your intention to enter. Well, we haven't entered it, but have been made to enter. You had just said this when I was grabbed from behind. I shouted, for I had turned my head and saw behind you a man reaching out with an oar to hit you on the head. The blow hit home and you dropped like you were dead. Three or four strong fellows held me. They wrestled me down. I fought with all my might, but in vain."

"I hope our two companions noticed what happened."

"I took care for them to hear, for when I wrestled with my attackers, I did not keep silent, but screamed loud enough for my grandfather to hear."

"Most likely he and the Djangeh returned to the ship right away for help. Keep talking!"

"You had mentioned a gap, *effendi*, and hit it right on. Once they had wrestled me down and temporarily tied me up, they pushed a bush aside and opened a gap through which a man could pass in a bent position. We were taken through this opening and carried here, where they tied me up more thoroughly and wrapped you completely with ropes."

"Was Murad Nassyr, the fat Turk, with them?"

"No. I only saw unknown faces."

"Fine. First, I want to find out what the men who attacked us were actually doing outside. Did they stand guard? That's a job for only one."

"I know, *effendi*. I figured it out from their talking. They were out to lance fish. You know that this is only done by night. A fire is lit by the bank or in a boat. Its light attracts the fish, which are then lanced. The men had just crept through the gap to go to the river when they heard the Djangeh's scream. They stopped, listened, then saw the two of us coming. We came up on the bright side of the *mishrah*. They retreated into the deep shadow on the right side, then let us come close in order to take us. One of them carried an oar. It was he, who clubbed you. Do you think we will be able to get out?"

"I always hope, just as I do now. The *amir* isn't far from here."

"But if they kill us before he comes?"

"We must take this into consideration. We have escaped our enemies repeatedly, and in order to prevent this, they may easily reach the conclusion that they must take our lives immediately. It is odd that they left us by ourselves and did not post a guard. Quiet, someone's coming!"

We heard steps. The mat at the door was lifted and several men entered, lead by the hefty Murad Nassyr, followed by the old sergeant, who I recognized by his limp. The Turk put himself before me, stroked his beard contentedly, and said derisively:

"You have come again. I hope you will visit us a bit longer this time. Or do you intend to also disappear as quickly today?"

I did not reply. He turned to the sergeant:

"Look, this is the Christian dog I told you about. This cursed creature is coming after us even here. But this will be the last route he will take in his life. I swear by Allah that he will not get away from here again! He and his companion must die!"

"I do not mind," replied the sergeant.

"You are in command here in Ibn Asl's place, which is why I must obey you. Shall we take them outside and shoot them right away?"

"Shoot them? That would be a death much too quick. They must die slowly, very slowly, and suffer several different kinds of pain simultaneously. This has long since been decided. We must come up with some kinds of death no one has yet experienced, the kind of death with pains no man has yet suffered. It is night now. I want to see their suffering, and every feature of their howling faces. This can only be done by day. Let us wait, therefore, until there is light."

"Shall we leave them here until then?"

"No. We will throw them into the *Jûra al-Jazâ*, where they will lie deep and secure so that we need not guard them. In the meantime, we can continue our interrupted fishing. Has the boat of the two dogs been secured?"

"Yes. It was tied to the foremost tree by the *mishrah*. We pulled it to the bank and can use it for catching fish now."

"This is good. Two boats will double our catch. We are ten *asakir*, plus the sergeant and myself. Five can man each boat, two stay at the *saribah* to guard it which, actually, is not even necessary."

"I feel just the opposite. I think it absolutely necessary," the sergeant objected. "Do you expect these two enemies are here by themselves? Could they not have arrived on the *raïs effendina's* ship?"

"I will ask them, and woe to them if they do not answer, or even tell me an untruth."

He turned back to me, kicked my belly with his foot, and told me, while he pulled his knife:

"Your silence to each of my questions will cost you a finger. Remember this! I do not lie. Look at this knife! If you do not answer at once, I will cut. When you escaped us at Fashoda you derided me openly. This will be repaid now. I shall prove to you that I am lord of your life and limbs. Did you come here alone?"

The Turk was serious. Since it was for my well-being, I didn't think it best to remain silent, yet was even less prepared to tell him the truth. Something was still inexplicable to me. They had found our boat and taken possession of it, however, no one had mentioned Abu al-Nil and the Djangeh, who had been in it. Where had the two disappeared? They must have left the boat. For what purpose? To save us? I did not trust the old helmsman to make such a decision. He was also not the man to follow through on it. The smartest thing for the two to do would have been to return immediately to the ship and bring it here by night.

That the Turk talked about catching fish in our presence was stupid. It told us the situation, and some kind of opportunity might offer itself to make use of it. I answered:

"I'm here only with Bin Nil."

"Where is the *raïs effendina*?"

I acted as if I did not want to let on, when he bent down, took my left thumb, put on his knife, and threatened:

"Answer, or I will cut! Where is he?"

"He is over there in the Bahr al-Jabal, looking for you."

"Why are you not with him?"

"Because I did not believe that your *saribah* was over there."

"Who told you that it was located over there?"

"A Bongo warrior, Agadi."

"Ah, after all! Where was he going?"

"To Fashoda to become a soldier."

"You must have taken him on board to check him out?"

"Yes. But we did not find anything."

"Did you ask him about the *saribah*?"

"No. we didn't know its name, but we asked him about Ibn Asl. He told us that he knew him, and that Ibn Asl had a *saribah* farther up in the area of Bahita."

"You believed him?"

"The *raïs effendina* did, but I didn't trust the man. When the *raïs effendina* sailed upstream, the Bahr al-Jabal, Bin Nil and I took the boat and came up the Rohl to look here for you."

"I heard that you visited Ibn Milawa, the *sangak* of the *Arnautlar*. How is he doing?"

"Fine. It was because of this fellow's doing that I had to leave Fashoda. I had discovered that he was in liege with the slavers. He had captured me and had me taken to you, where I succeeded in escaping. I brought charge against him in Fashoda, but he had the trust of the *mudir* to such a degree that the latter did not believe me, but him. I had to leave and was glad not to get the *bastonnade*."

"It served you right," the Turk laughed. "If you regret not to have been beaten there, rest assured that we shall make up for it here. So, the Bongo warrior wanted to become a soldier in Fashoda? Did he hope to be accepted?"

"Yes. He wanted to turn directly to the *sangak* of the *Arnautlar*."

"You are silly, exceptionally silly! You are the sons and grandsons of stupidity and foolishness. You think yourselves smart and wise, yet are so silly that one could feel pity for you. Do you know who this Bongo truly was?"

"Well?"

The fat Turk had assumed a superior, triumphant voice. He thought us conned which made him, whom Allah had not blessed with a first-rate mind, feel good. He replied proudly to my question:

"He is no Bongo, but a Dinka. We hired one-hundred-fifty Dinka, whose leader he is."

"By the Devil!" I exclaimed, acting surprised.

"Yes," he laughed. "You stepped into a beautiful trap. He carried an important letter. Had you found it, things would have turned bad for us. But you are much too stupid to find out something like this. He had been instructed to lead you astray, to send you into the Bahr al-Jabal."

"Well, not me!"

"But he did the others!"

"I found you!"

"What use is it to you? You two will be executed tomorrow. The *raïs effendina* will need an entire month to sail up to Bahita. From today, it will take at least fifty days for him to realize his mistake until he can then find us here. By that time, Ibn Asl will long since have returned and will welcome him happily that he will forget leaving here forever."

"Allah, Allah!" I exclaimed. "This Dinka was a real rogue!"

"He was a smart fellow, ten times smarter than all of you together. You were crazy enough to have the audaciousness to come with only two men to a hostile *saribah*. Now comes the reward – the punishment. You walked into certain death. Now, tell me, how was it possible for you to get from my cabin to the boat at Fashoda?"

"I had two knives," I lied, not wanting to betray his sister. "You did not find one of them. It fell from my pocket, which enabled us to cut our fetters. We then climbed down the anchor chain into the water and swam to the boat that was still attached to the ship."

"So, this is how you did it! Well, then we will take better care today. Although I was told that everything has been taken from you, I will check you once more, after which you will be dumped into the *Jûra al-Jazâ*. You will leave it tomorrow morning only to enter death."

Jûra al-Jazâ means 'Pit of Punishment'. The slavers' *asakir* are very insubordinate, gone-to-seed men, who, at times, do not mind rebelling against their masters. This requires prisons. But since a *tokul*, a fragile construct exclusive to this area, is unsuited as a prison, fifteen to eighteen feet deep vertical-walled pits are dug, into which the villains are dumped. They cannot escape being unable to climb the smooth, vertical walls. Such a pit is called *Jûra al-Jazâ*.

Since almost all *saribahs* are located on the Nile, with the pits being deep, one can imagine that their bottom is wet and moldy, even muddy. In addition, all kinds of garbage are dumped in them, and various types of vermin are found in there, as well. It did not fill me with joy when I heard that such a hole was to serve for our stay.

We were once more thoroughly checked, then dragged outside to the pit, beside which lay a ladder. Its length told me that the pit was very deep. The ladder was lowered into the pit; they let us slide down it, after which they pulled it up.

"Sleep well!" The Turk called derisively from above. "May Allah give you a pleasant rest and even more pleasant dreams!"

These were the same words that once before had been meant to anger me and which I had returned likewise. Would I also be able to return them today? Hardly. Yes, if only the old helmsman and the Dinka had returned to the ship, then we could have hoped for help. However, I did not quite give up courage.

The slavers left. The stars reached us even in the pit. Around us it rustled and crawled. We were not the only living beings in this nightly abode which, regrettably, was of no comfort to us.

We thought we were without supervision, however, some time later, voices sounded from above:

"How are you, you dogs? Have you yet made friends with the scorpions and rats?"

We did not answer. It was nonsense to put a guard up there. Even had we not been tied, we had no means to get up. We had understood that ten men were going fishing. Two stayed back. One sat up there with us, while the other had to be at the *saribah's* entrance. A few minutes later we heard our guard anew:

"Who comes there?" he asked.

We heard the reply he received but were unable to understand it.

"Did you change into different cloths?" we heard him ask. "I do not know you. One of you is a Black. Stop, or . . . oh, Allah, Allah!"

The last words were smothered by a rattle. We heard some stomping and struggling, then it turned quiet and a soft voice called into the pit:

"*Effendi*, are you down there?"

"Yes," I replied. "Who are you?"

"It is me, the helmsman, Abu al-Nil. Allah be thanked that we found you! Is my grandson with you?"

"Yes. Lower the ladder and come down to cut our ropes."

"Right away!"

He lowered the ladder and climbed down. A few seconds later we were once more in possession of our freedom.

"Are you not surprised to see me?" he asked. "We are . . ."

"Let's not talk now!" I interrupted. "First, we must get out. Until then, I will not feel safe!"

I climbed up, with grandfather and grandson following. Arriving at the top, I saw the guard lying on the ground. The Dinka knelt next to him, his hands on the man's neck.

"Is he dead?" I asked.

"No," replied the Black. "He is still moving his legs."

And the helmsman added:

"We did not want to throttle him completely, since he would then not have been able to provide us with information."

"This was smart of you. Let go of him! Let's see whether we can get him to talk."

The Dinka removed his hands, while I knelt next to the man, holding him by his arm so that he could not suddenly jump up and run off. He took a deep breath, moved his head, opened his eyes, and stared at me.

"Do you know who I am?" I asked.

"The *effendi*," he said with difficulty.

"Where is Murad Nassyr, the Turk?"

"Gone fishing, right by the *mishrah*."

"And where is the sergeant?"

"Also fishing with eight *asakir*."

"Then there is one more *askari* in the *saribah*. Where is he?"

"At the entrance. If I whistle, he will come."

"Where are the things that were taken from us?"

"In the Turk's *tokul*, over there, to the right, the second from here."

"This *tokul* is rather large. Is his sister living with him?"

"Yes, with her servants."

"Are the men who went fishing armed with pistols and muskets?"

"No. They carry only knives and the fish lances. Muskets and pistols are kept in the *tokul* we occupy. It is the first hut to the left from here."

I had not even urged the man to tell the truth. He responded from such fear that one could hear from his voice that he did not dare to invent a lie. I took all his possessions, and told my companions to position themselves for the time being behind the closest hut. When they had left, I ordered the *askari*:

"Now whistle for your comrade!"

He did and received an answer from the entrance.

"Now, quickly, down into the pit!" I ordered. "Be quick or I'll throw you in. And if you make a sound, it will be your last."

He disappeared quickly. I thought I could still pull the ladder up, but no longer found the time, since I saw the other *askari* approaching. I sat down, so that he would be unable to see my full figure and realize that he was dealing with someone else.

He saw the ladder's end sticking from the pit, which distracted him from me. He was still fifteen feet away, when he shouted:

"What is this? You put the ladder in. The prisoners must not escape! Out with it!"

He hurried up and grabbed the ladder. That's when I leaped up, took him by his throat, pulled him down, and demanded:

"Silence! Not a sound, or you are dead!"

Fear had struck his limbs; he did not move. When I let go of his throat, he stared at me and murmured:

"The *effendi*! Oh, Allah, Allah!"

I waved to my companions to come. We emptied the man's belt and pockets; then he, too, entered the infamous *Jûra al-Jazâ*, after which we pulled up the ladder.

Our first task now was to gain possession of the *asakir's* weapons, for which we went to the respective *tokul*. The Dinka knew his way around. He searched in the dark at a place where he knew he could find kindling. Then, he hurried to the *tokul* where I had woken from unconsciousness, where a fire was still burning. He returned with this makeshift torch, after which we had the necessary illumination. We also found a clay lamp filled with palm oil.

Ten muskets hung from the circular wall, plus an even greater number of pistols, all loaded. We took these weapons, then walked to the *tokul* we had been told was the Turk's living quarters. I looked forward to seeing his sister there. When we entered the 'foyer' it was dark, but through a mat curtain light shone from the second, the rear part. I pushed it aside and entered. The 'ladies' sat having coffee. Kumra, the 'Turtledove', the Turk's sister, sat in the middle on a rug. Next to her the four servants were squatting around a clay vessel in which charcoal burned. On it, stood a pot with boiling water into which Fatma was just pouring the ground beans. All five stared wordlessly at me, which meant they were frightened by my appearance.

Usually, I like to be as considerate as possible with ladies, but now I was very inconsiderate, which, to this day has never caused me any pangs of conscience, I can honestly admit. First, I did not come at the prescribed time of visitation; secondly, I entered a *harem*, which is strictly forbidden, and thirdly was my appearance not very presentable that, when writing this, I lower my eyes, however only for two seconds. If my suit had suffered on the long journey and by previous events, it had received its final impact in the muddy pit. My looks were less than gentleman-like. Added to this were my weapons. I had taken them from the two *asakir*, and now had three muskets draped over my shoulder and four pistols stuck in my belt – a Rinaldo Rinaldini bandit in mud! Despite this poor external appearance when paying a visit to the ladies, I crossed my hands before my chest, bowed, and said:

"Muhammad, the Prophet of Prophets, may confer the pleasant scents of paradise on your beverage! My soul thirsts for refreshment. May I ask you for a *finjan* (cup)?"

Now, the 'Turtledove' recovered her speech.

"The *effendi!*" she exclaimed, while she jumped up. "I thought you were kept imprisoned in the pit."

"You can see, it is no longer the case."

"I wanted . . . wanted . . . to free you, but did not know how to do it this time."

"I thank you, you loveliest and best of maidens. You showed me once before the greatest of good deeds, but today I could not expect you to do so again. I have come with another request, which is that you do not leave this *harem* until I have told you to do so. Then you can enter the frontal part of the *tokul* again."

"Why that?"

"You or your servants could be hit by a bullet."

"Allah, a bullet! You are going to fight? Against whom?"

"Against the sergeant and his *asakir.*"

"Also, my brother?"

"Yes, should he resist."

"Allah, Allah! You are a strong and bold man. You will surely over-come him, and you will kill him!"

"No. My gratitude forbids me to sadden your heart. I will spare your brother. But I can do this only if you keep totally quiet."

"We will, *effendi*, we will! We shall remain here. I promise it, *effendi*!"

She raised her hands solemnly to me. She forgot that she did not wear a veil, which gave me for the second time the pleasure to see her face, this strangely pinched face which, as I stated before, reminded me so vividly of the Saxonian spoon-seller from Beierfeld near Schwarzenberg. Even today, when speaking of Oriental female beauty, I involuntarily remember the features of the 'Turtledove'.

On the *sarîr*, a padded wooden frame, for sitting, lying on, and other purposes, stood a burning clay lamp, similar to the one we had found earlier in the *asakir's tokul*. I picked it up and stepped into the front par-tition, where, to my joy, I found everything that had been taken from me and Bin Nil. Several good muskets, a few pistols, and two sabers hung from a wall. We took took these weapons, too, and stepped outside after I had returned the lamp.

"Till now, everything's gone well," Bin Nil said. "Now the question is how we will overpower the ten *asakir* without endangering us?"

"The best way will be to gun them down," his grandfather remarked. "We have enough weapons to do it."

"We will do this only in an emergency," I told him. "You know that I don't like to spill blood. Let's first go to the *saribah's* entrance to see what the men are doing."

When we arrived there, the helmsman showed me the bush cov-ering the entry hole. I pushed it aside and looked outside. The two boats, the one belonging to the *saribah*, and the one taken from us, floated just before me at the *mishrah*. They had been connected by several cross-bracing boards on which a fire burned which spread its light across the water and attracted fish. The men stood in the boats to spear the prey with their barbed lances.

"We have time to think things over," I said. "Now that we are safe from falling into these people's hands, tell me how you managed to enter the *saribah* to get us out of the pit. Of course, you had heard Bin Nil's scream?"

"Yes," the old helmsman replied. "We not only heard, but also observed it. The moon had risen and was so bright that we were able to see everything clearly. The fellows crept through the hole with you. Agadi was aware of this gap. While he lived here, he had used it often, but forgot to tell us about it. He urged me to creep into the *saribah* through this hole to try to free you, insisting that only a few *asakir* remained in the *saribah*. I agreed. We climbed from the boat, darted across the brightly illuminated *mishrah* and crept through the hole. When we came out the other side, the moon shone directly into our faces. We hurried to get into the shadow of the trees. Then we observed you being carried from the *tokul* and dropped into the pit. After this, we saw the ten men leave the *saribah*. An eleventh sat down by the pit to guard you. Now, we did not lose any time and walked toward the fellow. He hailed us and ordered us to stop, but the Dinka leapt at him, pushed him down and throttled him. What happened afterward, you know. You must admit that we did right, *effendi*?"

"Yes, I gratefully acknowledge it and shall never forget it."

During this conversation we were sitting behind the gap's bush. From time to time, I pushed it aside with my rifle to observe the fishermen. The Turk had no experience; he always missed and had therefore left the boat to sit by the bank and watch the men's effort. After awhile, this seemed to bore him. He rose and walked slowly up the *mishrah*.

"Maybe he will come inside," Bin Nil whispered.

"Most likely he will," I replied. "Quickly, run to the pit, where you will still find the ropes we were tied up with. I saw that there are more in the *asakir's tokul*. You others, step aside so that he does not see you right away when his head comes through the hole."

They followed my request. Next to the bush, I pressed closely against the natural fence and put the muskets that were now a bother aside.

The Turk arrived, pushed the bush away, and crawled in, which could only be done in a bent position. Before he was able to stand up, I got hold of him, pulled him in completely and pushed him to the ground. Unable to scream, since I was squeezing his throat, he tried to defend himself, but Abu al-Nil and the Dinka came to help and held him by his arms and legs.

"One sound from you, and I'll kill you!" I whispered, all the while holding him with my left hand while I pulled out my knife with the right to put it on his chest. Thereafter, I risked letting go of his throat. He took a deep breath, looked terrified at me and didn't utter a word. My two companions squatted next to him with knives in hand.

"If you keep quiet, nothing's going to happen to you," I assured him softly. "But should you not obey, you will be sent instantly to *Jihanna!*"

Soon, Bin Nil returned with the ropes and the Turk was tied up. Barely finished, we heard steps, and a brief glimpse outside told us of two *asakir* approaching. They carried a large clay vessel, holding part of their catch. Filled, they intended to empty it inside the *saribah*. We made ready to capture the two without them being able to make a noise.

It was not an easy task. The gap was too narrow for both to enter together. I picked up one of the muskets, positioned myself to one side of the hole, pushed Bin Nil to the other, whispering:

"Pull the man away once I've clubbed him!"

The two *asakir* had arrived. The first crept in backward pulling the vessel after him. I clubbed him on the head and dropped him. Bin Nil pulled him aside, gripped one of the vessel's handles and pulled. The *askari* outside kept pushing, then crawled inside. When his head appeared, he, too, received a blow. He collapsed and remained lying in the gap. We pulled him inside.

Both were unconscious. We tied them up and put them next to the Turk, who had watched everything, not daring to warn the *asakir*. By now we had rendered five men harmless, leaving seven more to take care of. Bin Nil asked:

"Shall we catch the others in the same way, *effendi*? Yet, it will not succeed as well all the time."

"Quite right, but let's wait a bit."

We had time; there was no need for hurry. Each boat had carried a vessel like we had captured. The second was also soon filled. The carriers were expected back. They did not come. I heard the sergeant give a command, upon which two *asakir* picked up the second vessel, lifted it from the boat, and came walking to the gap. We were fortunate enough to overcome these two just as quietly.

Now, I was curious what the others would do. They didn't know where to put the additionally caught fish, dropping them into the boats, but could not avoid stepping on them. They looked repeatedly to the hole, expecting their comrades to return with the emptied vessels. The old sergeant repeatedly put his fingers to his mouth to sound a shrill whistle. When this brought no success, he left the boat and limped cursing up to the hole. When he pushed the bush aside and had come through with head and shoulders, he was instantly gripped by his throat. Bin Nil and his grandfather had already acquired some experience at it. They and the Dinka succeeded so well that it was a joy to peruse this hard work.

"This works as easily and orderly as rolling up a rope," the helmsman laughed. "Now, we have only four left to take care of."

"We will make short shrift of them," I replied. "I will now go outside to stand in the shadows. Then you call them to come up quickly."

"They will notice the strange voice, *effendi*."

"Unimportant! They will come. You three hold the muskets at the ready. They will see this, when they enter, and will immediately surrender."

"But if they do not come in? The first in will, once he sees us, warn the others."

"That's why I will go outside now and drive them in."

After picking up two of the guns, I crept outside and positioned myself in the trees' shadow, probably the same place the *asakir* had stood before they captured Bin Nil and me. Then, the helmsman stuck his head through the hole, calling to the others to come quickly to the *saribah*. There was no need for him to repeat his request. That five men, not counting the Turk, had already left without returning, told them that something must be amiss. They jumped from the boats and came hurrying up past me. The first crept in, with the second pushing after him. Inside, a scream rose. The third following, wanted to retreat, but received such a push from the fourth that he 'shot' through. There erupted another warning, sounding like a scream of terror. The fourth pulled back. He had seen what was happening inside and turned. That's when I faced him with gun aimed, and ordered:

"Inside, or you get a bullet through your head!"

"Heavens! The *effendi*!" he exclaimed.

"Yes, the *effendi*! In you go, if you value your life!"

I stepped closer to him and put the muzzle to his chest. He could have slapped the gun aside, but it didn't occur to him. He turned and crept through the hole with me following. There stood Bin Nil, the helmsman, and the Dinka, muskets raised with the sad figures of the *asakir* before them. I was unable to remain serious and broke into happy laughter. My companions joined in, and Bin Nil shouted:

"Yes, yes, you brave men, here we catch different fish than you have down in the water. You are these fish. Drop your knives or we'll shoot!"

They obeyed and we tied their hands behind their backs. Now, I checked on the four fish carriers who had received my blows. They still lay there but were likely conscious. The last four *asakir* did not get their feet tied so that they could walk to the pit, the others were carried. We lowered the ladder and let one after the other slide down. I kept the Turk and the sergeant for last, then pulled my knife out and told the former:

"Murad Nassyr, keeping silent to each of my questions will cost you a finger. I love to pay by the same coin. Answer therefore quickly and truthfully! When did Ibn Asl leave from here?"

"Five days ago," he hurried to say, "with more than two hundred men"

"Do you know the Dinka standing next to you?"

"Yes."

"You will get the idea now that I wasn't so stupid to be fooled by you. We read your letter and the *raïs effendina* isn't over there in Bahr al-Jabal, but lies nearby with his ship so that I can almost hail him. He will come tomorrow morning after which you shall be judged. You will die a painful death, like no man ever experienced."

"Have mercy, *effendi*, have mercy!" he exclaimed.

"Don't speak of mercy! You would not have had any for me. Life for life, blood for blood, like for like. You will be treated like you wanted to treat me."

"I would have forgiven you."

"Forgiven? What was there to forgive? Who is here to forgive? Is it you or is it me? How often did you think of triumphing over me, and yet always had to feel and experience the superior force of good. I was patient with you, but now my forbearance has come to an end. Your end is near. as soon as day breaks, the sun will shine on your death!"

"Do not say this! *Effendi*, do not speak such words! You are a Christian!" he wailed.

"A Christian dog! That's what you called me, just as you had earlier. Don't expect mercy from a dog. A dog fights his enemy, and when he's stronger, he'll tear the other apart. You folks appeal to our mild teachings only when it suits you. I will no longer have anything to do with you and repeat: it's your end!"

"*Effendi*, think of my sister! What is going to happen to her if I am killed?"

"Her fate will, in any case, be a better one than the one intended for her. To be Ibn Asl's wife is the most terrible fate I could imagine. Toss him down there; I'm done with him!"

I asked this of my companions, who once more lowered the ladder into the pit. Once he was down, the sergeant was sent after him. It wasn't callousness, not thirst for revenge that I talked to him like this, but rather was guided by the best of intentions. He was to go into himself while spending some terrible hours in the pit. He would become mortally afraid, and perhaps thereby gain some understanding and insight.

All twelve were now trapped in the pit. What a difference from when Bin Nil and I were down there! Bin Nil, despite his youth, was very deliberate, even prudent, and now drew my attention to another matter:

"Did you perhaps forget that the two asakir we dropped in, were not tied up? If they untie the others, they may be able to escape. If three stand on top of each other, the topmost can make it out."

"We will keep guard and send a bullet through every head that comes peering over the rim. Let them untie themselves; none of them will make it out of the pit."

We now had to inform the amir. I assigned this task to the helmsman with his experience in navigation. I accompanied him to the mishrah where the boats were tied together. The fire had died. We tossed the remaining fish into the boat belonging to the saribah, and untied ours. He climbed in and steered into the middle of the moonlit river. I returned to the saribah to pay another visit to the 'Turtledove'.

As earlier, she received me unveiled, telling me that because of her concern for her brother, the coffee had not tasted well.

"What did you do to him?" she asked. "Where is he? Why does he not come? Did you fight with him?"

"Yes, but I only tied him up and threw him into the pit. He's now our prisoner and will sleep very well in the Jûra al-Jazâ."

"In there? My brother is in the Jûra al-Jazâ? A man like him. Such a noble and grand master!"

"Do you think that I am a common man?"

"No, *effendi*, you are not, not at all. Were you not a Christian, you would be thought even more noble and of higher-standing than my brother."

"Yet, I was dropped into the pit. If I wasn't too noble for the pit, then he isn't either. I have always tried to walk the path of the law, but he is a criminal."

"Is the slave hunt truly a crime?"

"One of the worst there is."

"I did not know this. I always believed Whites had the right to capture Blacks and to sell them. Will my brother be punished?"

"He must be punished."

"Allah, Allah! But not with death? I know that the *raïs effendina* wants to catch him and that you are a friend of this terrible man. Is he here, by chance?"

"He is here. You will see him tomorrow morning."

"Then tell me quickly just one thing. I have been told that the *raïs effendina* kills all slave traders. Is this true?"

"I cannot keep silent. I did experience him having an entire group of slavers shot."

"What a fright, what terror for my soul! Will he also have my brother shot?"

"I am very much afraid that he will do so."

"Then you must save him, *effendi*! Listen, you must! I did save you!"

She raised her hands beseechingly, as she had done earlier.

"Yes, you rescued me from captivity, and I am not an ungrateful man. I shall ask the *amir* to give him his life."

"Then all is well, everything! I thank you, *effendi*. Now, I will make some more coffee. The previous one turned bitter from my fear, but this one I will enjoy with a calm heart, and its scent will increase the joy you have brought me. I remember that you also asked earlier for a cup?"

"I did indeed ask, but you did not respond to my request."

"I was oppressed by fear and concern, but now I have been comforted. You shall get some coffee."

"Make a big pot. I have two comrades, who, just like myself, long to be blessed by your kindness. Fatma, your favorite, may bring us the coffee and cups to the 'Pit of Punishment'."

"Are we now allowed to leave the *harem*?"

"Yes, I rescind my ban. But you must promise not to try to free your bother. If you did, the *raïs effendina* would have you shot on the spot."

I left. She was a genuine Oriental! Her brother was captured. Whatever would be done to him, what losses were awaiting him, was not her concern. He was permitted to live, so she made herself some coffee. And the sister of this indolent being had been intended to become my wife, had I been willing to become a slave hunter!

Now I sat with Bin Nil and the Dinka by the pit to await the Arabic beverage. When Fatma brought it, the two black servants followed her, bringing us tobacco and pipes, of course, the property of the Turk. We did not get the coffee ready made, but as boiling water and ground beans. I made myself a cup, drank it, lit a pipe, then walked away to learn the layout of the moonlit *saribah*. It was larger than I had imagined. The rear part was blocked from the front by a palisade for the herds of cattle taken at every slave hunt. The place was empty now.

The remaining hours of the night passed quickly. When day broke, the usual morning breeze rose which the *amir* could use to sail up here. I left the Dinka on guard by the pit and went with Bin Nil to check the *tokuls* in the light of day.

Most of them were empty since their residents had left for the slave hunt. Still, we found weapons and ammunition. One hut held provisions of all kinds, also a crate with clothing among which was a suit that seemed to fit me passably. Bin Nil also found one which pleased him. We changed, and when we left the hut, and because my appearance had changed so much to my advantage, I thought to pay the 'Turtledove' a dignified morning visit in my new costume and to express my gratitude for the coffee and pipes we had received. Unfortunately, a most energetic snoring quartet greeted me when I entered the frontal room, telling me that at least in this *tokul* the sun had not yet risen. Thus, I had to forgo her seeing my new external appearance which she would have recognized and appreciated.

It had been my intention to once more quiz the Turk prior to the ship's arrival, thinking to learn much more that was important to us. This is why I went to the pit. When I looked down, I saw that the captives had indeed freed themselves of their fetters but had not tried to escape. They lay next to each other in the dirt but were not asleep. Murad Nassyr saw me standing by the rim and called:

"*Effendi*, I beg for your mercy! Let me come up, if only for a minute. I must talk to you."

"You aren't worth it, but come."

We lowered the ladder and he climbed up. He was so worn out – probably more internally than externally – that he did not remain standing but sat down.

"You caused me some terrible hours," he sighed, putting an elbow on his knee to rest his head on his raised hand.

"I did? It's your own fault. Yours alone! We Christians have a saying: Do not do evil, so that no evil is done to you!"

"But I did not do anything that would justify my death!"

"And I did not do anything evil, only good, yet you folks had firmly decided to kill me."

"This is over, totally over, *effendi*! I realize that it was the greatest foolishness of my life to risk entering the Sudan. How very much would I like to leave, leave right away."

"To continue with the slave trade?"

"No. There are other goods one can buy and sell. *Effendi*, let me go! I swear to you by Allah, the Prophet, and the bliss of all my ancestors and descendants that I will never again sell a slave."

"This promise is not enough. It is insufficient payment for what I am accusing you."

"What else do you demand?"

"Actually nothing, nothing but your life."

He rested his face in both hands and remained silent. After awhile he looked up and said:

"Make it quick then and shoot me on the spot!"

What kind of a face was this? In these few hours, the man seemed to have aged ten, fifteen years. He truly looked as if wrinkles were now crossing his previously full cheeks. This made me glad; this I had wanted, and told him so in a less severe voice:

"Murad Nassyr, remember the hour we met in al-Qahira. I did not know you, but you had seen me in Algiers and had also heard of me. You told me about it and invited me into your house. I liked you and was willing to accompany you to Khartoum. We became friends. Then I leaned that you were a slave trader, something you had kept from me. You made me some very good proposals which I could not possibly accept. Thus, we had to part. We were actually done with each other, but you showed me hate and revenge and became a grim enemy. This was not good, not smart. You knew me as a man who goes his own path and has his own ways, who does not fear anything but God, and does not fold the sails from any cunning. You should not have become such a man's enemy from simple smarts and pure calculation. Still, you did, you lost card by card and today sit here with empty hands, after I took all your trumps. You pity me. I was your friend and am not able to forget this. Even now, at this moment, while I want to give you my hand in help, I cannot. But it is not I, but the *raïs effendina* who determines your fate. He will ask for your death. If I ask him for your life, I must be able to offer him more than the promise you just made."

"Then tell me, what?"

"Clear and secure proof that you are serious by going to give up the slave trade. Break with Ibn Asl! This is the proof I demand."

"This is what you demand? Nothing more?" he asked, while his eyes lit up. "Nothing is easier than that! I realized that this man was my evil demon and wants to remain my evil spirit. Why did he ask for my sister?

Why did he not take her when I brought her? Why does he lure us ever deeper into the wilderness? What can be his purpose?"

"Most assuredly an evil one for you and your sister."

"First, the wedding was to be in Khartoum, then in Fashoda, then here in Aliab. And now that we have arrived here, he has moved farther away and leaves us alone with people I do not know and do not trust."

"You do not possess the sharp-sightedness required to see through this devil. I, in your place, would have known for a long time already what he wanted for me. I would have set traps for him, he would surely have entered. I saw through you already in al-Qahira, without you suspecting it. You had to tell me what I wanted to know, without realizing that I was forcing you to do it. In the very same way, Ibn Asl would have had to communicate with me. Think of the hellish betrayal he plans for the poor Dinka! They are his allies. He promised them payment, yet later, after they have done their work and spilled their blood for him, he intends to make them slaves to sell. Isn't such a man capable of acting just as evil, even more so, toward you? He attacked Hafiz Sikhar and sold him to gain his fortune. You, too, are rich, while he has lost much, almost everything. He needs money! Why is he luring you on? Why does he remove you from areas and places where one would not notice your disappearance, your death?"

"*Effendi!*" he cried. "Are you certain?"

"Yes! Nothing else!"

"Maybe you are right. Yes, the more I think about it, the more it seems to me that as usual your insight has hit on the right thing."

"Then turn back! Do you know where Ibn Asl has traveled to?"

"To the Gohk."

"Can you describe the route he took?"

"I swore to him not to say a word."

"To keep such an oath is a sin. We want to come to the aid of the threatened Negroes. This will only be possible if you are candid. If you keep silent, all murders and other deeds will be your responsibility. I demand openness. This is the proof I mentioned earlier and on which your fate, your life, depends. Your oath was a poor choice and will become a crime, should you keep it."

"Realize, *effendi*, that I swore to it by the Beard of the Prophet."

"Nonsense!" I exclaimed angrily. "Your Prophet didn't even wear a beard!"

"What? What? No beard? Muhammad . . wore . . no . . ."

The words became stuck in his mouth and he looked at me uncertainly.

"Well, relax! Maybe he did wear one."

"Maybe? *Effendi*, you know so much others don't, and since you just claimed that he did not ha . . . Heavens!"

"My words slipped from me in anger."

"Then he did wear a beard?"

"Probably."

"Allah be thanked! I have never yet seen or heard of a person who doubted the Beard of the Prophet."

"Well, no one has seen him, at least no living person, and nothing's written in the Qur'an. If you then swear by such a doubtful thing, this oath has no value in my mind. You said it in a rush. Take it back! I advise you. It's for your own good."

"Can you not give me some time to think it over?"

"I agree to this, but only for a short time. The *raïs effendina* will demand your decision and may arrive at any moment."

"Actually, I have told you enough already, *effendi*, by saying that Ibn Asl has gone to the Gohk."

"I knew this already from his letter. The Gohk are the westernmost of the Dinka tribes. Their area is large with a number of rich villages that border the Shur. Such a slaver drive is always directed against a particular village, and so we must get to know this place with certainty if we want to be successful. Because you know the direction Ibn Asl has taken, this village must be known to you, as well."

"I do know it. Ibn Asl has maps of all the areas of the upper Nile, very accurate maps, which he draws from reliable information given to him by his agents. I studied them with him and was present when he determined the route to travel."

"Then you are able to give us this information. If you refuse to do so, don't expect mercy from the *raïs effendina*. Return now to the pit. I told you what I had to say. What you will do is your own decision."

"One more thing, *effendi*. How are you treating my sister? Are you treating her also as an enemy?"

"No. Rest assured there. I shall take care of her such that she will not miss you. As I found out, she loves to drink coffee, and for as long as a woman can and will do this, the heavens will not come falling down."

He climbed down and we pulled up the ladder. I stuffed my pipe again, lit it, then walked down to the *mishrah*. I had barely arrived there, when the 'Falcon' appeared, its sails blowing in the wind. It was a magnificent sight to see this rakish sailing ship. The *amir* stood at the bow. Seeing me, he shouted: "Hello, there stands the conqueror of worlds, smoking the victory pipe! Imprisonment does not seem to have harmed you."

"It was short enough," I replied, "that it was more entertaining than a nuisance."

"I heard so. Abu al-Nil told me. But now, I want to hear it from you. I will be there in a minute."

The 'Falcon' swooped closer, it's sails being dropped. Its momentum propelling it on, the ship drifted up to the *mishrah*, where its anchor was dropped. A boarding plank was lowered, and the *raïs effendina* was the first to the bank. He offered me both his hands, shook them heartily and said with an upright, straightforward laugh:

"With four men, one of them even a Negro, to conquer an entire, large *saribah*, and even at first being imprisoned, that is something to be proud of. I congratulate you. Now, let's have these dogs jump over the blade, all of them to the last, not excluding the fat Turk."

"Slowly, slowly! I don't want to hear this said so firmly."

"What?" he replied, while his eyebrows narrowed grimly. "Are you going to come with another of your philanthropic requests?"

Now, his first happy face had assumed a totally different expression when he continued in a gruff voice:

"Nothing will come of it. It has been decided. Such spawn must not stay alive. Come up to the *saribah*!"

We walked up the *mishrah* and crept through the entry hole. I now took him around without first entering one of the *tokul*. Then I settled on a tree trunk and asked him to join me.

"Sit down and let me fill you in."

"Fine. But first let me tell you that Ibn Asl sure knew how to set up a *saribah*. This is a true fortress! It is impossible to penetrate this woody wall. He only needed to position his defense at the *mishrah* for attackers to bump their heads there. You found a total of twelve men? Even those few, sufficiently supplied with ammunition, would have given my one hundred *asakir* and the few Takalah plenty of trouble."

"They were well equipped. I found a good supply of powder and lead."

"It would only have taken a prudent and attentive commander, and I would have had to leave without having achieved anything. We would have lost blood, plenty of blood, and all for nothing. And you got this done without firing a shot or a single stab with a knife! *Effendi*, you had immense luck, such luck that only the fear of God must have saved you. Should it once forsake you, you will be that much the worse. Beware, and in the future, do not risk as much as you did this time. But keep talking!"

He had already learned the facts from the old helmsman's report, so that I could be brief, not needing to add much. Now, my main intention was to induce him to be more favorably inclined toward the Turk. I did my best, gave a long speech, and presented all kinds of reasons to serve as an excuse for the prisoner. He listened without interrupting even once. When I was finished, he gazed sternly and wordlessly ahead, then said:

"I am obligated to you, however, you have such a peculiar way of using it for your misplaced humanity. I will accept one of your reasons, but only a single one, which is: He is a slave trader, not a slave hunter. He has bought and sold slaves, but has not caught one himself. Actually, the trader is not any better than the hunter, for if the former did not exist, there would not be the latter. But one does not treat him as severely as the hunter. Plus his sister is with him, with whom we would then be encumbered. What would we do with the girl and her four servants? We cannot simply throw them into the Nile to get rid of them!"

"No," I said, going along with his present mood. "If we leave him with these four wenches, he is punished enough."

"Oho! Is he otherwise to go completely free? To this, I must tell you my reservation, a serious one. The ten *asakir* and their sergeant must, by all means, be punished."

"To determine this is your business, not mine."

"Don't try to evade me! Of course they must be punished. I have decided to have them shot. But how can I do this if I let Murad Nassyr get off free? You must realize that your request makes me feel very uncomfortable."

"I realize this, and will count its fulfillment that much more in your favor."

"Do not speak of credit! Your gratitude will simply consist in that you will again get in my way at the very next opportunity. I know you. If this Turk would only be honest!"

"I hope he will be."

"He can also give us wrong information. Once he's gone, we can no longer go after him."

"There's an excellent solution for this: We won't let him go."

"Then we must also hang onto his six wenches."

"That can be taken care of. Keep them on the ship, which we will need to leave behind at some point. We cannot travel by ship over land."

"That is true. We will take him along. Should it turn out that he lied to us, he gets a bullet."

"I think we can now check his statements. The Dinka wanted to also lead us astray, yet did not succeed. I saw through him and told everything to his face that he wanted to keep secret. It's the same with the Turk. Do you recall this fellow, Malaf, who I came across between Bir Murat and the hidden well?"

"Yes. You were all alone yet took him and his companions captive. He was allowed to walk away, but the fellows had to give you everything they owned. He was the leader of Ibn Asl's advance party."

"You remember it well. Of all the weapons and other things I took from these people I did not keep anything for myself except several maps that I was interested in. They depict very accurately the areas Ibn Asl used to hunt in. They include also the Gohk's lands. I still have these maps. They are on board the ship; I shall get them. If the Turk's information matches these documents, there's no reason why we should not believe him."

"This is, of course, true."

"Then you are prepared to have mercy on him?"

"Not so fast! Although you have almost talked me into it, I want to hear him first myself. My decision will depend on his behavior. Go get the maps. I will have my *asakir* disembark and will interrogate the captives."

We returned to the ship, where he permitted the soldiers to go on land. The poles by which the entrance to the *saribah* had been blocked were, together with the thorny weavings, pulled from the earth, after which the *asakir* marched in in orderly fashion with muskets shouldered. They formed a circle around the 'Pit of Punishment'. The ladder was lowered and the prisoners climbed up.

They became scared when they saw the uniformed *asakir* of the Viceroy, knowing now their fate, their certain death, and almost collapsed to their knees in fear. Murad Nassyr stood with them and barely dared look up. Veiled, his sister waited with her servants in front of their *tokul*. I could not imagine what she presently thought and felt. Maybe, the sight of the soldiers interested her more than the fate of her brother which was now to be decided. I could not help thinking that she might come forward to ask the *amir* whether she would be permitted to make a cup of coffee for him.

The *raïs effendina* studied the Turk for a few moments, then asked him: "Do you know who I am?"

The Turk bowed deeply and silently.

"And you are a torturer of slaves I should actually slice the hide from your body, poisonous vermin, one must squash and exterminate. Admit to it that you trade in slaves?"

"Until now, yes."

"You are allied with Ibn Asl?"

"Yes."

"With that you spoke your death sentence."

"*Amir*, I did not know him well!" the Turk stammered, frightened.

"The worse for you! One does not follow an unknown deep into the Sudan. Where is he now?"

"Gone to the Gohk."

"What route did he take?"

"First by ship to Aguda."

Murad Nassyr now did not think of his oath, nor the Beard of the Prophet. He trembled from fear. The *amir's* tone of voice did not permit any resistance, no reflection. He answered every question instantly, not letting a second pass. I pulled out the map to compare it with his statements.

"Which village does he intend to attack?"

"Wagunda."

"Why it?"

"The local chief has gathered substantial ivory stocks and his subjects own large herds. Also, the Negroes of this area are known to be strong."

"And will bring a good price when sold! Oh, you sons of dogs! Ivory, herds and Negroes! *Shaytan* ought to take you away through the air! Are their other villages in the area of Wagunda?"

"Thuat, Agardu, Akoku, and Foguda are nearby."

"When did Ibn Asl expect to arrive there? How much time did he figure on?"

"We covered everything very well. He thought it would not take any longer than twenty days."

The *amir* gave me a questioning look. I nodded, telling him that I was convinced the Turk had told the truth. The consequence was that the *amir* continued in a much milder voice:

"I will believe you. You did not put anything in a favorable light, which will save you. The *effendi* asked for mercy for you, and I shall try to follow this request. Do you know the shortest and straightest way to the Gohk?

"Yes. From here, it is upstream to the Maiyah Samkat, were one arrives on the third day. There, one must leave the ship to travel for six days over land."

"Do you know the land route? Can you guide us?"

"Unfortunately not; I was never there."

"Have mercy, oh *raïs effendina*, and allow me to speak," one of the *asakir* called. "I know this route. Ibn Asl sent Malaf there to draw a map. He took me along. We walked everywhere to get to know every forest, river and lake."

Malaf was the one I had taken the maps from. The young man had his use. I gave the *amir* a signal. He understood and was going to continue speaking when his attention was drawn to a spot where the *asakir's* circle seemed to become disorderly. One could assume that someone wanted to get through. It truly opened. And who appeared?

Just like I had imagined it! Veiled Kumra, the 'Turtledove', appeared, a pot of steaming water in her hands. Behind her came Fatma, her favorite, who carried the ground coffee. Then came the two white servants with the porcelain *finjan*. They were followed by the black girls, one carrying the pipe, the other the tobacco crock. I could have laughed aloud. The *amir*, his face darkening, called to the beauties: "What are you doing here? Off with you! You belong in the *harem*, but not in this circle."

But the ladies, once on their errand, could not be restrained. They would not let themselves be put off and closed in in their wobbly procession stopping before him.

"We do belong here, oh lord!" said the 'Turtledove'. "We offer you refreshment after your travels; coffee, fresh and hot, like the lips of girls, and tobacco with its joy of scent and exquisite taste of paradise. Drink, smoke, and for it, release my brother, I cannot . . ."

She did not get any further. Right from the beginning, her arms had been kept in a peculiar position, also her hands. The steaming pot began wobbling to the right then the left, and while she spoke she lowered it, only to raise it convulsively again. Her torso bent forward, rose again, turned this way and that – one could see the catastrophe coming. The good 'Turtledove' was missing the charitable hand protection the Arabs call *tanjariyya*, which the English-speaker calls an oven glove. The water vessel was too hot for her tender fingers. She had suffered the pain for too long, and now, with the best of intentions, was no longer able to. She dropped the pot with all the water onto the *amir's* legs and hollered, while she ran away:

"Patience, patience, my lord; I will boil up another helping right away!"

Her five helpful souls thought to follow their mistress's example. They tossed, whatever they held, to the now empty pot and wobbled quickly after her. I bit my lips. The Turk emitted an angry curse. The *amir* looked at his wet legs, looked at me, noticed the irrepressible, convulsive tick of my facial muscles and – erupted in a loud, hearty laughter. I immediately joined in, being glad to catch my breath again. Bin Nil and his grandfather joined too, which affected everyone, so that even the entire circle of soldiers followed suit.

It was now impossible to proceed with the earlier severity. The *amir* took me by the arm and pulled me from the circle. Walking outside, back and forth, we conversed. The water pot had put him in a better mood. Of course I did my best to support it with the result that he returned into the circle and announced his judgment with a loud voice:

"In the name and orders of the Viceroy, whom Allah may give a thousand years! This *saribah* has, since its inception, been a place of crime. It must disappear from the Earth by putting fire to all *tokuls* today. Murad Nassyr, the former slave trader, must swear to renounce his trade forever. He will accompany us on our move to Wagunda. If he has told us the truth, he will be forgiven and his property will remain untouched. However, should it turn out that he has lied, he will get a bullet, and everything he owns will become the property of the *asakir's* cashier's office. During his absence, his *niswân* (women) will live on my ship. The eleven slaver soldiers have earned death, but this *effendi* has asked for mercy for them, and Allah will give them the opportunity to be put on the road to recovery. They, too, are allowed to accompany us. If they fight bravely on our side, they will be forgiven, and can, should they so desire, become part of us. But should just one of them display disobedience, all will be shot. This is why they should keep an eye on each other."

He was finished. An almost minute-long, silent pause ensued. Then the old sergeant, despite his impairment, jumped forward, swung both arms high into the air, and shouted:

"*Al-yawm, da'iman, abadi, amir!*" (today, always, forever) all voices rose in a chorus.

The Turk walked to the *amir*, bowed, and offered the demanded oath. He then shook hands with me, and said:

"I have to thank you for this, only you, and I will never forget it. I swear to you that you will never regret your intercession!"

So that the general pleasure would not miss piquant spice, out came the 'eternal female', once more on another 'pilgrimage'. The 'Turtledove' carried another steaming pot in her hands, which, this time, were not endangered. She had slipped them into her slippers. Need is at times a humorous teacher.

I hurried to her, took her – no, not by her arm – I wasn't permitted – but by her wrappings and pulled her to her brother's *tokul*, where she was allowed to present the *amir* and me with the festive beverage, without wetting the *amir's* pants this time.

A very lively movement now commenced in the *saribah*. The former enemy-*asakir* were treated as friends and helped assiduously with the work. All usable items found in the *tokuls* were either shared out right away or brought to the ship. When they had been emptied, fire was set to them. While they burned, we stayed put to guard the fire from spreading to the forest. In the meantime, a small cabin was erected with poles and mats as a *harem* on board ship. By noon, the *saribah* lay in smoking ruins. We embarked, the 'Falcon' weighed anchor and with sails billowing, we journeyed south.

What concern the Saribah Aliab had early caused us! Now, it had taken only half a day for it to fall into our hands and for us to destroy it completely.

GLOSSARY

Plurals in the Arabic language are not like those in Western languages. There are two broad categories: (a) 'regular' plurals, which are the least common, and (b) "irregular' or 'broken' plurals, which are occasionally encountered even in Western European languages. (An example of a "broken" plural in English would be "children" as the plural of 'child'.) Most Arabic plurals are irregular, e.g. "haïk"/ "hâka," or "aswad" / "sudân," and must all be learned individually. An example of a 'regular' plural would be 'fallahin' as the plural of 'fallah' (farmer, or peasant), i.e., the addition of an additional syllable to the singular noun.

The apostrophe symbol in e.g. "Ma'abdah" and the double-dot, in e.g. "haïk" (similar to the French/English term "naïve," represent glottal stops.

abu	=	father
al-	=	is the definite article in the Arabic language; its function is to render the noun on which it is prefixed definite. al- does not inflect at all – not for gender, plurality, grammatical case, etc., it is typically translated as "the" in English
al-Qahira	=	Cairo
amir	=	commander or general, also spelled emir
araki	=	a dry Turkish schnapps, also spelled "raki"
arnauts	=	people of Albanian descent, serving in the Turkish army
askari / asakir	=	soldier / soldiers
aswad / sudan	=	the color black, with Sudan meaning Land of the Blacks
bab / bawab	=	gate / gates
bakshish	=	a tip

bastonnade	=	a severe beating or whipping of the foot soles
bin	=	patronymic or series of patronymics, indicating the person's heritage by the word ibn (colloquially bin), son
bir / bi'ar or abar	=	a well
burnous	=	a hooded cloak
kandshi	=	servant
Chimborazo	=	Andean volcano, highest peak near the Equator
Circassians	=	North Caucasian people, displaced by Russian conquest
consumption	=	pulmonary tuberculosis
dahabiyah	=	a broad, shallow-draught vessel with a sharp prow and sails used for conveying passengers on the Nile
dragoman	=	interpreter, translator; often used to mean a guide
duar / dija	=	small settlement, usually of tents
effendi	=	meaning "lord" or "master;" Turkish title of respect and courtesy
façade	=	front
fallah / fallahin	=	a peasant or agricultural laborer
fantasia	=	elaborate Bedouin festivity with horsemanship displays, singing and dancing by women
faqir / fuqara	=	also spelled fakir, a Muslim mendicant, religious ascetic
fatum	=	fate, destiny, lot
Fatiha	=	First Surah in the Qur'an, often used as prayer
Freiligrath, Ferdinand	=	German poet, 1810-1876, admired by Karl May

giaur	=	also spelled giaour = a nonbeliever, an infidel
haïk / hâka	=	a long fabric - 7 ft x 20 ft - kept to size by a belt and brought back over the shoulders to be fixed there
hajji	=	Muslim pilgrim to Mecca
al-Hamdulillah	=	Praise be to God
hajin / hujun	=	camel / camels
henna	=	plant dye for temporary tattooing of skin, hair, and nails, but also of leather and wool
Hijra	=	The migration, or exodus, of Mohammad and his followers from Mecca to Medina in 622 AD
ibn	=	son – see "bin"
infidel	=	what Muslims call an unbeliever
jabal	=	hill
jalabiyya	=	a nightgown-like shirt worn by Arabs in Egypt and the Sudan
jihanna	=	Hell
Khalif / Khulafa'	=	civil and religious leader of a Muslim state, considered to be the representative of Allah on Earth (often written as 'Caliph')
khawas / khawasin	=	well-armed Turkish police soldiers, per J. Zeilinger the security guards assigned to European embassies at the time of the Ottoman Empire
Khedive	=	the Viceroy of Egypt under Ottoman suzerainty
khur	=	creek, often dry
kohl	=	an eyeliner
kismet	=	fate or fortune
Korosko	=	hamlet near Aswan, Egypt. Take-off point for crossing the Nubian desert to Abu

		Hamad in the Sudan, thus avoiding the Nile's huge bend with its cataracts
marabut	=	saint
Maria-Theresia-thaler	=	Austrian coin, at the time widely used in the Middle East
mudir	=	local administrator, governor
mukkadam	=	leader, chief, head; basically someone that is held in high regard who leads a group
musket	=	a smooth-bore, long-barrelled, single shot, front-loading gun
muza'bir	=	a pickpocket, tumbler, clown, charlatan
nargileh	=	water pipe (for smoking tobacco, etc.)
Padishah	=	a Persian title, equivalent to English "emperor," occasionally used also by the Ottomans
pilaf	=	rice with vegetables
onbashi	=	Turkish for corporal
'qadi	=	judge, sometimes written cadi or kadi
qaryah / quran	=	village / villages
qiblah	=	The prayer niche in a mosque indicating the direction to Mecca
raïs	=	chief, or leader; also a Muslim ship's captain
raqiq / ariqa	=	slave / slaves
rifle	=	a short- or long-barrelled fire arm with a "rifled" bore, rotating the bullet for better aim and range.
		Karl May's "Henry Carbine" and the "Bear Killer" were rifled fire arms. He mentions them specifically in his North African adventure, "The Gum."
		However, arriving in Cairo and narrating the story of "The Mahdi," he only refers to

his "rifles" and not specifically to the Henry Carbine and Bear Killer, although, when he shoots a lion, it had to be by means of the Bear Killer, his double-barreled rifle. The Henry Carbine is not brought to use.

It is peculiar that he did not mention his beloved fire arms by name in this trilogy.

sakkia	=	water lift, one of which is the "Archimedes screw"
samum	=	dust storm in the North African deserts
salaam	=	peace; also used as a greeting
sandal	=	fast Nile sailing ship; also a boat shoe
shaykh / shuyukh	=	in English usually spelled sheik, an Arabic honorific, but also a title, as for the head of a tribe
Shaitan	=	the Devil
sidi	=	masculine title of respect, meaning "my master"
Siut	=	Asyût is modern day name of Egyptian city
sura / suwar	=	Quranic verse, singular & plural
tachtirwan	=	a sedan chair, a covered housing for women, carried by camels
tel	=	archaeological site which time has turned into a mound or small hill
tshibuk	=	Turkish name for a smoking pipe
wadi / wudyan	=	valley, dry river bed, a wash
ya Allah	=	equivalent to English exclamation: Oh God!

The Arab language knows only three basic (short) vowels, "a," "i," and "u." Because the "a" is colloquially often pronounced like "e," Western writers have commonly transliterated Arabic words voweled written with "a" as "e."

(This practice has become so pervasive that the word "tel" has been universally accepted, which is why it has not been changed to "tal" in this narrative.)

The Times of Salah

The five daily Islamic prayers must also be made during specific times of the day.
These times are:

- Fajr – From the onset of dawn until sunrise
- Zuhr – From just after noontime until mid-afternoon
- Asr – From mid-afternoon until sunset
- Maghrib – From sunset until the full darkness of night
- Isha – From beginning of the night until the middle of the night (not midnight)

About the Author

KARL MAY (1842-1912) can be called the most widely read German author. The images he created enthralled generations of German readers young and old. His numerous novels, novellas, and short stories were translated into more than two dozen languages.

About the Translator

HERBERT WINDOLF WAS born in Wiesbaden, Germany, in 1936. In 1964 he emigrated to Canada with his family to provide his German employer with technical services for North America. In 1970 he was transferred to the United States to eventually become Vice President of the US affiliate. Retired, he resides in Prescott, Arizona, where he has taught courses on scientific subjects at an adult education center, has written science essays and, widely traveled, miscellaneous travelogues. He has translated more than 40 of Karl May's novels, novellas, and short stories, as well as a number of other publications.

Made in the USA
Charleston, SC
12 August 2015